Author Introduction:

Harold Shuler (aka: H), born as the ninth child of a large family in the summer of 1959 in Douglasville, Georgia, spent a few years in Augusta, Georgia, and then grew up in Cobb County, Georgia, where he attended South Cobb High School. His pen name, H. G. Shuler, was selected to represent his given name, Harold, plus the middle initial 'G' which stands for Gil, a shortened version of his mother's maiden name—Gilstrap. After all, the storytellers were on his mother's side of the family.

He now resides, along with his wife of 47 years, in a small rural town in North Georgia called Ellijay. This town reminds him of where he grew up, but which has lost that small-town feel as it was engulfed by Metro-Atlanta.

'H' has told stories his entire life, as a youth to entertain family, and as an adult to practice for the moment he became a published author. He has yet to run out of material and plans to be busy for years to come.

A NOTE FROM 'H':

I always wanted to be a writer, but it took me a long time to find my words. Every person I've ever had a relationship with is a part of me now. Some of these relationships were good, some bad, others were amazing, horrible, refreshing, or stressful. When I think of each of those people, I'm glad that I had all of them in my life because those experiences didn't break me or elevate me. Those people, all together, designed me, fabricated me, and placed me where I stand. Because of them, I found my words. And because of you, the reader, I have a platform and continue to exist as a writer. Many thanks to all of you, those who helped me find my words and those who give me a platform for writing.

Follow the Author at: https://hgshuler.com

The Seven Senses, *Book One of Girls, Guys, & Spies,* is another riveting Sci-Fi Thriller Series by H. G. Shuler that masterfully blends the worlds of high-stakes espionage and cutting-edge technology. Set against the contrasting back drops of Albuquerque, New Mexico, and Washington, D. C., this novel takes readers on a whirlwind journey through the eyes of Paxton Thomas, a young woman who regains her sight through advanced government technology after being blinded by an explosion at the tender age of ten. Yet, what initially seems like a miracle quickly spirals into a life-threatening ordeal, as Pax discovers that her new abilities extend far beyond mere vision.

Shuler's story telling is both thrilling and thought-provoking, as it delves into themes of identity, trust, and the ethical ramifications of technological advancements. The character of Pax is compelling--strong yet vulnerable, and her journey of self-discovery is as engaging as the intricate plot twists that keep readers on the edge of their seats. The novel's climax is a heart-pounding race against time, leaving readers questioning who can be trusted and whether Pax's newfound abilities will be enough to save her. The Seven Senses is a must-read for fans of sci-fi and espionage, offering a unique blend of action, intrigue, and emotional depth.

The narrative opens with Pax's transformative surgery in Albuquerque, an event that not only restores her sight but also endows her with extraordinary capabilities. As she begins to uncover these new faculties, Pax finds herself ensnared in a web of espionage involving the FBI, CIA, Pentagon, and numerous foreign spies, all vying for the groundbreaking technology implanted in her. The tension is palpable as Pax, along with a team of dedicated agents, must navigate carefully conceived double-crosses and clandestine operations to protect her and the advanced tech she harbors.

Sci-Fi Thriller Series
Girls, Guys, & Spies
Book One

The Seven Senses

A novel by:

H. G. Shuler

Novels by H. G. Shuler:

The Monsters of Mary Pursey, published 2023 ©,
ISBN: 979-8-218-10736-0; previously published as
  The Reconstruction of Mary published 2019 ©

Earth Chronicles, Series:
  The Fifth Pinnacle, Book 1, published 2019 ©,
ISBN: 979-8-218-30741-7
  The Blue Woman, Book 2, published 2020 ©,
ISBN: 979-8-218-30804-9
  Traces of Caledonia, Book 3, published 2020 ©,
ISBN: 9798218372552

The Last Sugar Baby, published 2020 ©,
ISBN: 979-8-218-22929-0

Man Seeking Life, published 2023 ©,
ISBN: 979-8-218-32951-8

Girls, Guys, & Spies Series,
  The Seven Senses, Book One, ©2021, registered by
Harold Shuler, under pen name: H. G. Shuler
  ISBN: 979-8-218-38652-8

Chapter 1

Twenty Years Ago

On the day that math prodigy, Paxton Thomas, turned ten years old, she started praying for a miracle. Her parents couldn't seem to get along. Every time they argued, she could strangely sense their blood turning from warm to cold. She could predict down-to-the-minute when her mother would leave the room and her father would get into his car and drive away. They seemed to think that separating at the right moment was like being saved from a burning house. When her father would return, her mother always met him at the door. They would exchange kisses and act like they were connected to a supply chain keeping marriages alive.

After praying every day for a week, Paxton got to see the other side of a miracle instead. Her parents separated. The following two months were filled with unproductive marriage counseling, telephone disputes, and differences of opinion. What she thought would get better did not. In only three more months, they were divorced, the supply chain cut off forever.

As part of the divorce agreement, the judge gave custody rights to her mother. Paxton spent every other weekend with her father, Gatsby, named after the book, because his father loved anything by F. Scott Fitzgerald. For months, the divorce defined her life, until one day, on a cold January morning, something more terrible and defining happened.

Paxton and her mother were living in a subdivision in Arlington, Virginia, just south of Washington, D.C. One day in early January, Pax, as she was known to the neighbors, was outside enjoying a recent snowfall. It was completely silent, no cars, no birds singing, no doors slamming, just silence and snow the size of nickels floating in the quiet afternoon. She sat, molding small snow animals with her hands, placing them side-by-side on the ground.

Since the divorce, her mother had been sinking into depression and tiredness. She had been living on the other side of the miracle Paxton had been praying about. When Paxton saw her mother come running out of the house it was exciting and mysterious. Her mother was shouting, her voice full of power.

Paxton did not recognize it as fear until she saw her mother running toward a man walking a small dog along the road. "Mister," her mother said out loud like shouting was part of the pronunciation. "I smelled it. Do you know how to shut it off?" She was upset, only half explaining herself.

The man stopped in his tracks, his head jutting back. His Yorkie Terrier gives out a shrieking bark. He reaches out lightly touching her arm. "What is it you smelled?" he asked softly, calmly, hoping to settle her down.

It's no use. She is terrified and trembling, attempting with little success to catch her breath. Carbon dioxide in her blood is dropping. She is on the verge of hyperventilating. With great effort she explains. "It's gas coming from the stove. Can you help?"

He rubs his forehead with his index finger. He says, "There should be a shut-off valve." Kneeling, he picks up his dog. When he stands, a serious, uncertain look is on his face. His eyes have widened, his brow severely wrinkled. He hesitates a moment, looking at the house with concern. "Show me to the kitchen."

As the two make their way to the house, Paxton's mother suddenly turns, pointing her finger like an upset teacher. "Pax," she shouts. "You stay here. You understand? I mean it. Don't you dare move."

Oblivious to what was going on, Paxton stands up, dropping some snow that lay clutched in her hand. Too tense to speak, she nods in confusion. In less than a minute, she hears shouting coming from the house and then a scream. She took two steps toward the house before remembering her mother's words. And then the most unusual thing that she has ever experienced happens. First, there was a loud pop, and the house bows slightly before bulging out like a pregnant woman. Curious, Paxton takes another half step toward the house when unexpectantly, all the windows shatter. Glass and flames shoot out like fire from a rocket launch. The super-heated air slams into Paxton. Her arms and legs fling out horizontally as she is propelled backward, an immense power knocking her off her feet. When she hits the ground, there is a ringing in her ears and numbness across her face. She can hear herself breathing like her brain has its own voice box, like the air is coming from her brain instead of her lungs. She listens as more explosions occur, some close by, others farther away. Rolling to her side, she braces herself with her hands, makes it to her knees, and stands up. Her vision blurs, comes back, and blurs again. She blinks hard several times and concentrates on the scene in front of her. She makes out that her house has disappeared. Strangely the foundation was wiped clean.

In the distance, behind her, she can hear voices. Slowly, she turns and sees a river of fire running along the street. The fire jets out and engulfs all the other neighborhood homes. A man and woman are walking frantically toward her. It's their voices that she hears. As they approach, she hears them say something about her safety. At the same time, she can smell burning tree leaves. She notices dozens of them like dots of flames blowing across the road, tumbling, and mixing with the snow. She is dizzy and confused, not understanding what is going on.

The woman has taken hold of her shoulders. Again, she hears the woman say something about safety. Paxton looks up at the woman's face. She notices the man has one arm wrapped around the woman's shoulder. He says something about the neighborhood not being salvageable and then about rubble and trapped people. Finally, he says something about the foundation giving way.

Paxton realizes there is pain across her whole body, especially her eyes. She tilts her head toward the street and sees the orange flames moving in waves, hissing, and blending with a darker gray. While she watches, the flames slowly turn more and more gray until they are no longer orange but only gray. Agitated sirens funneled down the street and blasted past, pushing a gust of wind into her legs. In awe she looks at the dark, blurry firetrucks, and then the whole street goes black.

Chapter 2

Albuquerque New Mexico,
Twenty Years Later

Dr. Tennison raised his clipboard, clasping it to his chest, hoping he could relieve some of the tension in the room. He stands next to a hospital bed, eyeing Paxton. Her caramel-colored hair droops down next to her green eyes as she lies there. Her eyes have a murkiness caused by opacification in her damaged corneas, limiting their transparency. "We're running a little behind," the doctor explained.

It wasn't anything she didn't already know. She had expected it to be done by now though, to see like all her friends and family, walking without tapping a cane in front of her. Her mind was doing that racing thing, picturing one scenario after another, all bad of course. She is anxious as she rubs her cheek. For a moment she gives in. Her face tenses up, her eyebrows squint, her arms and legs tighten. Her heart pounds, her breathing accelerates. It's a rush of emotions, a panic attack, she hasn't had one in a long time.

Something has gone wrong, it must have. They can't give her eyesight back. The surgery has failed, the technology flawed from the beginning. It was too good to be true. She will go on being blind forever. She never should have agreed to this. Suddenly, she remembers what her therapist had told her; fight back, challenge the negativity. Easier said than done. She tries concentrating on her breathing, longer, slower breaths.

The doctor steps back from the bed. He has a nervousness showing on his face. He wants to put her at ease, to make things better, to pump some air into her lungs, his lungs. He makes a fist, brings it to his mouth, coughs, and swallows. He says, "I can see you're worried, but I can assure you the surgery was a complete success. The chip installed on your occipital lobe has integrated perfectly with our computers. You'll have your vision back in another," he checks his watch, "in another twenty-five or thirty minutes."

Trying to settle down she continues working on her breathing. Slow, long breaths, patience, patience, patience. Maybe Xanax would help. Would the doctor give her one? Should she ask? She decides against it because she has heard they can be addictive. Instead, she reaches one hand to the right, feeling for the metal cart. "Could I have a drink of water?" she asked. "My mouth is dry."

Taking a plastic pitcher from the cart, the doctor fills a glass, and along with a smile he hands it to her.

She chugs it down hoping the smooth liquid stuff will help calm her. She hadn't drunk much today, maybe that was part of her problem. She never liked water. Anytime she has more than a few swallows her stomach gets queasy. Maybe she should have asked for Coke. She is overthinking it, a habit of hers, the dark side of her personality. She holds the glass out for him to take. She says, "Thank you. Oh, and I've been meaning to ask how big the scar is? Is it very noticeable?" She was picturing the scar as big as the bandage on her head. She had touched it, and it was half the size of her head.

Taking hold of her hand, the doctor lightly squeezes it, then checks her pulse while staring at his watch. He says, "I think you'll be pleased. The occipital lobe that controls vision is on the backside of the brain. Your hair doesn't hide the bandage, but the scalp only needed a one-inch by one-inch section shaved. In a few days the bandage comes off. No one will notice a thing."

Paxton gives a relaxed smile. The news calmed her. She was afraid she would look like a science experiment.

When operational, the sensory chip will act like a camera, feeding her brain video of her surroundings. Her father, Gatsby, had read the information to her from a brochure. But he was a lawyer, not a doctor and certainly not a brain expert. He had rushed through the technical jargon. In reality the chip is a miniature computer with liquid components housed in a flexible outer shell. It was quite different from the computer she used to connect to Facebook or YouTube. This computer was chemical based. Liquid mediums for computing have been around for decades. Among the advantages, liquid computers required very little material and space, which was essential when used on the brain. And their liquid components can assume any shape. The theory was that liquid computers, when used in other applications in the body, could tag-team with D.N.A. computers to turn the human body into a disease fighting supercomputer. To date, this technology has fallen short.

However, an area of success was sensory technology. The chemical gel chip, essentially a computer, had proven successful in two years of testing. Paxton is the first to receive the new sensory chip technology. The chip would feed her brain video of her surroundings.

She had been trusting her father to explain things. These days he was scatter brained and running around like a chicken with his head cut off. Her hands fall to her lap, her face softens, and she can be heard inhaling and exhaling slowly. She had given up trying to figure out what was wrong with him. And there were a lot of technical things, a real mapping of the eyes and brain. She points a finger at her face. She says, "The brochure spoke of cameras in my eyes. My father seemed confused. Did he read that right?"

Dr. Tennison nods. He grips his clipboard and says, "Yes and no. But don't worry, it's simple. Contact lenses house the cameras. When the technician gives me the go ahead, I'll install them. You never have to take them out, and they only need replacing every ten years. And you'll be happy to hear that the contacts are your original green color before the accident. We checked old photos for that. Your father brought them in."

"What if the power goes out? Does the chip have battery back-up?"

Dr. Tennison's eyebrows rise considerably. "That's a great question, one not found in the brochure. *No, it doesn't.* The brain itself acts as a semiconductor, powering the chip. We switch it on by adjusting the voltage levels in the brain fluid, much like those induced by salt concentrations in biological systems." A smile flashes across the doctor's face. He scratches his forehead. "I'm sorry if that's too technical for you." Dropping her hand, the doctor steps back and sits on the edge of a chair. "The technician, Fergus, is in the process of aligning the voltage now. He should be here shortly. Meantime, are you feeling any discomfort?"

She wanted to tell him, *hell yes, what's taking so long. I've been lying on my back for hours.* She was restless, growing more and more irritated, but he had been so accommodating. She says, "I don't think so. No, I'm good."

After nodding, the doctor glances over his clipboard before looking back at Pax. "While you're waiting, you might want to know that our previous device was more elaborate and complex. It was bulky and didn't work very well. That's okay because it did lead to the ground-breaking research now implanted in your brain.

The old design lost ions, which means it was constantly powering off. As you can imagine, it's a huge problem. You don't need your vision failing while crossing a street."

Pax reaches behind her head, pushing at the pillow. She asks, "How did you manage to correct that?" She lowers her hand rubbing her leg.

"I'll tell you, but I doubt you'll understand." He smiles. "Try to follow me the best you can. Okay, so, our scientist came up with a hexagon design, similar to chicken wire. This design allowed them to trap potassium chloride, a salt that splits into potassium and sodium ions. These have a positive charge, and the new model doesn't allow leakage. At this point, the power controlled by the voltage in the brain's liquids was like opening and closing a gate. Once we open the gate, it stays open until we close it. In other words, no recharging station required."

Suddenly the doctor hears a couple of knocks on the door. When he turns to look, the door is open, and two men are standing in the room. One of them is Gatsby, Paxton's father. Gatsby places his hand on the other man's shoulder, and they both turn around, their backs now facing Paxton and the doctor. Gatsby is whispering something in the other man's ear. After another five seconds, the two men turn around. "Pax, darling!" Gatsby shouts. "I want to introduce you to someone."

He notices she has pink splotches on her face, clear evidence that she is upset with him. The splotches appear quickly when she gets mad. It had been that way since she was a child. She crosses her arms. Her face tightens and her splotches darken to red. She had been waiting for this moment and doesn't plan on wasting it. "Where have you been, Dad? You were supposed to be here like three hours ago."

He waves a hand in hopes she will lighten up on him. "It couldn't be helped. Now don't make a scene. It's been one of those days."

"Why didn't you at least let me know something?"

Gatsby hesitates, rubbing his forehead. He frowns. His chest goes in and out quick and short. "Look, everything just blew up. First, I got a call from the Pentagon. There was a clerical error. They thought this was happening next week. They wanted to have a representative here." He frowns again and rubs at the side of his head. "Then I got a call from the office of the FBI, here in Albuquerque. The Pentagon called them and asked that they send one of their agents. He's to give a third-party report to them later today by video conference. That's who I wanted you to meet." He points with his whole hand. "Pax, standing with me is Special Agent Hawke Gentry."

For the next ten seconds, there is silence. Paxton was steaming. Her dad wasn't getting off the hook and neither was this FBI man. "Well, Hawke!" she shouts. "Are you mute? Say something."

Special Agent Gentry takes two steps forward and grabs the bedrail. His forehead is crunched up. His shoulders go up and down. He gives a slight sigh and says, "Right, sorry. I was waiting for you. I guess I thought you would talk first. Anyway, it's nice to meet you, Paxton. Gatsby's been getting me up to speed. Today is the first I've heard about your situation, and I'm afraid I've caused a delay."

Paxton makes a fist as if she's planning on taking a swing. She bumps it up and down on her right leg. "*So, you're the reason I'm still blind?*"

Hawke's face squints. His hands jerk back from the bedrail. He seriously doesn't know how to answer her. A numbing sensation rises up his spine, then out his extremities. It was only twelve o'clock and already it had been a long day. From the moment he walked through the doors at FBI Headquarters this morning everything had been a blur. He was shoved into a meeting with his superior. Instructions were given like artillery shot out of a cannon. The next thing he knew he was standing in a hospital with doctors and lawyers, even a general. By the time he was introduced to Gatsby his head was spinning like a weathervane in a dust storm. It had taken hours for him to be brought up to date on the significance of what was happening today. And now he was under attack from one of the prettiest girls he had ever seen.

"At ease, Pax." Gatsby blurts out. He pats her on the leg. "Hawke's just been dragged into the middle of this. It's not his fault. The technology used on you is government property. They want representation, which is understandable. It took a few hours to work that out. So, here we are. It won't be long now, maybe twenty minutes. First, I need to have a pow-wow with Dr. Tennison outside in the hallway."

Pax crosses her arms, slams them onto her lap like she's spiking a football. "Is there something wrong, Dad? If there is, don't keep me waiting any longer. Just tell me."

There was no time for a confrontation with his daughter. If he let that happen, he would lose miserably because she always had the last word. "It's nothing like that." He grits his teeth and glances over to Hawke. "Why don't you two get to know each other." He shifts back to Paxton. "And Pax, be nice. Like I said, it's not his fault."

Tension runs along the border of Hawke's cheeks where a few beads of sweat can be seen. He stares at Pax wondering what she must have been through. What it is like to be blind, he has no idea. All he knows is that he's in a situation he did not ask for and in no way wants.

When Pax hears the door shut, her face perks up. She releases the fist and moves her hand to the bedrail. Her eyes are wide open and looking straight up. Her hand moves farther and scrapes against Hawke's. Her touch is warm as she gently rubs the back of his hand. "Are they gone?" she asked.

Hawke swallows against the dryness of his throat. He glances around the room. The walls are white. There is a round clock and a machine he cannot identify. There is a tray on wheels on the other side of the bed. A carton of orange juice with a straw and a glass of water is on the tray. The room looked like he felt: clinical, depressing, and cold. "Yes." Hawke answered in a low, soft tone.

"I love him," Pax emphasized, still looking straight up. "But in case you haven't noticed, my dad can be an ass. I sent him like five messages, and he ignored them all, knowing I'm lying here waiting."

Hawke has decided he does not want to be here. He tries to think of a way out, but it's no use. He's stuck. His superior would have his badge faster than the blink of an eye. He reevaluates trying to have pity on the girl. But he is unsure about her attitude, not knowing if he is impressed or put off by her. Her father ignored her texts, and she didn't hesitate to call him out. That took guts. "Right, well," he spoke as he squeezed the bedrails like he's trying to choke the life out of the bed. "I noticed that he was ignoring his phone. But it's been a hectic morning, so I'll try not to judge him."

"Dad came from money. He was raised to think he's better. He doesn't realize how he treats me sometimes."

Hawke lightens up on the bed rail. He's trying to relax, hoping for some calmness in the room. A shot of vodka would hit the spot right now. No one could have prepared him for Paxton. He is trying to make sure he has complete clarity of the situation. "Did you know he used his contacts at the Pentagon to recommend you receive this new technology?"

Pax repositions herself on the bed. She isn't in the mood to hear compliments about her dad. "That doesn't surprise me. Dad has a softer side too." She sucks in a deep breath. "*But when he does things like today, I just get so mad.* Sorry you had to see that. Do you have any questions for me?"

"Questions?" Hawke responded, still a little uncomfortable.

"Yes. I've been in the dark for a long time, but I can feel you staring at me. No offense, but it's the freaking story of my life, people staring."

"No offense taken." Hawke swallowed again, a little moisture finally returning to his throat. And he did have a question. "How long has it been?"

"Twenty years. I was ten years old."

"Do you mind if I ask what happened?"

"Most people don't ask. They assume I don't want to talk about it. Truth is, I don't usually volunteer it."

Hawke loves her openness. It helps him to relax a little.

She grins and turns her head as if she can see him. "It was a house explosion. Gas lines sometimes wear out or rust, allowing gas to escape. They tell me when gas leaks into a confined space, it creates a mixture of gas and air. Any spark ignites the gas, setting off a conflagration." Pax thrust up her hand, pointing one finger at the ceiling. "Now, there's a word you don't hear very often. Basically, the gas expands as it heats, causing the pressure to reach intolerable levels. Any windows in the house then blow out, and, as you can imagine, the explosion causes great harm to people and property. I googled it using the voice activation app on my phone. You're still staring at me, aren't you?"

Hawke smiles. "I'm sorry. I don't know what else to do."

"It's okay."

The tone of her voice causes Hawke to relax more. He says, "Anyway, I can't believe you lived through something like that."

"I was outside when it happened. My mother wasn't so lucky. When the house exploded, it was like a miniature earthquake. The shaking caused the main gas pipe in the neighborhood to explode, destroying twenty-two homes. Twelve people died, and another eleven were injured."

"It's hard to imagine something so terrible."

"I came to grips with it a long time ago. Even so, there are important things that being blind causes you to miss out on."

Hawke blinks and tilts his head back. "You mean like going out, seeing a movie, visiting family, stuff like that?"

"Those things, yes. And it would be nice to know what my cousin looks like all grown up, or *what I look like.*"

Hawke continues to relax. He is seeing her from a different perspective, one of a beautiful woman instead of a spoiled brat. Maybe this is going to work after all. "That's easy. I can fill you in."

"Oh, really?" Even though unsolicited, she loved his teasing tone.

"Yes, descriptions are my specialty."

Paxton shook her head. "Whatever you do this had better be good."

"To start with your hair is Caffe' Mocha."

"No one's ever told me that before."

"That's what it reminds me of, and you have Native American cheekbones. You know, they're pushed up high just below your eyes. Your complexion is tan. Your eyes are gray with a slight green tint, and you have long maturity lines on both sides of your mouth."

"That's pretty detailed," she responded. It was all a ruse to compliment her. She knew it, and she liked it. She could smell his cologne, British Sterling. The same as one of her college professors. A very young professor. Hawke was growing on her.

He smiles and his eyes twinkle in the bright lights of the room.

She reaches behind her head, trying to adjust the pillow.

Hawke leans over the bed. "Here, let me help you." Sliding one hand under her shoulder, he lifts her while using his other hand to adjust the pillow. "It was pushed up too far. Better?"

She nods. "I've been really excited lately. Until four weeks ago, I never dreamed I'd be like others, like you. You know, with sight. Being blind, I always feel like an extra set of clothes lying around on the bed. But I've gotten good at pretending I'm like others."

"Seriously, pretending?" Hawke inquired. "I guess I don't know the first thing about blind people."

"That's okay. Anyway, pretending helps you to be like everyone else. Of course, it can get you into trouble if you're not careful. For example," hesitating, Pax angles her head to the side. "Could you lower my bed a little?" She points. "There should be a button under the rail."

Bending at the knees, Hawke eyeballs a series of icons located on a plastic strip. "Here it is." He presses it for three seconds. "Good enough?" He asked.

"Perfect."

Suddenly an army general pokes his half-bald head into the room. With three quick jerks he scans the room, nods, and backs out.

Paxton asks, "Is Dad here?"

Hawke touches her on the arm. "No, just an overpaid government employee. He's gone now."

She continues. "So, as I was saying, pretending can get you into trouble sometimes. When I was eighteen, we were at Virginia Beach. You probably already know we used to live in Virginia. Anyway, I was swimming and noticed something pulling me farther out."

"Seriously? You were swimming?"

Her face crinkles up a little. "Of course. Blind people can swim too. I heard someone, a man shouting, *swim sideways, swim sideways.* That's what you're supposed to do in a riptide. Unfortunately, I had already panicked. I struggled to get back to shore. Finally, I was so exhausted I just gave up and sank. It wasn't like I thought it would be. Underneath, it was calm, and I felt warm and at peace. I just wanted to let it happen. I don't know how long I held my breath. It seemed a long time. I could sense it, feel death getting close, but not in a scary way. It was more like relief, I think. Again, I found myself just wanting to let go. I almost did it, breathed in. That's when it happened, something that's hard to explain."

"This is interesting." Hawke perked up. "Go on."

Pax reaches over, finds the orange juice container, and slurps until it's empty. She feels for the tray and sets the container back. "One side of me wanted to just give up and die, but this other something was forcing me to fight. I was surprised when I suddenly started to kick my legs and feet. I was pushing with my arms, moving up fast. I couldn't stop. Whatever was causing this had taken control. When I reached the top of the water, I never stopped. I swam sideways at a furious pace. Within minutes I was out of the riptide, standing on the beach. To this day, I don't know where the energy came from. I honestly didn't know what it was inside me that saved me. Sometimes I think there is another person trapped inside me. I know it sounds weird, but I do wonder about that."

Hawke nodded to himself. He says, "That was quite an accomplishment." He wasn't sure which one he was more impressed with, her story, or her looks. He could hardly believe a girl this pretty couldn't see herself. He bit his lip thinking about it.

She continues. "Pretending to be like other people got me into trouble that day. Still, I wouldn't change it for anything. I found out things about myself that helped me move on with my life. Besides," her voice caught. Her lips turn down, and she sighs slowly, and deeply. "Have you ever had something happen to you that was so powerful it changed you?"

Hawke strokes his hair with his hand, combing it back. He says, "That's a deep question. Do you mind if I sit down? It looks like we're going to be waiting for a while." He doesn't wait for an answer, just reaches behind him, pulls a cushioned chair up to the bed, and sits. "Let me just say I've got nothing that compares to your near-death experience. I did have an incident, though, that shocked me pretty good. Did it change me? I guess. It sure sucked the oxygen out of me." He sinks back into the chair, deciding to alter the story to limit any questions later. He had done this before with others. Besides, the true story was too difficult to talk about. He still needed to come to terms with some things.

Pax reaches out searching for his hand. "Don't stop now. You got me wondering."

"You sure you want to hear this? It's dull compared to your story."

"Are you kidding? I live for stuff like this. Besides, I'm nervous. I'm afraid something's wrong, or there's another delay. So, talk to me."

"You needn't worry. Gatsby indicated everything is... You know what? Never mind that." The altered story was bouncing around in his brain. "Okay, we were in New Orleans, Callie and me. She had been my girlfriend since high school." Without knowing why Hawke starts gesturing. It's not like she could see him. He stopped when he hit his hand on the bedrail. He continues with only a slight hesitation. "I was serious about her. I had planned on asking her to marry me on that trip. For years we had talked about waiting to marry till after college. Anyway, that time had come and gone. Walking along Bourbon Street, Callie takes me by the shoulder and turns me toward her. It was odd timing, and I thought she must be going to mention the marriage thing. Really. I honestly thought that's where we were in our relationship. Instead, it was the moment I got my heart broke. She told me she was leaving, catching a plane back to Little Washington. That's what she always called Albuquerque. You know, because of all the government buildings. She said she thought the trip to New Orleans would make a difference. When I pressed her on the matter, she told me that she had been seeing a guy from work. That was it. She turned and left me on the streets of New Orleans. It hit me hard. For the next two days, I stayed drunk. Three months later, Callie's mother called me and told me Callie had been killed in a car crash. That was ten years ago, and I still get drunk sometimes thinking about it."

Pax reaches out searching. She finds his arm and squeezes it. If she could see, this would be a good time to slip out the door before she shares something she would regret. She had never been able to hold back. It was another part of her personality. "Okay, that's like, way worse than my story."

Hawke is surprised at her reaction. "What? No!"

It was too late. The floodgates were open. "Like, *YES!* I didn't die, but you did. I mean, you know, emotionally. And it sounds like you haven't recovered."

He responds quickly. "It's not like that. Everyone goes through stuff."

Pax can't seem to stop. She pours on more. "You're depressed, and you don't even know it."

Hawke removes her hand from his arm. "Hold on there. I'm not depressed!"

"Ten years later, and you still have issues about Callie. That's depression."

"That's not depression!"

"What else would you call it?"

"How about regret!"

"Ha-ha, that's so not regret. On top of depression, you got a case of denial."

In some odd way Paxton thought she was helping. At least that's what she kept telling herself. She had no idea that she had jumped from his good side to his bad. It had happened in a split-second.

Hawke forgot himself, what he was there for, how important it was. He felt threatened, and the need to defend himself. He had never been good at this kind of confrontation. Heat was rising into his face and there was some pressure around his eyes. "I'm not so sure Gatsby's the ass of the family!" It just fell out of him like a stone from a crumbling building.

As surprised as Paxton was, she wasn't backing off. The fight was on. "You didn't just go there!"

By this point Hawke is steaming. "Yes, well, it's just my opinion. Your mileage may vary."

"I think you had too much to drink last night. Or worse still, too much *to dream.*"

Hawke stares at her, wishing that she could see his face, how upset he was, the fire in his eyes. "For a while, I liked listening to you," he tried to explain. "But..."

"But what?"

"But now I want to run like hell."

"Why don't you then. Or even better, wait till I get my vision back. I'll run from you like Callie did!"

Hawke lunges up, turns, and slides the chair back, pushing it hard against the wall. He stands there in silence, staring out the window, his face burning red. He hates the fact that he had lost himself. He wasn't sure, but he thought the argument was his fault. She was just trying to help. Worse still, she was right.

"I might have overreacted with the Callie comment, Hawke." She was disappointed that she had gone too far, *that they* had gone too far. "Okay, I was out of line on that one."

There is a moment of silence before Hawke speaks. He shakes his head. His chest rises and lowers making a hushing sound as he forces the air out. He glances one more time around the room. God, he hated hospital rooms. He says, "It's fine. I could've handled it better. I'm supposed to be more professional. I've had training but... And you're probably right about me. My mother once told me that I live on the dark side of the street. Point being, I bottle things up and hold onto them." He smiles and walks back to the side of the bed. "I can be a bit of a downer sometimes. You might want to be careful how much time you spend with me. You might start believing in dragons, and bigfoot, and wooooh!"

Pax burst out laughing and reached out to him with her hand. "Give me your hand?" He places his hand in hers, and she lightly feels it. "Just what I thought. They're firm but smooth and soft."

"And that means, what?"

"It means I wouldn't mind visiting the dark side of your street sometime."

Disaster averted. Relief swept across Hawke's face. "And," he paused, thinking again about her good looks.

Realizing how he might be taking this, she tried to wave her hand cavalierly, but like Hawke, she awkwardly hit it on the bedrail. "When a man's hands are rough, it means he's a simple person. His interests are limited to a few things. He is easily content. I think those kind of men are boring. When a man's hands are like yours, it means complexity. You have many interests, and they can change. I've only known you for about twenty minutes, and I already see the complexity. You're funny, have depressive leanings, and are very intelligent and interesting."

"I think you just described an FBI Agent."

"Did somebody mention the FBI?" It was Gatsby. He and Dr. Tennison have come back into the room. This time the technician, Fergus, is with them.

"Don't be startled, Pax," the doctor announces. "It's time. I'm adjusting the bed, so you're sitting up a little more." He pushes a button, and the mechanism can be heard tilting the bed up. "There, that's good. Now…" Reaching into his white surgical jacket, he pulls out a plastic container. After unsnapping it, he takes one of the contacts from a Styrofoam insert and leans over Pax. "Are you ready?"

She gives a twitch with her shoulders. Her long wait was over. "I'm a little nervous."

"This will go smoothly," the doctor promises. "Now, don't be alarmed; I'm going to hold your eyelids open, starting with your left." He places the contact directly over her pupil, installs it, and repeats the process with her right eye. In less than a minute he was done. "Now, when Fergus punches in the code, things will get bright fast. We've darkened the room some to help. We've been over this. You know what to expect. You might get a slight headache, but your brain will adjust." He nods to Fergus and watches as he punches in the code.

Instantly the room comes into view. Pax has a video visual of everything. After twenty years, suddenly she can see. Doctor Tennison waves his hand out in front of her. "Give me some feedback, Pax. Too bright, too dark. Clear, not clear."

She lies there quietly at first, looking around the room. She remembers the explosion, the destruction of the houses and the shock that it gave her. She remembers the pain too, not just in her eyes but of losing her mother. And she remembers how Gatsby had taken care of her, day after day, year after year. So many years, so much grief. "Oh my God," she gasped. "Everything is perfect." When she notices Hawke, she stops. "Hawke?"

He nods. "Or you could just call me complexity."

"I didn't know you had a beard. What color blond is that?"

He shrugs his shoulders. "I never really thought about it."

"Ash blond, I think. And your skin is super white, which causes your eyes to sort of glow. They're blue like the sky." She turns to Gatsby. There were fine lines crinkled around his eyes. She recognized the nose, the high cheekbones, and the green eyes. Her small world had just gotten larger, her twenty-year prison sentence over. "Dad, you've aged a bit since I last saw you. You're more handsome than I remember."

Gatsby laughs. "You, my dear, are the pretty one in the family. Before you get out of that bed, Fergus has some instructions for you. I need you to listen to him carefully, okay?"

Trying not to tense up she takes a deep breath. "My life is about to change, isn't it?"

"Yes, it is."

"I'm ready." She looks at Fergus. He was average height and skinny. He had short black hair and a tiny mustache. His face was neither pretty nor ugly. If he were standing in a crowd, he would go unnoticed. He has a computer and a can of Red Bull. He was the perfect tech geek.

Fergus sets the computer and Red Bull on a table at the foot of the bed. He pulls his hand back and reaches into his pants pocket. He steps close to Pax and lifts a device from his pocket directly in front of her. He says, "This is your new phone. Consider it part of your vertebrae, it's that important. Everything in your field of vision is recorded, and you have video playback. The video is stored in what we call a holding room. It's like the cloud, only more secure. You can access it anytime with your phone.

We've installed an app just for that. There are two options. You can watch playback from your phone, much like a YouTube Video. Or you can watch playback directly through your brain chip. However, when you do that, your vision will be nonfunctional due to watching playback from the chip. Does that make sense?"

"Yes, I understand."

"Good. If you want to watch a video of something you experienced earlier in the day or up to thirty days prior, I recommend you use your phone. That way, your vision is not interrupted. Any videos you want to watch that go back beyond thirty days must be accessed and downloaded from the holding room. The brochure explains how to do that. Any questions?"

Paxton swallowed and felt a lump in her throat move. She wanted to memorize all the details, but all she could think about was getting out in the world and starting her life. Her body trembled from excitement. She was getting ahead of herself, turning a page, then another. She visualized dancing, driving a car, jogging in the park, the scenes photocopied in her mind. And although she didn't know it at the moment, there would be a learning curve to work through. She blinked, snapping out of it. "I can't think of any. No."

"Then, I'll turn it back over to Gatsby."

"Thank you, Fergus," Paxton's eyes were gleaming green.

"You're welcome. And Miss Thomas, you've got me on speed dial. Don't hesitate to call."

"I won't."

"Pax," Gatsby had excitement in his voice. "This is wonderful. We'll celebrate later with drinks and a steak dinner. But for now, you've already met Hawke. The Pentagon insists he sends them weekly reports on you for the next few months. They want to know how their new toy is functioning. You'll be seeing a lot of him, so get used to it."

Pax sits up and swings her feet to the side of the bed. "Dad, we've reached that point in time, haven't we?"

"What do you mean?"

"That point where blindness doesn't matter anymore."

"Yes, Pax, the world has changed."

28

Chapter 3

Six Weeks Later

When Hawke Gentry's alarm clock went off, he was in the middle of dreamland New Mexico. He didn't like to admit it, but he sometimes had trouble waking up. With an audible groan, he sat up far enough to see his desk. The night before, he had left his laptop open. The screen was dim but not dark, which meant he had a message, probably from FBI Headquarters here in Albuquerque. As soon as his feet touch the floor, he reaches over and wakes up the computer. Instantly a hotlink appears on the screen. Mildly surprised that there is no FBI identifier, he yawns and stretches out his arms. He needs caffeine and fast. He unplugs the laptop, closes the screen, and heads for the bathroom without thinking anymore about it.

While brushing his teeth, he hears a familiar voice. A little girl's voice. "She needs your help, Daddy. She's like a little girl. She doesn't know what the world can do."

Hawke spits into the sink, splashes water into his mouth, and spits again. "Ginger?" He turns around, and she's standing in the doorway. At seven years old, she is barely four feet with white skin, blue eyes, and blonde hair.

"She's got her sight back, Daddy. She's starting life over. She's a little girl again."

"I know. I was thinking the same thing."

Ginger continues. "She doesn't know what the world can do."

Hawke twists back around to the sink, scoops more water into his mouth, and spits it out. Looking up into the mirror, he can see Ginger still in the doorway behind him.

"You have to help her, Daddy."

"I know, sweetie. I will."

"Could I have pancakes this morning with blueberries?"

Squinting his face, Hawke glances into the sink. "Sure, if you like."

"I love you, Daddy."

His head slowly moves back up to the mirror. A softness in his heart, an overwhelming sense of love made him smile at her. "I love you too, Ginger."

"I'll get the blueberries out. Hurry cause I'm hungry."

"I promise I won't be long."

Suddenly she was no longer in the doorway, vanishing without moving.

Quickly turning, Hawke walks into the hallway holding his toothbrush. "Ginger? Are you there? Ginger?" No response. Disappointed, he leans back against the door casing. He wanted, needed, her to stay longer. His head droops downward. He rubs his face with both hands. Deep slow breaths he tells himself. He repeats it two more times.

Thirty minutes later, he walks into Café Bella in the small town of Rio Rancho, just outside Albuquerque. The Coffee shop was an agreed-upon place, halfway between Pax's apartment and his. The arrangement was for them to meet two or three times a week. He needed updates on her adjustment to visual life, and she needed to keep the Feds happy with their new walking video technology. She was playing it safe, trying to be as cooperative as possible. She didn't want to risk being transferred to Arlington County, Virginia, near Washington, D.C., home of the Pentagon. They preferred her closer, but because her father used to work for them and a Federal Agent was keeping close tabs, they allowed it.

In a short time, Hawke had come to love Café Bella's comfy ambiance. It was a great place for him to study his FBI tactics and procedures, AKA, *The Vault.* It was a Legal Handbook for Special Agents.

Since he had his master's degree, he went up the ranks fast, from FBI agent to Special Agent, in just over two years. Technically, he could be assigned anywhere in the country, but they were keeping him home for his first assignment. It seemed a simple, straightforward task. That was about to change.

He set his laptop on the table, opened it, and tapped on the hotlink. It was a message from someone at the Pentagon. The exact location within the five-sided building was encrypted, meaning someone covered their tracks. The defense headquarters covers twenty-nine acres, including seventeen separate buildings with five concentric rings connected by ten corridors. The corridors run like spokes, from the inner ring to the outer. All total, they are 17.5 miles long, with gross floor space of 6,500,000 square feet and 3,800,000 square feet of office space. Finding out who sent this would be nearly impossible.

Maria, who had quickly become Hawke's favorite waitress, arrives with his order (Carne Adovada Egg Bagel), which consisted of Red Chili Pork, egg with mozzarella, and sun-dried tomato cream cheese on a toasted parmesan bagel. She sets it down in front of him with a cup of RED EYE (a shot of espresso with drip coffee.) She shakes her head and frowns. She cannot help but notice him buried in his computer. She asks, "Did you know you order the same thing every time?" At first, he doesn't answer. She shakes her head a second time. "Do you want to be left alone?" Over the last six weeks, Maria had gotten used to friendly conversations with him.

Looking up, Hawke sees her brown eyes and jet-black hair. She was a beautifully tanned white Hispanic. And as usual, she was wearing a friendly smile. Hawke returns the smile. He says, "I tend to be like that, one who orders the same thing every time. It's just easier, I guess." He yawns. "Man, oh man, I'm still in wake-up mode. Do you recommend something else?"

"Of course, you'll never know if you like something else until you try it."

"That's why I order the same thing every time. I know I like it."

She tilts her head to one side, places a hand on her hip, and frowns.

Hawke throws one hand up in the act of surrender. He says, "Next time, surprise me. I mean it. Anything you want, as long as it's different."

Maria's head pops back up. "Deal, meantime, you need to get some sun. You're whiter than that napkin I left with your sandwich."

He glances at the napkin and a sly look comes over his face. "I should probably tell you that Marilyn Monroe was an ancestor on my mother's side."

"So?"

"She couldn't tan either. And besides, her skin was beautiful."

Maria places her other hand on her hip and her hip angles to one side bulging out a beautiful curve. Her voice deepens. "Are you implying *your skin is beautiful?*"

He hadn't thought this through. He says, "What I mean is...?" He's got nothing. His wittiness is waiting for caffeine.

Maria smiles and gives a half-laugh. She says, "It's not the same. Get some sun. Christ's sake, you live in New Mexico." She turns and walks away giggling.

Realizing his attempt at humor had backfired, Hawke plants his eyes back on his computer. The message was simple but worrisome. It read:

I recently found out about the new technology used on Paxton Thomas and want to inform you of a cover-up. For starters, investigate her mother. Don't try to contact me. I will be in touch.

He eyes the message, realizing that whoever sent this has violated agency policy by not identifying themselves. Hoping to wake himself a little more, he reaches for his coffee, turns it up and lets some of the warm liquid run down his throat. He didn't know he was being watched.

"Is that your first heavenly sip of the day?" It's Pax. She slides back a chair, slings her purse on the table and sits down.

Hawke makes a half-hearted attempt to smile. He yawns again. He says with a dull boring voice. "Okay, that was funny. I admit it. And now that we've got the showing interest and enthusiasm thing rolling, do you mind if we talk about your mother?"

Pax throws up a hand against the morning sun shooting through the windows. Her internal compass was starting to spin. He had just knocked her whole day out of focus. "My mother?"

"That's right."

"She died twenty years ago. What else is there to know?"

"Did she work or have any particular interest?"

"Why are you asking about my mother?" His question seemed unnecessary if not stupid. She's wondering if this is the way it's going to be working with an FBI agent; him speaking to her like she is in an interrogation room. She liked Hawke but doesn't want to put up with this kind of stuff.

Hawke just stares back at her.

She continues. "Well, tell me. Because I can't think of any reason why you would. Twenty-years dead pretty much nullifies anything you might be thinking about her."

He rubs at his neck, grins, and gives her one singular nod hoping the caffeine will kick in soon. He says, "I should never do business this early in the morning."

He sounded like he was reading from a book of statistics, and it was irritating her even more. "Nine thirty is not that early," she cried. "Tell me."

He swallows, takes another bite, and talks out the side of his mouth. "I'm not sure I should be doing this, but…." He grabs hold of his laptop and twists it around, facing her. "I read this just before you arrived. Something's been nagging my stomach ever since. And I don't mean something warm. I'm talking about ice forming in my gut." Before continuing, he watches as Pax zeros in on the message. He continues. "I keep telling myself, natural gas explosions are quite common. People like your mother die. There's nothing out of the ordinary about it. But this message is saying something different. What do you make of it?"

Focusing hard on the screen, she reads every word. It was mysterious and about her mother. She carefully considers the implications. It sounded like the story of what happened to her mother was fabricated. She says, "I don't know. Do you think someone torched the place, like murdered her?"

"That's exactly what I'm thinking. Your family lived in the D.C. area. Your father worked for the federal government. As one of their lawyers, he would have access to classified information. It wouldn't be a stretch that she overheard or stumbled onto something." Hawke's answer rung true. It was as good an explanation as any.

"I agree. But, God, Hawke, *someone murdered my mother?*"

"We don't know that for sure. A mystery person sent me that message, though. And they broke protocol by doing it. Whoever it is, they're not playing games. They know who I am and who you are. That alone says this is serious. Federal agents' email addresses aren't available to just anyone. Whoever it is either has a high-security clearance or works for someone who does."

"I see that Red Eye's doing its job." It was Maria with Pax's order. "One croissant and one Americano." She places them on the table. "You two are in some deep conversation." She tilts her head toward Hawke and asks, "He didn't bring up his complexion, did he?"

"What do you mean?" Pax asked.

"Better ask him. We're slammed. I gotta' go. Enjoy."

Pax looks at Hawke. "What's she talking about?"

He wasn't about to go through that again. He shrugs his shoulders, raises his cup, and takes a sip.

"Okay, if you don't want to talk about it." She scoots even closer to the table, pressing her abs tight against it. Ignoring her coffee and croissant, she leans over the table, nearly touching the laptop. She whispers, "The message. What do we do about it?"

Hawke takes hold of his computer, twisting it around he pulls it back to him. She isn't FBI. Is it a mistake discussing this with her. It didn't matter, he couldn't rewind the conversation. He says, "*We* are not going to do anything!"

"What? You can't just show me a message like that and expect me to forget about it!"

He knew if he was going to get to the bottom of the email, he would need her help. He wished it could be different. "That's not what I'm saying."

"Then what? Because I can talk to my dad. He still works for the Feds, just not in D.C. But he still has contacts there."

They were getting into something they knew nothing about. To make matters worse, Hawke suspected Gatsby was involved. That wasn't going to go over well with Pax. "For now, this is *my* investigation. I'm not putting you at risk."

"Then will you at least talk to my dad?"

"I'd like to wait to do that. I have some D.C. contacts of my own I'd like to check with first."

"Seriously, but you're like, what, twenty-five. Who could you possibly know in D.C.?"

"I'm thirty, the same as you. Okay, oddly, my beard makes me look younger. It usually works the other way. What matters is that I spent twenty weeks training at the FBI Academy. The bureau's training division is based in Quantico, Virginia. That's thirty-six miles outside D.C. One of my instructors at the Academy, Gideon, is an intelligence analyst. And I do mean for the FBI in D.C. That's just for starters. After graduation, one of my classmates was stationed in D.C. He and I became close friends. We keep in touch by text and email."

"Do you think Gideon or this friend of yours will know something?"

"My friend's name is Nate. To answer your question, I doubt it. But both are insiders there. In D.C., almost everybody is connected in one way or another. What they don't know, they most likely can find out. I'll have Nate put some feelers out and start sniffing around. I think that's a good place to start. Meantime, I'm keeping Gatsby out of this. Are we clear on that? I don't want him knowing what I'm up to."

"You act like he's somehow involved. Is that what you think? Hawke, *do you think my dad's involved?*" She looked at him like he was one of those smelly things floating in a toilet bowl.

His thoughts about Gatsby were not good. Was he innocent? Was he involved in a murder plot? He was leaning toward murder. He asks, "How was your mother and father's relationship?"

She notices his FBI handbook. For the first time it hits her that he's just relying on his training. He's looking for evidence so that he has something to follow. "Terrible." She answered. "Their divorce was final two months before the house explosion."

"Doesn't that make you the least bit curious?"

She realized there was a clear motive. Any law enforcement would have him as their number one suspect. It generally goes that way, and it made sense. She says, "I see your point. What can I do?"

"Make sure you don't mention anything to Gatsby. And tell me about your mother, anything you can remember. Where did she work? What were her interests? Other than Gatsby, did she have any friends connected to the Pentagon?"

What could she tell him that would help? At the time she was just a little girl, and anyway her mother had taken the secret to her grave. She says, "I didn't know much about those things. But after the divorce she would be gone for long periods, three, sometimes four hours or more. At the time, I was too young to question anything. All I knew was my mom was away a lot. Did she have a job? I guess, but she never talked about it, so I don't know what to tell you. I wish I could be of more help."

Hawke smiles bleakly at her. The email had upset her. He regretted having to show her. He knew that it was necessary, but, still. He watches her closely as she eats her croissant, butter oozing down one side of her face. She was a beautiful girl that hadn't escaped his notice. But she was sincere and genuine. More than that, she was passionate. And that is what attracted him the most. "You going to be alright?" he asked.

She nods, raises her cup, and sips on her Americano.

At the same time, Hawke receives another email. It's a reminder for his refresher course, a follow-up to his FBI training. He is to report back at the Marine Corps Base in Quantico, in one week. This was something he was expecting. There was a bonus, a real kick in the butt surprise. Pax is to join him. Someone in the higher-ups at the Pentagon wants to meet with her. They want to see firsthand how their new toy is operating. He will escort her to Arlington. She is to be assigned a driver upon her arrival to accompany her to appointments and give her a tour of the D.C. area.

Hawke waits until Pax has finished off her coffee. He says, "I've just been informed about something that involves you."

She picks up her cup, realizes that it's empty, and just holds it. "This wouldn't be from our invisible friend at the Pentagon, would it?"

"No. Sorry, I should have made that clear."

"Then, who?"

"FBI Headquarters in D.C. I hope this doesn't come as a surprise. Some big wigs at the Pentagon would like to meet with you. They want to discuss how things are going." He knows they'll have one of their doctors check her out. The bottom line: she is cutting edge technology. If things go well with her, then this newest wrinkle in science will be made available worldwide. At least that's what he'd been hearing. He was to escort her there and see her to her hotel room. From there, an aide and driver would take over. After three days, they fly home. That was about the size of it. "We leave in one week, so you have plenty of time to prepare."

"Will you be with me the whole time?"

"No. Well, we might have a day together. I have a two-day follow-up training course to attend. That kind of thing is ongoing. Someone must have noticed and figured this would be a good time to bring you in. So, that's it, then. FBI headquarters will make the flight and hotel arrangements. I guess we're done here unless you're experiencing any vision-related problems you need to talk about?"

"No, I'm good."

"Anything else that might be bothering you?"

"Of course not, why?"

Hawke throws a hand up. "Just checking, trying to cover all the bases. Do you have any questions for me?"

"Nothing I can think of."

He gave a large cunning smile, one that screams, *I know something you don't know I know.* He asks, "Would you like me to walk you home?"

Her face instantly warms and flashes red. She'd been bagged. She had lied about where her apartment was so she could meet him at Café Bella, a place close by where she felt comfortable. "How did you know I live close by?"

"I have your address."

"I know we were supposed to meet someplace halfway between our homes. I guess I lied."

"I guess you did."

"Anyway, I needed to be somewhere I felt comfortable."

"It's fine, really. My apartment is not that far away. And I meant what I said about walking you home."

"That's kind of you, but it's a safe neighborhood and," she holds her cup up at face level. "I think I'm going for a refill."

"If that's the case." He stands up. "You don't mind if I head out, do you?"

"Of course not."

"I need to send in my weekly report, and I have other things to finish. Paperwork is always stacking up. I'll check back in a couple days. Sound good?"

"Yes. Go, and do that thing you do, you know, that keep-the-world-safe thing. I'm all good here."

Twenty minutes later, Pax walks out of Café Bella heading for home. Her mind was doing that racing thing, trying to figure out her father's true motives, wondering if he would find out he was being investigated. She rehashed the conversation with Hawke, but this didn't make her feel any better. To keep herself from spiraling, she fixed her mind back on Hawke. His striking blue eyes matched up well with his blond hair. And his beard was irresistible. A girl could do worse. Passing through the parking lot, she notices a Hispanic girl waving at her. "Do I know you?" Pax asked, stopping before she walked past the girl.

"No," the girl answered, "but chill yourself, 'cuz I know you." The girl's voice is tight and raspy like she's been smoking since kindergarten. She takes a puff off a cigarette, angles her head to the side, and blows.

Pax looks closer at the girl. She asks, "Okay, and how do you know me?"

"You that blind celebrity likes Café Bella hangout."

"Celebrity? I don't understand."

"Yo, you the one. People sees', always talkin' you up like celeb of the century. You see now, no blind. It's cool, real cool."

"Thank you. I had surgery. You know, all new stuff. It's kind of like a miracle. They tell me it's going to help a lot of people." She reaches her hand out. "My name's Pax." The girl switches hands with her cigarette and the two shake.

The girl quickly takes another long puff, turns her head, and blows over her shoulder. After dropping what's left of the cigarette, she steps on it twisting her shoe. "I'm Josie."

"Good to meet you, Josie."

"Yo, same." Josie nods her head and smiles.

"Are you waiting for someone?" Pax asked.

"No, just contemplate. Been evicted, so guess back to mommas."

"That's tough, but it's good to have family." She reaches out, taking a lock of Josie's hair between her fingers. "How do you make it shine like this?"

Josie shrugs her shoulders.

Pax gives her hair a couple of strokes before letting go. As far as she could tell, Josie was two or three years older than her. She was athletic looking, and solidly built, like if she got you in a headlock, you would be in trouble. She was white Hispanic like so many others in this part of Albuquerque. Black hair, brown eyes, tan skin, and beautiful. There is a tattoo of a tiger on her left arm, and a dragon on her right. Both stretch out as if they are in attack mode. Pax stares for a second, in awe of the artwork. "Have you had breakfast, Josie?"

"No, but all's good."

Reaching for her purse, Pax flips open the leather flap, smashes her hand inside, and pulls out several bills. She separates a ten and hands it out to Josie. "Ten is better, right?"

Josie reaches out taking the money. "Thanks. I mean, I could eat, you know, that eggs and coffee stuff."

"I know." Pax reaches and feels Josie's hair again. "Wouldn't want you to lose that shine." They both smile.

Bullying his way onto the scene, a big, well-built man who looked like trouble comes walking up. He is wearing glasses, but they do not make him look any less intimidating. His baggy jeans and oversized t-shirt go perfectly with the piercing in the middle of his bottom lip. He is handsome in that grizzled sort of way. He stops next to Pax. "Yo, Lil'self, what's the deal?" He asked with a hard statue-like face.

"No deal here," Pax replies. "I'm just talking to Josie. Who are you?"

Instead of answering, he looks at Josie. He says, "She bout her lil'self, bro. Watch your backup."

"No more, Chili Pepper," Josie responds. "She just got her eyes back. She good now, all good."

Chili Pepper looks back at Pax and leans in about a foot from her face. "Whoa, true that, true that." Suddenly he snatches Pax by the arm. "Lil'self, you need to go, like now."

Paxton attempts to yank her arm free. It's no use, he has a vise-like grip. She says loudly, "Let me go, let me go, now."

"What she said, let her go!" Josie shouts.

Chili Pepper does not budge. "This not ya war, Josie. She movin on ya. You my turf."

"What'd I say, yo, back it, back it now!" Josie shouts.

He just stares.

"Yo, I won't ask again!"

Chili Pepper pulls Paxton closer, places his other hand on her chest. "No, she movin on ya." He grimaces and shoves her straight backward. She falls against a car fender, buckles forward before hitting the asphalt and lightly skins her knees.

Josie has had all she can take. She raises both hands chest-high and clinches them into tight fists. Slightly bending her left knee, she moves her other leg backward one step. Chili Pepper does not realize that Josie is gaining momentum with this move. Her weight is now perched on the ball of her left foot. For about three seconds, she twists the ball of her foot like a bolt being fastened down. Lightning-quick, her left leg straightens up, and, simultaneously, she lunges her right leg forward. All the strike power is concentrated in the heel. Like a spring-loaded dart gun, her heel lands in the middle of Chili Pepper's chest, sending him airborne and crashing him backward into the same car Pax had hit. His glasses fly straight up, twirling like a spinning ballerina before descending to the parking lot. This self-defense, axe-stomp maneuver leaves him lying on his side, groaning with pain.

Josie grimaces at Chili Pepper. She helps Pax to her feet. "Sorry, Pax." She says and begins dusting off Pax's shirt and jeans. "He overcome with me. You know, all jealous. He thinks you movin' on me."

"I understand. It's okay, just a scraped knee. How did you learn to fight like that, Josie?"

Josie glances at Chili Pepper. She shakes her head and frowns. "My Pappa's Navy Seal. He trained me to back myself up."

Paxton touches her knee, rubbing a tiny amount of blood between her fingers. She says, "Well, he's a great teacher. I think I've got a band-aid in my purse." She lowers herself and picks up the purse from the parking lot.

Chili Pepper rolls over and rests on his knees. He's still in some pain, but nothing he can't handle. After retrieving his glasses, he stands slowly, balancing himself with one hand against the car. Shaking his head, he looks at Pax. "Sorry, New-Eyes. I thought you were tromping my ground." Shaking his head in disbelief, he glances at Josie, then back to Pax. "Josie, she a thunderstorm, powerful, destructive, a spirit of justice. You good now, New Eyes. She got yur back."

"I'll try to remember that." Pax answered. Anyway, I'm not hurt." She feels the blood between her fingers. "Well, maybe I am just a little."

Pointing her finger at Chili Pepper, Josie lays into him. "I told you we keepin' it casual, yo, no meaningful."

Chili Pepper shakes his head again. "Chill, girl. Just one date, unless you got somethin' bigger happening, like another bro."

"I told you no interest. Why do you text me? What's up with that?"

"It's all like scrabble, girl. Just trying to figure you out."

As the two streetwise friends continue their verbal attack, Pax throws up a goodbye hand and starts walking. Crossing the street, she hears Josie shout one last time. "Yo, thanks for the green."

Pax hesitates, turning back, "Can you teach me to defend myself?"

"Yo, New Eyes, anytime, anywhere in the ABQ. (Albuquerque) I see you around."

Pax turns and darts into the parking lot of a large concrete building. Her apartment is behind the building, one block away. The neon sign of an arcade flashes on and off, gently lighting her face as she walks. The heat-faded building has the charm and color of dirty beach sand. Her mind drifts back, way back, to summers at Virginia Beach. She was seven years old, her family was together, and the future was bright and endless.

Chapter 4

Twenty Years Ago

Dear momma,

It's been six months since you died. Two weeks later, a preacher man came out to Daddy's house. He told me I would see you again someday. Daddy told me not to pay him much mind, because he never once opened that Bible he was toting. He just held onto that book so hard that his fingers turned white at the tips. And he kept looking up high in the sky, raising that Bible like he was seeing angels or maybe God himself. But I didn't see nothing 'cept some blackbirds and one of them long tail kites.

Just in case you do come back, I decided to record a letter once in a while on Daddy's Sony cassette recorder. Besides, he doesn't use it anymore, and there are lots of cassettes. I thought if you did come back, you would know what happened while you were gone.

I want you to know that after you died, I only cried for three weeks, which I think is good. You always taught me to be honest, though, so I probably should explain why. After three weeks of crying, I started noticing that my breasts were growing. They started itching one day, and I rubbed them and could feel that my nipples were poking out. I asked Daddy to buy me a training bra, but he just said uh-uh, and to wait a little longer. I started checking them every day, and I think that's why I stopped crying. I don't know if that makes any sense, but I think that's why. After six months, they felt like small water balloons. Even Daddy had noticed. He bought me my first bra, but I'm not wearing it cause I don't like how it feels. I think they are gonna be big'uns because they are growing really fast.

I probably should tell you that the explosion blinded me. I don't want to say much about that right now, other than the doctors say I'm adjusting to it really good. Oh, and Daddy still cries sometimes, but not as much as before. He says we are *gonna be okay. He says that we still have each other. I think if you do come back, you will like Daddy the same as you did a long time ago. And he still likes you, momma. I know because he talks about you and stuff.*

With love, your daughter Pax.

P.S. Yesterday my math teacher got so upset with a boy acting up that she farted, and it was very loud and the whole class laughed, and the boy that was acting up fell out of his seat next to the trash can. They took him to the school nurse, and he ended up having a broken arm. Daddy said that must have been some fart to break an arm, and that the boy probably will not be acting up again. I will record again when I have something I think you would like to know.

Chapter 5

Washington D.C.,
Now

After arriving at Reagan National Airport, Hawke rented a car and drove them to the Sheraton Pentagon Hotel. The room was an oversized suite overlooking the city. A large sliding glass door leading to a balcony overlooks the Potomac River. "When I was in Quantico undergoing training," Hawke paused as he gazed out the sliding glass door. "I don't mean to sound ungrateful, but the bureau never treated me like this. That's some view."

Hawke closed his eyes for a moment and let out a long breath, hoping to release some tension. The next three days would be divided between his training and searching for intel about the Pentagon email. Previous attempts hadn't resulted in much. A background check on Gatsby had some concerns, but nothing he couldn't explain if pushed in a corner. There was an investigation after the house explosion that killed Pax's mother and a neighborhood man. It was determined to be a gas leak. Not anything everyone didn't already know. Hardly anything remained of the bodies, only a few bone fragments. The families were interviewed, including Gatsby, but nothing came of it. That was the extent of the report.

Glancing down into a courtyard, Hawke sees a little girl skipping along a concrete walkway. Surrounded by summer flowers and scattered cherry trees, the girl stops abruptly and looks straight up at Hawke. "Ginger?" Hawke slid the door open and walked out onto the balcony. She waves at him and blows a kiss. Leaning over the balcony he rests his weight on his arms. He smiles and waves. "Ginger? How did you get here?"

After pulling at her skirt, she places her hand on her lips and blows another kiss. She says, "I'm always here."

"I guess you are."

Ginger continues, "She needs you, Daddy. She doesn't know what the world can do. Take care of her."

"I will. I promise."

Ginger turns to leave, glances back and vanishes.

Hawke considered their relationship a joint effort. It was failed logic, of course, but it made her seem more real. He needed her to be because he didn't want to give her up. He *couldn't* give her up. Every time he tried, he would unravel, get drunk on vodka, and wake up with a splitting headache. And the booze never worked. The only thing that did work was keeping her in his life. He had tried to ignore her, or at least not talk to her in public. It didn't last long. Ignoring her was like choking himself to death. He was settled with it now. She meant more to him than anything else.

"Who are you talking to?" Pax shouted.

He turns, looking through the sliding glass door. "No one. I mean, I thought I saw someone I knew, but I was mistaken." Walking back inside, he continues. "Anyway, this room's like the finest, most modern condo. When I was here, I had 300 square feet of bare walls and a roommate to maneuver around."

Standing in the kitchenette, Pax is staring at a piece of paper. "Would you like an espresso?" She asked. "There's a machine here with instructions."

Hawke turns, looking over his shoulder. "Seriously?"

"Yes, with Starbucks espresso."

"I could go for that." He found himself staring at her. Most girls he knew wore lots of makeup with heavily lined eyes, but not Pax. After years of blindness, she had never developed the routine. Her look was natural, and she seemed prettier than the day he met her.

"I'll get it started. Meanwhile, tell me about Quantico and your Special Agent training."

He hadn't expected to discuss his training, hadn't wanted to. As an FBI agent the training was important, but it was also boring. He closes the sliding glass door and says, "It's not as exciting as you think."

She takes hold of the portafilter. "Go on. I want to hear."

"Okay, but don't say I didn't warn you. They re-test us in certain areas and further our training; weaponry skills, surveillance, imminent danger situations. We'll probably spend a whole day watching right way and wrong way videos."

She opens the Starbucks pre-ground espresso and shoves in the measuring spoon. "Tell me about your instructors? Do you like them?"

"Not particularly."

She starts filling the portafilter. "Why not? I mean, they're there to help you, right?"

"That's true, but... Okay, I'll be *your* instructor. Let's see how you like it. Are you paying attention?"

Pax drops the measuring spoon and portafilter onto the counter and salutes. "Yes, Sir, Captain." Her hand falls down a little. "Or is it General?"

Hawke bursts out laughing. She was growing on him more each day. And she reminded him of Ginger, which only added to her appeal. He says, "It's not the army."

She drops her hand back to the counter. "Then what do I call you?"

"We have a couple of seasoned Special Agents that help us with the training. There's no title. They're just called instructors."

"Instructors?"

"Just say Special Agent Gentry."

She thrust her hand back up above her right eye. "Yes, Sir, Special Agent Gentry."

Hawke grins, connects his hands behind his back and starts walking back and forth. "Welcome back to the FBI Training Center in Quantico. You survived your training here one year ago, which was quite an accomplishment. Now you pathetic lizards are going to get some real training."

"Do they really treat you that way?"

"No, but I was trying to help you with the boring thing."

"I thought it was going fine."

"Are you going to let me finish?"

"Right, go ahead."

"You've been in the field for some time now, helping to protect your country."

"I'm starting to see your point."

"I know, right?" He makes a funny face. His shoulders raise and lower. He continues. "The focus of your training during the next three days will be technology, collecting intelligence, and conforming to procedure."

Pax interrupts, "Do they always talk like robots?"

"Always."

"Okay, sorry, go on."

"Since there are more threats than ever before, these three training areas can save your lives and that of others. Our number one game is investigation and subsequent apprehending."

"Okay, I might have to throw up." Pax interjected.

"I'm almost done."

"Okay."

"In nearly every investigation, there will be missing information. People forget things, withhold information to protect a family member or friend, or just lie."

"I don't think I can take anymore."

"Told you so."

In no time, the machine was oscillating smoothly, sending a deep coffee aroma into the room, dripping, and filling their cups. They stand at a coffee bar that has a marble top and wicker bar stools. The room is contemporary in its design, which lends itself to sipping and talking. "What do you like to do for fun?" Hawke asked.

Pax squints her eyes. She looks like a teacher contemplating a mathematical function. She says, "For fun? I guess just, you know, since I've got my eyesight back, so many things are changing. I'm still trying to figure that out. I'm getting out more, going to the movies. I even went bowling. You know, things like that. The thing I like the most is doing math computations."

Hawke chuckles. "No offense, but that sounds painful. You should stick to the movies."

Pax smiles. Her eyes open wider. She says, "For the average person, yes. For a mathematician, no. I love it more than anything. Since my first year in college, I've been working on a math computation that could prove time travel possible."

"I heard you were a mathematician. You really believe that time travel stuff?"

"It's sort of like the Bigfoot theory. It doesn't matter if I believe it or not. It must be proven."

"And you think you can prove it?"

"If I can make the math work and figure out a power source, it's not only possible, it's doable."

Hawke's brow raises as he chuckles. He scratches the side of his head. "No offense but I think Bigfoot will be discovered first."

The two are interrupted by a knock and look toward the door at the same time.

"It's probably your aide," Hawke treks the long walk from the counter to the door, squeezes the knob, and pulls. "Nate? I didn't expect to see you till tomorrow at Quantico."

Nate throws out his hand and the two shake. Nate was a little taller than Hawke and a little thinner. His black hair is extremely short, and he has a mustache. This, along with his white, long-sleeved button-up shirt made him look classic FBI. "I decided to show up early. There are some things we need to talk about. I thought it might be better if we talked here."

"Come inside. And how's Gracie?"

"Gracie?" Nate stops for a second. "I thought you knew." He walks past Hawke and turns around.

Hawke quickly shuts the door and asks, "Knew what?"

"Gracie left me. The divorce was final four months ago."

Hawke averted his eyes apologetically, embarrassed that he didn't know. His communication with Nate the last few months hadn't been very good. He would have to cut her out of the photos, or just throw them away. "Sorry, Nate, I knew she wasn't happy with the whole FBI thing."

"It's fine. I might have failed to mention it. This last year's been crazy. Gracie, she wanted me to quit the FBI. She, well, she more than wanted. She gave me an ultimatum. To be honest, I'm not sure she ever really loved me."

"*Maybe we never truly love someone.*" Pax whispered in between sips of her second espresso.

Hawke and Nate turn, looking at her. Was this her way of introducing herself or was she trying to mitigate or lessen his pain. Either way, she had surprised them.

Hawke says, "Nate, meet Pax. I've brought you up to date with her already."

Nate nods in recognition, and he and Hawke walk to the counter where Pax is seated. "I always believed in love," Nate said. "Or at least I thought I did."

Pax gives him a half-smile. "I probably shouldn't have uttered a word. It's none of my business."

"No, go on. I liked what you said."

"Well, it's a sort of theory of mine: we never truly love someone. Oh, we love them for *who we want them to be*, just not for who they really are. When *who we want them to be* doesn't work out, it all comes crashing down."

"Makes sense." Nate responded. "I'll have to remember to write it down." Twisting his head to Hawke, Nate whispers, "We *definitely* need to talk." He had questioned some Pentagon insiders, and his internet sleuthing had hit pay dirt. What they were up against was dangerous business. It was either to cease and desist or risk bodily harm.

"Relax, Nate. Pax already knows about the email. She knows you're helping me with this. So, what did you learn?"

Nate takes a moment, looking back and forth between Hawke and Pax. "I uncovered some pretty serious stuff." Again, he glances back and forth between Hawke and Pax, trying to make sure it's okay to continue. "It comes in the form of Chinese Espionage. The Chinese acted quickly to get a hook on this potentially valuable source." He focuses on Pax. "What I mean by that is the *sensory chip,* the vision technology implanted in you, Pax. They already had a man on the inside when the technology was still classified information. It's classic tradecraft."

Hawke isn't surprised. He kind of expected it. He places both hands on the coffee bar and asks, "Do they already have the technology to reproduce it?"

Nate answers without hesitation. "I think we can assume they do."

Hawke's next two questions were important. "Is this the cover-up? And if it is, how does Pax's mother, Sloan, fit in?"

Again, Nate replies quickly. "That's where this thing gets mysterious." He motions with his hands like he's measuring the size of a fish. "I'm talking full-blown enigmatic. Did you know that Sloan used to work for the Pentagon?"

Hawke glances at Pax, wondering if she had been holding something back.

Before he can say anything, she shrugs her shoulders.

He shakes his head and continues. "No, In what capacity?"

"That's the real kicker, the Department of Defense. She worked in defense counterintelligence. Sloan was CIA."

"Okay, that's surprising," Hawke responded. If Sloan was CIA, then this mystery would be way more than he had anticipated. The cover up could reach to the sky. Trusting anyone could be dangerous.

"My mother died twenty years ago," Pax blurted out. "Her involvement with this, I don't see how it's possible?"

"I get what you're saying. What you don't understand is the technology that gave your vision back was in the works by the time you were born."

"Seriously?"

"It goes back thirty years or more. The Chinese were onto it long before your mother died."

Pax continues questioning Nate. "Do you think they caused the explosion that killed her?"

"I don't know, probably."

"So, the cover-up has to do with the Chinese murdering my mother and stealing technology?"

Nate shakes his head. "As likely as that is, that's not the cover-up. If they killed her, it was *to hide* the coverup. She probably discovered who one of their spies was. They will do anything to keep their informants hidden. This day and age, espionage like that happens all the time. It's part of doing business in the twenty-first century. The email implicates someone either in the Pentagon or representing the U.S. at a high level. My guess is both."

Hawke speaks up, "It would have to be someone that's been around a long time and has high-level clearance." The situation is becoming more bothersome. The kind of person they were talking about meant all bets were off. They would have the authority to do some serious damage.

"Exactly," Nate replied. "At least thirty years, back to the beginning of the sensory chip technology. By now, this person would have the kind of clearance that makes them near untouchable."

"Should we try to do something?" Hawke asked. "Or should we leave this alone?"

"Are you kidding?" Pax pleads, "*We can't not do something.* A spy at the Pentagon is feeding technology to the Chinese and who knows what other countries."

"She's right, Hawke, no question about it."

"Then where do we go from here?" Hawke asked.

"My mother was murdered because of this guy." Pax shouted. "We find him, and hand him over for prosecution!"

Nate shook his head aggressively. "I'd like to make an observation first. Up to now, my digging around hasn't drawn any attention. If we proceed, that could change. *It could get dangerous.* Whether you like it or not, Pax, you are in the center of this. The Pentagon is watching you closely to see how their new technology performs. It's a sure bet that the Chinese are too. When I say, *it could get dangerous,* they've murdered people before. They wouldn't hesitate to do it again if they felt threatened. Or they may just decide to take you. It sounds crazy, but it would make applying the technology much easier for them. That thought couldn't have skipped the Pentagon's notice. So, if the Chinese feel we're on to them, all of us are in danger."

"You guys are trained FBI. You can investigate this without giving yourself up, right?"

"For a while," Nate said. "But I think we should take a week to think about it. If we proceed, sooner or later, the cat's out of the bag, and this thing gets serious fast."

"Hasn't enough time been wasted already," Pax interjected.

Again, both Hawke and Nate find themselves eyeballing Pax. "You're not scared?" Hawke asked. "Not even a little?"

"The only thing that ever scared me was being blind. I don't plan on being scared ever again." What Pax really meant was that she had been through a mind bending twenty years. Nothing she would go through could match it. Investigations were not her natural habitat, but she wasn't going to stop until she knew the truth about her mother.

"I should probably educate you on Chinese Intelligence," Nate responded. "They have an established network of spies in this country, and in recent years they've been increasing and intensifying their efforts. Their operation is second to none. They've been able to breach our defenses and steal targeted information repeatedly. They're a threat we should take seriously."

Pax continues her protest. "But they're in this country doing damage. Isn't this an opportunity to do something about it?"

Nate looked at her sternly. He was thinking about challenging her on her observation. A moment later, he glanced away, nodding in agreement. Dangerous or not, all things in perspective, she was right.

"Pax, you're not hearing us," Hawke said. "We're concerned about your safety." He felt she had enough details to leave this alone, that anyone half-filled with sanity would leave it alone. He was perplexed, and unsure how to read her.

"So, you're willing to risk your safety?" Nate asked.

"You're talking to someone who walked across streets without being able to see cars. If my mother was murdered, I want to know who did it and why."

Hawke was bothered and intrigued. This was more than finding justice for Sloan. This was about finding a leak in the Pentagon or, just maybe, the White House. He looks up at Nate. "Who do we know in Counterintelligence?"

Nate glances at Pax and then back to Hawke. "I guess this means we're proceeding. We know one of the top agents in Counterintelligence, Gideon."

"Gideon!" Hawke exclaimed. "I thought he was an intelligence analyst and trainer."

"Intelligence Analyst is his title. His department is Counterintelligence. Instead of broadcasting that, he errs on the side of caution. I think it's obvious why."

"Of course," Hawke said. "It makes perfect sense. We can arrange a meeting with him tomorrow after training."

"We can meet with him tonight," Nate responded. "He's one of the instructors at Quantico this week. Before I came here, I bumped into him in the parking lot. He had just arrived. I'll shoot him a text and arrange a meeting for tonight. Other than pizza and TV in his room, I doubt he has much else on his agenda. That might change tomorrow."

"Just let me know the time. I hadn't planned on leaving here for a couple more hours."

"I thought you could just ride with me?"

"No can do. My instructions are to stay with Pax until her aide arrives. I can just take an Uber."

"Hawke, have you checked in with the Bureau's headquarters since you arrived?"

"No, why?"

"With something this important, Pax's aide should have been here waiting."

"Are you sure about that?" Hawke asked.

"I'm sure. Occasionally I get the same kind of assignments." With a serious face he looks at Pax. "Your aide will be an FBI Special Agent. I probably know them or at least know of them. You'll be in good hands. Hawke, call headquarters and find out what's happened. I'm heading out now. I'll see you in a little while. Maybe we can discuss strategy over dinner." Nate smiles and tips his head. "Pax, nice meeting you. I hope to see you soon."

In the hallway, Nate is surprised by a woman opening a door across from him. "Special Agent, Nate Holder?"

Nate turns toward the woman. "Who's asking?"

She holds up her identification badge. "I'm Special Agent, Darcie Hannagan."

"You're Pax's aide, I presume?"

"That's right."

He recognized her. She was double digit years FBI with a whale of a reputation. Some say she twisted things to get justice. They say she came by it naturally like it was her given profession. Didn't matter. When it came to apprehending the bad guys, she was considered a god. "I've seen you around." Nate said. "You're the one they loan out to the CIA sometimes. They say you're the best interrogator in the FBI. You can get anything out of anyone."

"That's what they say?"

"Yes. And they say everything you do and say has a purpose."

"Well, if that's what they say."

"Aren't you supposed to be looking after Pax?"

"I'm doing just that."

"From my perspective, it doesn't appear that way."

"I suppose not. I'm following orders. I planted a bug in her room before she and Special Agent Gentry arrived. My orders were to listen in for the first couple of hours, then introduce myself and take possession of her visit." Darcie looks at her phone. "That's another fifteen minutes."

"So, you overheard our conversation?" Nate asked.

"Yes, everything."

"Are you required to report it?"

"Technically, my primary responsibility is to protect Paxton. Secondly, I'm to observe her socially. If anything seems out of whack with her, I'm to include it in my report. My first report goes in tomorrow. What they're concerned with is whether or not the chip is functioning properly."

"Then you don't have to mention what you overheard."

"No. But her life could be in danger. Investigating the Chinese and whoever the mole is feeding them information won't be easy. As far as I'm concerned, you and I are on the same side. I'll do what I can to help."

"That's a relief. We could use the help. And Darcie, you don't mind if I use your first name, do you? The formalities will just slow us down."

"I'm good with that."

"Darcie, other than me and the two people in that room," he points at Pax's door, "you can't talk to anyone about this investigation. Are we clear?"

"Don't worry. My priority is the safety of Pax. I've got a question, though."

"Go ahead."

"I didn't fully understand what the coverup is. Is this only about the Chinese protecting their spies?"

"Truth is, I just don't know."

"Then what makes you think there's a coverup?" Darcie points at Pax's door. "Her mother's death could have been an accident."

"I have information that points to other causes. And we can't just ignore the email sent to Hawke. Can we just leave it at that for now? I'm needed at Quantico."

"Sure. You go. And don't worry about Pax. I got it covered."

"Thanks." Nate throws up a goodbye hand, turns, walks down the hallway, and disappears into an elevator.

Back in Pax's room, Hawke was shaking his head. He says, "I'll warn you now. You should relax tonight and try to get some sleep. The next few days will be busy."

Pax is standing at the window looking out over the Potomac. "Don't worry about me. Sometimes, I feel like I've been sleeping for twenty years."

"Suit yourself. I think I'll call the Bureau's Headquarters. We need to know what's up with your aide." Just as Hawke gets the words out of his mouth, he hears a knock at the door. When he answers, he sees a sharply dressed woman. She's medium height, solidly built, with black hair and black eyes.

"Hello, I'm Special Agent, Darcie Hannagan. I'm to serve as Paxton's aide."

Chapter 6

Now

Darcie and Pax sit in a waiting room outside the office of Three Star General Robert Stackhouse. Classical music filters down softly from a speaker in the ceiling. A security guard, dressed in red and green fatigues, stands next to the door. To the right of him a pretty secretary sits at a desk curling a few strands of hair around her finger. She stares attentively into a computer. There is very little furniture in sight: a desk, four hardback chairs and an end table. The room is so clean that it glows. And there is an odor. Apparently, there has been a fight with a battalion of germs and a can of Lysol. Lysol won out. On the walls hang military pictures, some in combat fatigues, some in officer's dress, one of a family complete with grandchildren.

Darcie moves forward in her seat and twists sideways looking at Pax. She nudges her with her elbow. "Do you like bats?" she asked.

"Bats?" Pax replied. She had just reached over to an end table and picked up a People Magazine.

"Yes. You know." Darcie raises her shoulders until her head is resting on them. She moves both her hands beneath her chin and starts fluttering them.

"Oh, *bats.*" Pax opens the magazine, looks down and starts flipping unconsciously through pages. "Why would you ask me about bats?" She knew that Darcie was just trying to be nice. She was one of those people that tried too hard, like it was her calling, in her DNA. After arriving at her room, the day before, she had acted like a mother hen, taking care of their dinner, cleaning up, and asking over and over if there was anything she could do. She even did a bathroom check to make sure Pax had everything she needed. She knew she should be happy Darcie cared so much, but she hadn't had a mother in twenty years.

"Bats see without seeing," Darcie said. "They live in darkness as easily as we live in light."

Pax looks up. She closes the magazine and holds it in her lap. "And you think since I was blind for twenty years, the darkness would endear me to them?"

Darcie grins. "That's right. Last night in my room I took a headband from my suitcase. I use it when I jog. I placed it over my head and pulled it down over my eyes." She moves her hands, reenacting. "Then I slowly walked through the room. It was easier than I thought it would be."

"Really?"

"Yes."

"You didn't bump into anything?"

"Only twice. The chair that goes with the desk scraped my knee, and so did the corner of the bed. But I made it to the bathroom, opened the door, and stood in front of the mirror."

For the second time Pax looks down and opens the magazine. She says, "Next time, try it on a sidewalk full of people."

"Seems like you would hurt yourself." Darcie responded. "Could you describe it?"

Pax pumps her head from left to right, trying to relieve tightness in her neck. In truth, she was buying time trying to figure a way out of the conversation. Recognizing her rudeness, she moves awkwardly readjusting her seating position. She finally gives in. "It's scary." She glances up making eye contact with Darcie. "If you have a seeing-eye dog, it's better, but you still get bumped into." She tightens her lips and takes a deep breath through her nose. "It's not like on TV where everyone gives blind people several feet of space. Most people aren't even paying attention. Getting bumped into by people you can't see is unnerving. You get used to it, though, with experience. When I first started going out in public, I viewed it as an experiment, which was a big help. I was still scared but excited too."

Darcie nods in recognition. "People are afraid of bats. Do you know why?"

Growing more relaxed, Pax crossed her legs and folded the magazine. "I guess not."

"It's because they live in the dark. They aren't blind the way we think of blindness. They have their unique way of seeing. They use sound waves."

Again, Pax unfolds the magazine and looks down at it. She nods. "When you put it like that, bats are pretty interesting."

"I thought about it for a while last night. I was trying to understand what you've been through to get to know you better." Darcie is determined to break through Pax's outer shell and befriend her.

"Did it help?" Pax asked.

"I think so. Blind people have their unique way of seeing things too. They don't use sound waves, but they see the world through their other senses. They use them to determine the location of objects. Is that how it was for you?"

Pax places the magazine back on the end table. She moves her hands to the arms of the chair. "For me, yes. But it's not that way with everyone. I think it depends on each one's circumstances. If you have too much help, your senses have no need to change. I think it's important for a blind person to learn to do everything for themselves."

"Like bats?"

"Yes, Darcie, like bats."

Darcie touches Pax on the shoulder. "I have a confession to make. I do want to know you better, but that wasn't the real reason I put the headband on."

"Then why would you do something like that?"

"My father has Alzheimer's. He doesn't know who I am. I've been obsessing over it. I was trying to think about something else, anything else."

Suddenly, the secretary interrupts. "Miss Thomas, General Stackhouse will see you now." The secretary stands up from her desk, reaches next to the security guard and opens the general's door.

Pax motions for Darcie to lead the way, and they enter and stand before the general's desk. It was impossible to miss the rows of achievement plaques hanging on the wall behind his desk and a U.S. flag standing tall in the corner. Not to mention a half-smoked cigar in an ashtray and a glass of Brandy. Pax lowers her chin and gives a slight grin. This is what it's like to be a high ranking general at the Pentagon, she thought.

"Please, have a seat." The general spoke in a kind but authoritative voice. "Miss Thomas, welcome to D.C. I hope your accommodations are suitable."

She straightens her head. "Thank you, Sir. They are. My room is well stocked and comfortable. And the view is amazing. I can see the Potomac."

"I'm glad to hear that. I'll get right to the matter at hand. Here at the Pentagon, we view you as a new species. You can see without the natural use of your eyes. You are *very special* to us. How would you say your vision compares to the way it was before you lost your eyesight?"

Pax glances around the room as if she's giving the general a demonstration. "From what I remember, I would say it's the same. No. I would say it's better. It's perfect."

"No glitches with depth perception or going from dark to light?"

"I haven't even had to think about that."

The general clasps his hands together, forming a tight double fist. He taps them up and down on the desk and nods. "I was hoping you would say that." Unfolding his hands, he spaces them apart and places them palms down on the desk. "You also have video playback. It doesn't take the place of your memory; however, in some ways, it's better."

"Better, sir?" Pax asked.

"That's right. Yesterday my wife asked me what dress she wore at our last anniversary party. Here in D.C., we go to a lot of social events. It can get confusing. She wanted to make sure she didn't wear the same one this year. Later, she looked at a picture taken on the day of the party. Pictures don't forget or get details wrong. Our memories don't work that way. Have you been using video playback?"

"Lately, yes."

"How's that working? Any glitches you might have noticed?"

"I can't think of any, no."

"Can I report that the computer chip is recording properly, and the playback is functioning smoothly?"

"Yes, Sir. The smartphone makes it easy."

"Well, if you're satisfied, then I'm satisfied. Our doctors have some tests to run, so I'm having you escorted to another building. Things might get a little uncomfortable. They tell me you'll be there for about three hours. If everything goes well, you can spend the rest of your stay touring D.C. Your aide here, Special Agent Hannagan, will be your driver. That's about it. Miss Thomas, do you have any questions for me?"

Pax was concerned about a Pentagon power move. They had regretted not requiring her to move here before the surgery. She wondered, since she was here in Washington, would they try keeping her here. Their leverage was her eyesight. After twenty years she had it back. She didn't want to lose it again. She says, "It's not a question as much as a request."

The general raises the glass of Brandy and takes a sip. Slowly, he sets the glass down, carefully using the coaster, then he smiles. "And what would that be?"

"I've been told that it would be easier for the Pentagon if I lived here. You could see me regularly and all that. It's understandable, and originally, being born here, I was a D.C. girl. But after I graduated from college, Dad was transferred to Albuquerque. That was seven years ago. It's my home now, and I want to remain there. Can you reassure me that I can stay in Albuquerque?"

Tapping four fingers on the desk, the general's lips curl downward. He glances at a clock on the wall behind Darcie. He says, "I can't promise you. However, as of now we've no plans currently to move you here. If everything keeps going the way it has been, then it looks like you've nothing to worry about."

"Thanks. I needed to hear that."

"You're free to go now. Oh, and enjoy the D.C. sites. I recommend the Smithsonian, and you wouldn't want to miss the Lincoln Memorial and Washington Monument. There's also a tour here at the Pentagon if the military is something that interests you."

"Growing up, I spent some time here." Pax replied. "So, I know most of the sights. My father is closely connected. He's one of the Pentagon lawyers or used to be. He still works for the government."

"Yes, I know him personally. How's Gatsby doing these days?"

"He's busier than a mosquito on a nudist beach, Sir."

The general picks up a pencil, taps it on the desk and smiles. "I thought as much. Tell him his old drinking buddy misses him."

"I'll do that, Sir."

Chapter 7

Three Hours Later

A series of exhaustive tests were nearing completion. "You appear to be the picture of health, Paxton." Dr. Simmons was one of the three doctors. "You're five foot seven and weigh 134 pounds. Does your weight fluctuate much?"

While buttoning up her blouse, Pax replies, "No, it's always about the same."

The doctor hesitates while looking over some test readouts.

Pax tucks in her shirt, zips her skirt, and slips into a pair of black, medium heal shoes.

"A little fluctuation is normal." The doctor explained, "Your vitals are pretty good. Your heart rate is near-perfect, 68 bpm. But your blood pressure is a little elevated. It's probably nothing to worry about. I'll send a blood pressure monitor home with you. The ECG came out clean. Both the 12-lead and rhythm strip showed no interference. We did a print-out just in case your doctor in Albuquerque needs it. Most importantly, your vision chip is operating smoothly. It's continuing to integrate with your brain. It's receiving the wireless signal from the cameras built into your contacts with no interruptions. The bottom line is your vision is perfect, which is nothing new to you. You already know how well you can see." The doctor holds an object up that looks like a tiny hearing aid. "Have you ever seen anything like this before?"

Pax squints her eyes, moves closer and inadvertently brushes against one of several medical machines. She touches it. "I can't say that I have." She was ready to get away from this place. During the last three hours they had taken every conceivable measurement and transferred them to a stick figure poster of a human. There were 'X's documenting every part of her body. There were line drawings connecting each part to her brain. There was a timeline beginning with her surgery. And there was a blood analysis chart. Nothing was explained to her, only that it was all necessary.

The doctor points to the side of her head. "It fits in your ear. It's going to monitor your vision chip. I can track it from my phone or computer. Would you mind wearing it for a few days? Before I file my report on you, I just want to be sure."

For a second, she hesitates, looking down and brushing stiffly at her skirt. "Is it uncomfortable?"

"No. And once you put it on, it's hardly noticeable. After you get back to Albuquerque, you can take it out, or you can drop it off here on your way to the airport."

Pax stops brushing and looks up. "Okay, sure." She wanted to be as cooperative as possible. It was still stuck in her mind that they might force her to move here.

"Before you leave, there's someone who would like to meet you." The doctor motioned to the door. "He's in the waiting room. Do you mind?"

She shrugs her shoulders while giving a confused look. "Who is he?"

"He's an important man. He invented the technology that gave you back your vision."

Pax gives a smile that spreads across her face. "Hey! This is an awesome surprise." She follows the doctor to a waiting room down the hall.

Inside the room, a fair-skinned lightweight man stands up from his chair. He clutches his hands together and looks at Pax like he knows her. He is short with graying hair and has unusually round eyeglasses that speak to his education level. He is dressed in a sharp-looking three-piece suit. It would be easy to take him for a professor. Dr. Simmons reaches out like he is pointing. "Paxton, this is Edward Cotton."

She nods, and the two of them shake hands as she says, "Nice to meet you, Mr. Cotton."

"The pleasure's all mine, Paxton. And please, call me Edward."

"I love your suit, Edward." Pax asked, "What color blue is that?"

Looking down for a moment, Edward analyzes the suit. When he looks up, he's smiling. He says, "I don't have a clue."

Pax softly rubs a finger on his arm. "Looks similar to Royal Blue." She pulls her finger back. "So, you're the one that invented the tiny computer in my brain?"

Edward shakes his head. "Oh, heavens, no! I invented the technology that makes the connection. The technology interfaces the computer with the part of your brain that deals with vision, the occipital lobe. It uses the body's magnetic field as a sort of telecommunications center. The short version is: it opens a portal that the computer chip uses to communicate with the brain. I'm currently applying the same technology to give deaf people their hearing back. Testing patients starts in another three months."

She places her hand on the side of his arm. "That was a little above me but thank you a thousand times."

"You're welcome. Would you mind if I asked you a question?"

She releases his arm. "You gave me my sight back. You can ask me anything."

"I don't want to pry. However, there is one thing. I've been wondering about this for weeks now. After you regained your sight, what was the first thing you did?"

She pauses, looks down at his shoes, and notices that they are a perfect match for his suit. This adds to her favorable impression of him. She says, "When I got home, I rushed into my apartment and changed into a dress." Raising her head, she gazed helplessly around the room. "You know what, I probably should back up a minute and explain. I had my dad drive me to The Wild Rose in anticipation of the big day. It's a cool place to shop. They have lady's apparel, boots, and jewelry. The manager, Lisa, helped me pick out a red dress and turquoise boots. I wanted to know what I looked like in a red dress. So, that's what I did. I rushed inside and put it on. Then I spent like twenty minutes just looking at myself. It might not be what you expected. Maybe I should have had my dad drive me to Santa Fe for some eye candy. The Camel Rock formation is there. And I always wanted to see the Woodpecker Arch over in Ramah. But before I did anything else, I wanted to see myself in a red dress."

Edward tilts his head and looks Pax straight in the eyes. "Makes perfect sense. You're a pretty girl. I'm sure you looked amazing."

"Thank you. You lose your compass when you're blind for a long time. When I gained my sight back, my sense of direction was way out of whack. It took about a week and a half before it returned to me. After that, I just wanted to go a hundred miles per hour. I wanted to do some fast catching up and do things I hadn't been able to do. So, I did. I started a Facebook account and Instagram. I even got my driver's license. I haven't got a car yet, but it's in the works. I want to live a totally wired, plugged-in life."

"Sounds like your life has completely changed."

Pax nods. She didn't mean insinuating that blind people can't live a happy, fulfilled life. But all the things concealed from her for so long, she sees now, and it feels incredible. From the fifth grade through her high school and college, she never knew what any of her teachers looked like. Her friends, either. She made so many during her school years. She had already connected with a few of them, through Facebook. "I can't tell you how good it feels to finally be able to put a face to someone I've known most of my life."

She gestures with both hands out in front of her, palms up. "I want to say, Edward, I was nervous about making the trip to D.C. I felt like a bumblebee trapped in a bug zapper when I got off the plane. I was speed talking and repeating myself, thinking they might keep me here. Maybe in time, but it's too soon for me to leave Albuquerque, my home. Then I found out they're not keeping me here, which was a relief. And now this, meeting you, the one responsible for giving my vision back?" She touches his arm just below the shoulder. "It's such a privilege."

"I feel the same way about you." No sooner than Edward spoke, his phone began vibrating. He punches the button. "Mike, I'm busy right now. Can I call you back?"

Pax can hear a voice on the other side but can't make out the words.

"Mike, slow down. Okay, I'll break it off here. I can be there in thirty minutes. If there's traffic, maybe an hour." He punches the phone again. "I'm sorry, Pax. I've recently completed a book, and my publicist needs to meet with me. I was hoping to have more time with you. Could we arrange to meet for cocktails and dinner tonight?"

Again, Pax's hands go out in front of her. "Are you kidding? It would be an honor."

"There's an Italian place called *The Red Hen*. It's on North West Street in D.C." Edward grins and reaches out his hand. "I'll see you there around seven, if that's okay?"

"Seven it is," Pax replied while the two shook.

Outside, a warm breeze curled around the building, blowing, and fluttering their clothes as they walked to the car. The breeze carried the strong scent of Gardenias, which added to the nice day Pax was having.

As Darcie turned on the engine and pulled out onto South Washington Blvd, she realized she needed to say something to Pax. She knew Hawke and Nate's digging around might uncover something. If it did, she didn't want to look like a fraud. She needed to be a friend, a super close friend to Pax. She needed Pax to believe in her at all costs. She watched as the forceful breeze blew grass clippings onto the road. In her mind, she was compelled but was having trouble choosing the right words. She was hoping what she was about to say wouldn't change Pax's perception of her. She kept driving until she finally just blurted it out. "*The moment they catch on to you, you're dead!*"

Mildly surprised, Pax turns looking at Darcie. "You think that's what's going to happen, don't you? You already have it cataloged in your mind."

"Just let me say one or two things, and I won't bring it up again?"

Pax twisted her head, looking out the window. "Fine, go, get it out of your system."

"This investigation that Hawke and Nate are involved in."

"And me."

"Right, and you."

"So, you know about that?" Pax asked.

"I talked to Nate in the hallway before he left yesterday. It's okay. We're all FBI."

Pax looks back at Darcie. She says, "I bet this is going to be good."

"I understand that it looks like someone murdered your mother. Anyone would want to find out what happened. I know I would. The people you're looking into, though. These people, it's not like opening a locked storage compartment to see what's inside. Once you unlock it, you can't change your mind and lock it back."

Pax uses the lever to tilt her seat back. The situation was threatening, menacing, and intimidating. Darcie didn't need to tell her. She knew that already. But she wasn't about to stop the investigation into her mother. Nothing was going to stop her, including Special Agent Hannagan. Tension is building behind her eyes. She closes them and tries to make light of it. "I see. Is that it then?"

Darcie was just getting started. She says, "No. You don't want to put yourself in a situation you can't get away from."

"And you think that's what I'm doing?"

"Of course, why else would I even bring it up? I usually keep work and personal stuff strictly compartmentalized." Darcie gives a quick, concerned glance at Pax. "I can't handle knowing what I know. Every email, every phone call, text message, everything Hawke and Nate do will leave a trace. They'll probably use one of the bureau's tech guys to hide their tracks. In a situation like this, you need better, a lot better."

Pax tilts the seat back further. She rests her head on the headrest. Maybe Darcie wasn't trying to stop the investigation. Maybe she was trying to help it along. "And by better, you mean what exactly? Or maybe I should be asking who?" She tilts her head sideways looking at Darcie. "Who do you have in mind?"

Darcie's hands are clamped like a vice grip on the steering wheel. She says, "Somebody off the radar. Somebody that knows how to keep *you* off the radar. You need a hacker, a good one. You need a leave no trace, expert hacker."

"Okay then. I'll mention it to Hawke next time I see him."

"If he's like other FBI Agents in his age bracket, he won't know a hacker. At least not one good enough to keep you off the grid."

"You act like Hawke is just a kid on a bicycle." Pax felt incredibly defensive toward Hawke. Darcie hadn't really meant it that way or had she. Pax was confused. A fog was descending onto her brain and the tension behind her eyes was engulfing her head.

Darcie picked up on her discomfort. "I didn't mean it like that. I've been an FBI Special Agent for fourteen years. That's a lot longer than Hawke or Nate. The longer you're on the force, the more connections you make. And I have a pocket full, some of them with the D.C. underground."

Pax's eyes flash open. "Who is he then? Who's your D.C. hacker?"

"*It's she*, and I don't know her real name. I just know her as *Nutty-Buddy*."

"And you believe this Nutty-Buddy is the way to go?"

"There are 10,000 spies at any given time in the D.C. area. It's been that way for years. It's the only way to keep your tracks covered."

"How do we get in touch with her?"

"We don't. She gets in touch with us."

"How's that work?"

"I leave a specific phone message at Mac's Computer Repair. *I have a silver dinosaur that needs repairing.* I'm not sure if someone there relays the message, if she has a way of checking in, or if it's something else. All I know is if she takes the job, I will get a text with instructions. When we get back to the hotel, I'll get in touch with Nate and explain things. If he's agreeable, then we move on it. Does that sound good to you?"

Pax leans forward, then uses the lever to move the seat to its original position. "If it keeps me safe, yes." Pax's phone starts buzzing in her hand. She holds it up for Darcie to see. "I don't recognize the number. Should I take it?"

"Looks like a local number. It could be important. Answer it."

"This is Pax. Yes, I understand. Sorry, I just got busy. No, I won't forget. Again, sorry about that. Okay, goodbye." She crams her hand into her purse and starts feeling around.

"What are you doing? Darcie asked.

"Trying to find something."

"Why don't you just open your purse and look?"

Pax removes her hand. "Right, old habits." She opens the purse wide, looks in, and pulls out a small device. "Here it is."

"Here what is?" Darcie asked.

"Dr. Tennison gave it to me. It's to monitor my computer chip. I forgot to turn it on and put it in my ear."

"Could you wait on that?"

"Why?"

"I'm not sure the good doctor was upfront with you. When he showed it to you earlier, I had my suspicions."

"I'm not following you."

"If that thing was really to monitor your vision chip, why didn't they give it to you right after surgery? They could have been tracking the chip for the past seven weeks."

"Good point. What do you think it's for?"

"I've never seen one like it, but I think it's for audio surveillance. Once you put it in your ear and turn it on, they hear all of your conversations. I didn't tell you this, but my superiors had me bug your room before I introduced myself to you. I was to report back directly to the Pentagon."

"Did you tell them about our investigation?"

"No."

"What should I do?"

"If you don't use that thing, they'll want to know why. We don't have a choice. Just do what I say. Now, text Dr. Tennison. Ask him if you should take it off in the shower or swimming pool. But first, install it in your ear and turn it on."

Pax follows directions, tilting her head to the side, pushing the device into her ear, and flipping on the tiny switch. She takes her phone, punches in the doctor's number, and starts texting. *"Dr. Tennison, this is Pax. Should I take this ear device out when I'm showering or swimming?"* In less than a minute, her phone starts ringing. *"Hello, Dr. Tennison. Yes, I can hear you just fine. Okay, that's cool. I just wanted to be careful. No, it's comfortable. Yes, sir, I'll wear it straight through until I'm ready to return to Albuquerque. Okay, thank you."*

Darcie gives a thumbs-up and then puts a finger vertically across Pax's lips, signaling her to remain quiet.

Once they arrive at the hotel, Darcie turns on the car radio and increases the volume. She leans over and whispers in Paxes ear, the one without the device. "Just what I thought. He didn't text back. He called you so he could check how well the bug was operating. If you need to say something without them hearing, make sure the radio or TV is on and the volumes up, then whisper."

At exactly 6:55 that evening, Pax and Darcie arrive at *The Red Hen*. Before exiting the car, Darcie gets a phone call. She is instructed to drive to the Pentagon and meet with one of their intelligence agents. She's to give an update on Pax. "Looks like I'm dropping you off. I have to leave and give a report on you at the Pentagon. I don't think there's anything I can tell them that they don't already know. You going to be, okay?"

Pax opens the door and steps out of the car, then leans her head down, looking through the window at Darcie. "Go, give your report. All good here."

Darcie nods. "You got my cell number if you need me."

Pax waves her off, shuts the door, and watches as Darcie drives away. She takes a moment to look around and sees the entrance to *The Red Hen*. A hazy, neon red sign points the way, and a man and woman snuggling tight open the door and enter. She begins walking, and within five seconds, a Black Mercedes-Benz pulls into the parking lot. A hand waves from inside the vehicle, and it's clear that Edward Cotton has arrived. Pax waits as he parks about twenty feet away.

Suddenly a blue and red motorcycle carrying two men comes whizzing into the parking lot. It screeches to a stop, almost hitting Edward's car. The driver has a blue and red striped helmet that matches the motorcycle. The man on the back is wearing blue jeans and a long red sleeve shirt that is made more noticeable by his muscular build. A solid blue helmet is clasped firmly in his hands. While the driver stays with the bike, the strongly built man jumps off, runs to Edward's car, rears back, and smashes the driver's window with the helmet.

Pax stumbles backward in shock at what's happening. She leans against a yellow Toyota as she watches, not knowing what to do.

The man drops his helmet and, with both hands, reaches into the car, grabbing hold of Edward. He pulls him through the shattered window. Pax can see miniature pieces of glass cutting into Edward's suit and other shiny pieces flinging into the parking lot.

Once he pulls Edward out of the car, he drops him to the ground. Lightning quick, he moves one of his legs back and shoots a high-kick karate move at Edward's face, blasting his head straight back. Moans coming from the injured man sicken Pax's stomach, and she wiggles, pressing herself tighter against the Toyota. Again, the muscular man moves his leg back, gaining momentum. His next strike explodes into the same spot-on Edward's face, and the sound of breakage reverberates through the parking lot.

Pax almost screams, but instead, she throws a hand over her mouth. The brutal man reaches down, rummages through Edward's pockets, and takes his wallet. After checking it for money, he picks up his helmet and surprisingly looks straight at Pax before running back to the motorcycle. In another five seconds, it's all over, the men on the motorcycle having sped away.

Chapter 8

Now

A crowd of ten or twelve had gathered before the police arrived. A tall, overweight man approaches Pax. "Are you alright?"

Pax turns away from him. She places her hands on the Toyota, leans over, and presses her forehead against the top of it. She made a stifled sound that could have meant anything.

The tall man continues. "Did you know the deceased? Are you his daughter or a friend?"

Pax whirls around, facing him. Her face is flushed, her cheeks swollen from crying, "That bastard on a motorcycle killed him!" She's gasping for air as she leans into the man, nearly falling. A fierce shudder plunges out of her as air returns to her lungs. She keeps trying to catch her breath, breathing hard and deep.

"That's good. Keep breathing. You've had a panic attack. Here." He takes a disinfectant wipe from a small container. "Let's get your face cleaned up." The man starts gently wiping. "My name is Earl. I used to be an EMT. You're doing good. You're going to be okay."

Her complexion returns to her face. She steps back from the man, takes one more broken breath, coughs, and her breathing returns to normal. That's when a policeman comes walking up.

He stops directly in front of Pax, points behind him and says, "I was sent your way by a man and woman over there. They tell me you witnessed the crime. Is that true, Miss?"

Pax glances at the police officer. Her eyes opened wide, filled with anger. She says, "What the hell took you so long? I called 911 like thirty minutes ago!"

The officer tilts his head back in surprise. He reaches into his pocket, pulls out a handkerchief, and wipes his forehead. "Could I get your name?"

"Paxton Thomas. Are you going to answer my question?"

"The patrolman in this area was detained. Now, back to *my* question? *Did you witness the crime?*"

"Yes, there were two men on a motorcycle."

The officer throws a hand up in the stop position. "That's good enough." He turns, motions for a man in a black suit, and watches as he walks over. When he gets within ten feet, the officer continues. "We got a witness. Her name's Paxton Thomas. Unless you need me for something else, she's all yours. Forensics needs my help with this one."

The man in the suit stops a few feet from Pax. He says, "You go ahead. I got this now." As the officer turns to walk away, the man in the suit looks at Pax. He tries to grin but doesn't quite make it, his head tilting slightly down instead. "I'm sorry you had to witness this. You've had one hell of a tough day."

Pax doesn't waste time answering. "Would you mind telling me how something like this can happen in broad daylight? And right here in the freaking capital of the country?"

The man in the suit attempts another smile. He looks around at the smashed window, the broken glass, the corpse. He motions with his thumb for Earl to give them some privacy. He says, "Paxton, that's what we're going to find out. I'm Detective Dawson Slater of the D.C. Police Department. If I'm to catch the thug that did this, I'm going to need your help."

Pax steps back and leans on the Toyota. She reaches up and puts a hand on her forehead. "I can't believe this. It was like, you know, a good day, and then, suddenly," she removes her hand from her forehead and points to Edward's dead body, "this happens."

Again, the detective twists his head and looks over the crime scene. He says, "Once in a while, we get a reminder of how fragile life can be and how close we are to that other side." He twists his head back, staring straight into Pax's face. Reaching into his suit pocket, he pulls out a small notebook. "Can you tell me the name of the deceased? They stole his wallet, and we couldn't find any other identification on him."

"Edward Cotton."

"Thank you." He jots it down. "What is your relation, girlfriend, sister, wife?"

"No relation. I was meeting Edward for dinner at *The Red Hen* across the street."

Detective Slater glances over at the Restaurant, nods, and looks back at Pax. "How did you know him? Were you co-workers or just friends?"

"Friends, I guess. I only met him today at the Pentagon."

"The Pentagon?"

"That's what I said."

The Detective grins. "I'm sorry about all the questions. The information is critical to the investigation. I appreciate all your help. Are you going to be okay?"

Pax nods. Momentarily she covers her face with her hands. She is stunned by the past hour's events. The man that restored her eyesight is suddenly dead, murdered right before her eyes. She looks the detective back in the eyes. "Sorry, I still can't believe he's dead. He invented something that helped me with my vision. We met earlier, but he was called away. So, we made plans to meet at *The Red Hen* to talk over dinner. I'm sure the Pentagon could tell you more. He's connected to the federal government somehow. I believe he's one of their research scientists."

"That's a big help. I'll look into that. Can you tell me what happened here?"

"Of course. Edward had just arrived. He was still in his car when these two guys on a motorcycle came rushing in behind him. One of the men jumped off the bike and ran up to Edward's car. He took his helmet and shattered the windshield. Then he just dragged him out. It was horrible to watch. After that, he started kicking him. I think he broke his neck."

"It's not confirmed, but it looks that way. The motorcycles, we run into that a lot. The traffic can get pretty bad in D.C., so criminals use them to maneuver around. Muggings or robberies by these motorcycle bandits are common. They have an easy escape. But this is the first murder I can remember. Can you give me a description of the assailants and their motorcycle?"

"I can do better than that." Pax holds up her phone. "I have it on video."

"That was risky. If the assailants had seen you using your phone to video them, we probably wouldn't be talking right now."

"That's not exactly what I did."

"I'm not following you. Were you hiding?"

"No, I was standing where we are."

The detective hesitates, turns, and looks at the crime scene, visually measuring the distance. "If what you say is true, they had to see you."

"They saw me. Do you want to watch the video or not?"

"Yes."

She punches her phone and starts the video.

"Looks like you were videoing before they arrived. Here comes the motorcycle. The thugs don't seem to care if you record them. It's obvious why you're so upset. There they go. That was fast. Those guys were in and out in like thirty seconds." The detective pushes back his coat jacket, reaches around with his other hand, and unsnaps his phone from a plastic case. He punches at it and holds it up to Pax. "Here's my number. I'm going to need you to text that video to me. It'll be a lot easier than me confiscating your phone."

"Give me just a minute." She punches away. Almost there. Just a second. Got it. You should have it any time now."

"It just came in." He starts reviewing it to make sure it's all there. "I still don't understand why they let you film them."

"They didn't know because I didn't film them with my phone."

The detective tilts his head to the side. "What you're saying doesn't make sense."

"What doesn't make sense!" It was Darcie. Pax had called her just before the police arrived.

"Who's asking?" the detective asked.

"I'm Special Agent Darcie Hannagan of the FBI."

"What's the FBI doing at a robbery/homicide."

Darcie motions with her head to Pax, "This girl is a very important person. I'm her driver while she's visiting D.C."

"Why's the FBI providing a chauffeur service? And where were you when all this went down?"

"I'm not required to answer any of your questions."

"Okay, can you tell me how she was able to record the homicide without using her phone?" He looks around the area, "Because even if her phone has access to surveillance cameras, there's none anywhere in sight."

Darcie looks at Pax. "You haven't told him?"

Pax shakes her head. "I wasn't sure what to do."

"He has a right to know." Darcie glances at the detective. "Before I tell you anything, I need to see some identification."

He reaches into his suit pocket, pulls out a leather case, and flips it open. "Detective Dawson Slater of the D.C.P.D. Special Agent Hannagan, I could use your help on this one."

"Right, well, brace yourself, Detective. This girl has special technology built into her eyes. She doesn't need a phone to record. Basically, her eyes *are* cameras."

The detective shoves his badge back into his suit. "I don't suppose you'll tell me how this came about?"

Darcie shakes her head no. "Even if I understood it, I probably couldn't explain it. You have an explanation of where the video came from, and you have the video itself. If you're as good as I think you are, you'll make an arrest in a day or two."

"So that's it then," the detective replied. "Because I watched the video, and some things don't add up. The robbery seemed like an afterthought. I'm sure it was just to create a motive. This crime was all about committing murder. And why would the murderer look an eyewitness directly in the face and then leave her unharmed?"

"You're barking up the wrong tree, Detective," Darcie answered. "I don't have the answers. I'm sure when you make an arrest, you'll get to the bottom of it. If you want more on the video technology, you'll have to talk to the Pentagon."

"I plan on it. But if it's classified, I won't get anywhere."

"At this point, it's for certain ears only. I think it's worth a try, though."

"Talk with General Robert Stackhouse," Pax exclaimed.

"Stackhouse?"

"Yes."

"Thank you, Paxton. I'll do just that. And just to let you know, it's likely the assailants have an arrest record. If so, we'll bring them in by tomorrow morning. Again, Paxton, I'm sorry about your friend. I'll let you know if we make an arrest."

"Thanks, Detective."

The detective nods, "Paxton, Special Agent Hannagan, I'll see you soon." He turns and walks back to the crime scene.

Darcie takes Pax by the arm. "It's time to go. General Stackhouse wants a briefing. Earlier, when you called, I had to break off a meeting I had with his assistant. I informed him about Edward. We're to go straight to his residence. He wants us there, pronto. And Paxton, I agree with the detective. None of this adds up."

After fifteen minutes of weaving through a maze of roads, they are parked on a concrete entryway waiting for an iron gate to open. When it does, Darcie drives past the gate, veers right, and follows a shrubbery-lined wrap-a-round driveway. The general's assistant greets them and escorts the women through an oval portico inside to the foyer. They are quickly whisked away into a large wood-paneled room where the general is waiting.

At first, the general is silent. He sits behind a large mahogany desk shaking his head in disbelief. His assistant, Henri, seats Pax and Darcie in blue leather chairs directly in front of the desk. "Henri," the general says, "would you mind fetching the decanter and pouring us all a drink? I hope both of you like apricot brandy. I always keep some on hand for times like these. It helps with stress. Your visit, Miss Thomas, I hoped it would go better here in D.C." He leans back in his high-back chair and places his hands behind his head, locking his fingers together. "Oh, what the hell? It's time we admit that crime is getting out of hand in D.C."

The general unlocks his hands and swings forward, picking up his freshly poured drink. After taking a generous sip, he continues. "The public attention has been fixed on the crime rate for a while now. There's so much going on here. And then you mix in the enormous number of tourists. The urban D.C. area covers 1,400 square miles, so it's hard to contain the criminal element."

The general notices Pax is looking up at the ceiling. There is a triangular-shaped skylight that covers a large portion of the roof. The general points to the corner of the room, where a nice-sized telescope is sitting on a tripod. He asks, "Do you like astronomy, Miss Thomas?"

She lowers her head and smiles. "In Albuquerque, we have lots of stars. I only got my vision back seven weeks ago, but I've been noticing how beautiful it is."

"I enjoy viewing the night sky," the general motions with his head. "In those cabinets to your right, I have charts and maps that tell you anything you want to know about all the heavenly wonders. You should get yourself a telescope, a good one, and take up stargazing. It helps to decompress.

Now back to the business at hand. I just got off the phone with a few others representing the Pentagon. What I mean is others who are overseeing your situation. They wanted me to extend sincere apologies for what has taken place. I do not doubt that the D.C. Police Department will handle this in the utmost professional manner. It's such a pity. A great man, an important man, was lost today. And all for the price in his wallet."

"General, sir," Pax interjects, "Detective Slater of the D.C. Police Department seems to believe it was more than a robbery."

The general glances at Darcie. "Special Agent Hannagan, what do you believe?"

"Something seems off about it, but I'm not sure, sir."

"I see. Miss Thomas, you were the only one to witness this. What do you believe?"

"I'm not sure either, sir."

"From my point of view, and I'm not claiming to be an expert, it appears to be a robbery that got out of hand. These thieves on motorcycles have become a real problem. In any case, when they bring him in, he's going down for murder. If we're not careful, we'll end up in a pointing contest. It's the Russians, no, the Chinese, no, it's an Islamic terrorist group. It wouldn't be the first time, and it never gets us anywhere.

Miss Thomas, murder is a terrible thing to witness. I wanted to see you in person to ask you if you're alright?"

"I just want to get back to my room."

"Are you sure there's nothing I can do? I'm not claiming to be the repairer of broken-down walls here, but I could have a Pentagon Psychologist visit you in your room. I'm not going to force it on you, but I strongly recommend it. It would be mandatory if you were on the Pentagon payroll after something like this."

"No, really. I just want to grab a bite to eat and relax in my room. You don't have to worry about me."

"I understand. I'll acquiesce to your wishes. You should know, though, that at the moment, it's my job to worry about you. They want me to keep you around for a few more days where I can keep an eye on you. My peers want this thing to be deader than dinosaurs, or disco, before you leave town. Until then, I'm staying awake, sober, and nervous."

"How long do you plan on keeping me?"

"This should all blow over in five or six days. Maybe a week. By then, we should know who's responsible. I know you want to get back to Albuquerque. I promise to have you on a plane as soon as possible. It's just hard to say when. Meantime, just try to enjoy the rest of your stay."

"Is that everything, then?"

"Unless you'll reconsider the psychologist visit?"

"No, Sir. I'm good. I've got Darcie and a bottle of gin in my room."

The general pressed his hands down on the desk and stood up. "Then you're free to go. I'll be checking in. Oh, and Special Agent Hannagan, I don't want her left alone again. Is that clear?"

"Yes sir."

"Good. Now, Henri, could you see them to their car?"

In less than three minutes, Darcie sped the car around the circular drive, past the iron gate, and onto the two-lane road.

"We can order room service," Darcie glances at Pax as she drives. "I hear the food's top-notch. If that's not to your liking, there's an Italian place two blocks from the hotel."

"Room service is fine. I want to get back. I'm looking forward to a gin and tonic."

"Do you have limes?"

"I haven't seen any, no."

"I'll have room service send some up." Darcie didn't waste time after arriving back at the room. As soon as the limes came, she went into mother hen mode, heading straight for the bottle of gin. She pours two glasses at a one to three ratio and adds ice and lime wedges. She set the two drinks on a coffee table near the patio door.

A few feet away Pax noticed something. She pulls the patio curtain open. The door is partially open. "This morning, didn't I close this before we headed out?"

Darcie looks and sees Pax pointing at the door. "That's odd," she answers. "I made sure the no service sign was on the door. I guess housekeeping could have ignored it, but that almost never happens." She walks toward the curtains and notices the partly open sliding glass door. Reaching her right hand across her chest, she unsnaps her shoulder holster and takes out her 9MM Glock Gen 5. She grips the plastic pull handle on the curtain with her other hand. She counts to three under her breath and swings open the curtains. Quickly she shoves the sliding glass door farther open. A drone, three feet in diameter, is hovering like a spaceship just off the patio. Its distinct, low-frequency whizzing is clear and loud. Darcie is a little unnerved because the drone is looking right at her. Realizing it is spotted, the drone shoots several feet upward before making a U-turn. With a rush of adrenalin and both hands firmly on the gun, Darcie aims, blasting three consecutive shots as the drone attempts its escape. The drone takes a direct hit and warbles back and forth while losing altitude. Its buzzing sound goes quiet. Darcie rushes to the patio's edge, looks over the railing, and watches the drone crash land onto a sidewalk some twenty feet below.

The mind-numbing situation over with, she tries to relax, leaning her body into the railing and catching up on some missed breaths. She almost placed her Glock back into the holster but thought better of it. Behind her, Pax is standing in the opening of the sliding glass door. "What just happened?" she asked. "Was that thing here to harm us?"

"It didn't have a weapon attached to it, just a camera." Darcie never takes her eyes off the drone. "Someone is monitoring you."

"Someone dangerous?"

Darcie glances at Pax. "The safe thing to do is consider them dangerous, yes."

When Darcie looks back at the drone, she sees a man running from the parking lot.

He's headed in the direction of the drone.

"Freeze!" she screams and shoots one round into the sky.

He never flinches, reaching the drone in less than five seconds.

Darcie fires one more warning shot. "I said, *Freeze!*"

Reaching down, the man takes hold of the drone.

Darcie unloads two more shots, both hitting the man in the leg.

He hobbles backward, twisting sideways, losing his balance, and drops the drone next to a cherry tree. Wasting no time, he grabs hold of the tree and uses it to pull himself up. His attempt to walk results in him falling again. By now, doors are opening, and people are watching in surprise.

Darcie shoves her gun back into the holster, pulls out her phone, and starts punching away. It goes into voice mail. "Hawke, you, and Nate need to get over here right now! This afternoon all hell has broken loose. It landed at Pax's feet. I need you here, and I need you now!" Darcie races across the patio and past Pax into the hotel room. "Lock the door behind me." She hesitates, turning back. "I mean it, Pax. Lock all the doors behind me, and don't open them until I get back. Are we clear?"

"Lock the doors. Yes, I understand."

Outside the hotel, Darcie walks tensely with her gun drawn. Up ahead, she sees the drone and scans with her eyes, searching for the injured man. People are standing outside their doors. Darcie throws up a hand, encouraging them to go back inside. She hears the faint sound of sirens. She looks around for the injured man. She can't find him. She grabs the drone and heads back to Pax's room. As the sirens grow louder, she picks up her pace, not wanting to be spotted by the uniforms. She wanted to keep this a G-man investigation, not chancing the local police confiscating the drone.

She hears a car driving by. Glancing to her left, two men are in the car, one closely watching her, the other slumped over. It's the man she's been looking for and his accomplice. She stops in her tracks, pulls her Glock out, and shows it to the driver of the car. "Don't get too clever," she shouts and watches as the car speeds away. She can tell by the sirens that the police are pulling into the hotel parking lot. She places the gun back in the holster, swings open a door and enters the building. At the elevator, she waits anxiously for a group of tourists to exit, steps in, and punches button 3.

By the time she reaches the room, her eyes are ablaze with tension. Her breathing is quick and uneasy. She pounds on the door and shouts for Pax. Upon opening the door, Pax sees Darcie stooped over and holding a piece of paper. "What are you reading?"

Darcie stands back up. With one hand, she holds the drone, with the other a handwritten note that she had found at the base of the door. Her face is covered in apprehension and concern. She looks at Pax. "It's addressed to you."

"What does it say?"

Darcie lowers her eyes and raises the piece of paper. She hesitates a moment and squeezes the piece of paper tight. *"You might be a D.C. girl, but if you know what's good for you, you will go back to Albuquerque, take that brain chip with you, and stay the hell away from D.C. Your life is in danger!"*

Chapter 9

Twenty-Years Ago

Dear Momma

    When you come back, I can't wait to show you Daddy's house. I should probably warn you that it's much bigger than the one that exploded. Besides nineteen rooms, it has a giant creepy-smelling attic. When I told Daddy I went in there, he locked it up and told me I could get hurt. I asked him why his house was so big, and he said, because he grew up in a prominent place, and that's what he liked. He said if he lived in the Biltmore, he would still want one more room. I don't know what the Biltmore is, but I guess it doesn't have many rooms.

    Anyways, this house has seven bedrooms and four bathrooms, if you don't count the one that Daddy calls a closet. There is enough space for more little girls and maybe some big people too. The house is very old, and my room has a built-in marble washstand, which I like and am very proud of. I think you would be proud of it too, momma, because you can wash your face before getting into bed. And there is a pot-bellied stove in my room. It is one of five in the house, and in the old-timey days, it was used to heat the place. I managed to open the door on it but had to bang it shut, so I'm not doing that again. Daddy said this used to be a boarding house, and people would come into this room and sit around talking and warming up and stuff.

    The other day I heard voices, and since my room is on the second floor, I walked to the stairs and sat down on the top step to listen. I could hear two women talking to Daddy, and one of them sounded a little like you. It sounded like they were all in the parlor. The one that sounded like you said she remembers holding me when I was a baby. After she told me that, it got really quiet. I was trying to hear, so I leaned forward and almost fell down the steps. When they started talking again, I didn't think she sounded much like you anymore. Those two women got in a battle with their words, and both showed great courage. It was wonderful to hear them, and it made me feel strong like I could do anything. And I thought that I would like to be like that too. I did not call out to them for fear I might be summoned and not make a good impression. That night at supper, I talked to Daddy about them. He told me they were from work at the Pentagon. He said he had known them for a long time. He said that there was three women, not two, but that one of them was shy and soft, and I probably could not hear her.

We are having a hard winter with lots of snow like last year. Daddy paid someone to shovel a path from the house to the sidewalk so that I could go out and play. I can still make little snow animals, but they probably don't look as good as before I was blinded.

I've been sitting here rambling and trying to talk to you about my blindness, so, here goes. At first, I didn't know if I wanted to keep living, but I tried. And then the next day, I tried again. And then I woke up one day and thought that trying was not hard anymore. For a long time, all I could dream about was the house exploding. Then, one night I didn't dream. I stayed awake all night, wondering why bad things happen. I used to believe that everything in life was going to work out. Then you and Daddy got divorced, and the house exploded. Now that I know things don't always work out, I think that means I'm grown up.

One more thing, momma. The day before you were killed, you said you was making hot chocolate, and we were gonna sit at the kitchen table and talk. But it was snowing, and I begged you to let me go out and play. I thought about it a lot, and when you come back, I would like to have a do-over on that one.

See you someday, I hope.

Your daughter, Pax.

P.S. I still have my memories from before things didn't work out.

Chapter 10

Twenty-Two Years Ago

The Thomas family lived on the outskirts of Arlington, Virginia, just outside the heartbeat of D.C. Not far from them were some of the more popular tourist attractions. Within this megalopolis of millions, they were part of one of the most affluent metropolitan areas in the U.S. Their house was an eleven-room colonial style, which, if not for its white exterior and black shutters, would be nearly impossible to distinguish between the other two dozen or so on their street. Though the house was quite old, it had been updated with new wiring and plumbing.

One afternoon, Gatsby drove his Mercedes Benz onto the vintage brick driveway and eased his way underneath a sizeable arched carport. After walking inside, he took a glass, added three cubes of ice, and poured himself a generous portion of scotch. When he hears a voice calling out to him, he walks from the kitchen to the den. Sloan was there doing some straightening up. Pax sometimes uses it as a playroom, and Sloan was a stickler for unnecessary clutter. "Where's Pax?" Gatsby asked.

Sloan rises from a kneeling position, holding a plastic horse and a barbie doll. "She's in her room doing homework."

Gatsby smiles and takes a sip of scotch. "Still doing math?"

Sloan tosses the toys into a cardboard box. "No, English, but it's simple stuff. It's what she needs the most work on."

"That's why I love her," Gatsby said. "She never gives up. Most kids would be outside playing. It's a beautiful day out."

"Would you mind if I change the subject?" Sloan asked, giving him a sharp, serious look.

Instinctively, Gatsby's brow raises, wondering, hoping it's not what he thinks it is. He lifts his glass, takes another sip, and enjoys the warming sensation as it eases down his throat. He says, "Of course not."

Sloan leans her legs into the side of a sofa and crosses her arms. She glances around the room. "I accepted their offer to receive the training."

Gatsby starts to talk but then stops. He sets his drink on an end table, raises his hands, and massages the side of his head, giving out a rusty groan. He says, "I thought we were going to discuss it more."

"We were, but I want this. Without the training, I can't be an agent."

"Are you sure you know what you're getting yourself into?"

"I've worked in intelligence for nine years," she responds with a noticeable attitude. "I know what the job involves, Gatsby."

"There are dangers, serious risk-taking. It's different than staying in one place, mostly behind a desk."

Sloan reaches over, grabs his drink from the table, and takes a sip. She sets it back down and crosses her arms again, only this time tighter and with a deep serious breath.

Doing this was a characteristic of hers, a defensive position, and a habit that Gatsby did not care for.

She says, "I know I should've talked to you about this first, but look, I know what the hell I'm doing!"

"No, you don't!"

"Yes, I do, and anyway, you've never even worked in intelligence!"

"I know more than you think."

She knew he was right, but she had to take a stand, and this was the time to do it. Enough time had been wasted. "Really! How's that?"

"I cover the field agent's asses! I'm the one that makes it look like they have halfway regular jobs when what they really do is illegal!"

To Sloan this was a personal shot, or at least that's how it felt. "What they do is necessary and vital to the country's security!"

"I'm not questioning that, Sloan. But espionage against another country is a crime. A spy violating another country's laws may be deported, imprisoned, *or even executed.*"

"I'll mostly be doing surveillance."

"Depending on what the surveillance is used for, it's still spying." Gatsby throws his hands up and lets them fall. Shaking his head he says, "In a few years, they'll have you involved with hostile acts. Sloan, I know how it works! I've been covering their butts for years!"

"It's what I want. I think I'll be good at it."

"I don't doubt that, not for one minute. But that's not the point. Look, you're wound tighter than a jack-in-the-box. Have a drink and think about this. We have a nice life here, working 9-to-5 with weekends off. Field agents' lives are unpredictable. They're always in and out, not knowing where they'll be from one day to the next."

Sloan uncrosses her arms. She wasn't giving in. That time had passed. "Are you going to support me on this or not?"

"Doesn't matter. I've seen you like this before. When you get your mind set on something, you lose track of everything else. Come hell or high water, you're pushing forward."

"I still want your support."

"You should have thought about that before agreeing to the training!"

"Stop being an ass!"

"I'm tired of you calling me an ass every time we disagree. I have the right to be pissed off!"

"And I have the right to follow my dream!"

"What's the matter, momma?" Pax had overheard them and came to look. Her mother and father never used to argue, but the last few weeks had changed all that.

"It's nothing," Sloan responded. "Go back to your room, honey. I'll be there in a minute."

"I don't want to."

Gatsby walks over, kneels, and looks her in the face. "Would you like to go outside and play?"

She nods.

"She has homework to finish," Sloan interjects.

"No, momma. I'm finished."

"Go on then, but don't leave the yard. Do you want your horse?"

Pax nods again, and Sloan reaches into the box, pulls out the molded plastic toy and hands it to her. "Don't let me catch you outside the yard. And stay away from the gardenias and peonies."

As soon as Pax closes the door behind her, Gatsby lifts his drink, takes two swallows, and again hesitates while the stiff potion burns a pathway to his stomach. He glances hard at Sloan. "When's your training?"

"Three weeks."

"Langley?"

"Yes. I'll be home every evening."

"How long?"

"The usual is 18 months. But I've had at least half of that training already, including the uniform police, criminal investigation, and federal law enforcement. They tell me 8-10 months, depending on how well I adapt. They signed me up for the STD program (CIA Special Activities Training), so that means an extra three months."

"The SAT program?"

"Yes. So, altogether, I'm looking at one year of training."

"Did you request the SAT program?"

"No. My superior said he thought I would be a good fit."

"You know that's the CIA's most secret operations."

"Yes, deep undercover, I know."

"You'll be deployed 60-90 days at a time."

"That's at least two years down the road, and only if I don't end up opting out."

"Is that possible?"

"I accepted the SAT training with the understanding that if they convert me to an operative, I will remain stationed here in D.C. Any covert assignments would be of the shorter versions. It should stay that way for the first two years. At that point, I either opt-in or opt-out. I can still be a CIA operative without being in the SAD program. I just thought it would be good to get the training and make that decision later."

"It surprises me that you would consider it."

"I've been thinking about this for a long time."

"How long?"

"Since like, I don't know, forever. I'm tired of being a pencil pusher." She jerks her hand out and starts counting with her fingers. "I got the smarts, athleticism, and looks to be an excellent operative. And I'm fluent in five languages, which will make my assignments that much easier."

Gatsby nods in agreement. He says, "I understand why the higher-ups want you. But you have a family."

"Most operatives do, and they manage."

"You don't have a clue how they manage, not really."

"What the hell is that supposed to mean?" Sloan grabs the drink from Gatsby's hand, slams her head back, and finishes it off like it was a glass of water.

"It means their families are probably a wreck," Gatsby still tries to convince her. "I've heard stories of problem children, separations, and divorces. That's the reality of spending so much time from home!"

"And you think that's what will happen to us?"

"I don't know, Sloan, I hope not. But this has already caused a rift between us. That's as plain as day. Lately, all we do is pick at each other."

Sloan sets the glass back on the end table, lunges forward, and places both arms around him. "I'm not going to let that happen."

Gatsby pats her back. He rubs her silky hair between his fingers. He gently moves her head off his shoulder and kisses her on the cheek. Not letting up, he tilts his head until their noses touch and he lays a deep, satisfying one on her lips. They stood there for the next couple minutes, alternating kissing and hugging. When they finally let up, Sloan points a finger to the coffee table in front of the sofa. "Have you ever seen one of those?"

"I can't say that I have. What is it?"

"It's a microfilm reader."

"Seriously? That's the old-fashioned way of stealing information."

"I know. The U.S. hasn't used them in decades. I'm getting familiar with it because some backwoods countries still use primitive technology." She holds the empty glass out in front of him. "Could you get us a refill?"

Outside, Pax was filling a round plastic swimming pool with water. She leaves the hose in the pool and goes running around the yard, picking wild bluebells that have sprung up in scattered patches. She plucks dozens of the horn-shaped blooms and begins tossing them one by one into the pool. When she has emptied her hands, she runs cautiously over to the Gardenias, scours the back windows of the house in case her mother is watching and plucks two handfuls. After running back to the pool, she tosses them in, plops down on her butt, and begins stirring her hand in the water. Gazing in awe, she watches, smiling at the sight of dozens of blue and white flowers dancing in circles and sending their fragrance across her delicate young face. She is captivated, unaware that her parents have begun to argue again inside the house.

It used to be that sipping scotch together was a unifier for Sloan and Gatsby. They would sip and talk about their government jobs, their financial security, their living in one of the most politically exciting areas in the world. Now, instead of the calming effect, the alcohol was broadening and intensifying their agitation with each other. Sloan wanted to make the most of her CIA career, training for and becoming a deep-cover operative. Gatsby, who had always supported her, was drawing a line, insisting her career change was too radical.

"I recollect the time when you supported everything I did." Sloan holds a tight grip on her scotch.

"I still do," Gatsby responded quickly, strongly. "Just not this." Gatsby knows operatives get caught and imprisoned often, and sometimes killed in the line of duty. As a Pentagon lawyer, he knows that when things go wrong, the government must extract itself from the operative agent, denying any involvement.

Since the CIA is directly under the Pentagon's authority, Gatsby has first-hand experience.

Sloan plops down on the sofa, kicks her shoes off, and throws her feet on the coffee table. She says, "And now you're going to abandon me!"

Gatsby walks around from the backside of the sofa and stands next to the coffee table. "That's not a fair summation."

Moving her feet off the table, Sloan leans forward and sets her drink on the table. "What do you think is fair?"

"I'm not sure."

Sloan shakes her head in agitation. "Do you remember where we first met?"

"Of course I do."

"Then say it!"

"The Pentagon."

"That's right. You were an intern, and I had a clerical position, mostly delivering mail. We were both fresh out of college, and I had already applied for acceptance into the CIA."

"I remember. I think I was assisting one of the Pentagon lawyers. You were pushing your cart and stopped at the desk where we were standing. I noticed you were eyeing me. I nodded and smiled."

"You had on a charcoal grey, three-piece suit with a cobalt blue tie. You looked incredible. I mean, God, you were so sexy."

"And you had legs as long as a Pentagon hallway."

"I still do."

"I promise you it hasn't escaped my notice."

"Good. My point is you knew when we met, I wanted to work for the CIA."

"That's true."

"And you didn't have any hesitation to date me and marry me."

"For heaven's sake, Sloan, I'd do it again!"

"I don't think so. If you knew then what you know now, you'd have handled things differently."

"But how can you say that?"

"I told you when we were dating that I would be an operative one day. Do you remember we were at the Lincoln Memorial sitting on the top step?"

"Yes, but I thought you were just imagining. I didn't think your mind was made up."

"You thought I was too fragile, too pretty to ever make it. You weren't threatened by it because you didn't think me capable."

"No. You've got me all wrong. By that time, we were the best of friends. We were in love. I would have married you no matter what."

"I don't believe you!" Sloan is fighting to keep her emotions under control. Her body is starting to tremble. She snatches hold of her scotch, guzzles a large swallow, and falls hard into the sofa. The magic potion is affecting her senses. She raises her glass, leans her head back, and downs another swallow. Instantly her face turned pink. "If you," she breaths in deeply to maintain speech control, "still feel the same way," she inhales again, "you'll stop being AN ass and just support me."

"You're drunk! And I told you once already. I don't like being called an ass, especially not by a bottle of scotch!"

Sloan doesn't respond; instead, she stares at Gatsby, her eyes giving a silent appeal. For about a minute, both say nothing. Finally, he kneels, leans in, hesitates a moment looking at her, then kisses her brow. Slightly backing up, he rubs his finger across her lips and kisses her brow again.

Sloan shook her head and blinked her eyes, trying to clear her head. "Please, Gatsby. I do have rights."

"Of course, you do. You're not thinking clearly. It's the scotch."

She continues. "The guys at work." She places her hand on the side of his face. "They ready 'spect it." She hesitates and shakes her head again. "They already expect it. And I have the right."

Gatsby removes her hand, then uses the coffee table as leverage to push himself up.

Instinctively Sloan scoots forward. She locks her eyes onto his. "Aren't you going to say," she closes her eyes, takes a breath, and opens them right back up, "anything?"

Gatsby nods in irritation. "Yes, you have rights. I don't own you. You can do as you please."

"You'll support me then?"

Now it's Gatsby trying to hold it together. He looks up to the ceiling, then around the room, concentrating, trying to think of another way. When he plants his eyes back on Sloan's, they are filled with a world of pain. "I'm sorry, darling. I can't. I wish I could. I do. But my time at the Pentagon tells me this isn't going to go well for you."

She reaches out, places her hand on his leg, and gently squeezes. "But if you could just put yourself in my place. For just a moment, think about how I feel. I love you, and I love Pax. I love the family we've made. I would never let anything happen to that."

Gatsby pushes at her hand and shakes her off. "I said, 'No'!"

His voice is filled with so much power that Sloan snatches her hand back and starts to cry. With mascara easing down her face, she stands up slowly like she barely has the strength. Suddenly the alcohol kicks in, and her eyes light up. "You don't love me! You never freaking did! You got your career, but the hell with mine!" At this moment, they hear a door slamming shut from inside the house.

"Did Pax come back inside?" Sloan asked.

"If she did, I didn't see her."

"My God, Gatsby. Do you think she overheard us?"

Gatsby walks over to a window and looks outside. He says, "She was in the backyard, but there's no sign of her now."

Suddenly they hear a movement and the sound of feet running up the stairs to the second floor. Gatsby starts toward the stairway. There is another much louder banging sound outside.

"Gatsby, recheck the backyard," Sloan shouted, the effects of the scotch having been frightened away from her. "It must be Pax."

Gatsby looks hard at Sloan. The two stand there, frozen, staring at each other. Gatsby swallows hard. He says, "But if Pax is outside, who just ran up the stairs?" Another loud sound causes him to run and glance out the window. "The winds picked up. The trash cans are blowing around, and the Crepe Myrtles are brushing the house." He notices the door going from the kitchen to the backyard is open. "Someone left the door open. It must have been Pax. She probably came in while we were arguing."

"Why didn't we see her?" Sloan asked loudly.

Suddenly Pax is standing in the room. Her t-shirt is wet. She is crying. On the left side of her face, there is blood.

Gatsby and Sloan both run to her. Sloan reaches her first, rubs her finger on Pax's cheek, and examines the blood. "What's happened to you, child? Why is there blood coming from your eye?"

Gatsby reaches her next. He examines her and says, "I don't think the blood's coming from her eye. I think she has a cut." He points closely. "See right here. It's right in the corner next to her eye socket. Who did this to you, Pax, darling? Is there someone else in the house?"

Pax rubs her eyes, and the blood comes out even more. "You don't like each other."

"What are you talking about?" Sloan asked.

"You don't like each other anymore," Pax repeated.

"Of course, we do."

"No. I heard you."

"We were just having a disagreement. It doesn't mean anything. Who did this to you? Is someone else in the house? Answer me!"

"You don't like each other anymore. I heard you. I ran. When I got to my bed, I tripped."

Sloan places her thumb over the cut, temporarily stopping the bleeding. She glances back at Gatsby. "In the kitchen, the first aid drawer, could you get the gauze and one of those butterfly bandages?"

Shaking loose from her mother, Pax falls back on her butt. "You don't like each other anymore! You can't lie to me! I heard you!"

Sloan tries to scoop her off the floor, but Pax starts screaming even louder. "Don't touch me! Don't touch me! Don't touch me!"

Chapter 11

Now

Café Bella was its usually busy place. Blue-collar workers came and went while locals and tourists sat eating freshly prepared food and drinking the best espresso drinks this side of Albuquerque. Pax was one of them, and nobody was more surprised to see her here than herself.

She had fled D.C. in the middle of the night without telling a soul. One minute she was lying in her hotel bed, the next, she was slipping quietly down the hall and into the lobby. She overheard a man talking to his wife about driving straight through to Philadelphia instead of getting a room. She quickly offered them 300 dollars to let her tag along, and instantly their decision was made. Once in Philadelphia, she boarded a plane with a half-hour layover in Chicago before heading to Albuquerque. She had no idea how she was going to explain herself. She only knew that she needed to be where she felt comfortable, and D.C. wasn't it.

She sits sipping on a caramel iced coffee and gazing out the window. Across the street, an enormous white concrete building is blocking her apartment from view. The computer chip manufacturing company is one of the major employers in the Albuquerque area. Pax's vision is unusually sharp today. In the parking lot of the block building, she can see five employees standing next to a Ram 4-door pickup truck. Even though they are tucked between other cars and are over 50 yards away, she can see close-up details. For the first time, she notices her eyes have the ability to zoom in close as if she were standing with the employees. She sees that one of them, a White Hispanic girl, has brown eyes, hair dyed blue, and arms covered in tattoos. A girl standing next to her has a pierced nostril ring. In the middle of her bottom lip is a shiny labret. She keeps sticking her tongue out and licking it. Pax sees all of this with perfect clarity. She concentrates and zooms in super close. Nuances in their facial features expand like they are under a microscope. There are distinctions in skin tone, small pores, and what would normally be invisible hair in plain view on the outer portion of their cheeks. She looks closely in amazement as all of this blends with imperfections, scars, darkness under eyes, moles, and freckles.

While staring across the street, Pax feels an insistent tug on her arm. "Yo, New Eyes, you like all dreamed up. You spaceship gazing, a floating fantasy." It's Josie. With one hand, she sipped on a Frappuccino, with the other, she continues to tug on Pax's arm. "Come back, girl, to Café Bella landing pad."

When Pax looks up, she immediately notices several fresh cuts on Josie's face. She asks, "Did you get into it with Chili Pepper again?"

"No, we good. He like all up in my stuff, but we good." She points through the window. "See him there, Chili Pepper intexticating with his I-Honey."

Pax twists her head around and sees him on his phone. "Oh, I get it. He's thumb lashing on his electronic leash, probably gaming." Turning back, Pax points at Josie's face. "So, what happened?"

Josie angles her face and pushes some hair behind her ear. More cuts are showing. She says, "All weird, lightbulb exploded in momma's house."

"You're lucky it didn't get into your eyes. Is your face going to be, okay?"

"Doc says all super, sixty days, no trace, no scars."

"That's good to hear." Pax slides her empty plate away. She crosses her arms on the table, and rests on her elbows. She places her lips on the straw of her drink and takes a generous sip. "I've been wondering about you, Josie. You know, about your martial arts training, the way you held your hands up and combat kicked Chili Pepper in the chest." She hesitates, taking another sip. "Can you teach me?"

Josie gives a big smile, displaying her pretty face. She nods. "Yo, just say, girl."

"There's no time like the present," Pax responds. "We could take our drinks outside to the other end of the parking lot. There's plenty of room. I think it's safe."

Josie doesn't say a word. She takes a sip of her Frappuccino, turns toward the door, lifts her hand, and waves for Pax to come.

Outside, the sky was a cloudless, clear blue. No white haziness from pollution could be spotted hanging around like would sometimes happen. It was one of those days you thought you could dip your finger into the sky and fingerpaint your name right into the air.

They stood between an old truck and an SUV and had three empty parking spaces to go to work in. Josie stands facing Pax. She takes Pax's arms and holds them up. "Time for some straight talk. We are getting' serious now. You ready?"

Pax nods. "I'm ready."

"Make two fists," Josie said, holding her hands slightly to the side of Pax's hands and analyzing them. "Thumbs center of your knuckles, jive that?"

"I understand."

"Right-right. Now tighten them. No, no' yo, harder! True that true that, perfecto. Now, up-up in your face, 6-8 inches spaced. Yo, your elbows need to be tighter, closer together. Tight band, tight band, go girl, much better. Otherwise, if you take a strike, they'll be easily displaced. Keep them tight, pretty face between them. Now, bend your knees like New Eyes riding surfboard, trying to stay balanced. Always keep your knees bent or risk getting knocked off balance. Too much, too much. Come up a little. Good, awe inspire, double perfecto. In this position, you ready to back yourself up, attack like spinning Ninja. Now, take two quick fight jabs."

"Okay. Like this?" Pax blasts away.

"Go, girl. True that. Now, more speed, Pax. Both should land one after another in the same spot. Use quick jabs to gauge distance. Navy Seal attentive, feel the landing, repeat blows."

Pax swings away. Two swings at a time, ten times in a row.

"Next, relax like momma's old dog," Josie continues. "Go on, relax, arms down, loose up, loose up. Now, quick, right back into combat stance and jab. Nice, girl, inspiring. Practice in and out combat stance, jab and jab, and jab. I want you in and out quick, no thinking. When threatened, yo, automatic. Now, practice-practice, girl. Go on, practice-practice."

Pax went right at it, moving more smoothly than Josie expected. She took to it like it was her given nature. She looked like she had been doing it her whole life. The more she went back and forth, the faster and smoother she became. "Yo, girl, what the hell!" Josie shouted. "You been holding out! Who trained you? Give it up!" She starts laughing.

Pax hesitates, relaxing her stance. She says, "I've never done this before."

"Chill, just kidding," Josie chuckles. "You like lightning in a bottle, like reflex heaven. Way faster than me."

"What? No!" Pax interjected.

"Yes. You ready for more?"

"I think so, yes."

"If attacked from the chest up, move arms side to side. If attacked from the waist down, block by raising the leg. See if you can block me." Josie throws a punch at half-speed, and Pax easily cuts it off. Josie incrementally starts throwing one punch after another, each time speeding up the pace. Soon she is whaling away, mixing in feet attacks. Pax is locked in, blocking all punches as easily as the first. Within seconds Josie is doing everything she can to get through Pax's defense, but it's no use. She starts swinging wildly, trying different angles.

Pax is moving so fluently it's like she is hardly moving at all. Strangely, she feels her mind racing, calculating, processing, and storing information like some kind of advanced supercomputer. Just as strange to her is she's not stressing the least bit. She's moving, accelerating with hyper bursts of speed, and she feels wonderful. Her velocity is smoothly meeting speed and direction, no matter how much Josie changes things up. Once Josie realizes that it's no use, she just stops. She places her hands on her knees, huffing away, trying to catch her breath.

"You deadly action, girl. All smooth, sexy, resourceful. You a star fell from heaven. We chillin' now, yo, all loose, all fun."

Pax relaxes and breathes freely, smoothly. She looks like she's been doing nothing but standing around idle. "I don't understand. It felt good, I mean *seriously, incredibly,* in every part of my body good. I want to learn more. Can we do more?"

"Yo, Miss Hercules. Give me a minute to rest. I gonna show you how to reverse yourself, get behind your attacker, take him down. After that, six Navy Seal attack moves. I feel you, girl. You born kick butt; G.I. Jane combat ready."

One hour later, the two girls are leaning against a rusty old truck. By the look of it, the truck has been broken down and parked here for months. Pax is digging into her purse. She pulls out a wad of cash. After counting it, she says, "Here, I want you to have this."

Josie places both hands behind her head and locks her fingers. "What's up with that?"

"They evicted you. I think it's unfair."

"Yo, you didn't just say unfair to make yourself feel better?"

"What are you talking about?"

Josie removes her hands from her head, moves them around to her stomach, and crosses her arms. She says, "Take some of that money of yours, and like, jump an airbus to the beach. Drink Mai Tai's and get that pretty face tanned. Or cruise a floating hotel and get all pleasured by a sea prince."

Pax smiles at Josie. She reaches out smashing the money between Josie's arms and says, "You know what? You're just going to have to deal with it. Think of it as payment for kicking Chili Peppers butt for me."

Josie doesn't respond. Instead, she just stares at Pax.

"I know you're a tough, proud girl, Josie. You should be. You're nice-looking and got kick-butt abilities. But at the end of the day, you're just a person with needs like everybody else. I know you could use the cash."

Still nothing from Josie but a stare.

"No offense, but am I talking to myself here?" Pax looks hard at Josie. "Okay, well, I think you should know something about me. After I went blind, I could still see for a while in my dreams. And then slowly, more and more, I was, you know, blind. It was four or five years when it started. First, the color faded, and I dreamed in gray. Then everything went black, and I could hardly tell the difference between when I was dreaming to when I was awake. Twelve years ago, I stopped dreaming altogether. They tell me now that I can see, the dreams will come back. They're right; I just had a couple of dreams this past week. The night before last, I had another one."

Josie scoffs at Pax and turns her face away. She asks, "Oh yeah, what did you dream?"

Pax smiles really wide. "I dreamed you had a sense of humor."

Josie jerks her head back. She giggles. "That was a dream, alright."

"That's what I'm saying." They both burst out laughing. When they settle down, Pax continues. "I'll make this simple for you. My dream was about you, and I think that means something. I think, no, *I know* that you're someone I want in my life."

"Yo, did you just compliment me?"

"It's more like, just the way it is."

After Pax got her sight back, she had no real connection to the world. She was just going through the motions for a month and a half. It was like she was in flux, trying to get her bearings. Everything was one giant haze. And then she met Josie. When she saw her handle Chili Pepper the way she did, the blood started pumping faster in her veins. It was that connection to the world.

"Yo, D.C. girl. Why you all talkative today?"

She spoke harshly, but Pax didn't take it that way. Her throat tightens and there's a rush in her chest, a good rush because she's happy. *"Josie, it's called letting someone get to know you."*

Two iced teas from Cafe Bella gave the girls energy for another intense self-defense session. When the sun had moved past the midday point, Josie walked away more convinced that Pax and fighting went together like hammer and nail. She could not wait to see Pax throw the hammer down. She had no doubt that she would wipe the floor with almost anyone.

Chapter 12

Now

Later that day, Pax sits comfortably in Cabezon Park near the center of Rio Rancho. She watched frequent walkers and mothers looking over their children as they run, dart, and swing on the monkey bars. Pax had started visiting the park a couple of weeks after her vision was restored. She is eyeing a middle-aged man; she doesn't recognize him as a regular.

He walks up, holding a small box, glances at her, and sits on the same bench with her. After setting the box next to himself, he fans out his arms, placing them on the backrest. He looks far off into the distance.

Pax is suspicious of him because he wears a sharp-looking black suit with shoes that stick out like a sore thumb. They are pretty but bright blue and don't match his suit. He could be a politician looking for votes, but even then, he wouldn't need the jacket.

"Beautiful day, don't you think?" When he asked the question, he didn't turn to look at her.

"Yes," Pax replies, resisting the urge to stare at him. "The weather's one of the reasons I love Albuquerque. It's like this most of the time. But you're not from around here, are you?"

"It's that obvious?"

Pax nods. "Even if you weren't wearing those shoes, you'd look totally ridiculous."

The man still doesn't look at her. He says, "That's funny as hell, and I hardly ever use that word." He finally turns to look in her direction, and they both burst out laughing. In a few seconds, he continues. "Way over there, past the pavilion," moving his arm off the backrest, he points. "Can you see the elementary school? You have to look hard. Most people aren't able to see it, not from this distance, but it's there."

"I can see it just fine," Pax replies.

"Of course, you can. You can probably see past the school, maybe all the way to Camacho Road or Walsh Loop. Can you make out the street signs?"

"That's over two hundred yards away."

"I realize that, but I bet you can if you focus."

"Yes, I can. Who sent you? Was it General Stackhouse?"

"No, coming here was my idea. However, you might want to know that the general is slightly bothered by your running off."

"And the FBI agents?"

"Them too."

"How much do you know about me?"

"Everything, which is a lot more than you know about yourself."

What did he mean by that, Pax wonders? Wherever this was going, she knew she needed to follow. Angling her shoulders, she turned toward the man and asked, "What is that supposed to mean?"

The man frowns. "It wasn't my intention to upset you. I was just stating the truth. You already know that you can see far better than any other person. You have fantastic zoom capabilities. Have you noticed anything else about yourself that's improved?"

Stunned by his knowledge of her, she felt her jaw dropping open. She needed to play this out to the end. "Now that you mention it, yes. My physical speed and reflexes. It's like I'm another person."

"Oh, I can assure you that you are the same person. Only now you can out-see and out-maneuver anyone else on the face of the earth."

She knew he was right. There was something, a strange feeling, reinforcing his words. And it wasn't in her mind. *Something inside her was physically changing*, but how? Had blindness been holding back her abilities all these years? Had she been more than just a math prodigy all along? Her questions were piling up. It was time for answers. She asks, "How is that possible?"

"Surely by now, you've figured it out." He taps the side of his head.

"You mean the chip in my brain?"

"I mean the sensory chip that I invented and had installed in your brain, yes."

"Well, why wasn't I told? I thought it was just for vision."

"Are you complaining?"

"No. Really, I just meant, well, telling me ahead of time, it just makes sense."

"The technology in your brain is being guarded. Only a select few know about it. Not even the surgeon that operated on you knows all your capabilities."

"I don't think your secret is as secret as you think," Pax said.

"You're referring to the incident at the Hotel Pentagon?"

"Yes, someone's trying to kill me and extract the chip."

"And that's why you came running back home to the ABQ?"

"I needed to be somewhere I felt safe."

"And you feel safe here?"

"Yes, D.C. was a disaster. Edward getting murdered, people watching my every move."

The man nods in agreement. "For the time being, I can arrange for you to stay here."

"Thank you."

"You're welcome."

"You never introduced yourself. What's your name?" Pax asked.

"I'm not sure you're going to like my answer."

"I don't follow."

The man shifts his hands from the backrest to his side, pressing his palms down on the bench. His face squints, and wrinkles pop out on his forehead. "Paxton, my name is *Edward Cotton*."

Startled, she quickly stands. She says, "Edward Cotton was murdered. I saw it happen. I was there."

"It would seem so. Yes."

"Are you going to tell me what's going on?"

"The man murdered was not the real Edward Cotton. He was part of my security. Sort of like a person who tastes food for someone else to make sure it's safe. He was to be the one communicating with you. That was before the unfortunate incident in D.C. Certain parties would like to take my invention and see me dead. At this point, at least one of them thinks they've been successful."

Pax eases back down, sitting on the bench, and looks straight ahead. "How does it work?"

"What exactly are you asking?"

"I want to know how a computer chip can give me the abilities I have. It must be amazing if others are willing to kill for it."

"Don't underestimate how easily others will kill for the newest technology. However, what you say is true. What is in your brain is truly amazing."

"I was told you didn't invent the chip, that you created the vision part of it or something like that."

"The chip itself is sold all over the world. What I created, as you say, is the communication center, the software that interfaces with the brain. As remarkable as it is, the chip is just a computer that houses it."

"I understand how it works to give me eyesight. The videos from the cameras in my contacts are wirelessly sent to the sensory chip. From there, they go to the occipital lobe. What I don't understand is how I can move so incredibly fast and smoothly. I can even anticipate on a different level. How is that even possible?"

"The sensory chip is interfacing with other parts of your brain. If you wanted to, you could distinguish every ingredient in a homemade apple pie and smell it baking from two blocks away. All your senses are heightened. All you need do is focus."

"I still don't understand," Pax looks puzzled, "how I can move so much faster. Movement isn't one of the senses."

I'll try to explain it. Most people only think of the five senses: sight, hearing, smell, taste, and touch. In reality, there are two more, seven total."

"And movement is one of those?"

"That's correct. The technical term is vestibular, the movement and balance sense. This sense gives us information about where our head and body are in relation to space. It helps us stay upright when we sit, stand, and walk."

"I see. And what would the other sense be?"

"It's called proprioception. It's just a fancy name for body position. The body awareness sense tells us where our body parts are relative to each other. It also gives us information about how much force to use, allowing us to do something like crack an egg without crushing it."

"So, seven senses, not five."

Edward smiles and nods. "You can Google it if you like. In most people, these senses are limited. With the sensory chip, your senses come together on a level never seen before. It wouldn't be fair for you to enter a gaming contest. You would obliterate your opponents. I would love to see it, though. It's just that it would draw too much attention. Our enemies might discover you. In every way, your brain will work smoother and faster. If my calculations are right, it will do this trouble-free. And that includes any math functions you may be working on."

"I should have known."

"Should have known what?"

"That you already knew I'm a mathematician."

"We both know you're not the ordinary mathematician."

"How long have you been hacking into my computer?"

"We don't consider what we did hacking."

"*Then what do you call it?*"

"Surveillance."

"Since you did it without my permission, I'm pretty sure it's hacking. And that's illegal."

"Yes, from your perspective, it is. However, the Pentagon runs by a different set of rules. What we did with their involvement was surveillance."

"You know what I've been working on, then?"

"We know."

"You must think I'm crazy."

"Pax, your math skills have always interested us. Whether time travel is possible, nobody knows. However, math indicates it's theoretically doable. There is a certain general relativity spacetime geometry that permits traveling faster than the speed of light, such as cosmic strings, traversable wormholes, and Alcubierre drives. We've been attempting it for a long time now. I brought you a gift." Edward slides the box along the bench until it touches her leg. "The sensory chip makes you the foremost mathematician. If anyone can figure time travel out, it's you. The instrument in the box is the latest version."

Pax lifts the box, flips a latch, and looks inside. "What's it called?"

"Technically, it just has a number, but we nicknamed it *The Time Ship.* We thought it would open a portal to go backward or forward. It doesn't work. We know the sensory chip in you is functioning correctly. Right now, that's our main concern. We would be interested in anything you could tell us about *The Time Ship.*"

"I'll see what I can do." Pax closes the box and scoots to the edge of the bench, shifting to cross her blue-jean-covered legs. She looks Edward in the eyes and asks, "How on this green earth did you ever come up with something like the sensory chip to begin with?"

Edward's face and hands have relaxed. For the second time, he places his arms on the backrest and begins, "What seems dull to one person can be pretty fascinating to another. My college days were like that for me. After receiving my Doctoral Degree in Chemical Engineering, I added courses to do the same in Cell and Molecular Biology and Biomedical Engineering. Over ten years of my life were in college, and I loved every minute. I spent half my time studying for classes and the other half attending the classes. I walked away with a folder full of degrees and offers to teach, which I did for a long time. I had to make money while I worked on my theory.

One day General Stackhouse came knocking at my door. Until that moment, I had no idea how to keep my research secret. They had known about my studies since my days in college. That came as a great surprise to me. My trial phase had just started. From that point on, the Pentagon made sure my discovery stayed out of the public eye and under a stash of other military secrets. If it weren't for the Pentagon, I probably wouldn't have made it this far."

"Why me?" Pax asked. "I don't get it. Why not a Pentagon security guard or another soldier? Or even better, why not a CIA Agent? It would be the perfect testing ground."

"Of course it would. It would also be the quickest way to allow our enemies to secure the technology."

Pax wasn't sure she wanted the particular details, but she couldn't resist. "Are you telling me the Russians have spies in the U.S. Military?"

"The Russians, the Chinese, and at least three other organizations that steal and sell technology. It's big business. Neither Intelligence nor Counterintelligence works the way it used to. Today, everyone has a cyber spy network. There are cyber wars taking place in little offices way out in the middle of nowhere. I don't mind telling you, sometimes we get our butts kicked, especially by the Chinese. Even the Pentagon is compromised. What I've told you today about the true nature of the sensory chip is only known by a handful of people at the White House and Pentagon.

We needed to keep this off the grid. With you, we could do that. You were a civilian that needed eye surgery. It was the perfect situation. Even Gatsby hasn't lived in D.C. or worked for the Pentagon for a number of years."

Pax stood up. She walked a few feet away, her back turned, her arms crossed. She looks out over the park and sees a mother playfully pushing her daughter on a swing set. That mother-daughter connection, she hadn't had much of that growing up but thought how nice it would have been. "I've got more questions."

Edward stood up from the bench. "I've got a security team here with me, ensuring you're safe."

Pax roves her eyes around the park.

Edward continues, "I can assure you, you won't spot them. Nobody is better at surveillance. I'll be here until tomorrow afternoon. About your questions, we could meet up tonight if you like."

"No. I need to get some rest. It's been a busy couple of days. Maybe in the morning. Could you meet me at Café Bella, say, nine o'clock?"

"Café Bella, nine o'clock. It's a date."

"GPS will get you there."

"Thanks, but I'm already aware of Café Bella, your favorite hangout."

Pax turns, clinches her hands together, and slyly eyes Edward. "Why am I not surprised?"

Chapter 13

Now

To say Hawke was bothered by Paxton's actions the last thirty-six hours would be an understatement. His frustrated voice cuts through the chatter of customers that has Café Bella humming like a beehive. He says, "You're one heck of a person to keep track of." His voice sounded strong but strained. Rushing back from D.C. the night before, he hadn't had much sleep.

She raises her pretty, green eyes from a table where she was texting Josie and takes a sip from her caramel iced coffee. Peering into his accusatory face, she knows her relationship with him right now is tenuous at best. She doesn't have a clue what to say to him after she slipped off in the middle of the night, and with no warning whatsoever. She says, "I guess you're pretty pissed-off?"

Hoping to stamp an exclamation point to show his disappointment, he crosses his arms tight and shakes his head. He says, "Pissed-off, maybe. Double-crossed, definitely." He drops his arms, pulls out a chair and twirls it around with the seat facing him. Straddling the seat, he sits down and swings his arms up on the backrest. He says delicately, in a low, serious tone, "There are bad guys out there who are ready, willing, and capable of killing you."

To Pax all the bad guys were in D.C. And anyway, what right did he have to talk to her like that? When she needed him, he wasn't around. If it weren't for Darcie, she'd be taken hostage by now, or, maybe worse. She had to save herself. She had to run. And she had to do it quickly.

She takes another sip, glances at her phone, and looks back at Hawke. She asks, "So, what are you going to do about that?"

He gives her a smug look followed by a snippy quick sigh. "If you keep running away, then probably nothing."

"Do what you want. I don't care." She continues with her texting while placing her lips on the straw of her iced coffee. She likes Hawke a lot. He is a good man and he's cute. His FBI training, however, was lacking. She felt she was in better hands with Edward Cotton and his team of G-men. "Besides," she says, "I'm not afraid. Right now, I'm waiting for someone who's watching over me."

"Pax. This is serious," Hawke replied. "Will you look at me?"

She doesn't respond. At the moment ignoring him feels pretty good. He was the one who had taken her to D.C., then unceremoniously dumped her to run off and play his FBI games. If it had not been for someone whom she had only known for one day, who knows what would have happened. She can still picture Darcie on the balcony shooting away with her Glock. All the while she stood only six feet away, her mind and body going numb. She had not calmed down until she made it back to Albuquerque.

"If I leave here, you're on your own." Hawke oozed with agitation. In reality he felt bad for what she had gone through. It had scared her so bad that she ran. And it must have been tense escaping D.C. without notice. But the mouth full that his superiors had given him before he headed back to Albuquerque was still ringing like angry bells in his ears.

She hesitated. Then she glances up from her phone and says, "I told you I'm covered. Someone's watching over me."

"You don't seem to understand that *someone* is *me*!"

Again, she goes back to her texting. "That shows how much you know. By the way, after that drone attacked me, Darcie called you for help." She glances up at Hawke a second, then right back down to her phone. "You never showed."

"The drone, it's not what you think. And I couldn't respond because my phone was off. I didn't even have it with me. It had to do with my training. When I checked in with Darcie the next morning, you were already gone."

"You can go now. I'm all good here."

Hawke was getting tired of her blowing him off. For a second, he thought about just walking out and leaving. He seriously wanted to, but if he did, it would mean being insubordinate to his orders. He could be demoted. And in his heart, he recognized the situation for what it was. Whether she knew it or not, Pax needed him. Then there was this mystery thing involving her mother. He was itching to get to the bottom of it. He says, "Edward Cotton is boarding a flight to D.C. right now. I have orders to watch over you."

Pax jerks her head up and her phone skips on the table and falls into her lap. Was she being dumped a second time. "What? No!" She screamed, her confidence dissolving like an Alka-Seltzer in water.

Hawke gives out a half-hearted laugh. "That's the same reaction I had when I received the orders."

It seemed Pax couldn't trust anyone to keep their word. She had questions only Edward could answer. She had changes taking place inside her, epic changes, changes Hawke knew nothing about. Now what the hell was she going to do? "Edward and I had plans to talk this morning. He wasn't leaving till this afternoon."

"He was called back to D.C. by the Chairman of the Joint Chiefs of Staff. In case you didn't know, that's the highest-ranking military officer in the country."

She couldn't understand what could be more important than the technology they had implanted in her. "What are they meeting about?"

"I don't know, probably the Chinese. There's a lot of talk about them lately. Word is they were behind the recent murder you witnessed."

That made sense to her. Edward was being targeted. His life was in more danger than hers. They had put his self-preservation first. "Did they make an arrest?" She asked.

"Yes, but those guys were just the hired help. They claim they had nothing to do with it. They told the D.C. Detective that the video was doctored, and they were set up. But the video's solid, so good luck with that line of defense."

"I hope they get cancer and rot to death in jail. They're merciless."

Hawke shifts his hands to the side of the chair. A rush of emotions shoots through him. The kind that makes you ache for someone. What she had been through, seeing a murder with no one around to help, was heart wrenching. He says, "I don't know about cancer, but the jail part is a sure bet. They're going away for a long time. I heard it was gruesome."

Her expression was telling him yes, absolutely, but she was exasperated with the whole conversation. "I guess it's back to you and me here in the ABQ. Do I have that right?"

Hawke nods. "I thought Homeland Security might get involved, or at least the CIA. Right now, it's just the FBI."

"I think I know why. Edward said that they want me off the grid as much as possible. They don't want the attention the CIA would bring. They're worried about spies. And the talk you heard about the Chinese is probably correct. Edward seemed especially worried about them."

Hawke had been wondering why they were leaving her here in Albuquerque. Now he understood. Internationally, the ABQ was a nothing town. It has a lot of government buildings and so forth, but that just goes back to the days of the atomic bomb experiments. Chinese spies here, maybe, but not likely; D.C. was the hot spot.

He says, "I received another untraceable email. I didn't tell anyone at the Pentagon about it since it's coming from that location. However, I did inform Nate and Darcie and requested they be sent here for better security."

"What did the email say?" Pax asked. She was calmer now, more under control.

"It said to bring you back to Albuquerque and keep you away from D.C."

"When did you receive the email?"

"Night before last. Why?"

"That's when Darcie found a note at my hotel door. It stated the same thing, only more bluntly. Didn't she mention it when you checked in?"

"No, her superiors gave her an ear full. She panicked over you disappearing, and I haven't talked to her since. But she and Nate should arrive by plane this afternoon. Tonight, I've arranged for all of us to meet at my place. If it's the Chinese we need to be worried about, I want to be as prepared as possible. If they find out about you, it could get crazy. They might try to take you hostage."

"Hawke?" It was Maria, the waitress. She's holding a pencil and pad. "I didn't see you come in. Did you want to order something?"

Hawke gives her a wide smile. "Do you remember our last conversation?"

She nods and slides her pencil and pad into her apron. "Anything I want? Seriously?" She asked.

"As long as it's not my usual."

"I know, right?"

"Could you put a rush on it? I'm so hungry; I almost stopped at McDonald's."

Maria grins. "No prob. Be right back." Walking away, she added, "This is going to be fun."

"What was that about?" Pax asked while watching Maria leave.

Hawke shrugs his shoulders. "Maria thought I needed to change my choice of breakfast food."

"And how do you feel about that?"

"I'm just trying to survive and be happy. According to her, trying something new will help me out with both of those things."

"But what if you don't like what she brings?"

Hawke's lips press together tightly. He places his hands out in front of him and starts strumming his fingers on the tabletop. He says, "You know, I really hadn't thought that far ahead. Besides, I like to try new things?"

"*You* like to try new things, seriously? And I enjoy *tap dancing in poop*. Hey, genius! Maria loves pulling that on people. It's one of her things."

"Any chance of getting out of this unscathed?" Hawke asks.

Pax is the next to shrug her shoulders. "I doubt it. In a forest fire, people get confused. They turn the wrong way and burn up."

"What's your point?"

She taps the side of her head. "I think Maria confused you."

"Aren't you the witty one?"

A few minutes later, Maria returns with Hawke's breakfast. Quickly, she slides the plate in front of him, then the cup of Red-Eye.

"This looks like what I always order," Hawke said.

"Try the Redeye," Maria replied, giving a big smile.

Hawke picks up the cup and takes a slow sip. "There's something different, it's..."

"I added a pinch of cinnamon and a bit of cayenne pepper for flavor."

"It's really hot."

"Take a bite of your sandwich," Pax encouraged. "That usually helps."

Hawke grabs hold of the sandwich. He takes a large bite and begins chewing. At first, he nods his head, indicating all's well. But then his complexion changes. He swallows hard, sets the sandwich back on the plate, and looks up at Maria. "Did you put something different in the sandwich?"

"It's our special hot sauce. Do you like it?"

"I'm going to need a glass of water."

Maria could see red splotches popping up all over his face. She puts her hands together in a fist and cringes. "You're not a hot-sauce person?"

"No."

"But like, you know, most of our customers are."

"I'm going to need that water really fast. Apparently, I just ran into a forest fire."

Maria turns and takes off for the water.

Hawke looks at Pax. "Is it possible for the inside of your mouth to fall off?"

She can hardly answer for laughing. She says, "Your face looks like a red glow stick."

"You got no argument from me." Involuntarily, tears are dribbling down his cheeks.

Maria arrives with the water, and Hawke downs all of it. "Sorry, Hawke." She sounds anxious, speaking in an apologetic tone. "Mateo thinks he might have added the hot sauce twice. And, okay, I added a little extra because it's the way I like it."

Hawke wipes his eyes with a napkin, then looks back at Maria. "I totally believe you. Could I have another glass of water?"

"Yes, and anything else you want to eat. No charge."

"Maybe you could bring me the same thing all over again, but without the hot sauce, or cinnamon, or cayenne pepper."

"Crap, Hawke, I'm so sorry. I'll get right on that."

After Maria leaves, Hawke wipes his eyes again and tries to smile at Pax. "How come every time I get around you, crazy, no, bizarre things happen?"

Pax is trying not to laugh again. "Maybe you should have stayed in D.C."

Hawke gives her another smug look and tosses the napkin on the table. He says, "Or maybe I should have stopped at that fast food place on the corner." They both burst out laughing. He continues, "And anyway, *if it weren't for you, I'd still be in the nation's capital.*"

"I know."

Chapter 14

Now

After breakfast, Hawke and Pax stood outside Café Bella. Pax leans back against the block building and Hawke stands in front of her with his hands in his pant pockets. It was another cloudless, crystal blue day, with several sandhill cranes huddled together, not more than fifty feet from them. The elegant giant birds were considered a priority species and would often wander away from the freshwater reservoir to hang out in Rio Rancho. The cranes resembled a group of teenagers standing idle after school, wondering what kind of trouble they could get into. They eyed Hawke and Pax as if the two were intruding on their space. They stood there without even the slightest hint of movement, resembling marbleized statues.

"I hate it when they stare at you like that," Hawke pulls his hands from his pockets, trying to wave them away.

"I think they're amazing," Pax replied. "We're lucky to have them. And anyway, they're harmless."

"I was thinking creepy." Hawke interjected.

"They're probably thinking the same about you," Pax replied.

"You mean us, right?"

"You're the one that tried to scare them away. They know who their friends are."

"I just wish they would move once in a while, do something different. Every time I see them, it's always the same. They stand there like zombies, just staring. I feel like I'm caught in a freaking Groundhog Day repeating time-lapse. I think we need them like we need a hole in the head." He waves his arms and shouts. "Eeeeee, eeeeee, eeeeee!" He takes a step in their direction. "Eeeeee, eeeeee, eeeeee!" The cranes remain motionless. "Why don't you fly to *The Fe!"* (Santa Fe). He screams. "It's hippy town, extraordinaire! You'd fit in perfectly!"

"Could you dial it back a little?" Pax asked. "That thing you said about creepy. People are starting to stare. Just saying."

Hawke looks around. A few people in the parking lot are staring at him. "Right. Dial it back. Got it." He turns back to Pax and sticks his hands back in his pockets. "Have you talked to Gatsby since you've been back in the ABQ?"

"No, why?"

"Just wondering if he knows what's been going on."

"I doubt it. If Dad had heard anything, he would have called."

"You're probably right."

"You're still suspicious of him, aren't you?" She asked. "You think he caused my mother's death?"

He was thinking, yes, but could not bring himself to say it. Pax was Gatsby's daughter. He needed to tread lightly, stay on her good side. And it was early in the investigation, he could be wrong. "I don't know, maybe. Whoever's been sending me those emails knows something. By that, I mean something very few others know. I think she was murdered, and I think whoever sent the emails is trying to lead us to something significant. They want you in Albuquerque, which tells me they're trying to protect you."

"You don't think it's possible they could be a threat?" Pax asked.

"Maybe, but I don't think so." Hawke glances up along the side of the building, all the way up to the sky. When he tilts his head back down, looking across the parking lot, he sees a little girl. She's licking an ice cream cone. "Ginger?" He said it out loud, almost shouting.

Pax turns, looking in the same general area that Hawke is. She asks, "Who's Ginger?"

He doesn't answer, just keeps looking at Ginger. Ginger points at Pax and shouts to Hawke. "She's like a little girl, Daddy. She doesn't know what the world can do."

Hawke takes a step in the direction of Ginger, and Ginger shouts again. "Are you helping her? You have to. She needs you, Daddy."

Pax places her hand on Hawke's shoulder. "Who's Ginger?" Tugging at him, she firmly pulls him around, and the two make eye contact for a moment.

Quickly, Hawke turns back to Ginger, but she's no longer there. He looks around for her.

Pax asks sharply, "Are you going to answer me or what?"

He looks back up into the sky. "Sorry, for a moment there, I was confused. I thought I saw someone I knew."

"No kidding. So, who is this Ginger person?"

"She's a girl I once knew. At one time, we were very close. That's been a few years now. Anyway, could you tell me about Gatsby?"

"What do you want to know?"

Hawke lowers his head and looks her in the eyes. He cups his hands and puts them over his face.

She can hear him breathing deeply.

"Anything," he answers, lowering his hands. He is trying to shake off the emotions of seeing Ginger. "After Sloan's death, did he change?"

"I guess. We both did."

"Just tell me about him."

"Right, well, I had a simple childhood. Dad never did anything to cause me harm. It did get rough after he and momma started having marital problems. I guess that's to be expected. After he noticed how it was affecting me, he seemed more afraid about it than concerned. If that makes any sense."

"It does. Go on."

Pax crosses her arms and looks past Hawke into the parking lot. She turns, looks at the cranes, and focuses. "Sometimes, the silence would be so intense at the supper table. I was just a kid, but I wanted to say something, I don't know, to help them, reassure them. I didn't want them to break up. I knew they were going to. All I wanted to do was stop it from happening. But when I tried to say, you know, that it would be okay, it felt like I had taken a shot to the stomach. My voice would crack, and oddly I could feel my face distorting like it was falling away. I would end up crying every time.

One night my dad came into my bedroom and sat on my bed. He told me that he and mother had been talking about me. They have a therapist friend, and they were going to bring me to see him. When I went to the therapist, he was a kind and thoughtful man. He was much better to me than I was to him. I told him on the first visit, *don't you think you should be talking to my parents?* He asked me what I meant? He didn't know they were having marital problems. When I told him, he said *grownups get to make their own decisions. But if what you say is true, then, yes, I should be talking to them. For now, though, all I can do is try to help you get through this.* I was so mad. Dad was upset that I had told the therapist about all the arguing. He was still caring, but in a harder way after that. I probably should explain what I mean.

Things gradually got worse until one day, years later, he did something that caught me by surprise. It was one of those things that shock you and changes how you think of a person. We were sitting on the patio one afternoon. It was a fall day, and the air had that crisp feeling going on. The temperature was comfortable, and the mugginess, the stickiness which had been hanging out in D.C. all summer, was finally gone. Dad was nervous about something. I could tell because he kept repeating himself. You know, things that only need saying once, but you repeat them anyway. *You look lovely today,* he said for like the third time. *Maybe next week we'll take a drive to the beach. I think the air will do us both some good.* And he kept asking me how I liked my glass of wine. After I turned sixteen, he would sometimes pour me a drink, and we would sit and talk.

I said to him, *Dad, why don't you tell me what's going on?* He just smiled and told me how lovely I looked. He kept on with *there wasn't a prettier girl in D.C.* I kept pressing him because I knew there was something he needed to get off of his chest. He started getting agitated. I misread it, though. I thought he was on the verge of opening up. When you can't see someone's face, sometimes that happens. So, I kept pressing him. I felt like I was the only one he had to talk with. I told him, *Dad, tell me, tell me what's going on?* That's when I heard glass shatter on the concrete patio. I think he stood up fast because right after the wine glass shattered, his chair crashed flipping backwards to the concrete. It was like one loud sound back-to-back.

That's when it happened, the thing that changed my thinking of him. He shouted, *Hell no! You think you're a freaking psychologist! You think I need fixing! You can't see, so you think talking is the answer to everything! The sky's not blue all the time. It's not supposed to be.* The next day he apologized. He said he didn't know what came over him. He asked me to forgive him, said I had to, pleading with me. I told him I forgave him, but I never looked at him the same after that day."

Hawke stepped closer to Pax. He put his finger under her chin and raised her face. He could tell she was dejected. For some reason he wanted to kiss her right now. He bit his lip to keep himself from doing it. He asked, "You going to be, okay?"

She grabs his finger and just holds it. "I've had a pretty screwed-up life, haven't I?"

He steps a bit closer, their bodies lightly touching each other. "You've had more than your share, but..." He leans in, and their noses touch.

"But what?"

He kisses her cheek and whispers in her ear. "Most people don't try to be terrible. Most people are trying their best. Sometimes their best is terrible. I think Gatsby loves you. I don't know what happened, but I think he got in over his head. It only takes a split second to cause someone pain. I don't think he meant to change your relationship. He just couldn't stop himself."

Her heart softens in the face of his serenity.

He says, "I hope you get what you want."

She whispers back. "What makes you think I want anything?"

Hawke's head tilts back a little. "Because you came back to Albuquerque. And because you're talking to me about your father." He can't hold back any longer. He kisses her lips, soft and light.

Still leaning her back against the block wall, Pax raised one foot, placing it on the wall. "Was that a pity kiss?" She asked.

Hawke rubs his knuckles softly on her cheek. "Absolutely not." He lays another one on her, long, forceful, and wet. While kissing, they hear the flapping sound of cranes flying away. When finished, Hawke lifts his head and sees the cranes shrinking and fading into the massive blue sky. "If that's what it was gonna take for them to leave, I'd have kissed you twenty minutes ago."

Pax smiles. "Hey, if I had known, I would have told you." She moves her hand around to the back of his head, pulls him in, and plants a wild one on him.

A shout comes from the parking lot. "Yo, New Eyes!"

Both Hawke and Pax turn to look. "Yo, Chili Pepper!" Pax shouts. "Why'd you interrupt me?"

"You all tangled. Thought maybe you need backup."

"No, Chili Pepper. My life is perfect, isn't yours?"

He throws up his hand. "I know, huh. True that. It's all sick. You caught Josie today?"

"I texted her earlier, but she's not been around."

"Yo, thanks. See ya on the flip." He turns and walks into Café Bella.

Hawke releases Pax. He asks, "*Chili Pepper*, seriously?"

Pax grabs Hawke by the chin and squeezes. She says, "Personally, I think it's a cool name. Not everyone is as smart and interesting as you. Not everyone gets to go to museums, meet diverse people, or understand politics. People like Chili Pepper just want to control some little part of this out-of-control world, and they're doing it."

"Well, if it means anything, I do think he's diverse."

Pax lets go of his chin. "Do you want to go to my apartment?" She points in the distance. "It's not far."

Thirty minutes later, Hawke sits on the sofa, and Pax comes walking out of the bedroom. He scoots up to the edge with a surprised look on his face. "Are you trying to seduce me?"

"Isn't that obvious?"

"*You're wearing a negligee and holding a glass of wine.*"
"Am I overdoing the friend thing?"
"No. I like this kind of friend thing just fine."

Chapter 15

Now

Hawke and Pax walked beside each other in silence, past a laundry mat, a convenience store, and a Mexican restaurant. Earlier, they had decided to take a walk in the beautiful Albuquerque weather. Being together was something they had grown accustomed to. When they reached Hawke's apartment, an elongated sandy-brown two-story building, Hawke grabbed Pax by the arm, stopping her in her tracks. "Have you told anyone where you are?"

She shook her head and took a drink from a squeeze bottle. She and Hawke had bought identical ones the day before at Dick's Sporting Goods. The air was super dry, so they had filled them with Gatorade for the walk. "No one, not even my father." She replied.

He was on high alert, looking out for anything suspicious. He had to be. His first important assignment was to protect Pax. If something happened to her, it would be a big blow to his career. He lightly squeezed her arm, before releasing it and says, "Somebody is messing around my door. Looks like a girl trying to jimmy the lock." He glances around scanning the area, checking for other assailants. Nothing, just the one. "She's trying to break in."

It was time to put some of that FBI tactics training to work. He made eye contact with Pax and signals with his hand for her to stay put. After a serious grin followed by a nod from Pax, Hawke cautiously walks away.

Less than thirty feet of space separated them from his apartment door and the girl. Hawke needed to know what the girl was up to, and he wasn't going to wait around to find out. Stealthily slipping up behind the girl, Hawke positions himself, lunges, and grabs her by the shoulders. What happens next is swift and painful. In their struggle the two smoothly flip forward and Hawke is catapulted into the air. He does a somersault and lands hard on the concrete, one arm twisted behind his back. The girl is sitting on him with one hand on the back of his head, pressing Hawke's face into the concrete.

Adrenalin spikes in Pax, her senses connect, her reflexes align. In a move that more resembles a nimble-footed animal, she springs into action. In under two seconds she grabs the girl by the waist. Immediately, the girl thrusts an elbow backwards in defense. With her new abilities on display, Pax easily blocks the attempt and effortlessly tosses the girl to the ground. Josie's Navy Seal training was already paying off. She secured the girl by locking her legs around the girl's arms and clamping her hands on the girl's throat. "Darcie!" Pax shouts.

"Paxton?" Darcie replies.

Hawke rolls over, pushes with his hands, and stands up. His nose is aching, his face a bulbous red. He rotates his arm in a circular motion and moans in pain. "You nearly broke my arm."

Darcie, sitting on her butt, quips back, "You shouldn't surprise me like that."

"You were breaking into my apartment. And where've you been? You were supposed to be here yesterday."

"There was a delay. I told you. I left a message on your phone."

"Message?" Hawke snatches his phone from his jeans and starts punching. "I missed that one. My phone's on silent mode. Anyway, where's Nate?"

"General Stackhouse wanted to see him today. It was all on the message."

"Do you know if he's coming?" Hawke asks.

"I'm not sure. The general's upset. He wants Pax and the rest of us back in D.C. He's not going to let us stay here very long. There was a man with the general that bought us some time. He wasn't in the military, but he had some authority. He insisted they leave Pax here, at least for now."

"The man is Edward Cotton, the *real Edward Cotton.*" Pax exclaimed.

Darcie gasps, her brow crinkles and her head swings back. "What?"

Pax offers her hand to Darcie. "The man murdered was a plant to keep the real Edward hidden. I'm not going back there. It's too dangerous." Darcie grabs hold of her hand, and Pax helps her to her feet. "Somebody in D.C. is trying to do me harm. Darcie, you said so yourself."

"No, Pax. What I said was *the safe thing to do is assume it.* The drone was just a couple of guys messing around, having some fun."

"But they ran!" Pax shouted.

"I was shooting at them." Darcie glances at Hawke. "You didn't tell her we looked into it?"

"I told her it wasn't what she thought."

Darcie shakes her head. "Okay, I think it's time we had a strategy meeting."

Hawke unlocks the apartment door. They all shuffle inside. The living room is open to the kitchen, giving it a roomy feel. There is a black lacquer dining table set in front of a matching China cabinet, and in the living space, a brown leather sofa with two wingback chairs. It wasn't the trendiest décor, but it wasn't awful.

Darcie likes the layout. "This should work. Other than, you know, it could use some straightening up. How many bedrooms?"

Hawke glances around. Other than a pizza box left out from a few days ago, everything looked fine. Certainly not out of order, at least not by his standards. "Just one bedroom."

"If you have an extra pillow I can sleep on the floor," Darcie said. "Pax can have the couch."

"Didn't you book a hotel room?" Hawke asked.

Darcie squints her eyes and shakes her head, no. "Until we head back to D.C., we stay together. The general made that clear. Pax isn't to leave my side."

"My place has three bedrooms," Pax interjects. "My dad insisted I get the biggest apartment in Rio Rancho. He can't stand small places."

"How many actual beds?" Darcie asked.

"He had it completely furnished, three bedrooms, three beds. He doesn't do anything half-ass. It's nice."

"Then, we're moving our headquarters to your place," Darcie insisted.

In less than an hour, they were at Pax's apartment with a New Mexico map spread out on the kitchen table. Darcie points to a spot on the map called Bear Canyon. "We need to go through this canyon," she says. "Eighteen miles on the other side is a man by the name of Rosie."

Hawke didn't understand how this tied into their investigation. He's irritated that Darcie has rank and is taking charge. This was his town, not hers. "Makes perfect sense." He was being sarcastic. "The first thing we do is go looking for a man named Rosie."

Darcie ignored his jab. "We need his help."

Rosie's real name was Henri. He was a southerner from Georgia. Darcie had obtained his information from her contact in D.C. He was the best hacker on this side of the Mississippi. Twenty years ago, he caused havoc on the New York Stock Exchange. That got him in some serious trouble. After changing his name, he headed for the desert. From that point on flying under the radar was his preferred way. He is always suspicious, into conspiracy theories, and would want some serious cash to help out.

"What do we need him for?" Hawke asked.

"He's the one that's going to hack the Pentagon for us." Darcie replied.

Hawke was trying to make some sense of what he had just heard. It sounded like Darcie was writing her own strategy. Involving someone else could be dangerous. It was a bad move, he thought. His blood moved faster, pulsating through his veins. "Why do we need to hack the Pentagon?" he asked more forcefully.

Darcie glared hard at him. He was well-built and handsome. And like her he was a special agent, but his training was lacking. She had just flipped him in the air like a rag doll. She had little to no respect for him. She says, "For starters, to find out who's been sending you those emails. After that, I want Pax off the grid. And that's gonna take some nifty computer work.

I don't want the Chinese or anyone else to find her. She's not in D.C., but she's still in danger."

This wasn't what Pax expected or wanted, but she trusted Darcie. And at least D.C. was behind her now. In a day or two she would be back in her apartment, her information on the internet wiped clean. "Do we leave now?" She asked.

"No," Darcie answered. "It's gonna be dark soon. We don't want to get caught in the desert at night. It'll be difficult enough to find him in the daylight." Darcie turns her attention to Hawke. "Is your car a four-wheel drive? Rosie's way out there off the grid. All I have are the coordinates. It could get a little rough."

Hawke would be more comfortable working with Nate, someone he trained with and knew well. And he was still uncertain about Darcie's makeshift plan. It didn't matter, though. It was the only plan they had, so he might as well get behind it. He answers her. "I've been sent out between the prickly plants more than I care to admit. Doing grunt work for the higher ups is part of my job. It's a four-wheel-drive. Anything else would be a waste of my time. My Hydration Backpack is always in my car, and an emergency pack with granola bars. You don't want to be caught in the desert with car trouble and no hydration or food."

Pax shifted a backpack off her shoulder and set it in a chair. "Okay, guys," she points across the room to a back hallway. "There's a bathroom there if you need it. Farther down are your bedrooms. Hawke you take the first one on the right, Darcie, the one at the end." They had a plan, now it was time to settle in.

Three hours later Pax is sitting at a small desk, gazing into a computer screen. Next to her sat the Timeship Edward had left with her. The mathematical function calibrated into the machine was inaccurate. She was working and reworking the computation. Her brain was moving at a speed she had never experienced. Grasping math had always come easy to her, but now, with her seven senses working so closely together, she was experiencing something different. The computer screen could not move fast enough. She closed the laptop, leaned back in her chair, shutting her eyes. In less than two minutes, a lifetime of math computations raced through her mind. She opened her eyes, stood up, and jotted down the correct calibration figure; she was sure of it. She grabs the Timeship, unhinges the latch, opens it, and makes the necessary adjustments.

A knock on her door diverts her attention. She was hoping Hawke would come, was sort of expecting it. "Come in, handsome," she shouts. The door swings open. It's Darcie. She has that mothering look on her face. Pax braces for a lecture.

"If you like Hawke in that way," Darcie says, "so that you know, he's got some baggage."

"What do you mean?"

"I do a background check on all agents I'm assigned to work with. Hawke's been through some stuff. His wife and daughter were killed in a car crash three years ago. They were in the middle of a divorce when it happened. It shook him up badly. He barely passed his psych evaluation at Quantico. If it weren't for his other areas being so strong, he might not have made special agent status. Sorry. I thought you should know. Do you mind if we talk about what happened in D.C.?"

"Of course. And thank you for telling me about Hawke. I wasn't aware."

Darcie takes a few steps toward the desk. She says, "I don't mean to spoil your party with him." She cocks her hand and points at her head. "But I don't think he's ready mentally for another relationship. Just saying. Now, about D.C. Why did you run? Were you afraid I couldn't protect you?" She is standing in front of the desk noticing the odd-looking device.

"I needed to be somewhere I felt comfortable and safe." Pax replied. "That wasn't D.C. And General Stackhouse made it clear I would be there for another week."

"I wish you would have told me how you felt."

"Darcie, you wouldn't have allowed it if I had told you. If I'm wrong, tell me."

"You're not wrong. What is that thing you're holding?"

Closing the Timeship, Pax latches it back, and half covers it with her hands. "Oh, it's one of those things you thought would never exist, then one day you get out of bed, and there it is staring back at you. Do you believe in time travel, Darcie?"

Darcie scratches the side of her head. "I get it. I messed with you; now you're messing with me. Okay, I'll play along. In the movies, yes, in real life, not particularly."

"I didn't think so. Most people don't. They don't understand that the math involved says it's possible."

"I'm not so sure it matters what the math says."

Pax raises the device for Darcie to see. She turns it back and forth. "It matters a great deal." Pax understood that everything has a mathematical function, even gravity. Gravity gives weight to physical objects on earth, and the moon's gravity causes ocean tides. According to the math involved, gravity came into existence ten seconds after the birth of the universe. It's explained by Einstein's theory of relativity, which describes gravity not as a force but as a consequence of masses moving straight ahead in a curved spacetime continuum. Einstein's theory also makes it possible to travel at the speed of light. Pax was a mathematical prodigy. She understood this and a lot more. "Do you believe in gravity, Darcie?"

"Of course."

"Why? You can't see it, and before it was proven *by math*, it seemed like it came out of someone's dream."

Hawke interrupts as he walks into the room. He asks, "Is she talking that time travel stuff again?"

Darcie turns and smiles. "Yes, she is."

Hawke continues. "I told her I'd believe in time travel when they capture Bigfoot."

Again, Pax turns the Timeship back and forth. "The Pentagon doesn't agree with you, and neither does Einstein or Edward Cotton."

The theory of time travel was more respected in the science community than most people realized. It was fruitless to try and persuade ordinary people, Pax knew that, but it was only a matter of time before someone crossed that threshold. One day it would be looked back on like many other breakthrough discoveries. When the first cars started showing up, most people didn't believe it was possible. In a short time, everyone was driving one. It's the same with any new technology, the airplane, the computer, the internet.

Opening a desk drawer, Pax lowers the Timeship into it and closes the drawer back. She says, "One day, everyone will believe in time travel, the same as gravity."

Chapter 16

Now

The next morning at 8 a.m., Darcie dragged Hawke out of bed. It took another hour to get him moving. Finally, he slid behind the steering wheel, and eased his Nissan Rogue out of the parking lot. After a quick stop at Café Bella for coffee, they were buzzing down the road. The next fifteen minutes, the three looked through deeply tinted windows as the Nissan maneuvered its way through the backstreets of Rio Rancho. Darcie had insisted they make sure they weren't being followed. Both she and Hawke knew the protocol well. Drive for five minutes. After backtracking for three miles, with seven right and left-hand turns, followed by a U-turn, proceed cautiously outside the city. During the elaborate sequence, they keep their eyes on the lookout.

Forty-five minutes later, they turn onto a sandy desert road. Winding their way through scrub bushes and lots of cactus, they make another turn, and the wide-open desert is stretched out in front of them. Before long, they top a rise in the road, and in the distance, they see a clearing. Darcie double-checks the coordinates, and they soon arrive at a spot with two RVs and a military-grade, four-wheel-drive Hummer.

Piling out of the Nissan, they are confronted by a middle-aged man. He points a wicked-looking gun at them. Darcie moves her hands up in the surrender position. She recognizes the gun, a nice fully automatic AK-47 with a seventy-five round drum magazine. It was a serious piece of equipment, only available on the black market.

"Y'all government?" The spunky man asked.

"Two of us are," Darcie replied. "Are you Rosie?"

"Y'all know who I am, or you wouldn't be here. And you'd be Homeland, FBI, or CIA?"

"FBI." Hawke replied.

"I been clean for years. Mostly, anyhow. Now go. Git yore butts outta' here."

"We need your help," Darcie exclaimed.

Rosie jiggles the gun. He says, "I been itchin' to use this thing. It's outlawed in the U.S., which is funny, y'all being FBI and such. If you don't want your grave to be the baking desert and leave your momma's wondering what happened when y'all don't come home, then do like I said and git!"

Darcie raised her hands higher. *"Nutty-Buddy* sent us."

Rosie shifts his face away from the gun. "Say again?"

"Nutty-Buddy sent us."

Rosie lowers the gun. "And?"

"She says to tell you, *the cow jumped over the moon."*

The gun lowers farther, finally pointing at the ground. "Y'all in some deep doo-doo. I'd say up to your ears in it. D.C. headquarters or the ABQ? Show me, now!"

Darcie lowers her hands. She promptly slid her hand into her back pocket. After pulling out a leather-encased badge, she flips it open, moves it forward and shows it to him. "I'm D.C." Angling her head sideways; she points to Hawke. "He's Albuquerque."

"Who's the looker?" Rosie points to Pax. "The pretty one. Who's she?"

Darcie glances at Pax and gives her that motherly smile. "She's the reason we're here. We need help keeping her off the grid, out of sight."

"Easy peasy. Fifteen hundred. Now. And cash only!"

Darcie unzips a small pocket on a backpack, reaches in, and pulls out a wad of money. She hands it to him.

"Anything else?" Rosie asked.

"I'll take this one," Hawke says, keeping one eye on the gun. "We need you to hack the Pentagon."

"The Pentagon? I haven't heard a good one like that in ten years."

"I know, right?" Hawke continued, "The question is, can you do it or not?"

"Can I do it?" Looking down, Rosie shakes his head in disbelief. "Can I do it! Sonny, water seeks its own level. So does mediocrity. That's what the computer geeks at the Pentagon are." Raising his head back to Hawke, he continues. "Why would the FBI want to hack the Pentagon? Don't answer that! It's as plain as the nose on my face. Or is it your face? Doesn't matter. It's clear you're looking for a spy, probably Russian. Cyber-espionage is serious biz these days."

"We were thinking Chinese Intelligence, not Russian," Darcie interjects.

"Then you need my help more than you think. I'm talkin' like a duck needs a pond. The Russian military has been in the computer game longer than anyone. Deflecting guilt is what they do best. They keep their finger pointing at the Chinese while they fly under the radar. It sickens me how far ahead of the Pentagon geeks they are, those propeller heads, those nooshbags, those bio-snakes. I can do it. The cost is five thousand. If there's something you're not telling me, the price adjusts accordingly."

"We agree with your terms," Darcie replied, peeling off more of the green stuff.

"Do you mind if I ask you a question?" Pax asked.

"Missy, no pretty girl *has ever* had to ask my permission for anything, not for computer repair, not for a hack-for-fun. Okay, just so you know, the hack-for-fun, it's mostly how I make my living these days. So, go ahead and shoot."

"Why are there two RVs?"

"That's a good question. I especially like it because it has nothin' to do with computers. Does seem funny, don't it, two RVs in the middle of a desert? One would be strange enough, but two? The simple answer is I live in one, and I work in the other. I like to keep my work life separate from my life-life or is it home-life? You know what I mean. And your name would be?"

"I go by Pax." Pax motions with her hand to Hawke and Darcie. "This is Special Agent Hawke Gentry and Special Agent Darcie Hannagan."

"Two special agents and a pretty girl. It's like a sign," Rosie clenches his jaw as he speaks, "one of those telling you your whole *freaking world is about to change*! Nobody from the government has showed up at my door in years. It's a sign, alright."

Suddenly a buzzing sound can be heard above them. It's high pitched and unmistakable. "It's a drone!" Rosie shouts, as everyone scans the sky. He points to the south. "You've been followed. Everybody down behind the Hummer, I want it to come in close."

They collapsed to the sand. They can hear the buzzing growing louder. Rosie tilts the AK47 straight up. As the drone comes in, he suddenly springs to his feet, takes aim, and presses the trigger. There is only about 0.02 of a second from the recoil of the bullet until the impact of the bolt hitting the back, and then 0.06 of a second later, it hits the chamber. Another 0.03 seconds later, the hammer hits. All said and done, the AK47 shoots 600 rounds per minute. Each bullet takes only 0.1 of a second to cycle—the results are a smooth pop-pop-pop, pop-pop-pop. The spitting bullets leave no chance for the drone. It's hit multiple times, careens skyward, then spirals to the left before plunging straight down into the sand.

Rosie runs like a madman to the drone. He uses the butt end of the gun to smash the camera. He flips over the drone, kneels, and inspects a series of numbers on the main body. The others come running up behind him. "Is it Russian or Chinese?" Darcie asks.

"The Chinese make 'um all," Rosie responds. He points his finger close to the drone. "See here. Somebody filed off the number identifying the purchasing country. I think we're dealing with the Russians, but there's no way to tell." He shoots a sideways look toward Pax and Darcie. "Your phone batteries, take them out." His gaze moves to Hawke. "You, too. Now! And can you drive an RV?"

Hawke kneels next to Rosie. "I can drive practically anything. It was part of my training."

"Then we're moving out. If we stay, we risk being found. But first, there's something I gotta do." Rosie calmly stands and walks over to the Nissan. He places his hand under a fender well and begins searching. Finding nothing, he goes to the next and then the next. "Jackpot!" he shouts. He yanks a small box-like object from underneath the fender well and holds it up. "It's a GPS tracking device. From the looks of it, it's been here a while." He looks straight at Hawke. "Any idea who put this here?"

Hawke nods his head. "I don't have a clue."

"Then, after we've moved to another set of coordinates, we'll just have to do a little snooping and find out."

Chapter 17

Twenty Four Hours Later

Edward stood in the hot desert sand, his eyes looking reflectively at the busted-up drone. His left eyebrow raised; his breathing nearly stopped. He couldn't have felt any worse than if a lightning bolt had struck his heart. Directly across from him, was Nate. After spotting the drone, their conversation was interrupted. With the disdain for losing track of Pax embedded in both of their faces, their eyes lift upward from the drone until they stare in disappointment at each other. Instinctively, they draw apart at the sound of a car driving up. They walk several steps in the car's direction, abruptly stop, and wait while a man wearing a general's uniform exits the vehicle. It was General Stackhouse. Closely behind, three soldiers piled out, all carrying automatic weapons. With one motion of the general's hand, both Edward and Nate approach. With a second motion, one of the soldiers runs, picks up the drone, and delivers it to the general.

Edward could feel his heart race. The drone itself wasn't important, but Pax was a different matter. With years of research implanted in her, she was valuable. There was no way around it, her disappearance was on him. Worst case scenario the Chinese had taken her. He thought not but couldn't be sure. He tried to keep his composure as the general looked over the drone.

"Somebody shot it up pretty good," the general said. "Edward, any idea who? Nate?"

Both shake their heads and the general waves off the soldier. Turning and inspecting the area, he continues. "And the video?"

Edward shifted his body backward wishing he had a better response. He crosses his arms and leans against a government-provided Grand Cherokee. "We have our best tech guy working on it back at Quantico. He's running it through the facial recognition software." He hesitates, shaking his head in disgust. "The video's not clean. Even with the filters, we don't expect too much. It was shot down before it zeroed in on them. Maybe we'll get lucky, maybe not. We could sweep the area, but it's doubtful we'll find anything."

"Do it anyway!"

"We'll start today."

"I want four drones covering every direction. Am I clear?"

"You got it," Edward responds. He glanced at the drone. He peers around for clues that might help them. All he sees are tire tracks heading nowhere. The general no doubt had noticed the same. He was worked up and had every right to be.

The general goes on, "And I don't mean the toy ones. The military base is a 45-minute drive from here. You got all the soldiers, and all the big boy drones you need. Your clearance is top-level. You won't have any trouble. When we find her, she goes right back to D.C. There's no more time for appeasing her."

Edward's belt buckle squeaked as he squatted down, resting on his heels. The extra weight of his blunder had ripped a scar inside him. He couldn't stand the thought that Paxton could be in enemy hands, or worse. "And if we don't find her?"

No answer. The general was so wound up his voice cracked and whiffed. His face turned red and stern. He just turned his attention to Nate. "This morning, when I looked at my computer, freaking *moans* were coming from my inbox! My superiors were blindsided and wanted answers. You and Edward, find the girl!" He looks back and forth between the two disappointed men. If you don't, we'll all be subject to a judicial hearing. Edward, Nate, I need to talk to you privately." He motions with his hand, and all three walk away from the guards.

A few minutes later the general looks behind them. He needed to be sure their conversation would be private. He says, "They're threatening to cut the argonaut program."

Edward lifts his hand and pulls at the sleeve of his shirt, revealing the tattoo of an octopus. "You mean the President?" He asked.

"And the Vice President, yes."

He jerks his sleeve back. "It's the only edge we have."

The general sighs. "I know."

"What about private funding?" Nate asked.

The general eyed Nate curiously. "If we go that route, it could be risky. Our cover could be blown. If that happens, it's all over."

"If they cut the program, we don't have a choice. Do we agree?" Nate asked.

Both Edward and the general nod. "I'll check with the others," Edward said. He takes a handkerchief from his shirt pocket, wipes sweat from his face, and again shakes his head in disgust. "Is that all, then?"

"No," the general continues. "If you hear from Agent Gentry, I want to be the first call you make. And Agent Hannagan, she's gone silent too. Any idea what they were doing out here?"

"No Sir, Edward responded. "If their phones power back up, we can track them. For now, that's about it."

The general nods and glances around the desert landscape. "I'm going back to the hotel. If I stay out here, I'll dry up and disappear. My hands and breath are already scorched by the heat. Why the hell do educated people want to live in the desert, anyway? I want a report by tomorrow night. And gentlemen, this is no time to worry about breaking the kitchen China. I mean it. Use whatever means necessary but find Paxton and bring her to me." In less than a minute, the general and his men are driving away. In another two, Edward and Nate follow suit.

Chapter 18

Now

Twenty-two miles away, at coordinate's south-southwest of Bear Canyon, the two RVs sat on a lonely stretch of desert road. The location change had taken a little over three hours to complete. That included towing a fifty-gallon fuel tank, disconnecting, and reconnecting the generator. Finding a remote spot was easy because everywhere you looked was remote. It hadn't taken long for Rosie to spot a patch of the hot soft stuff he was comfortable with. A rising berm of sand and a hedge of cactuses hid them from the main road. And in this location, the main road was rarely ever used. Unless the drones find them, they are safe.

Four hours later, Rosie sits at his computer with a four-pack of Red Bull. With poetic rhythm, he punches the keyboard. Three minutes of typing followed by one quick sip of the energy drink, stop and repeat. When he hears the door open, he looks over with red, strained eyes. Pax is holding a glass bowl. She sets the bowl next to the Red Bull, squats next to him, and shoves hair behind her ear. "I made mac-and-cheese," she says. "You had like twenty boxes. You can't live off energy drinks." Pax taps the side of the bowl. "You haven't eaten all day."

Rosie doesn't miss a beat. He keeps blasting away at the keyboard. "I'm dadburn close." He spoke with his eyes glued to the screen.

Pax grabs his face and turns him toward her. "You've been going *dadburn* non-stop since this morning. If you don't take a break, your brain's gonna come oozing out your ears. Eat."

He nods, takes the bowl, and scoops a spoonful into his mouth. "I always did love this stuff." He scoops another spoonful, then another. "As long as I can remember, since I was a kid. And it has to be the powdered kind." Smashing another spoonful in his mouth, he chews away. "That real cheese stuff doesn't cut the mustard." He leans back in his chair, bear-hugs the bowl and keeps eating.

"You're a disgusting eater, Rosie." Pax crosses her arms. "You know that, right?"

He nods in agreement. He says, "I done took after my pops. My momma once told him that he spit more food on the table than he swallowed. And she told me once, *When I told you to wash your hands, I didn't mean with your food.*"

"Hacking the Pentagon. How do you do it?" Pax asked.

Rosie finished off the mac-and-cheese. He set the bowl down, burped and took a sip of Red Bull. "I make it look like I'm employed there and lost my password. From there, password recovery software makes it easy. The hard part is covering my tracks. I learned a long time ago it does no good to hack somebody if they know you did it. To accomplish that, I build an elaborate trail that eventually leads to a server in China. By the time their hound dog techs snoop their way to the end, they won't be any the wiser because they expect it from China."

"That's really smart. Do all hackers use fake names?"

Rosie leans farther back in his chair. He spins it around and stares straight at Pax. He wipes his mouth with the back of his hand. "I haven't been around someone like you in 'bout two or three presidents."

Pax smiles. She repositions hair behind her ear. "What do you mean?"

"Your brain, it's different. You think about every-darn-thing. And you ask a lot of questions."

"Is that a problem?"

"That is definitely not a problem. To answer your question not all hackers do it. Only those good enough to have gotten into some serious trouble."

"Did you do any jail time?" Pax asked.

"Some, yes." Rosie pushes back in his chair. He rocks back and forth. It was his misfortune that someone is always looking for a way to capitalize on his expertise. An ex-friend of his turned him in for a reward. Easy money was too big a temptation. She was his really close friend, a let's get physical, kind of friend.

When the FBI found him, he was caught off guard and stumbled around, grasping for answers. He didn't want to believe the truth. He couldn't accept that the closest one in the world to him gave him up. For a long time, he didn't. He had it all worked out in his mind. There were a dozen scenarios that could have led the feds back to him. *Maybe things would have been different if a butterfly in Australia had flapped its wings differently. Maybe if he had nuked that butterfly from orbit, everything would have turned out roses.* A year later, he realized that grasping at butterflies wasn't the answer. He's been much more careful with friends ever since.

"Why didn't you just stop the hacking?" Pax asked.

Rosie ceases rocking, draws his head back, and stares at his computer. He says, "A long time ago, I had a feeling in my stomach. That feeling has calcified, fossilized, and has dug so deep inside me that I can't even pretend anymore. On the surface, it may look like I'm a hack addict. But in my stomach, it doesn't feel that way. It feels *wonderful.* I could no more stop hacking than I could stop breathing."

"I think I understand." Pax knew that Rosie's profession was frowned upon, that people hated those involved with it. In a way, she felt camaraderie with him. She had wanted to prove time travel for years but received laughs and jokes every time she brought it up.

"I had to give up a lot to keep doing what I do. I had to give up everything."

"Are you happy, Rosie?" Pax asked.

"If I wasn't hacking computers for a living, I could never be happy." Rosie tilts his head to one side. He looks away from the computer and concentrates on Pax's eyes. "The people after you, I know a little about them. They won't stop. They'll keep coming at you the way people crave chocolate. Seriously they won't stop. They'll poke and poke and poke until you bleed. Even if I'm successful at helping you, you're going to look up and see doom one day. When that happens, you'll either suffocate or go out of your mind trying to stop it."

"I don't plan on suffocating!"

"Course not. Nobody does. But then that day arrives, and it's like holding water back with your hands." Rosie rises to his feet and helps Pax to hers. "Why don't you give me 'bout an hour. Go spend some time with those friends of yours. By then, I'll be inside the Pentagon cyber room, worry-free. Then maybe we can find out a few things. Bring Hawke back with you. I got some news for him, too."

Once Pax steps outside, Hawke shouts at her. "It's hell out there in the sun!" He is sitting under the canopy of the second RV. He points at a chair next to him, holds up a can of beer, and watches as she walks over and sits down. "It's the cheap stuff," he hands her the beer, "but Rosie keeps them cold."

She pops the top, presses the cold can to her face, then chugs a swallow. "Any idea what the temperature is?" she asked.

"The RV radio said 105, but that's the least of our worries. Someone's got their claws out looking for us. On top of that, we have no communication." His face is freshly washed, and even in the shade, his beard glistens. His jeans and t-shirt show off his athletic build.

Pax heard very little of what Hawke just said. She sips beer and stares at his T-shirt.

"Have you talked to your father lately?" Hawke asked.

She gulped another drink of beer. The heat of the desert made the cool liquid more refreshing. She couldn't have enjoyed it more if it was champagne at a wedding. For the second time she presses the cold can against her face. "The answer's the same as last time. Why?"

"Just wondering."

She touches his arm with her finger. "You think he's the one with the claws, don't you?"

"I'd feel better if we knew what he's been up to, that's all."

"My dad's harmless. That FBI training has made you paranoid."

"If it seems like I'm putting him under a microscope, I am. It's my job to decipher the facts and be on high alert. I'm assigned to protect you. To do that, I have to look at things with a critical eye."

"I understand that. I think you're barking up the wrong tree, but I get it. It's something you have to do." Moving her fingers to his head, she starts stroking his hair. "Tell me something about yourself nobody knows."

"Why?"

"I don't know. Maybe I want to play. Maybe I'm bored. Just do it."

"So, this is like a game?"

"Right. Go on, tell me."

"Okay, I have really weird dreams."

"Give me an example."

Hawke turns his beer up and chugs a swallow. He peers at Pax giving her a sly look. "Last night, I dreamed a pack of dogs was chasing me."

"That's not cool. But it's not weird, either."

"I'm not finished."

"Sorry."

"The dogs were drunk and kept stumbling and falling."

"Okay, that's weird."

"I'm still not finished."

"Sorry again."

"When I reached my house, the door was locked. Before I could get my keys out, the dogs were on me."

"Okay, and..."

"My fault this time. I was waiting for you to interrupt me. Anyway, I thought I was done for and panicked and fell backwards on my butt. Then the dogs took my shoes off and started licking my feet."

"Is that it?"

"My fault again. I should have given you a signal. Yes, that's it."

"That's a really weird dream."

"Told you. Anything else I can do to un-bore you?"

"Hey, are you like this bad with all the girls?"

"I thought I was excellent with girls."

"Really!"

"Yes."

"You think you would be good at marriage?"

"I know I would."

"Even with like, arguments?"

"I would be an expert at settling arguments."

"Then why don't we give you a test?"

"Fine by me."

Pax stood up and began pacing back and forth. "Alright, let's say we've been married for five years." She throws up her hands gesturing. "By this point, the whole rose-colored glasses thing has worn off. Your job keeps you away a lot, and it's caused a rift."

"Are we poor or rich?"

She stops pacing. "Um, upper middle class. You know, making it pretty good."

"Any kids?"

"None."

"Okay. I'm ready."

Pax throws her hands up again, gesturing frantically. "This is the third time this week you've dragged your butt home late for supper! You could have at least called! Supper's ruined, and I'm sick and tired of this!"

Hawke stands up, pulls Pax close, hugs her, and pats her back. "You're right, dear. I'll make it up to you. Tomorrow, you can order a shipping container of stuff off of QVC."

She pushes Hawke back and stares at him. She says, "Okay, my mistake. You're freaking good at this."

"Are you still bored?" He asked.

"No." Leaning in, she kisses his cheek and gives him a different kind of hug. "I like your face."

"Do you know why I wear a beard?"

"No, why?"

"Because my face cheeks are so big, they're like a butt with a nose and eyes."

She bends over laughing, nearly falling. "Ha-ha-ha, ha-ha-ha. That makes me want to shave it just to find out." She gives him a quick kiss on his lips. "I'm glad we're friends."

"I'm glad too."

Moving back, she lets go of him, and asks, "Do you mind if I ask you a personal question?"

"You have a habit of doing that. Go ahead."

"You used to be married and had a little girl. Why didn't you tell me?"

"How did you find out?"

"Does it matter?"

"I suppose not." Hawke sits down, grabs his beer, and chugs another swallow. Other than with the psychologist, he had never had the courage to talk about it. It had happened before his official FBI days. "Sometimes we wait so long to find out what we want that what's right for us passes us by. My wife, Callie-I loved her more than anything. But she was totally against my applying for the FBI. I had no idea she would leave me and take my daughter. And I had no idea she was stepping out on me.

The night after she left me," Hawke stares deep into Pax's eyes, rubbing his thumb across her eyebrow and holding his hand to the side of her face. "I told the truth about that part. *It did happen in New Orleans.*" His hand falls away and an attempt at a grin doesn't materialize. "That night I couldn't sleep. I sat at the hotel window. Twice I think I actually stopped crying. When I turned in that application to the FBI, I didn't know I was burning one bridge and crossing another. When I finally realized it, it was just too late."

"What was your daughter's name?"

"Ginger Rebecca Gentry."

"I've heard you call her name."

"I didn't realize I was saying it out loud. About that, Callie made her choice, but Ginger didn't have one." After finishing off his beer, he hesitates, pointing to his head. "Her dying, it affected me up here. Sometimes I see her."

"How so?"

"Oh, just walking in a group of people or waving at me. Sometimes she talks to me."

"You can get help with that."

"I know. I lied about that too. I've been seeing the bureau's psychologist for over a year now."

"How's that going?"

"Mona, the psychologist, she's been great."

Hawke's hallucinations were not normal, but neither were they abnormal. In her office Mona had explained things very carefully. She had helped him understand that traumatic experiences like the loss of a loved one could cause off and on periods of induced anxiety. Because we see with the brain, the eyes only being the lens or camera, then severe emotional stress can elicit hallucinations. People often think they see a dead loved one. It's fairly common. Hawke's issues go a little deeper because he often hears her. The good thing is Mona had already ruled out schizophrenia or manic-depressive psychosis. And there were no neurological problems caused by physical trauma. She helped him understand that he didn't have to get over Ginger entirely. But he did have to move on with his life. Hawke rubs both hands on the temples of his head.

"Are you alright?" Pax asked.

"I think so. Just a little woozy."

"Your face is flushed." To Pax it seemed he was trying to hold his breath. "You're not breathing normally. Does this happen often?"

"No," he's twisting his straight blond hair between his fingers, hoping this conversation would just go away. "Okay, yes, the episodes, I..." He coughs trying to clear his throat, as if this is going to make him breathe any better. "I used to sit up all night thinking about them. Why does Ginger visit me, talk to me?"

Suddenly a backward rush of remorse and agony blindsides Hawke. Brought on by their conversation and the resulting deep feelings of guilt. Another dizzy spell is induced. He hears the sound of a child playing. He turns around and sees a little girl peeking out from behind the RV. She giggles and waves.

"You're doing good helping her, Daddy. She's like a kid. She doesn't know what the world can do."

"Ginger?" Hawke whispered and watched as the little girl ran in front of him. She keeps giggling and running.

"Keep helping her, Daddy," she yells. *"She doesn't know what the world can do."*

"I will, darling. I will." Ginger turns facing him, making this cackling giggle that is both embarrassing and sweet at the same time. She touches her lips, blows a kiss, and vanishes into the desert.

Hawke wonders what Pax is thinking of him. He hopes this is not something that will scare her. When he looks at her, she is staring back at him, her face concerned but smiling.

Before Pax or Hawke can say another word, they hear the sound of a door flinging open and Rosie shouting and waving passionately. "Grab Darcie and git in here now!"

Pax shifts her shoulders around and pounds her fist on the RV. In less than five seconds, Darcie was outside. Together they walk in Rosie's direction. In another twenty seconds, all four crowd around Rosie's computer.

"I'll start with your emails." Rosie spoke while glancing at Hawke. "Do you know a General Stackhouse?"

Rubbing the side of his face, Hawke nods his head. "I've heard of him."

"Pax and I know him," Darcie said. "We've been in his office. Is that where the emails are coming from?"

"It's where I traced them back to, but it's not where they originated from. Someone is trying to implicate this Stackhouse fella. Whoever sent the email is good. It has more trails than a national park."

"Were you able to trace down the source?" Hawke asked.

Snatching the Red Bull, Rosie downs several swallows before answering. "I said they were good. I didn't say they were as good as me." Rosie gives a devilish smile, takes one more drink and continues. "You might have heard of this place before. The email is coming from a town in Prince William County, Virginia."

"What's the name of the town?" Hawke asked.

"Quantico! The email is coming from inside the Marine Corps Training Base. I don't know how, but I think the Russians have a man at Quantico."

"Why do you think the Russians are involved?" Darcie asked.

"Because it's what they do; it's their calling card. Pointing the finger is classic Russian espionage. I'm surprised, though, that they didn't implicate the Chinese. That's their norm. Most people think it's the Chinese doing the most damage, cyber hacking in the U.S., but it's the Russians. They just make it look like the Chinese."

Hawke shakes his head. "None of this makes sense. I was sure the emails were from a friendly source."

"Well, I can't say for sure it's the Russians, only that it's got their mark. Are you sure the emails are friendly? Could they be leading you into a trap?"

"Anything's possible," Hawke replied. He thought the emails were designed to help Pax and to uncover the truth about her mother. Now he isn't sure what to think. He doubted it, but if the Russians were involved, then this thing was getting more serious by the minute. If Nate was correct, the Chinese had been after the sensory chip technology for a long time. For now, he was leaning toward the Chinese.

After opening a desk drawer, Rosie takes out a pencil and jots down something on a sticky note. He hands it to Hawke. "Here's the location inside the Marine base. It's office 4S7." He points a finger at the computer and continues, "See the flashing red dot? That's the fourth floor, south side, office number seven. Can you get in Quantico without arousing suspicion?"

"I've got contacts there."

"That's good. You'll want to drive, though. They've probably got a team looking for you at the airport. Next thing, I've hacked into the Pentagon." Rosie punches the keyboard, and the logo of the Pentagon appears on the screen. "Give me a name or department."

Darcie places her hand on Rosie's shoulder. "Start with General Stackhouse. Can you get into his personal computer?"

"If he's connected to the Pentagon mainframe. Just a sec." He continues punching away. "Got it."

Darcie directs him. "Look for any documents connected to Paxton Thomas."

After several more keyboard entries, they are staring at documents labeled *Top Secret.* "Pax, your name's all over these documents. This Stackhouse fella is a three-star general. That kind of hardware makes a man think he can do whatever the hell he wants. There are instructions, threats, and intimidations. Does anybody know what the Timeship is?" Sliding to the side, Rosie allows the others to have a closer look. Reaching back, he points to a paragraph. "Whatever it is, this says the sensory chip in Paxton Thomas will make her the driver."

All at once, Darcie, Hawke, and Rosie look at Pax. "What?" Pax asked. "What do you want from me? Okay, I know what the Timeship is. I have it with me in my backpack. But if I tell you what it is, you won't believe me."

"Sooner or later, you're going to have to tell us." Darcie spoke in a serious motherly tone. "It might as well be now."

"First," Pax responds, "let me tell you they plan to use it for the country's defense. You know, to keep ahead of the Russians, the Chinese or any others that might be a threat."

"What's the Timeship, Pax?" Darcie asked. "Just tell us."

"Precisely what its name indicates. It's a device that travels through time."

"Tell me this is just in theory," Hawke says, shaking his head in disbelief.

Pax continues, "For a while, they couldn't get the math right. When they left the Timeship with me, I didn't realize they were just using me to complete the math. With the help of the sensory chip, my mind is a thousand times sharper and faster."

"What's the sensory chip?" Rosie asked.

"I used to be blind. The sensory chip was installed at the back of my brain to give my vision back. What they didn't tell me until recently was that it enhances all seven senses. With all my senses working together at a different level, I was able to complete the mathematical computation in less than two minutes. I opened the Timeship and made the adjustments. If I'm correct, *and I am*, the Timeship is now operational."

"Let me get this straight," says Darcie. "This is Pentagon technology that you helped complete?"

"Yes."

Darcie continues. "But it hasn't been tested?"

"No, but I guarantee it will work."

Darcie points her finger at the computer. "This paragraph here in the document. It mentions the Argonauts. Who are they?"

"I don't know. I only know what I've told you."

"Who gave you the Timeship?" Hawke asked.

"Edward Cotton. He said it didn't work and left it for me to play around with. I think he realized I could make it work. They already knew I was a prodigy mathematician that had a strong interest in time travel. I was the perfect host for the sensory chip technology."

"Sooner or later, they're gonna find you," Rosie exclaimed.

"No, they won't!"

"It's only a matter of time. Like I told you a while ago, they'll poke and poke and poke until you bleed."

"They want me back in D.C. They want to use me as their guinea pig. But I won't do it. I won't."

"Then, use what they did to you as motivation." Rosie continues, "Turn the tables on 'em. Use the technology against 'em. Travel back in time. Find out who's behind this and what they're up to."

"You mean like right now! Like today?"

"My pops always said *no time like the present.* Of course he was talkin' about drinkin' beer, but you get the point. If it doesn't work, no harm is done. But if it does, advantage, Paxton Thomas! Hawke, you go with her. If the Timeship works and she disappears, we need a witness to confirm. And keep up with the time. Darcie, you stay with me. Let's see if we can find out more about the Argonauts."

Chapter 19

Time Travel
Twenty Years in the Past

"**W**hat are you doing there?"

Ten-year-old Pax did not hear the question. She stands under the limbs of two cherry trees, picking up fallen blooms, thinking she's alone. She is in the backyard of her mother's house a few months after her parents' divorce. "I'm waiting." This time Pax registers the presence of a person behind her and turns around.

A young woman stood before her, gripping something narrow in her hand.

"Is that a toy car?" Pax asked.

The woman raises her hand and looks at the object. "No, it just looks like one."

Pax releases several cherry petals, and as they fall to the ground, she takes a couple of steps toward the woman, her eyes locked on the object. She wipes her hands on her dress and then rubs one of her eyes. "What's it for?"

"It's a device that helps me keep track of where I am and where I need to go next."

"Like a map?"

"That's right, it's a new kind of map."

"My daddy likes maps," as Pax speaks her eyes widen, and her brow raises. "He has lots of them."

"Really?"

"Yes. Daddy says you can never have too many maps."

The woman steps closer to Pax, kneels to her level and smiles. "Your father sounds like a smart man."

"He is. He's a lawyer at the Pentagon."

"You don't say?"

"Uh-huh, he's met the President. That means he's important."

"I guess you're right. You don't get to meet the President unless you're important."

"Do you know me?" Pax asked while reaching her hand toward the narrow object.

"I kind of know you, yes," the woman responded. "Oh, go on, you can touch it if you like."

Pax curiously rubs her fingers over it. Her head tilts from one shoulder to the other. "It's made of metal?"

"That's right."

"I never saw a map made of metal."

"That's because it's a new kind of map."

Pax looks down at the strange object. She pulls her hand back and looks the woman in the face. "I don't remember you."

"We haven't met before, but I know people at the Pentagon, and I've heard about you."

"What did you hear?"

"I heard that you were very good at math. Is that true?"

"Yes, it's my favorite subject. I'm gonna be a mathematician. That means at least six years of college. I don't care because I like school."

"That's something we have in common," the woman replied. "I loved my time in school."

"Did you like math?" Pax asked.

"It's the reason I'm here. I'm also a mathematician. I think mathematicians should stick together. So, when I heard about you, I wanted to come to see you for myself." All at once it hits her what she was going through at this age and how she can be of service. "I want to tell you something, okay?"

For a moment Pax looks away from the woman toward the ground. There are pink blooms half tucked into both pockets of her jeans, and thousands more spread around the base of a cherry tree.

The woman is watching her closely when suddenly an inspirational feeling hits her. It tingles her skin, shooting through her extremities. She is nearly overcome by the emotion of being in the presence of her ten-year-old self. It's like she's looking at a Monet or Van Gogh for the first time.

Pax wipes at her face and looks back at the woman. "What do you want to tell me?"

The woman still stares at her in awe. *Just look at her,* she thinks, her heart fluttering girlishly. *She's so young, so pretty, so amazing.* "I want to tell you that sometimes life gets tough. Things can happen that make us want to quit. Do you understand?"

Pax's lips curl downward. "I think so. My parents argued a lot, so they quit liking each other and got a divorce."

The woman reaches out and brushes her hand through Pax's hair. "That's precisely what I mean. When things get hard, that's what people tend to do." She draws back her hand. "But no matter what happens, you still need to go to college. You still need to be a mathematician. Will you promise me that?"

Pax nods, and another voice shouts in the distance. "Can I help you with something?"

The woman stands and shuffles her body around. She places a hand up to block the sun. She can hardly see. She steps into the shade of a cherry tree and just stares. It's Sloan. She wanted to shout, *Momma I've missed you,* but realized how insane that would sound.

"I asked if there's something I can help you with."

Pax lowers her hand. She had been so optimistic about traveling through time. She had imagined it playing out like a movie, smooth and exhilarating. And to some degree it was. But she hadn't planned on what to say, thought it would come naturally. But seeing her mother seemed awkward. Even worse, she hadn't remembered how beautiful she was. Why hadn't she remembered that? She was unconsciously holding her breath, *panic setting in.* Was her mother going to call the police? Would she recognize her? Surely not because she had changed drastically from the girl with cherry petals in her pockets. "Is your name Sloan?" Pax blurts it out; catching air from her lungs, she is breathing again.

"It is. Now would you mind telling me what you're doing here?"

Pax takes one step forward. She just needs to make conversation. Beyond Sloan was the house, just the way it was before the natural gas explosion. She can see a southern magnolia stretching up above the house in the front yard. It too, had been destroyed in the blast. "The magnolia tree is beautiful," Pax said.

Sloan looks at the tree. "It's what drew me to this house in the first place: The magnolia and all the cherry trees."

"Would you mind if I talk to you about your daughter?"

"Why? What's this about?"

Pax begins walking toward Sloan. She needs to keep talking. She can't tell her who she is, not now. It wouldn't make any sense to her. She asks, "Have you considered which university she'll attend?"

Sloan's head jutted back. She places her hands on her hips. Her face crinkles up. "University?"

"Yes." Pax stops several feet from Sloan and gives a big smile. She is anxious, wondering how this is going to play out. She needed to find out some things, but how. Just keep talking. "I'm in town for a few weeks visiting family. Yesterday, I was touring the Pentagon and overheard a conversation. It was about your daughter, Paxton Thomas. I think it was her father talking with several others. Apparently, she has incredible math skills for a girl her age. Have I got that right?"

"Her English still needs improving, but when it comes to math, she's off the charts, top in her school."

"That was my understanding. It sounds like Paxton is a child prodigy. I was wondering if you would consider a local school. I mainly had in mind Johns Hopkins. It's close by in Baltimore."

"Johns Hopkins?"

"Yes. With her math skills, she's guaranteed a full scholarship."

"Are you a recruiter or something? We've always thought it would be Harvard. Her father went there, and it's a great school for mathematics."

"That's true, but so is Johns Hopkins, only it's much closer. It has a beautiful urban campus with excellent public transportation. You don't need a car, and it's a quick and cheap train ride from D.C. to Baltimore. She could spend weekends at home, or you could visit her anytime you wanted."

"Her being close to home, *that is* appealing. I think Gatsby, that's her father, I think he would like that too."

"You'll talk with him about it then?"

"Yes. Gatsby picks her up tomorrow for the weekend. We recently divorced. If you're not a recruiter, could you tell me why it is you have such an interest?"

The questions were getting easier. Of course, she knew. She says, "There aren't too many child prodigies. I wanted to meet her. I'm a mathematician myself."

"How did you find us?"

"I started asking questions. When your name came up, all I had to do was check the directory."

"I didn't get your name?"

Trying to remain calm, she smiles to buy some time. Should she give an alias? Would lying cause more awkwardness? Would it complicate matters? Her senses are coming together, functioning in conjunction. A calmness spread over her. "That's another reason I wanted to drop by. My name is going to sound strange." Pax sticks out her hand, and the two shake. "I'm Paxton Thomas."

Sloan gives a half disbelieving laugh. She cocks her head to one side, "You're serious, aren't you?"

"I know, it's crazy, right?"

Sloan glances past Pax over to her daughter. She watches as she plays in a pile of cherry petals. "Pax," she shouts. "Don't pick any more cherry blossoms. Okay, darling?"

In the distance, Pax waves one hand up high.

Sloan looks back at the woman, still not knowing it is Pax as an adult. She says, "That girl's always picking blossoms off of something." She rubs her hand across her cheek and grins. "I see now why you had to come. The connection is just too bizarre. I would've done the same."

"I'm glad you understand."

Sloan reaches out, placing her hand on Pax's arm. "Paxton Thomas, would you like to come inside? I've got freshly made iced tea."

"Thank you. I would love that."

Once inside, they sit across from each other at an oak kitchen table, sipping iced tea and taking turns talking. From her vantage point, Pax can see into the den. She notices several elegantly framed citations hanging on a wall. Sloan catches her staring at them and realizes she might have made a mistake hanging them there. "So, Paxton, how long have you been a mathematician?" She was trying to divert her attention from the plaques. She was hoping she wouldn't notice the citations were for the CIA.

Paxton keeps staring at the citations. "Oh, in my mind, *I've always* been a mathematician." She raises her hand and starts rubbing at the base of her neck. "It's that way with your daughter too, isn't it? I mean, she's a girl like that, right. She lives and breathes it?"

Sloan gives a prideful smile. "Pax can sit for hours doing math. It's the darndest thing I've ever seen. Sometimes I think she's only happy when working out abstract math problems. I mean it, she's already working on that stuff. We have her in the best private school we can afford. They cater to gifted children. A professor of mathematics there spends two hours a day with her. He's been having her do mental math computations for two years."

Paxton finally breaks her gaze away from the citations. She says, "I remember."

"What do you mean?"

She has the urge to say, *because she is me, haven't you figured it out?* "I was like her."

"Do you mean a child prodigy?" Sloan asked.

"Yes."

"I see. Well, I have to admit, I don't always understand. I haven't been able to help her with her math since the first grade. Was it like that for you?"

Paxton drifts back, remembering how she loved it, how she would get lost for hours doing math. "Yes, my mother was the same. You don't have to worry about that, though. Pax understands who she is. She knows she's different."

"It can't be genetic."

"No. It's more an anomaly. In the whole world, there are only about three or four others in her age bracket with her abilities. The brain's like that. It just happens sometimes, and nobody knows why." Paxton hesitates, looking around the room. She remembers playing with her toys, these same toys, then stacking them in a corner to make it look like she had put them away. She remembers how patient and loving her mother and father were until their marriage fell apart. She looks back to the den. She says, "I wasn't allowed to play with other kids."

"We've been instructed to do the same with Pax. They say too much stimulation from other kids could severely stunt her mind. I sometimes wonder about that. But you seemed to have turned out just fine."

"I was so young when it started. I never really knew what I was missing."

"So, you agree then."

"I wouldn't worry about it. People like your daughter and I are like abstract poetry. Some people don't get us at all, but others love us. Just keep loving her."

"That sounds like good advice."

"Your daughter's gift with math is essential to the world. She's very important."

"I guess you're right. I figure she'll teach at a university one day."

"If she wants to, yes. But she's going to do much more than that." She wanted to tell her more, that she would make history by being the first to time travel. She wanted to shout it and tell her, *It's me, mom! I'm from the future.*"

For the first time Sloan appears confused. "I'm not sure I follow you."

Paxton leans forward, reaching across the table, and places her hand on top of Sloan's. "Let me see if I can help you with that." She draws her hand back, sinks into her chair, and takes an audible breath. "I don't think anyone would argue that the world needs help. Think of it as pieces of a broken coffee mug lying everywhere. You're standing there in amazement, watching some dumb ass poring coffee, hoping the mug will still work. Without people like your daughter, this scenario would continue to repeat itself."

"Do you believe that?" Sloan asked.

"Math prodigies have *always* affected the world. Nobody can stop that reality. I bring it up because I don't want you to be blind where Paxton is concerned. No field of study, not the sciences, biology, physics, or chemistry, would be worth a dime if not for applied math. It's how ideas get tested and accepted based on evidence. Mathematicians work on problems that help us understand and explain the natural world. Even if they fail to be proven, mathematical ideas are testable. When we have breakthroughs in other fields, it's usually through applied math. And a math prodigy like Paxton is always at the forefront."

"I hadn't thought about it like that before."

"Can you see now that your daughter's future is of the utmost importance?"

"I suppose I do, yes."

"Then, would you mind if I get more personal?" Paxton glances again at the plaques on the wall. It was time to broach the subject. And her mind was razor sharp, the sensory chip working flawlessly. Words were coming to her, falling in place like a completed puzzle. It was like she knew ahead of time how the conversation was going to go.

Sloan follows suit, looking at the plaques on the wall. "I was hoping you wouldn't notice those. I can't discuss my employment with the CIA. I'm going to ask that you keep that information to yourself."

"I didn't need to see the plaques. I already knew your profession before I arrived."

"I see." Sloan falls back on her training. The statement shows a knowledge of her that would be impossible for a civilian background. She has been misled. She is either being tested by her superiors or is in the presence of an enemy spy. "Then do you work for the Chinese or the Russians?"

"I promise you I don't work for any government."

"Then you mind telling me what's *really* going on here because you're either a foreign operative or someone at the Pentagon is checking up on me. Or maybe my own superiors at Langley."

"I don't represent the Pentagon and I've never been to the CIA headquarters. My being here is not about governments duking it out through espionage. Look, Sloan, I'm not a spy, but you are!"

"That's where you're wrong. I'm not an operative."

"Let me rephrase that. You work for the CIA, and your goal is to be an operative. They enrolled you in the operative training program but have yet to offer you the position officially. You finished your training months ago."

"Who are you, and how do you know these things?"

"If I told you, you wouldn't believe me. What's important is that I'm here to help."

"I get it now. Gatsby sent you. He's never supported my being an operative. It was the last straw in a bad relationship. I'll tell you the same thing I told him. I want this more than anything, and I'm going to see it through. So, stop interfering!"

"I'm not disputing that it's your choice. Of course, it is. I just want you to see that while you're crawling through your dreams, you're dragging Pax with you. This decision will affect her tremendously."

"You can tell Gatsby to piss off!"

"I'm not here for Gatsby."

"If you're not representing Gatsby, what's your angle?"

"I already told you. I'm here to help."

"What is that supposed to mean?"

"I thought I made that clear. What you do affects your daughter. Sometimes, when we make a choice, we lose something we can't replace. Don't you think this is one of those times?"

Sloan stands up from the table, crossing her arms. "Gatsby sent you alright. He thinks our daughter, the prodigy, will suffer. He believes my being an operative will stunt her. Is that it?"

"You have a responsibility toward her. And putting yourself in danger isn't being responsible. If something happens to you, it will have a lasting effect on her. I just want you to see that and to understand it. The choice is yours, Sloan. No one, not the Pentagon, not Gatsby, and certainly not me, can control you."

"I've already made my choice. It's all planned out. I have a wonderful neighbor across the street. She's agreed to take care of Paxton during my stints away from home."

"I'm sure that arrangement will work just fine, but what if something happens to you?"

"Nothing's going to happen."

"What if something happens to you?" You and I both know how dangerous the job is."

"If something happens to me, then Gatsby would take her in. He already gets her every other weekend."

"Losing her mother would destroy her."

"Maybe, but that's not going to happen."

"Would you at least reconsider your decision? Giving it some more thought can't hurt, can it?"

"Fine. I mull it over and talk to my superior. I can still opt out if I want to."

"Is General Stackhouse your superior?"

"No, but I've heard of him. He just got promoted to Director of National Intelligence. His new office is at the Pentagon."

"If he's head of intelligence, what's he doing at the Pentagon?"

"I thought you would've known. The CIA is under the control of the Pentagon. So are the FBI and all of the nation's security."

"If General Stackhouse isn't your superior, then who is?"

"Gideon Romanoff."

"I thought Gideon was FBI."

"No. He's CIA in charge of clandestine and covert actions."

"So, he has no connection to the FBI?"

"None that I know of personally. There have been rumors about a new program where the CIA will begin working closely with the FBI. I think that's a few years off. Traditionally, the two haven't communicated very well. There's been a conflict between U.S. domestic law enforcement and foreign intelligence. The wedge goes back to Pearl Harbor. Adding to that wedge were the Kennedy assassination and Watergate. The two organizations not working well together directly affect the country's security. I guess they want to improve that."

"Makes sense. What's your opinion of Gideon?"

"As my superior, he's sharp, really knows his stuff. He's probably the smartest man I've ever known. And he doesn't fold under pressure. I think he thrives on it."

Suddenly the TV turns on, the sound blasting through the kitchen. Sloan looks toward the den. "Pax," she shouts. "Is that you? Could you come here?" Within ten seconds, Pax comes walking in. "Could you turn the television off?"

Pax frowns so hard that her eyes almost close. She says, "But SpongeBob is on."

"Then could you at least turn the volume down? We're trying to talk in here."

"Did she show you her map, momma?"

"Map? Pax what are you talking about?"

Pax points to Paxton. "She has a map made out of metal."

Sloan glances at the object in Paxton's hand. Earlier she had noticed it but didn't make a connection. She rubs at her forehead, shakes her head, and turns back to Pax. "There's no such thing. Now go back in the den and turn that TV down."

"But momma!"

"If you want to watch SpongeBob, you'll do as I say." Pax slumps her shoulders and walks away. Turning back to Paxton, Sloan sighs audibly. "That thing in your hand. It's not what I think it is, is it? I mean, it can't be possible." She backs up a couple of steps, turns, and opens one of four drawers on a rustic-looking kitchen Armoire. After reaching in, she looks back to Paxton. "How old are you, Paxton?"

"I'm thirty years old."

"If I'm correct about your current incarnation, that would put you roughly twenty years ahead of today."

"I'm sorry. I don't follow."

Sloan's eyes raise, and her forehead wrinkles. "Nobody wants to be trivial. Certainly not me." Reaching her hand farther in the drawer, she continues, "So, I will have to ask that you stop playing games with me. I'm serious. I understand why you're doing it, though." She pulls her hand out from the drawer, displaying a narrow, oval-shaped metal object. "But if you keep playing games, I'm going to get pissed off." For a few seconds, Sloan waves the metal object. "This one doesn't work, but I have a feeling yours does."

Paxton sets the Timeship on the table and places her hands palms down next to it. She leans in uncomfortably, pushing down, rocking back and forth a couple of times. Her mother having an older model Timeship was a complete surprise. Was Sloan a part of the Timeship program in its early stages? Nothing else made sense. What else was she secretly a part of? Her head is beginning to ache with pain around the temple area. She peers at Sloan. Her new computer-like brain function is not helping her. She had questions and needed answers. She says, "I didn't know you had one of those."

For the second time, Sloan waves the metal object. "And yet here we are."

"Would you mind if I take a closer look?"

Sloan steps back to the table and places the object in front of her. "Go ahead. You know a lot more about these things than I do."

Paxton picks it up, twists a lever, opens it up, and glances back at Sloan. She asks, "What were they planning on using it for?"

"I'm a little fuzzy on the specifics, but the Pentagon wants to stay ahead of our enemies."

"By that, you mean the Russians and the Chinese?"

"Yes. The only way to defeat a disease is to stay in front of it."

Paxton looks down into the mechanics of the metal object. "Is this a battery I see in here?"

"Yes." Sloan continues, "My understanding is if used to travel back far enough, there wouldn't be an electricity source. The battery would give them several hours before they had to return."

"It wouldn't work," replies Paxton.

"No?"

"No. To slip through time, you have to open up an electromagnetic field. The magnetism would almost instantly drain the battery. And the power source used here is electricity. That's not enough power to open a time slip. If you managed it, it would only be for a second or two."

"As I told you already, it doesn't work."

"It's easy to see why. And looking at the preset coordinates, they got the mathematical function wrong."

"Did they get anything, right?"

"Yes. The Pentagon scientists figured out time travel is possible. My guess is this is their first attempt. When you look at it like that, it's pretty impressive."

"It takes them twenty more years, then?"

"I guess you could say that." Paxton continues, "But the Pentagon scientists aren't the ones who figure it out."

"Then, who?"

Paxton looks into the den and stares. She allows several seconds to go by before glancing back at Sloan. "That little girl in there sitting in front of the TV watching cartoons."

Sloan jerks her head toward the den. "My God, it can't be. That means." In a split second, she goes from surprised to being startled.

Paxton raises her hand and points it at Sloan. "Go ahead and say it. You already know the answer."

Sloan points a finger right back at her. Her next few words come out slow and shaky, "You're Pax twenty years into the future?" She adds breathlessly, "You're my daughter?"

"That's right, mother. And the powers that are so important to you at the Pentagon, and I might add, Quantico and Langley, those powers helping you today are the same ones in my time."

"I see. Well, are you happy with your life?" Sloan asked.

"Yes, I live in Albuquerque now."

"But didn't you like D.C.?"

"D.C. is wonderful. I like everything about this town, even my brick prison of high school, but Albuquerque's my home now. Do you have something against Albuquerque?"

"No. Albuquerque's fine. It's not dead. It's just that there are other places that are more alive. I guess I'm just surprised, is all."

"It's dryer than D.C., and the sun is almost always shining. Not to mention I have good friends. I have a good life, Mom. You don't have to be concerned about that."

"Maybe, but none of that replaces the excitement of D.C."

"Are we having our first argument in twenty years?"

"I guess we are. What now?"

"Make sure Gatsby sends me to Johns Hopkins. Harvard is a great school. But for the reasons I mentioned earlier, it's not for me."

"I thought you weren't supposed to change anything when you jump through time," Sloan said. "Wouldn't that be taking a big risk? It can change people's lives for the worse. It can even eliminate some people right out of existence."

"It doesn't work like that. That theory is all wrong. History will adapt and work around the change. Some details will be different, but the overall record doesn't change. I spent two years at Harvard. When I switched to Johns Hopkins, it was a much better fit."

"Fine, then. I'll insist on it with Gatsby."

"And for reasons I can't explain, the CIA Operative thing is a bad idea."

"I'm not making any promises there. I've wanted to do this since they hired me out of college. It's practically all I think about."

"I see. Would you at least tell me how you got your hands on this time slip device?" Paxton asked.

"My superior, Gideon. It was to be used by the CIA for espionage and counterespionage. The implications for a secure U.S. would have been incredible. Infiltrating and gaining secrets would have been as easy as 1-2-3. Of course, it didn't work, so they scrapped the project. They were going to toss the device. I don't know why but I took it home."

"Have you ever heard of a scientist by the name of Edward Cotton?"

"There are lots of scientists that have connections with the Pentagon. His name doesn't ring a bell, but that doesn't mean much. I only know a couple of scientists personally. It's hard enough keeping up with the contacts I already have. No, wait, wait. Cotton? Yes." Sloan reaches across the table and picks the oval-shaped device back up. Lifting it, she continues, "A scientist by the name of Cotton, *this was his project!*"

"Edward Cotton?"

"I don't know the first name. I only know him by *Professor Cotton.*"

"You're sure about this?"

"Yes. I only met him once at CIA headquarters. He told me he teaches math at the University of Maryland. He asked me about Pax. It was probably Gideon, but I'm still not sure how he knew about her."

"None of this seems to add up. Gideon Romanoff was an FBI instructor at Quantico in my time. And Edward Cotton is the inventor of a sensory chip technology that works with the brain."

Sloan sits back down and slides the metal object in front of the other. She gives a small smile, acknowledging both of them together. When she tilts her head back, looking at Paxton, she has a serious look. "I've done a lot of training this past year at Langley. I'm qualified for foreign operations. Basically, I'm an operative trained for deep undercover." She leans forward and lowers her voice. "I think in your time, Gideon is CIA disguised as FBI. The FBI only deals with U.S. internal investigations. They're not a threat to the Russians or the Chinese. He would be off their radar."

"And Edward Cotton? Could he be CIA also?"

"That's exactly what I'm thinking," Sloan answered.

"Do you know anything about something called the Argonauts?"

"Argonauts? I've heard that name a time or two. I can do some snooping around. I'll need some time. You *can* return, can't you?"

Smiling, Paxton holds the Timeship up. "Absolutely."

Chapter 20

Now

Hawke Gentry was thoroughly adapted to desert life. His parents had moved him to Albuquerque when he was only two years old, so it was more a law of nature instead of his choice. If it was good enough for mom and dad, it was good enough for him, and he absolutely loved it. The rules of hydration were engrained in him. Drink water every thirty minutes, fifteen if you are working out. Replenish electrolyte levels once a day, which means consuming a bottle of Gatorade, Powerade, or coconut water. Always know what your sweat is telling you. If it is salty, make sure to replace salt, magnesium, and potassium levels by rehydrating. And always stay tuned into the four things that determine how much of the liquid stuff you need: body size, climate, activity level, and overall health. It was rare that he ever met another person as adapted to desert life as himself.

Sitting in a plastic chair, he watches as a flock of sandhill cranes drift southward along the ridge of a group of cactus-covered dunes. About to set, the sun hangs behind the cranes like an enormous Norman Rockwell painting. The beauty of the desert has always impressed him with its weather-beaten colors and calming larger-than-life feel. Far off in the distance were the Sandia Mountains, some appearing bareheaded, others with hoods, and still others with stubby crowned hats—all of them with beards and sandy-colored garments. Not too many places could brag about originality and virgin ground, like the deserts of New Mexico. Altogether, it was as utopian a scene as the world could produce.

Invariably, Hawke's mind drifts to Pax, who had used the Timeship to slip back some twenty years and visit her mother. It was a good first test for the Timeship. If it worked, she might even find out some things that would help her in the present time. She had been rooted for several hours on one side of the portal while Hawke nervously awaited her on the other. Could it be that she had reached her mother, who at present was deceased and who she had not seen since she was a ten-year-old? Or had she been unsuccessful and was now trapped behind time, without a way back? Were her calculations off, were there other factors she failed to consider? Or did time move slower in the past, so they grossly miscalculated her return time? Had she not survived, her body composition being obliterated in the space-time continuum? Hawke's questions were piling up. All he could do was wait and hope the answers came soon in the form of a tall, beautiful girl with mocha-latte-colored hair.

In the back of his mind, he believed she would survive whatever sort of wilderness she had fallen into. Closing his eyes, he forced himself to stop trying to determine the outcome. Not more than three minutes later, he hears the relaxing sound of a soft wind blowing through trees. It hits him that there are no trees anywhere close by, and like a photon hitting the speed of light, his eyes open instantly. What he now sees is mystifying. Directly in front of him, thin blue lines are twirling clockwise inside an oblong sphere that resembles an open-ended horizontal tornado. Suddenly there is a surge, and the thin blue lines grow and become one large beam of blue. Pulsating and intensifying, the light seems on the verge of exploding. The wind sound has increased too, whipping in spurts like an angry hurricane. Twirling at break-neck speed, the blue light suddenly blasts into thousands of tiny particles and disappears. Left standing in the same spot is Pax. At first, her hair looked like a blue waterfall of fire. Hawke groans at the sight of it, but then it subsides and becomes the silky brown color he has become so fond of.

Pax swipes her tangled hair away from her face. It looked like a hurricane had combed it. "Next time, wear barrettes with a bobby pin," Hawke shouted. Despite his tenseness, he smiled to welcome her back.

Waving, she starts walking toward him, and as he realizes that she's back safe, a rush of feel-good relief sweeps over his body. Springing from the chair, he gives her a hug and asks how she feels.

"A little stiff," she answered, bending sideways at the waist. "It was the same when I arrived at my mother's house. It goes away quickly, so no biggie. I feel good, though, you know, lots of energy. I think time travel pumps positive ions into you. I feel like I could run a marathon or do a thousand pushups."

Hawke steps back eyeing her, sizing her up, making sure all body parts are present and accounted for. "You seem okay. Were you successful?"

She grabs him by the arms. "You can put your doubts to rest. *Time travel is real.*"

"So, describe it for me?"

She throws her hands out in front of her. "It was one of those situations where words can't do justice. When I first arrived, I recognized my old house because I had landed next to it. I overheard a little girl. When I turned to look, I was blown away. It was me at ten years old." Pax's hands, still raised, fold into tight fists. "Hawke, *I was staring at myself.* It was an indescribable feeling. And I had a conversation with her, or is it me? I don't even know how to say it! Then my mother showed up. At first, I didn't know it was her. The sun was in my eyes. When I realized it, I thought I would faint."

Taking her by the hand, Hawke tries to calm her down. "Easy there. Take a deep breath. Did she recognize you?"

Pax's breathing slows a little. Her eyes are focused straight into Hawke's face. "No. She figured it out later, but she had no idea."

"And when she realized it, what did she do?"

"Better than me, I think."

"I wish I could've been there to see that."

"About that, Hawke, I've decided to go back to the day my house exploded. I think there's a way I can save my mom. I could use your help. Will you, do it? Will you go back with me?"

Hawke had just watched her materialize out of a swirling mass of blue. Describing it as dangerous would be an understatement. And he didn't know the first thing about time travel, had never thought much about it. "Could I have some time to digest the idea?"

"Take all the time you need, but tomorrow I go with or without you."

"Fine by me. Are you hungry?"

"I could eat."

"We could send Rosie to Bear Canyon. I think it's safe. He's off the grid, and nobody knows he's helping us. He can get whatever we need. It's about fifteen miles. If he hurries, he could be there and back in an hour."

Rosie had been digging for information about the Argonauts. When Pax and Hawke walked into the RV, he turned to look.

"She's back," Hawke shouts.

Rosie looked uninterested. "Where's Darcie?" he asked.

"Didn't you hear me," Hawke exclaimed? "I said, it's Pax. She's back. She time traveled. It was a success."

He glances at Pax. "Bless yore little heart, girl. *Bless yore little pea-picking heart.* Now that we done got that out of the way, we got bigger fish to fry." Opening a desk drawer, Rosie reaches in and scoops something up. Extending his hand, he displays several phone batteries. "Do you notice anything unusual?" he asked.

"There should be four," Pax replied.

"Exactly."

"Where's the other one?" Hawke asked.

"We need to ask Darcie because the missing battery is hers. If she's installed it in her phone, we'll all be in danger, *and I'll be madder than a hornet stuck in a Coke can.* The last thing I wanna do is pack up and move again. So, where the hell is she?"

Looking behind him, Hawke combs the area. "I thought she was with you."

"She disappeared two hours ago, claiming she needed to rest." Rosie replied.

"Hawke, your car's missing." Pax points past the Hummer.

Stepping out of the RV he combs the area and catches sight of his car returning. "Here she comes." He is already worried about her being followed. He walks quickly to the car. When the door flings open, he tilts his head, eyeing her, hoping she will take the initiative to explain herself.

Nothing, not a word.

"Why did you leave without telling anybody?" He shouted loud enough for everyone to hear.

She throws up a hand trying to blow him off. "I walked right by you and waved when I left."

"No, you didn't!"

"Yes, I did. You must have been napping."

Hawke walks around the vehicle, bending down and checking underneath every wheel fender. If he finds a tracking device, they will need to pack up and leave immediately. There is nothing, so he walks toward the RV. Thirty seconds later, they all stand underneath the shade of the canopy. "You put us in danger, Darcie!" Hawke points his finger in her face.

She shakes her head, turns, and sits in one of several plastic chairs. "No, I didn't."

"Yes, you did."

"First off, I'm a seasoned agent, and I know what the hell I'm doing. And secondly, you're not my babysitter so let it go."

He doesn't take the hint. "That's all you got to say for yourself?" He glances at Pax, then looks back at Darcie in the shadow of the canopy. His face is slightly crinkled, his eyes have an animal-like glow. "Do you have anything else to say?"

She purposely looks away from him and says, "You might be a Special Agent, but you still got a lot to learn."

"So that's your next move, to turn this on me?" He crosses his hands at the waist, takes hold of his t-shirt, pulls it up and flips it off. Holding it up with one hand, he shouts, "Who did you call? And don't act like you don't know what I'm talking about. One of the phone batteries is missing." He wanted to snatch her out of her chair.

Tossing his shirt into the sand in exasperation, he bends down, kneeling in front of her, and grabs the sides of her chair forcefully. "*Who-did-you-call?*"

"I don't have to explain myself to you."

Pax grabs Hawke's shoulders and pulls until he stands up and backs away. She taps Darcie's chair with her foot. She asks Darcie, "Was it D.C.?"

No answer.

Pax lightly kicks her chair again. "I'm not mad at you, but I need to know if you've still got my back. Was it D.C.?"

"It wasn't what you think." Darcie switches roles, using her motherly voice. "I was checking on my father."

Picking up his shirt, Hawke uses it to wipe sweat off his neck. "So, you thought a little socializing with the family would be, okay?" He pats the shirt across his chest.

"Her father has Alzheimer's," Pax said without looking up. Grinning at Darcie, she continues. "She had to put him in a nursing home."

Hawke shakes his head and looks into Darcie's smoky dark eyes. "I'm curious. Why didn't you think you could tell us?"

The lines next to her mouth shifted slightly, caught between a smile and uncertainty. "Pops was thirty-five when I was born. When I was twenty-four, the doctor diagnosed him. That was eleven years ago. A while back, they told me it was day-to-day. I've been trying to stay in contact."

"How long?" Hawke asked.

A lack of sympathy in his voice made Darcie and Pax look at him. "What are you talking about," Darcie asked.

"The battery, it's not still in your phone, is it?"

"Of course not."

"How long?"

"I talked with the administrator at the nursing home for maybe five or six minutes. After that, I took the battery out."

"If they're tracking our phones, they would've known." Hawke glances around the area for the third time. "It doesn't look like you were followed, so, we're probably good. How long did you stay in town after the call?"

"An hour, maybe less. I went into a grocery store and picked up ten gallons of water and some protein bars. I would've noticed if someone was watching me."

"With your experience, you should know better. The people after Pax are the best of the best. You wouldn't have seen them coming, and you wouldn't have noticed them placing a tracking device on the car. That said, it looks like we're in the clear."

Rosie had been keeping his distance to see how this was going to play out. He has a 9 mm Glock 19 stuffed into his jeans under his shirt. He had learned a long time ago to take no chances and always be on guard, to expect the unexpected. For now, it looked like things had settled down.

A half-hour later, Rosie sits with Pax at his computer. "I wanted you in here for a reason. I need you to understand something. Twelve years ago, I began developing a computer program. Seven years ago, I completed it, and three years ago, I improved it. This program allows me to infiltrate any website and extract whatever I like. It still doesn't cover my tracks. It's possible and even probable, they could find out I had been there. So, I still have to take the time to point the finger at someone else, which, as you know, is usually the Chinese. What I'm getting at is I'm not so sure you can trust those two FBI agents. I done background checks on both of 'em. Darcie checks out the best, but she has some close contacts that are Russian. The emails I uncovered pointed to them being friends, but you can never be too careful. Hawke is perfectly clean, which is a major red flag. And there are gaps where he seems to go off the radar. I think someone's covering for him. He could be deep undercover of the Russian variety. Or it could be he's used for covert assignments, and there's nothing to it. I tend to doubt that due to his age. He's a young'un."

Pax shakes her head in disagreement. "Just so you know, he's older than he looks."

"Have you seen his driver's license?"

"No, but he told me he was thirty."

"According to his files, no discrepancy there." Rosie squints one eye like he's aiming to shoot. "But for what he's used for, he's a young'un. He's only been FBI for three years, half of that as a Special Agent. With his experience, it's doubtful he's placed deep undercover, which leaves gaps of weeks at a time where he seems to disappear. And another thing... after only three years, FBI, he wouldn't be used to guard someone as important as you. Darcie, yes, but Hawke, no. Do you have any idea what he could be up to?"

"No."

"When you first met him, what were the circumstances?"

"I was in the hospital awaiting the procedure that gave me my eyesight back. It was military technology, and the Pentagon wanted a representative there. Somehow there was a mix-up with the date of my surgery. It was too late to send someone from D.C., so the Albuquerque FBI was authorized to send an agent. That's when I met Hawke."

Rosie moved his shoulder like a tic or a nervous twitch. "No way to tell for sure, but it looks orchestrated."

Pax turns around and walks a couple of steps, stopping at a small aluminum sink. "Your wrong about Hawke. No way he's working the other side."

Rosie groans and falls back into his chair. "And you'd know this: how?"

She turns back around. "I just know."

He shakes his head, blinks his eyes, and groans again. "Girl, I hate to have to tell you this, but when it comes to spies, intuition is as useless as square wheels on a sports car. Everything is pointing to him playing for the other side. Have you been cuddling up to him or something?"

She drags her hand across her chin. "I guess so, yes. We're sort of in a relationship. I like him, and I don't think...."

"You don't have to say anymore. I got the picture. We like to believe we know those closest to us, that the boundaries between us are small, maybe even insignificant. What we don't understand is that love blinds us. It blinds us so completely that what we see as being a good person is actually a monster. Take it from someone with experience. He's playing you, and if he's working for the Russians, it's only a matter of time before they show up and take you. Can you drive?"

"Yes."

Rosie reaches into his jean pocket and pulls out a set of keys. He dangles them in front of Pax. "Take these and sneak out after dark. If Hawke follows you, go off-road. He'll never keep up in that thing he's driving."

"But what about you and Darcie? You'll be stuck out here without transportation."

"I'll call an Uber."

"Seriously?"

"This might be the desert, honey, but we got Uber's out here too."

"What about the Hummer? How will I get it back to you?"

"Leave it in the Walmart parking lot with the keys on top of the front left tire. Put your battery into your phone, call for an Uber, then take the battery back out. Whatever you do, don't go home. Go somewhere safe, somewhere they can't find you.

One more thing. I dug up some information on the Argonauts. Mind you, there's not much to know. They came into existence during WWII. Initially, they were to combat the infiltration of spies that had swept into the country. They were also to curtail technology theft. Both the Japanese and Germans managed to place numerous spies in a quick amount of time. President Roosevelt and Vice President Wallace formed the top-secret government agency. They called them the Argonauts for two reasons: one, they were to be completely underwater or invisible, and two, like an octopus has eight legs, there were to be eight members only. Today, if they still exist, which I doubt, they would probably be based in D.C. After WWII, in 1947, the CIA started up. My guess is this intelligence agency replaced the Argonauts. Although the name still surfaces from time to time, I think it's probably just a code name for the CIA."

"Rosie, how did you ever become so adept with computers?"

He hesitates, remembering his teacher. She was young with a pierced nose, short black hair, and legs like twigs. Her intelligence did not match her looks. There was nothing she didn't know about operating a computer. She had told the class there would be a learning curve, but not to worry, she was there to help. He expected a few bumps, but the speed of which he learned was unfathomable. He took to it like he had been doing it his whole life, like it was his career or given vocation. "For some people, these things come naturally," he responded. "When I realized I was one of 'em, I signed up for night classes. In two years, I was hacking major corporations. The first time I managed it, I got hooked. It felt like a thousand suns were rising in the sky above me."

"Well, I'm glad we found you. Thank you for all your help."

"I wish I could do more." Rosie taps his fingers on the computer desk while gazing out the tiny RV window. "I once walked into a spider's web and did a week's worth of cardio in thirty seconds." He twists his head and looks Pax straight in the eyes. "Point being, if you find yourself in a web, you best be doing the same."

"Do you think that's about to happen?"

He taps his fingers several more times and attempts a half-hearted grin. "People act like there's never been any trouble at the Pentagon. How could there be? It's the freaking security blanket of the country. The truth is people are bought and sold there every day. Like it or not, you are one of the most sought-after people in the world." He raises his hand to the window and points. "Out there right now, someone is spinning a web. It doesn't matter if it's D.C. or Albuquerque. Hell, maybe it's both."

Chapter 21

Twenty Years Ago

Sloan paced the floor of one of the Pentagon's spacious suites. Ten minutes earlier, she was escorted here by armed guards. It was a top-secret, hidden suite within a suite, completed in 1935 as part of the original building. The President, Vice President, and Joint Chiefs of Staff, along with General Stackhouse and his team, are the only ones with clearance to the room.

"Heaven's sake," she hissed between her teeth, thinking she was in some serious trouble. She stops, looking over some nicely framed pictures of past Presidents. Trying to relax, she shrugs her shoulders, moves her neck back and forth, and stretches her arms out like a hang glider. It's not working; her nerves are getting the upper hand.

"What the hell is happening? I've done everything asked of me, *everything!*" It hits her that she's talking out loud. Catching her by surprise, she hears a voice coming through a connecting door.

"Agent Thomas, is everything alright?"

When she looks toward the voice, she sees the unfamiliar face of a man. Her arms fell quickly to her side. She says, "It's just a relaxation technique. I learned it in training."

"Yes, I've used it myself, but these days I prefer liquor or Xanax."

Before replying, Sloan takes a slow breath and cringes. "No disrespect, but who am I talking with?"

"Just a second." He turns and addresses two armed guards standing just beyond the doorway. "I don't want to be disturbed. Is that clear?" The two guards nod, close the door, and station themselves on both sides of it.

After walking across the room to a minibar, the man looks over his shoulder. "In a while, we'll be joined by one of the

Pentagon's top-ranking generals." He squints his eyes at her, "Would you like a glass of wine? It might help you to relax."

Sloan's arms tightened and, trying to corral her nerves, she crossed them. "Are you going to tell me who you are?"

He reaches for a glass. "Yes, but first drinks. Wine or something else?"

Despite the unanswered question, she was looking forward to a drink. Maybe it would knock the top off her nerves. "Do you have scotch?"

Reaching for a second glass, he chuckles. "That's what I'm having." When he finally handed the drink over, his eyes narrowed, giving her a serious grin.

Immediately turning up the drink, she allows half the magic potion to slide down her throat, burning a beautiful path as it goes. Again, she turns it up, finishing it off. The 57% alcohol content quickly hit her. She says, "That's not a pretty smile. Do you have bad news? Am I being demoted?"

He gently eased the glass to his mouth. "It's quite the opposite." He tips the glass, enjoying the scotch. "My name is Edward Cotton. Have you heard of me?"

After grinning, she peers into the empty glass. "I have to admit, in passing a couple of times, yes." She grins again. "I ended up with one of your machines."

"I only built three of them."

"None of which work." She responded quickly.

"I'm not worried about that. Most new technology has its failures. What's science fiction today will be mainstream tomorrow. People are walking around with wireless phones. Not too long ago, that would have been impossible. My Timeship is a work in progress."

"So, you're an inventor for the military?"

"Something like that. I prefer Technology Engineer. I work under General Stackhouse. They brought him in from the Marine Corps Air Station in Miramar, California. He's new here, so you may not have heard of him. We've both been reviewing your record."

"If you're military, why aren't you in uniform?"

"I never said I was military."

"But you said…"

"I said I'm under General Stackhouse. As part of the CIA, you come under the Pentagon, but you're not military."

"That's true, but…" A ripple of suspicion sweeps across Sloan. She knew well enough that something was wrong. Langley must have spotted a red flag in her, maybe her confidence was interpreted as arrogance. Arrogant agents are more likely to flip to the other side. They usually feel underappreciated, and when approached by a foreign entity, the money is too much to turn down. She noticed her glass was empty, "Okay. I'll play along. What did you find out about me?"

He takes another sip and draws a steady breath. He says, "Your hands are never still."

Growing more nervous, she looks at the minibar, focusing on the decanter of scotch.

"Would you like another drink?" Edward asked.

She was impelled to speak up, to defend herself. But it could be viewed as being more arrogant, "Yes," she answers without hesitation and holds out her glass. After handing him the glass, she continues. "Why did you mention my hands?"

"Because you're never complacent, always going above and beyond." When he turns back to the bar, he keeps talking. "You're far above average in compliance, you speak five languages, and to top it off, your stature, five foot nine, which is tall for a girl. You're a busy girl, thus the hand's reference. It's no wonder the CIA wants you as an operative."

"They never offered me the position. You know that, right?"

"Yes, but they still might. Are you *certain* it's what you want?"

"I've never been more certain about anything in my life. Anyway, I finished my training, and they didn't offer."

"The process can be slow at times." Edward hands her drink back, "Sorry, it's not as much as the last one. You can drink all you want, but first, we need to discuss something, and I need you clear-headed."

She takes a quick agitated breath. Who was this man? Was he interfering? *Was he the reason they hadn't offered?* "My application was accepted a long time ago. I've had all the training. I'm ready for this. Edward, look, don't interfere. Not now. I've come too far."

"I promise you that's not what I'm doing. We need you in the CIA. And we need you to be an operative. It's part of what drew our attention."

"Who are we?" She watched him move uncomfortably a moment before taking a sip.

"If you can believe it, we are the most secret organization in the U.S. Government. And right now, (he holds his drink out as if pointing) at this moment, we are recruiting you."

"For what? What is it that you do?"

He moves his head like he's adjusting his neck, shrugs his shoulders, turns up his drink, and finishes it off. He says, "We hunt spies, especially those seeking to steal technology."

It made sense, an undercover operation to catch spies. It was usually the FBI that protected foreign soil, but everyone, including spies, knew that. Nevertheless, she had never heard the first word about this secret part of the government. She was more than intrigued. To be a part of something like that would be like living a fantasy. She says, "A group of spies who hunt spies."

"We're not spies. W*e're spy hunters.*"

"Spy hunters? My God, Edward. That's brilliant. Go on; I want to hear more."

"We've been around since the second world war. The Japanese and Germans were infiltrating and doing a lot of damage. Today it's the Chinese, the Russians, and a few independents who steal and sell. Because there are only eight of us, and we're in different branches of the government, our enemies don't know who we are. They're not even sure if we exist. We aim to keep it that way. We use the pseudo name Argonauts."

"Why, Argonauts?"

His eyes and lips narrow again. "Argonauts are a special breed of octopus. Unlike other octopus, they live close to the ocean surface, just out of sight, hunting their prey. Like the Argonauts, we are a special breed of hunters."

For a moment, Sloan's gaze goes across the room. "That's why the serious face."

"Yes."

She looks back at him in silence.

"We want you to join us, Sloan. If you decide to do so, you need to understand that there won't be any monetary reward. Your CIA salary will remain the same. If our enemies don't already know you're CIA, they'll figure it out sooner or later. If your salary is significantly higher than other operatives, it could tip them off. You're probably thinking they don't have access to that information, that it's top secret. But they have their ways. We must be extremely careful."

She did not care about a monetary reward. "Would I have any restrictions?"

"We have a protocol to keep from being found out. Other than that, no."

"I'd be allowed to kill?"

"Yes, you're free to make that choice without checking in."

"Where would I be stationed?"

"CIA headquarters here in D.C. But you would be out of the country a good bit."

"That's going to be hard. I have a daughter."

"It's a sacrifice. Of course, we could provide a full-time nanny. Still, you have to be certain because your life will change forever."

"No nanny. I have a neighbor, and my daughter's comfortable with her. It wouldn't draw any suspicion. And I don't want to be babied."

"A neighbor's perfect. Are you telling me you accept?"

She wanted to think about it longer because she had just made another commitment that she now regretted. She was already thinking of a way to get out of that. Afraid they wouldn't wait, she was backed into a corner and had to decide now, so she panicked. "I'm in. When do I start?"

"Do you mean, when do you get your first operative assignment?"

"Yes."

"In three weeks. To avoid suspicion, we'll send each Argonaut mission through coded information to your personal email account. The codes are directions appearing in the form of jokes, poems, short stories, and that sort of thing. They originate from a legitimate website where people post creative writings. We simply post our own and make sure you receive them. You've got three weeks to learn the code." Edward holds out his glass again, motioning to a desk. "The deciphering instructions are in the top drawer. *They never leave this room*. You're to come here every day until you're fluent in deciphering the codes. Any questions?"

Sloan liked what she heard. It was precisely the kind of thing she wanted to be a part of. Her hand tightened around her glass. "Something this big, how do you know you can trust me?" She was thinking about her recent decision and how she could get out of it.

The question did not surprise Edward. He expected it. "We've had you under surveillance for a year now. During that time, we even made sure you received the Timeship. You could have made some serious money selling that thing to the Russians or Chinese. You've had no contact with either of them that we know of. Of course, if you had, the technology wouldn't have helped them much. After all, it doesn't work. It was the perfect test, and you passed. Any other questions?"

"Who supplies me? Does everything come through the CIA? I'm talking about passports, fake IDs, weapons, or items specific to a job."

"I won't lie to you; this could get a little tricky. You're the first Argonaut in the CIA. Our enemies have eyes everywhere. If we try to get too hands-on, they'll know something's up. Most of the time, your standard CIA equipment will be all that's required. Otherwise, the first course is to improvise. Always at your disposal are the eight legs of the Argonauts for anything you need help with, but we *never* go through the CIA." Edward looks deep into Sloan's crystal green eyes. What he hopes to see is staring back at him, determination, and grit, mixed with a tinge of excitement. He shifted his feet and looked around the room before settling back on her. "I guess we're good here then. I recommend you get started on memorizing the code."

Suddenly, Sloan's mind goes to her daughter, Paxton. It was an old argument, with nothing new involved. What would be the least destructive way to handle this? She would see her very little from this point forward. She knew this was coming, and now it was here. Her face shifts because someone has just entered the room.

"General Stackhouse," Edward continued. "We've been expecting you."

Chapter 22

Now

Hawke covered his face while a stiff breeze blew sand past the RV. He is thoroughly pissed to learn that Pax and Rosie's car are missing. When the wind lets up, he looks over to Rosie, who is making quick work of an early morning beer. "What's wrong with this place? Every time I turn around, someone's disappeared." His words echoed and re-echoed in his mind. Pax was a little wild sometimes, but she wasn't flighty. And Rosie didn't seem the least bit worried.

Rosie tosses the empty beer can next to a cooler and pops the top on another one, saying, "You haven't heard? Albuquerque is sort of like the Bermuda triangle. There are places 'round here where you can put a bottle on the road, and it will roll uphill." He was happy that Pax had acted quickly, leaving unnoticed while the others were asleep.

Hawke rolled his eyes and rubbed his cheeks wearily. He had spent half the night hashing out the best way to handle the situation. And now, just when he has a plan, Pax is missing.

"You kind of look like you been rode hard and put away wet." Rosie turned up his second beer of the morning.

Biting his lip, a clench grips Hawke in his stomach. He needed to contact Nate, but even if he could, he had no explanation. Where was she? What had happened to her? He needed answers because the baggage on this one was getting heavy. He says, "You don't seem to be bothered. Why is that?"

Rosie frowned and gave out a loud grunt. "I'm more experienced at pretending everything's okay, even though we know it's a lie."

Hawke could sense he was involved. It was too simple; her taking his car. And other than nonsense, he wasn't saying much. Hawke says, "Lie. Now there's an interesting word. Is there something you're not telling me?"

Although he hid it well, Rosie was becoming impatient. Losing it, he slams his beer down next to his seat. "I should be asking you that question. Because from my point of view, it's a miracle she's not dead and the technology extracted already."

Hawke looked at him for a long, tense moment. "You sure this is the route you want to take?"

"You're a young'un. And a young'un would sell his poppa's ranch for next to nothing."

Any doubts that Hawke had were now obliterated. Rosie was involved. "You say that like you've been rehearsing it all morning."

Rosie didn't bother to answer.

Then Hawke's phone rang, and all hell broke loose.

"I missed you taking the battery. Mighty sparkly of you. How long you been playin' the other side?"

"You're wrong," Hawke said roughly, punching the phone and putting it to his ear.

Rosie jerked his head like he'd been slapped. "I'm not wrong! You've given away our location, you lousy gut eater!"

Hawke turns his back to Rosie, pressing the phone tight to his ear. He says, "The vanguard is missing! I repeat, the vanguard is missing!" There is a brief pause. "Yes, yes, yes," he shouted. "Anything else?" There was another pause. "I'll take care of it. I got an ETA of one hour." Placing his phone in his jeans, he runs ten yards and stops, looking into the sky. After doing a three-sixty, he throws his hand up, blocking the sun, and combs the area.

Rosie rubbed sweat from his face, jumped up, and ran to the first RV. "Darcie," he shouted while pounding on the door. "Darcie, we got a situation!" When he turns the handle, a sudden gust of wind flings the door open and slams it into the side of the RV. He sees Darcie standing with both hands wrapped around her Glock.

"I hate getting up to trouble," she said. "Don't tell me there's no bacon for breakfast."

"Are you trying to make a joke or piss me off?" Rosie shouted. Turning sideways, he waves her out. "Get ready for fireworks. Hawkes double-crossed you. He done gave us up."

Without a word, she runs out, still clinching the Glock with both hands. The brightness of the sun nearly blinded her. Through fuzzy eyes, she notices Hawke still searching the skies. "Stand down," she shouts, pointing the gun at him. And then a drone some twenty feet in diameter buzzes over the top of them.

Rosie, who by now has a foul taste in his mouth for the whole situation, has managed to get back to the second RV. He comes running out of it with his AK-47, pointing it wildly into the sky. The drone has come back and is hovering above them.

"Rosie, don't shoot!" Hawke shouted. "That thing's got four guns pointing at us! And it's equipped with a rocket launcher! Put the gun down!" He reaches out his hand, motioning downward. "I mean it! Slowly, lay-it-on-the-ground!"

Seeing the seriousness of the situation, Rosie complies, and the giant drone lowers to about twenty feet above them.

As if the suspense wasn't enough, three black Hummers come blasting to within thirty yards of the RVs. A small army unloads, all equipped with military-grade rifles. Within five seconds, the drone has locked onto them. It shoots straight up fifteen feet, avoiding rapid fire from the soldiers. In response, it fires a rocket, and one of the Hummers is blasted, turning into a mini mushroom cloud. The drone follows this with machine gun fire and a second rocket. After another Hummer goes up in flames, the soldiers run for their lives. The drone lowers again to about twenty feet above the ground. It spins quickly, keeping its camera on the retreating soldiers.

Shaking off any leftover sluggishness from a night's sleep, Darcie drops her Glock, does a tuck-n-roll, and snatches up Rosie's AK47. With deliberate aim, she pulls the trigger, and a smooth pop-pop-pop reverberates from the gun. In ten seconds, all 70 bullets had spat out, most of them hitting the target. The damaged, smoking drone lowers ten more feet before careening outward and crashing to the right side of the RV camp.

Questions battered Hawke's mind more than any illness he ever had. He knew Rosie was involved, but nothing seemed to make sense. It was time for some straightforward dialogue. After retrieving a handgun from his car, he points it at Rosie. "Who are you working for?"

Before Rosie can answer, Darcie makes a move for her Glock lying in the sand.

Hawke blocks her by stepping on the gun. "Easy there," he says. "I'm not the enemy." With his gun, he motions to Rosie. "But I think he is. I'll ask you again, Rosie. *Who are you working for?*"

No answer, only a sharp movement of his head as he looks over to Darcie.

Hawke abandons the old question and asks another. "Are you two working together?"

Darcie is furious that she has no weapon. "Stop the games, Hawke." She shouted while kicking sand into his legs. "It's obvious you called in the militia. What's your next move?"

"Nothing's changed with me." Ever careful, and with his gun aimed at them, he moves slowly, very calculated, stepping back, opening the door of his Nissan, reaching into the glovebox, and pulling out a set of handcuffs. "Until I know what's going on, you two are my prisoners. I'm taking you in. Step over here."

Darcie scoffs at him and laughs. "We're not going anywhere with you. And you've got a lot more problems than us. Whatever time you got left, I suggest you use it wisely by putting that gun down."

Suddenly, there is the familiar pop, pop, pop sound of rapid gunfire. Several bullets hit the Nissan's fender, and one sent a sharp pain through Hawke's left arm. He's been grazed and is bleeding. When the drone went down, the soldiers decided to make their way back. They seem determined to take Hawke out. He falls backward into the Nissan, twists quickly into the driver's seat, and hits the push-button starter. In three seconds flat, tires are flinging sand. He blasts the Nissan forward, maneuvering it through a barrage of prairie bushes and rows of cacti right out into the wide-open desert.

Darcie snatches the Glock from the ground and, along with the soldiers, starts shooting at the Nissan. The back windshield shatters, and a few more bullets pelt the car, but it's not enough. Hawke escapes when his car goes past several large rocks, down an incline, and out of sight. In no time, he meets up with the road and disappears into a cloud of dust. Darcie kicks sand and shouts profanities at the top of her lungs. Realizing Hawke has escaped, she twists in a 180 and runs like a man on fire up to Rosie. "Where the hell is Pax?"

Rosie falls back against the RV, trembling at the sight of soldiers making their way over. "I know'd she was in trouble, so last night, I slipped her my keys and told her to skedaddle.'"

Six soldiers with rifles walk up right behind Darcie. Slowly, she brings the Glock up and rubs the barrel on her chin. "Four of you take the Hummer and get after Hawke. Do it now!" After a few seconds, she points her Glock at Rosie. "Just tell me where she is!"

Chapter 23

Now

Several miles down the road, Hawke's Nissan is trying to stall. Before it stops completely, he juts to the side of the road, slows the vehicle, and manages to get it partly hidden behind a grouping of bushes and rocks. After exiting the car, he opens the hood and instantly jumps back as steam shoots from the radiator. It had taken more bullets than he realized. Reaching back inside the car, he slaps at the glove box, presses a lever, and pulls out a map. He estimates 18 miles to the city of Bear Canyon. Examining the map, he sees a small town some sixty miles west of Albuquerque called Sky City. It was a tempting detour. From his location, it was only three miles away through a narrow pass called Slot Canyon. He could walk there in forty-five minutes. Since it was off the main road and the chances were good, he wouldn't be spotted. He grabbed his camelback, two protein bars, and started walking. Along the way, he tried his phone but without success.

Within a minute, he hears an alarming sound. It's a car, but more specifically, a Hummer. He has been spotted and knows he is in real danger. He pulls his gun and fires three quick rounds at the Hummer. It slides to a halt, the doors fling open, and four soldiers come barreling out. Hawke quickly combs the area and notices an opening in the canyon wall. If he can make it, he can hide and defend himself. Half stumbling and half running, he dodges his way to the entrance of a cave. Once inside, he aims and waits for the soldiers. Soon he can hear them arguing just outside the entrance, not more than twenty feet away. When the loser of the argument attempts to enter, he fires two shots catching the soldier in the arm. The soldier falls back, and Hawke can hear them arguing again. When the arguing stops, there is silence for the next few minutes. Thinking they might try to rush him, he falls farther back into the cave. Entering a large opening that is partially lighted from the other side, he sits, and rips open a protein bar. He is hoping his adrenalin is done spiking, and his heart will stop pounding. From his vantage point, he can easily defend himself.

While eating, he notices stunning stalactites dripping from the tall ceiling and fat stalagmite mounds rising from the cave floor. It was the perfect place to contemplate human existence or maybe those little green visitors. Hawke sips from his camelback, finishes the Protein bar, and cautiously moves up toward the cave opening. The soldiers are driving away. Since he is in the middle of nowhere, they probably no longer see him as a threat.

Before he can leave, he is surprised by a blur of thousands of bats emerging from the cave. A spooky blast of wind swirls around him while their wings bump, slap, and kick him. He darts to his right, trying to keep his balance and escape. Instead, he falls face first, landing at the base of a large rock. He gets his bell rung and is knocked unconscious.

When he woke up, the first thing he did was check his phone. It shows he'd been in a dream world for ten minutes. Wiping a little blood from his cheek, he canvasses the area known for its volcanic rock formations, cave dwellings, and scattered dunes; they could have been imported from the Sahara or maybe another planet altogether. Happy that he has his camelback filled with water, he heads in the direction of Sky City.

Sky City took more time to reach than expected. It sits perched atop a 367-foot tall golden mesa. Adobe bricks padded its tiny box-like homes. Walking along a reddish dirt road, Hawke sees signs of electricity in the small town, which is a relief. The town appears trapped in time, right out of the 1800s.

Soon he notices a local native girl with braided hair as long as a horse's tail. She stands at a sun-worn table painting pottery with an older man. Beaded jewelry hangs from her neck, wrist, and ankles having all the colors of a rainbow. And her nose and ears are pierced with shiny pearl-colored rings. She is barefoot, and her only clothing is two wide strips of turquoise leather. As he walked closer, the girl shouted out to him, "The tourists usually stick to the center of town!"

"Thank you," Hawke replied. "But my car broke down." Lifting his hand, he motions behind him. "It's like two miles on the other side of Slot Canyon. So, I had to walk."

She makes a funny confused-looking face. "That's a wilderness out there, not for the unknowing."

"I found that out the hard way. Is there a place around here where I can make a phone call?"

"Just a second." The girl dips her hands in a bowl of water, takes a hand towel, and dries them off. Walking a little closer to Hawke, she continues. "Out here, you should carry a phone. A person can get into trouble super-fast."

Hawke smiles politely and nods in agreement. "I should have been clearer. I have a phone. It just doesn't have a signal."

The girl points to the other side of the town. A cell tower can be seen over the tops of the adobe buildings. "It doesn't work in the canyon, but everywhere else, no problem."

Hawke immediately reaches into his jeans and pulls out his phone. "Five bars! Okay, now I do feel like a tourist." He reaches his hand out to her. "I'm Hawke, and you?"

She shakes his hand, laughing at the same time. "I'm Kasa. Sorry, I didn't mean to laugh at you. It's just that your name is that of the big bird."

"That's right."

"To the Native Americans, the hawk is all-seeing, all-knowing. When one attains the name of Hawk, it means they display great wisdom."

Hawke moves his arms out like an airplane. "That's so totally me!"

She smiles. "You're funny. I didn't expect that."

"Funny is more natural, but I can be wise. You know, like in an emergency."

She smiles again. "Maybe you could give me an example?"

"I can do that." For the second time, he motions behind him. "About a mile that direction is a turtle big enough to bite your hand off. You should stay away from there. How's that?"

"It was super-fast and accurate. Of course, I never go through the canyon because it would be incredibly stupid and dangerous, but that's just me. I could show you around town if you like."

"I'd hate to take you away from your work."

"I'm not on a timetable like they are in Albuquerque. Besides, maybe some of that amazing wisdom you've got will rub off on me."

"Okay then." They turn to walk, and Hawke continues. "You don't strike me as a local girl."

"There goes that wisdom thing again." She answered. "I was born and raised in Albuquerque. I'm a graduate of the University of New Mexico. For the past year and a half, I've been learning Native American traditions and art like pottery and jewelry making. I plan to move back to the ABQ and do my part in preserving them."

"You mean you're going to teach the old ways?"

"Sort of. It's more of an awareness program. I've petitioned the governor for a start-up program in our elementary schools to ensure that these old traditions never die out. I would train others in the fundamentals, and we would spend time in the schools educating the children. The goal is to install a sense of heritage."

"Sounds like an honorable undertaking."

"Thanks. Someone has got to start giving back. In another fifty years, nobody will care. Like everything else, the native traditions will be a thing of the past." Kasa points to the east of town. "Over that way are some ruins left behind by the ancestral pueblo. I'm hoping to get a law passed to protect and preserve them. It's not easy, though, because it takes money, and nobody wants to spend it. Oh…" she stops Hawke. "If you need anything, this is the place."

He is surprised to see a small general store. "I could go for something cold. What about you? Would you like a Coke?"

"Yes, and they have the best kettle corn. They make it here."

"Before we go in, I need to make a phone call. With my car breaking down, I'm pretty much stuck. I need a tow truck and a ride."

"Go right ahead. I'll see you inside."

Hawke punches his phone and walks onto the wooden plank walkway in front of the general store.

"Hello, Edward speaking."

"This is Hawke."

"You're late by over an hour. General Stackhouse said this whole thing's going up in smoke. You pissed him off."

"I thought he was always pissed off."

"Why aren't you here?"

"I ran into some trouble. They shot my radiator out. I'm on foot in the town of Sky City. It's something like twenty miles outside of Bear Canyon. Can you send someone to pick me up?"

"Nate's here. I'll send him. Gideon's here too. He wants to talk with Pax, and so do I. We need to find her before the Chinese do. If they get to her first, they'll have her on a plane faster than a blond driving a red sports car. He'll be there in about an hour. Where's the pickup?"

"Just have him come to the center of town. There's a general store. I'll be inside."

When Hawke enters the store, he quickly catches sight of Kasa. She's paying for a bag of popcorn. As he approaches, she smiles and holds out the bag. "You should try some. It's the best I've had. And here." She picks up a bottle of Coke from the counter and hands it to him. "You know, we talked about me, but you never said much about yourself. Do you live in Albuquerque?"

"Yes, for most of my life."

"And what do you do. Don't tell me you're a teacher."

"No." Reaching around to his back pocket, he pulls out a leather book-style ID case. Flipping it open, he holds it out so she can read it.

She winces and then smiles. "I guess your name fits you, after all."

Meantime, back in Rio Rancho, Pax sits in Café Bella, sipping an iced coffee and enjoying a bagel with cream cheese. She had just come from Cellular Boutique, where she had purchased a pay-as-you-go phone. She was upset, had questions, and wanted, no, deserved answers. After chewing her last bite, she swallows, punches a number into her phone, and takes a long sip of coffee. It says the number is not in service. She punches in another number.

"Hello," a voice said.

"Dad, it's me. I had to call your home phone."

"I'm in the process of changing numbers. Pax, darling. For two days, I've been worried sick. You don't answer your phone, and you don't return messages. You never used to be like this. What's happened?"

"I got my sight back. And along the way, I learned a few things. You knew what they were doing to me, didn't you?"

"What are you talking about, child?"

"You know exactly what I'm talking about."

"No, child."

His voice had changed. With all her senses perfectly aligned, it was easy to detect. "You're lying. You know everything they did to me, *everything.*" There is a long pause, and she can hear him breathing, thinking. "Are you going to say something?"

He wanted to tell her the truth, to lay it all out there, to stop the charade. He almost did but stopped himself. If he told her the truth, things would get worse, the kind of worse that would cost her everything, including her life. He had to be disciplined. He had lied to her for years, and he had to keep it up. He says, "It was the only way, child, all or nothing." He needed to be forceful, so he raised his voice sharply. "*You know as well as me that you're damned happy to have it!*" Saying these things made him want to cry. "Not only can you see again, thanks to me, but you have powers far above any others. I'd say that's a might better than a couple of months ago."

There it was--her dad's excruciating honesty. It was that other side of him that she never understood. "I was hoping you would say *I did it because I love you.* But there it is, that acting like an ass thing you like to do. Were you planning on handing me over to the Chinese? Or maybe it's the Russians."

"Why would I do that?"

"You're *lying* again!"

"Okay, what's wrong if they get the technology anyway? It's only a matter of time before everyone has it. So why not benefit from it?"

"I agree with you, Dad, that everyone should have it. But it's not up to you to decide when that happens. It's up to the Pentagon. It's their technology. They get to decide what happens to it. And right now, I'm pretty sure they wouldn't want you to give it away. For God's sake, they trusted you." Her disappointment in him was like a shiver she couldn't control. But at least now she knew the truth.

"Where are you?" Gatsby shouted. "I'm tired of talking over the phone. I'll come to you. Tell me where you are?"

"First, tell me who you've cut a deal with? It's the Russians, isn't it?"

"No." After he answers, there's another long pause.

"I'm waiting."

"I'll come to you. Then we can discuss the whole thing. They're not going to hurt you. They just need to examine the chip. Afterward, they reinstall it, and that's the end of it. Just tell me where you are. I'll come right now."

"First, tell me who the deal is with?"

"Not that it matters, but Iran."

"But they're not a world power."

"As I said, it doesn't matter."

"It's probably a control thing," Pax said. "Iran already has the largest standing military in the middle east. They could leverage the technology to keep them from being interfered with. That's it. They plan on ruling the middle east."

Gatsby spoke as he walked to his car. "Tell me where you are?"

She can sense something is wrong. He's not telling her something, or maybe he's lying again. "There's something else you're not telling me."

"I don't know what you mean."

"Tell me, or you'll never see me again. I mean it. If you ever want to see me again, tell me."

He stops abruptly at the car. "Fine, it's the Russians. They're just making it look like the Iranians in case I get caught."

"I got one more question. Your decision, how did you make it?"

"What do you mean?"

"Your decision to sell the technology, how did you make it. You didn't just let a cat step across your computer board. What was the determining factor?"

"I don't know. After they contacted me, I just went for it."

"That's what I thought. You grew up rich. You've always drawn your dignity from your income."

The conversation was killing Gatsby. But he couldn't stop, not now. "So, what! You haven't ever complained about it before!"

"There's that attitude again. If you spend your whole life, letting money make your decisions, it'll catch up with you when you least expect it."

"It hasn't so far, so I think I'm good."

"You think you can trust the Russians?"

"I know I can!"

"My God, Dad, this isn't the first time you've sold them technology, is it?"

Pax could feel herself, with all her senses, as if a veil lifting. She was having an epiphany, a new understanding of Gatsby. There was a time when he was all she had. He raised her, giving moral support, paying for her education. He was everything to her, like a god. She is jolted in her seat when she hears him scream at her on the phone.

"*I'm glad I did it!* Others in the Pentagon and White House do it every single day."

"Dad, do you even know how to feel shame?"

"I'm in my car. I'm backing out of the driveway. Tell me where you are. It's not as bad as it seems. We can work this out."

"This is that split second, Dad, when your being pissed off at me turns into pain." With those words, Pax punches her phone off and sets it on the table.

Chapter 24

Twenty Years Ago

Dear Mommy

I wanted to let you know some things because I haven't made a recording in three months. So, here goes. Yesterday a man visited Daddy. It was a nice spring day, so they were sitting at a table on the patio. I was in the yard in a patch of grass sniffing cherry blooms and playing and stuff. The man's name was Mohammad, and I think that's Indian or Arabian or something. It was very exciting because he had a strong accent that I had never heard before. So, I tried to listen closely to see what he was saying. He spoke about the brain, and technology. He said we are standing on a threshold. I think he meant outside. He spoke of the future, how we will 'make every known malady extinct including death.' He said that technology will make us creatures. Or was it creators? I don't know. I think what he was trying to tell Daddy was that one day nobody will die anymore and that we will all be inventors. I hope that Mohammad is right because I would like to live in a world like that. He came and visited once before, but they were in Daddy's office, so I didn't hear nothing.

Last week me and Daddy were in the kitchen, and I opened the refrigerator. I felt around and pulled out a gallon of Neapolitan ice cream. I wanted the chocolate, but I remembered something you told me one time. You said, what you give away is yours, what you don't is lost. So, I asked Daddy which side the chocolate was on. He explained that it was the middle. I scooped a bowl and slid it to him. I think what you were really saying was that giving makes everybody happy, which I think is good.

Last night I stayed up late. On TV, I was watching a police show, and I heard a man say, justice is justice. But I think that if *justice is justice that you would not have been killed. I admit I'm not sure I know what that means. So, I guess I could be wrong.*

I don't think that I told you they had me try out a seeing-eye dog. It didn't work out, and Daddy gave it back, but I should probably tell you why. On the first day, the dog broke away and started running down the street. Daddy ran after it and was gone for a long time. When he came back with the dog, he was grunting and breathing very hard. The neighbor asked him if he was a smoker. Daddy said no, and the neighbor told him, maybe he should take up jogging. Daddy was not happy about the whole thing. Then the neighbor's dog started barking and didn't stop for four days. Daddy could not sleep and thought that the neighbor's dog was barking because we had a dog in our house. I think Daddy was right, because when he gave the dog back, the neighbor's dog stopped barking. I don't mind Daddy giving it back because all that dog did was sleep and snore at the foot of my bed.

Anyway, Momma, it's turned into a gloomy day with the rain. I'm getting sleepy, so I will end the recording and talk to you soon.

Your daughter, Pax.

P.S. If I get to see you again, maybe you can tell me how come after I eat ice cream, I can taste the chocolate on my lips for a whole hour afterward. I'm not complaining. I would just like to know how it's possible is all.

Chapter 25

Now

The coffee-scented aroma of Café Bella wasn't having its usual relaxing effect on Pax. She sits with closed eyes, filled with anxiety, wondering if she had been too hard on Gatsby. She thought about calling him back, but it could be dangerous. If the Russians caught up with her, the technology would be used to hurt people. That was something she couldn't allow to happen. She regretted allowing them to surgically implant the chip. If she had not agreed, the weight of this would have been on someone else. Suddenly she feels the presence of another person at her table. When she opens her eyes, she sees Josie holding up a phone and punching in a text.

"You cruisin' on overload, New Eyes," Josie said before pulling out a chair and sitting down. "Yo, you think Café Bella, your bedroom. New Eyes all sleep, dream, like Café Bella her Xanax world."

"Hi, Josie. No, I just haven't had much chance to rest lately. Do you know what happens to an animal when you pack too much luggage on it?"

"No, New Eyes, what happens?"

"It just stands there staring. I guess I feel the same way."

"True that; true that." Josie looks back into her phone.

"Are you texting Chili Pepper?" Pax asked.

"No, but we good. He all charming and stuff. He know things I never say. I don't know how, but he know."

"Sounds serious, like he really knows who you are. Before long, you'll be reaching across a pillow, staring into his eyes."

"I know, huh. But he all mad sometimes, so irresponsible, disagreeable, but we been havin' fun." Josie looks beyond the table toward the entrance. She recognizes someone, someone important, someone she had just been texting. Standing up, she glances at her phone one more time before sliding it into her jean pocket. "Yo, New Eyes, don't mean to be tight, but gotta go. Momma all doped up, a temporary backtrack. She usin' again. See you on the flip."

"Sorry about your mother, Josie. Say hello to Chili Pepper for me."

As Josie walks away, she grazes the shoulder of a man. Both make a special effort to ignore each other. The man stops abruptly at Pax's table.

"I was hoping I would find you here."

It's Edward. As usual, he is dressed in a sharp-looking suit and is smiling down at Pax.

"Do you mind if we talk?" he asks.

She motions for him to take a seat. "Edward, how did you know I was here?"

He places his hands on the table and intertwines his fingers. "I hear your senses are coming together, working better than anticipated."

"And *I know* you're dodging the question. I'll ask again. How did you know? Is there a tracking device in the sensory chip?"

"I'd love to say, yes, to that. But you'd just know I was lying. All I can tell you is that we have eyes on you that you don't know about."

"Your pupils stayed the same. You're being honest. Tell me straight one more time. Can I trust Hawke? And I want you to know that I ask even though I'm not sure I can trust you."

"That question is not as simple as you think." Edward replied. "However, the answer is, yes. You can trust Hawke. You can trust me, too. But I understand if you don't."

Strumming her fingers on the table, she stares at Edward. She sinks back in her chair and hesitates before raising her hands, gesturing emphatically with open palms. "Why all the mystery? Tell me. Seriously, because I'm getting tired of all the freaking secrets!"

"You're important, Paxton, but you're not the center of the universe."

She slaps her hands on the table, sits up, and slides closer, her head and chest now leaning forward. "I basically tell you that I'm pissed about all the mystery, and all you do is talk in riddles. What the hell is going on?"

Edward smiles and shakes his head at the same time. He is trying not to tick her off any more than she already is, but he cannot give her what she wants. "I didn't mean to upset you. Nevertheless, there are other factors involved, factors that are more important than you."

"I see. And you don't trust me with that information?"

"No, but don't take it personally. For the past twenty-five years, I can count the people I've trusted on one hand."

Her temper eases up. She leans back in her chair until it rests on two legs. "Why did you want to see me?"

"It's time for you to go back to D.C."

"Why?"

"I think you know why."

"Humor me."

"Okay. You're in danger here. In D.C., we'll place you in a secure location, out of sight from those after you."

"You're going to hide me?"

"Yes."

It was the last thing she wanted, and it bothered her. Still, she realized without help she would eventually be taken by the Chinese or Russians. "How long?"

"I can't answer what I don't know."

Another voice enters the conversation. "You'll be comfortable and safe. That's what matters most?"

Looking up, Pax sees an unfamiliar face staring back. It's a well-built man in his early fifties, wearing a sharp-looking blue suit. He's African American with a shaved head and thick mustache. He says, "I promise you it's the right thing to do if you want to be safe."

Edward interrupts. "Pax, I want you to meet Gideon. He's an FBI instructor at Quantico, the best we've got. We flew him in to see you back to D.C."

"Nice to meet you, Gideon." She reaches out her hand. While the two shake, Pax's eyes pivot back to Edward. "Do all you guys wear suits? And why are they always blue or black?"

He doesn't answer, only gives a smile and a shrug of his shoulders. Her eyes rolled back to Gideon. She says, "You might as well take a seat." She motions for Maria, the waitress. "I need a refill, and you two might as well get something to drink. I've got some news. I think you're going to want to hear it."

"What might that be?" Edward asked, just as Maria arrived at their table.

"What can I get you?" Maria asked, ready to go with her pencil and pad.

"Just coffee for me," Gideon responds.

"Same here," Edward said. "And do you have those little honey packets? I use those in place of sugar."

"Honey packets." She jots it down. "Pax, you need anything else?"

"Could I get a refill and a slice of pumpkin bread? I'm still hungry."

"No problem. It won't be long."

After Maria leaves, Edward wastes no time prodding Pax. "*What news*?"

She glances at Gideon and then back to Edward. "Does he know about the Timeship?"

"He knows. Anything you can say in front of me, you can say in front of him."

"I made some adjustments, and it works."

"Does that mean what I think it means?" Edward asked.

"Yes. I traveled back twenty years. To be honest, I surprised myself. When I looked the Timeship over, I could see the math figures were wrong. I just knew. I made the adjustments and got it right the first time. I've always been super sharp with math, figuring nearly anything out. But each time I work on a project, the process takes time."

"You're a math prodigy, Paxton." Gideon goes on. "It's one of the reasons you were chosen, *the main reason.*"

"I understand that. What happened when I studied the Timeship, though, was different."

"How so?" Edward asked.

Pax turns around, looking for Maria. "God, I could use more coffee." She thinks back to the stretch of time when she figured everything out. It wasn't normal. It had happened fast, too fast. For a moment she wondered if someone had given her the mathematical function. And even the coordinates to her childhood home, the numbers came to her instantly. "Okay, so, you know how when you're dreaming, you just know things?"

Before Edward responds, he glances at Gideon, then back at Pax, but with a flushed face. "Go on."

"Well, in a dream, sometimes you just know someone's with you even though you can't see them. Or there's a dangerous situation, but you're calm because you know nothing will hurt you. That's the way it was when I analyzed the Timeship. It was like I didn't need time to grasp the math involved. I just knew."

"Three coffees, one iced, and one pumpkin slice." Maria appears before them suddenly, setting the tray on the table and sliding the coffees off.

"Could you put those on my bill?" Pax asked.

"No problem. I'll put it all on your card."

"Thanks." Pax's eyes settled back on Edward, imploring him. "You need to tell me what's in the sensory chip? Was someone sending the calculation through the chip to me?"

"Of course not. We've already been over this. Your senses are better aligned."

"No. There's more to it."

"You're being difficult."

"I can tell you're holding back. What is it you're not telling me? You can't expect me to go back to D.C. without me knowing the whole truth. For heaven's sake, tell me!"

"Very well." He was yielding with reservations and, to a degree, ill grace because she was forcing his hand. "What I'm about to tell you should be tempered by the fact that we are still learning ourselves. What's happening to you has easily exceeded expectations." He raised his cup and, frowning, took a drink.

"Have your coffee and pumpkin bread," he urged. "You'll need the energy to decipher what I'm about to say. Well, go on. I'm serious."

In two minutes, flat, she had devoured the bread and drank half her coffee.

"Now, don't drink anymore."

"Why not?"

"I need you to just listen."

"Okay, then, get on with it."

Edward was about to go where he had not intended, nor had he ever thought he would need to, at least not this soon. At first, nervousness showed in his eyes, but then he softened. She had been through a lot already and really deserved to know. Sooner or later others would know, eventually, the whole world. It might as well start with Paxton.

"I said get on with it!"

He gives her one last look and then starts. "How does one come up with the sensory chip? I've been asked that question before without ever really answering. I've already told you about my degrees in chemical engineering, molecular biology, and biomedical engineering. Before I finished my university training, I was already working on a theory that eventually led me to create the sensory chip. It has to do with how the senses do what they do. How do they take in their surroundings, understand them, and subsequently react? The answer lies with the truth about consciousness. My theory about consciousness, when proved true, brought about the sensory chip technology. Any questions so far?"

She remains silent, just shaking her head.

"Good. Now finish your coffee, go on, drink up."

Still, she remains silent, turning it up and drinking it all down.

"Now, here's the part where you need complete focus. I don't want to have to cover this twice. You think that consciousness is continuous, where you are conscious at every single point in time. *This common understanding is wrong.* We are, in actuality, in continuous consciousness only at certain times. If it didn't work this way, humans would be a mess, barely able to survive."

"Could you give me an example? I want to make sure I understand."

"I would love to give you an example. Continuous consciousness is like a movie. In a movie, we think we see the changes in a scene moving on continuously. But that cannot be true because change cannot be perceived immediately. It can only be perceived after it happens.

We've always known that we move from unconsciousness to consciousness when we wake from sleep or anesthesia. Most people believe freely in continuous consciousness because it follows basic human intuition. We have the feeling that we're conscious at each moment in time, so we must be, right?

Contrary to this assumption, I discovered that humans are only conscious at certain moments in time. For each individual, there is no universal standard of how long these conscious points in time last. My studies proved that what we have are unconscious periods, albeit, they are very brief, where things around us are happening, and we are in an unconscious processing period. After we process, then we perceive and react. The processing and then perception and reacting are two separate states of mind. In the first one, the processing is done by the subconscious in an unconscious state. The second, perception and reacting, is done in a conscious state. The brain cannot process something and perceive it at the same time. And it needs to be unconscious in order to process."

"I'm still not sure I'm following you."

Edward nods and smiles. "Imagine riding a bike. If you fell and then waited every second or two to respond, there would be no way to catch yourself before hitting the ground. It's good it doesn't work that way. By pairing short conscious moments with unconscious processing moments, your mind integrates the information just processed. You perceive it and catch yourself. All of this happens much too fast for the eyes to see. The action, thoughts, or sounds are unconsciously updated, and your conscious self uses these updates to determine if they make sense. If they don't, you slow the bike down, speed up, or change your route. The unconscious processing period is critical to our conscious state. And the two states of mind work together flawlessly. One would never know that he's in a continuous state of being conscious and unconscious.

Now, Paxton, the explanation you've been waiting for. With the sensory chip we've implanted in your brain, you can move a hundred, maybe a thousand times faster, between the unconscious and conscious periods. It's not that you just knew the correct math involved with the Timeship. It only seemed that way. When you focused on it, your mind was reacting so fast the answer was instant. Your body movements work in a similar way.

The Pentagon's plan is to observe you. If they like what they see, they'll start up a new division that focuses on in-country defense. It's a no-brainer. America's security would be number one in the world. Who wouldn't want to live in a world protected by the sensory chip?"

Gideon followed Edward with a few well-intentioned remarks about the military benefits of the sensory chip. His words, however, felt listless.

Pax was thinking about something else, about the Russians. All eyes were on her, expecting her to say something. For the moment, she was only giving an indifferent stare. She could not decide if she should give Gatsby up. For the longest time, he was all she had. Now, it seemed to be reversed; she was all he had. The silence lasted for another minute but seemed much longer. And then suddenly she speaks. "What happens if your enemies manage to steal the technology?"

"We don't intend to let that happen," Edward said uneasily.

"That's not an answer. The sensory chip could be used against America. That must worry you. Just drop the façade and answer the question. What happens?"

"Well," he admitted apologetically, "of course, it worries us. There's always that possibility. If it happens, I suppose it would be one of those monumental feelings like when someone dies. You think the feelings will never end, but then time goes by, and life carries on."

"You say that like it's happened before."

"It's happened many times."

"And it's going to happen this time, too. Technology can be purchased. All you have to do is offer the right person enough money."

"That's true," Edward continued, "but it's not about money. It's not even about technology. It's about control. If you control technology, you control the conflict between countries and the chase for power."

"Do you even know who's involved in the chase?"

Edward releases an exhausted breath. He can hardly believe this conversation is happening. He taps the table with his hand. "*Everyone* is involved. When one country gets the upper hand, it doesn't end. The chase just resets and continues. Look, Paxton," he takes one more long-frustrated breath, "you're too new to this. You don't understand how espionage and intelligence work. And you certainly don't know how counterintelligence works."

"No. That was my mother's line of work and probably what got her killed."

"I knew your mom. You look a lot like her, top to bottom."

"Nice try. I don't blame you for trying to change the subject," Paxton continues. "Let me give you my take on it. If the sensory chip falls into the wrong hands, a lot of people will die. In fact, even if it doesn't fall into the wrong hands, a lot of people will die. How am I doing?"

"You're right, but no one's arguing that. The truth is, it's necessary."

"You're telling me you're proud of killing people?"

"I'm telling you: my research is going to help everyone. It's already benefitted you. I hate to be the bearer of bad news, but you're not the FBI or CIA. It's not your job to protect the country."

Her lips tightened. "It's *everybody's* job!"

Edward shrugged off her forceful comment. "No, Paxton, it's not. Especially for someone in your situation. We've established there's an element of danger for you. Are you willing to do as we asked?"

Her eyes glittered with moisture. She did not like being the guinea pig, and she could not stop asking questions and answering them in her mind. Ultimately, she knew the trouble she was in, and she knew Edward was telling her straight. "I'll do it," she said firmly.

"Good, we'll escort you back to your apartment, and you can pack some things for the trip. From there, we go to Kirtland Air Force Base. That's here in Albuquerque. I want you on a plane in two hours."

Pax nodded. "If that's the plan, let's get on with it."

In a sudden move, Gideon reaches out, placing his hand on Edward's shoulder. "We got a problem. Outside in the parking lot." He motions with his head. "They're on the approach. We need to hit the back exit fast."

Edward glances outside. "How many?"

"Looks like six."

Edward jerked his attention back to Pax. "Change of plans. We're going straight to the airport. This could get rough. Are you ready?"

She stood up from her seat. "Give me a gun."

After standing, Gideon quipped back, "This isn't the time for you to play soldier. We need to leave now!"

"If you want to make it to the plane, you'll give me a gun. I just scanned the area. There are ten of them. Unless you got a sensory chip in your brain, I'm our best option."

Edward's face was flushed with anxiety as he glanced at Gideon. "She's right. Give her your gun."

Reaching inside his suit coat, he pulls a Glock from a shoulder holster. He says, "Careful, this thing can shoot as fast as you can pull the trigger. I'm taking the safety off." He hands it to her. "The magazine holds 33 rounds. Make them count."

Edward was the first to the exit. Before pushing the door, he hesitates, looking outside as best he can. "Remember, Pax, they only want the chip. They don't care if you die." He leans into the glass door and shoves it open.

Once outside, Pax's senses were controlling her every movement. Not waiting to be attacked, she shoots two rounds into the sky. Immediately, ten men dressed in military fatigues come barreling in her direction. Three more shots send them frantically moving behind several parked cars. As Edward and Gideon race toward a gray Landcruiser, Pax walks swiftly behind them, unloading a single round per second and keeping the aggressors at bay. Quickly, Edward and Gideon are in the car with the engine roaring. They are both surprised to see Pax drawing close and firing shots without the benefit of looking toward the target. Her senses, having already locked into the positions of the ten soldiers, allowed her to hold one arm out, systematically shooting one round per second while facing the car. Pressing the doorknob, she opens it and slides sideways onto the seat. With her arm still extended and aimed, but without looking, she shoots away, keeping the soldiers in hiding. Finally, she draws in her arm, yanks the door shut, and shouts at Gideon for another magazine. He snatches one from the glove compartment and tosses it to her. She ejects, loads, and presses the window button, waiting for the mechanism to lower it. In a total of eight seconds, she resumes shooting while the Landcruiser carries them away. After a series of street turns designed to elude, they head for the airport.

Chapter 26

One Year Ago

Hawke sits in a psychologist's office, watching a dark-headed woman as she combs over some paperwork. He stirs uncomfortably in his chair and waits while her milky-white hands drift from one paper to the next. Behind her, on the wall, is a framed graduation diploma from Yale University with the name Mona Abercrombie in bold print. On both sides of the diploma are certificates of achievements arranged in a three-tiered design. He shifts again in his chair and says, "I don't know why I'm here."

The doctor's eyes rolled up above the papers, quickly followed by her head. She lays the papers on her desk and smiles. "I've been asked to evaluate you. Your superiors want to know if you're mentally fit to do your job."

Hawke scoots up into his chair. "I have a perfect record." The words shot out of his mouth as if this were proof of a misunderstanding. He continues, with hardly a pause. "My work speaks for itself."

The doctor lifted her hands, curling them together in a ball, placing them under her chin while she rested her elbows on the desk. "While that's true, Mr. Gentry, you have been exposed to a traumatic past. Your wife left you, and a month later, she was killed in a car crash along with your daughter. I know we have talked a few times, but there are concerns about how you're handling *all of this.*"

For about ten seconds, he gazes helplessly around the room before standing up suddenly. He says, "I've been on point with all of my assignments."

Unfolding her hands, the doctor quickly glances at the paperwork. "Your work is good, Hawke. That's not in question."

"But you just said."

"You're not thinking of walking out, are you?"

"This is a load of crap." He turns around and starts for the door.

"God, Hawke, you can't just leave. You need help holding it together. *I know* why you don't like being here."

Stopping abruptly, he turns back around. "I'm not even sure of that myself."

She motions to the chair. "Please, I think I can help you."

Whether he likes it or not being here is mandatory. Leaving would cause a reprimand, maybe even a suspension, or worse. He's not sure he cares about his job or anything anymore, but he decides to hear her out and gruffly takes a seat.

The doctor continues. "You don't like being here because it reminds you that they're dead and you're alive." The room fell quiet. She was waiting to see if he would respond, but he did not. "Do you read much, Hawke?"

"No, there's not much time. In the FBI, you work all the time God gives."

"Reading helps you focus on other things. Maybe you could give it some thought. For now, I have some questions for you. How did you feel when you found out about your wife and daughter, intense fear, helplessness, or horror?"

Hawke sat upright so suddenly that a pen from his suit coat jumped like an animal to the floor. "Why are you doing this?"

"I'm not doing this to upset you. These questions are important. They help me to evaluate and understand. They are a starting point."

He slumped back in his chair. "Alright. First horror, then helplessness."

"Thank you for that. Now, on several occasions, coworkers have witnessed you talking to yourself. Were you hallucinating?"

"Yes."

"Do you still hallucinate?"

"Yes."

"Do you see people who aren't there?"

"Yes."

"Do you see dead people?"

"Yes."

"Do you think you see ghosts?"

"No, I don't believe in them."

"What do you think you're seeing?"

"I'm manifesting them."

"That's good, Hawke, that you recognize it for what it is. I know we've talked about this before. However, I didn't expect the hallucinations to last. If I'm to help you, we need to go deeper. My records show that it's been two years since they died. A deep sense of loss can bring on hallucinations. The resulting sadness and the current love you have for your wife and daughter come together to form a sort of trench. The emotions can get pretty deep and trap you. My job is to help you out of that trench. Even though your wife left you, you still loved her, correct?"

"Yes, but when it ended, it felt like poison."

"Loving someone is a big risk."

"What happens now?"

"We work on your brain. It still feels that horror and helplessness. We prefer it to understand that what it feels is just a part of being human. And your being happy is what your wife and daughter would want for you. Do you talk to yourself?"

"No."

"But you've been spotted talking to yourself by multiple people?"

"*There's always someone there when I'm talking.*"

"Of course, the hallucinations?"

"Yes."

Dr. Abercrombie shifts some papers in her hands. "It says here that your grandparents raised you. Is that right?"

"My grandmother, from the time I was seven."

"Were you in the room when it happened?"

Hawke clamps his hands on the arms of the chair, squeezing tight. Instantly he is sweating. He says, "This is crazy!"

"*Were you in the room when your parents were murdered?*"

"Yes."

"It's been a long time. Can you tell me what you were feeling?"

He doesn't answer. He shifts his hands farther up the arms of the chair and clamps down again.

The doctor continues, "I need to do this report. If I don't, have they told you what will happen?"

"I could lose my job."

"If that happens, what would you do?"

"I guess drink vodka, probably a lot of it."

"Then why don't we continue."

"I was behind the sofa when I heard gunshots. I peeked out, and there was so much blood I just went in shock. I think I stayed there for a while, afraid to move. They tell me I went to the neighbors, and they called the police."

"And then you lived with your grandmother. How was that? Did she like you?"

"She liked to go out a lot and resented having to take care of me. So, she didn't. She would go out and leave me by myself. After a few months, I was lonely. I don't mean like regular lonely. I mean like, you know, that dissolving into nothing lonely. One day while she was out at a bar, there was some noise in the kitchen. When I went to see what it was, I saw my father. After that, he would come to visit me, and sometimes my mother would be with him. I wasn't lonely anymore."

"That's helpful, Hawke. Thank you. Could you tell me about your daughter, Ginger?"

He sighs audibly and looks around the room.

"Go on, tell me."

Suddenly there is a force pulsating inside him. He thinks panic attack, but no, it's not in his chest. It's in his arms, legs, and even his face. But mostly the pulsating is in his head. It hits him that it's just his heart beating strongly through his veins. He tries to focus on the doctor but ends up looking around the room again. He breathes in deeply, and says, "Sometimes, she was the little policeman, telling me where I needed to improve. It could be annoying. She was witty and fast and, sometimes, would even finish my sentences. And she loved chocolate." Hawke looks up to the ceiling glancing around as if searching. "*God, she loved chocolate.* She didn't want to go a day without it. Other than that, there wasn't anything to dislike."

"Have you been talking with her?"

"Yes."

"When did it start?"

"A few days after she died, maybe a week."

"Do you talk with others in the same way?"

"Yes."

"How long has this been going on?"

"Since I was seven when my father visited me."

"Once people start visiting you, do they remain in your life?"

"Only for as long as I need them."

"Do you trust them? What I mean is, do you believe everything they tell you?"

"No, not always."

"If I'm to help you, I need you to *trust me over them.*"

"I trusted my wife. Look where that got me. Why should I trust you?"

"Many reasons. First, when you listen to them, you're really just listening to yourself because your brain is making it all up. I want you to consider this, too. They are dead, and I'm alive, which means their perception of things is different. And remember, I'm trying to help you keep your job. It's up to you. Only you can make yourself trust."

"You'll just try to change me the same as my wife did."

"As I said, it's up to you. Trust is a very personal thing. It shouldn't be given blindly. Generally speaking, we trust only those who are honest with us, and, to a lesser degree, helpful. Can you say sincerely that your wife was these things? You don't have to answer, just think about it.

I want you to know, Hawke, that you're not insane. Your grief and loneliness brought on your hallucinations and interactions with people who aren't there. As a child, it helped you to cope and is probably what kept you sane. However, you're not a child anymore. You're an adult with a fully developed brain and the ability to function normally. In time, if you will let me, I'll help you through this."

Hawke sits up to the edge of his seat. He says, "I was an idiot. She was having a relationship with another man."

"Yes, I know. It's in the report."

"*For a year.* And she kept telling me she loved me. Why would she do that?"

"She did it because she didn't know what else to do."

Hawke sighs again and stands up. "I know you're right, but it's still hard to take."

"There's a group of people like you, Hawke. They meet once a week, sometimes twice." She hands him a card. "I mediate the meetings. You can just listen, or you can talk. It's up to you."

"I like to picture myself in that world before they were dead. Usually, we're talking and just having fun. I know everything about them, what they like, where they like to go. I could write a whole book with just them and me and that world."

"It would do the group some good to hear those things. It would do you some good too."

Chapter 27

Now

Nate had never seen anything like it, didn't even know a place like this existed anymore. The dirt roads were surprisingly hard, like earthenware clay or porcelain. Oxidation had taken over the centuries-old adobe buildings, leaving them with a muted, dusty terracotta coating. They seemed cut to shape, joined together with wet clay, fired in a kiln, then draped along the rolling terrain. A giant horizon connected the quaint town to the sun as if it were hanging from an invisible necklace. Sky City was as adorable as it was old, a picturesque gaze into the past.

His jeep crept along the satin-glazed road until he spotted the general store. Pulling it over next to the wood-plank walkway, he opens his car door and steps out into a piece of history. Once inside, he quickly looks around for Hawke. He noticed him halfway down an aisle filled with shoes and boots. He is talking to a local Native American girl, dressed in colorful leather strips and moccasins. Walking up behind them, he taps Hawke's shoulder and says, "Those cowboy boots you're holding will only slow you down."

Hawke turns and smiles. Holding out the turquoise-colored boots, he glares at the enjoyment of the situation. He says, "I thought they'd be perfect for an FBI agent in the ABQ. Maybe I'll splurge and buy you a matching pair."

"No, thanks. I don't think my D.C. counterparts would appreciate the western appeal. But you, go-ahead. If we get chased by the bad guys, I'll outsprint you by a country mile."

Hawke dangles the boots in front of him. "Last chance. The girls love 'em."

Nate's face crinkles up as he shakes his head. "I hate to have to bust up your shopping, but the team needs us. They want us back asap."

In two quick moves, Hawke placed the boots back on the shelf and motioned at Kasa. "Nate, this is Kasa. She's been a bright spot since I got myself stranded. And Kasa, this is Nate. By now, you already know he's FBI. We bunked together during training."

Kasa reaches out her hand. "Two FBI agents in Sky City at the same time. I'm not sure if that means things are starting to get exciting around here or if you two need more training."

Nate shakes her hand. "I don't know about the exciting thing." He points with his head to Hawke. "But *he* definitely could use more tactical training."

While Nate and Kasa enter a brief conversation, Hawke notices a little girl run past the aisle. She stops, backtracks, and stares at him. "Momma did love you. She just made a mistake."

"*Ginger*," Hawke whispered very softly. Walking down the aisle, he stops in front of her.

"Momma loved you. She wanted to get back with you, but then that bus hit the car."

Hawke kneels in front of her, sinking further into the hallucination. "You're wearing the yellow dress I bought you." She smiles, and he reaches out, placing his hand on her shoulder. "You should wear it more often, sweety. It's a perfect fit and so beautiful." Moving his hand upward, he begins stroking her hair.

"Momma loved you," she says again.

He keeps stroking her hair. "She did once, yes."

"She loved you and was coming back to you."

"I wish that were true."

"If you want it to be true, then it's true."

People were starting to notice Hawke talking to someone who wasn't there.

"It's more complicated than that, darling."

"No. If you believe it, then it's true." She removes his hand from her hair. "You have to believe it. She just made a mistake." Turning sharply, she runs away, and he stands back up.

"Hawke, are you okay?" It's Nate. He and Kasa are staring at him.

At first, he stands there silently. Then he walks up to them, reaches beyond them, and takes the boots off the rack.

"I've decided to purchase them, after all." After hesitating a moment, he glances at Kasa. "Kasa, thanks for everything. You've been a big help. Both she and Nate watch as Hawke walks to the register.

"Hey, FBI guy!" Kasa shouts.

Stopping abruptly, he twists around with the boots tucked tightly under his arm.

"I've got a *save the ruins party* planned for next month. It's in Albuquerque. I've invited the mayor, the police chief, and the city manager—also, a few others with connections, including the governor and a couple of representatives. I'm trying to be constructive and make something happen. I just don't know a more dignified way, so it's a party. And truthfully, I don't know who'll show. I'd love it if you could come, and," she turns to Nate, "you too, if you can work it out."

"Did you say next month?" Hawke asked.

"Yes, on the 15th at six o'clock. That's a Saturday. It's in the old library building across from city hall."

"They keep us pretty busy, but I'll try to make it." After throwing up a hand and waving, he turns toward the register.

In ten minutes, Hawke and Nate are driving down the road away from the old town of Sky City. Hawke hears a bouncing sound, so he looks over his shoulder to the back seat. "Stop jumping and sit down, the car's moving. You could get hurt."

Ginger plops down and crosses her arms. She says, "You never let me play in the car."

"Do you know what that means?" Hawke asked.

"No, what does it mean?"

"It means that I love you more than anything in the world."

A smile burst across her face. "I love you too, Daddy."

"Good, it's the way it should be." He settles back into his seat, looking at the road in front of him. "And why do girls cry for like no reason at all?"

"I'm not crying, Daddy."

He twists back again, momentarily making eye contact. "Yes, you are."

Nate slowed the jeep, made a sharp turn onto another road, and headed for Rio Rancho. "When we were in D.C. training," he spoke cautiously, "I didn't notice anything. I thought maybe you were over that by now. You still seeing that doctor? What's her name, Mona, or something?"

"Mona Abercrombie."

"Right. I thought she was helping."

"She is."

"Then why are you still talking to yourself?"

"I'm not talking to myself. When I talk, there's always someone there."

"Are you telling me there's someone in the back seat right now?"

"Yes."

"Who?"

"Ginger."

"And you're okay with that?"

"Of course, why wouldn't I be?"

Nate glances at Hawke, then back to the road. His face cringes, and his shoulders tighten up. "Because she's dead, Hawke, and because you see things that aren't there. It's the reason you saw Mona to begin with."

Ginger sits up in the seat. "Tell him he's wrong, Daddy. Tell him it's none of his business."

Hawke glances over his shoulder. "But it is his business."

"No, Daddy. Why would you say that?"

"Because when I talk with people that no one else can see, it makes him wary of me. It makes him think that I don't have his back, that if we get in a bad situation, I'll let him down."

"Then tell him you're good. Tell him you got his back."

"It wouldn't do any good."

"He's going to report you."

"Probably."

"Then what will happen?"

"They'll do another evaluation."

Suddenly, Callie, his wife, is sitting next to Ginger. She says, "You never stand up for yourself. For once, will you grow a set and take a freaking stand!"

He is still looking over his shoulder but now with an angry face. "Growing a pair is way overrated. I got where I am without having to grow anything!"

"Maybe so, but if you don't take a stand right now, your career is going to fold like a sheet of single-ply toilet paper."

"You always hated that about me."

"I just wanted you to stand up for yourself."

"I do, just differently than you would like. So, could you stop trying to change me?"

"I'm not trying to change you."

"Then what?"

"I can't stand to see you…"

"To see me what?"

"To see you wronged. You get walked on because you are kind and thoughtful and just, you know, nice."

"And you want me to change that?"

"No! That's what I love about you."

"You're not making any sense." Hawke turns back around in his seat, takes a deep breath, and gazes out the window. "Then why did you leave?"

"Maybe because every time we started to get ahead; you would give what we had away. Oh, I know that you're generous and all that. Maybe I am too. But you never once asked me."

"I feel like I'm being punished all over again."

Nate makes another turn; this time it's onto the highway that runs through Rio Rancho. He says, "I'm getting pretty lonely sitting here while you talk with people that don't exist." There is concern in his voice.

Hawke glances at him, and they both smile. "Were you able to get what I requested?"

"I thought you might ask about it. It's in the glove compartment."

"Let's see what we got." Hawke pulls out a folder and flips it open.

"That's a verified intelligence report," Nate said.

Hawke licks two fingers and starts flipping through pages. "I need the source, the one that's not documented, the real source."

Nate wiggles anxiously in his seat. "It wasn't easy to obtain. Do you know how sensitive this is?"

"You're the Pentagon's top debriefing guy, their freaking go-to guy, and you can't even access your own source?"

"They only use me for certain cases. Besides, it takes time. I've given you everything I got."

"That's a load of bull, and you know it. I don't like walking around in the dark."

"I'll see what I can do, but I think the report's solid."

"Right, meantime, I'm taking all the heat. I got a briefing to handle in two hours."

"The report I just gave you is all you need. You got a source, a high priority target, and a country of origin behind it."

"And who would that be?"

"It's in the report."

"It's the Chinese, isn't it?"

"Yes, the Chinese."

"It's a logical choice."

"I told you, the intelligence is good."

Hawke paused, rubbing his face with both hands, and taking a deep breath. "I got a bad feeling about this. Something's wrong. It doesn't add up. The technician, Fergus, is sitting in jail right now for selling information to the Chinese."

"That's true, but they still don't know how it works."

"They're probably manufacturing the vision chip as we talk. In a couple of months, maybe less, they'll be testing it in their own patient. Killing the man behind the technology, how does that help them?"

"They only think they killed him," Nate says. "Edward is very much alive."

"It's the same thing. The FBI is the number one authority behind conspiracy theories. I'm not letting this go until I get to the bottom of it. If it's the Chinese, then fine. But maybe it's the

Russian Federation. They've been known for this kind of thing since the beginning of the cold war. They're experts at pointing the finger somewhere else."

"I trust our people. A lot of work went behind that report."

"It has to be confirmed. If we get this wrong, you and I both know the implications. In a war with Russia, we'd probably lose Alaska right off. And the fight would be in our own country. If they somehow got their hands on the sensory chip, they could be building a super army right now. I need to talk with Pax. Have we got any leads on her whereabouts?"

"We caught up with her," Nate confirms. "She made the mistake of going back to Rio Rancho. She's lucky we got there before the Chinese."

Hawke states loudly, "I'm still not convinced it's the Chinese."

"Whoever it is wasn't far behind. Gideon gave his gun to Pax, and she held ten men at bay while they escaped Café Bella. At this moment, they're enroute to Kirtland Air Force Base, and so are we. The whole gang is headed back to D.C. You can talk with her on the plane. There's plenty of time."

"I guess my briefing will have to wait."

"General Stackhouse will see you tomorrow morning. Five of the team will be there. We're keeping three in Albuquerque, just in case. Maybe they pick up on something that helps. I want to make something clear right now, though. When we get to D.C., Pax goes to the Pentagon safe room, and you go straight to Mona's office. I'm going to insist they fly her in tonight."

"You want me reevaluated?"

"It's the only way. I don't want your invisible family on my conscious. I'm the first to admit that what's happening to you is something I don't understand. If Mona clears you, then I'm good with that." Nate reaches over, placing a hand on Hawke's shoulder. "Are we good?"

He nods, smiles, sinks into his seat, and closes his eyes. "It's been a tough day. I've been shot at, had my car break down, chased into the desert, trapped in a cave, and stranded in an ancient town made of clay. I need some rest. Oh, and get a tow truck out there to pick up my car."

Chapter 28

Now

One hour later, Hawke sits in an airport hangar directly in front of Pax. There are twenty armed guards inside the hangar and at least that many on the outside. The makeshift table and chairs are half covered in pizza boxes, chips, and soda cans. He watches as Pax takes a sip of her Coke. "I guess you know Rosie thinks I'm playing the other side," Hawke whispers.

Setting the drink down, she shoves her hand into a bag of chips. "He did a check on you. There were some red flags." She pulls out several chips and just holds them. "He said there are weeks, months, where you fall off the grid. That's not classic FBI."

"I am a special agent."

"That doesn't explain it. If you were a CIA operative, maybe, but not the FBI. Would you like to tell me what's going on?"

"I'm not at liberty."

"Rosie was right to suspect you?" Shifting forward, she lifts the chips, shoves several into her mouth, and chews.

"If I were him, I'd feel the same way," Hawke says, snatching a few chips of his own and eating them.

After swallowing, Pax takes a long drink. "Hawke, you and Edward are the same. I can tell you're both being honest with me. At the same time, you're admittingly holding something back."

"In time, it'll all work itself out."

"How much time?"

"I'm not sure, Pax."

"Of course not. Somebody schooled you and Edward at the same place."

"I have a question for you, an important one."

"We're in the middle of a conversation. What are you waiting for?" She bites into another chip.

"Have you talked with Gatsby today?"

"No," she answered, half speaking, half chewing.

"Now, who's holding something back?"

"Are you saying I'm lying?"

"I'm saying a daughter might protect her father. It wouldn't be the first time. Have you talked with him today?"

"We haven't had a decent conversation in weeks."

"*Did you talk with Gatsby today?*"

"You've been suspicious of him from the beginning."

"I'm trying to determine some things."

"The email wasn't his, and he had nothing to do with the attack in D.C. He's not a murderer."

"No, probably not. How did he seem when you last saw him? Were there tensions between you? Did you argue?"

"Yes."

"What was the argument about?"

"That's between him and me."

"Tell me. Maybe we can clear him. If not, sooner or later, you're going to have to choose between him and us."

Pax's hand comes flying off the table, sending the bag of chips skirting over the edge to the floor. Her finger is pointing at Hawke's face. "Why would I choose the FBI?"

He takes her hand in his and gently moves it away. "Because we're the ones trying to protect you. And there's evidence we've known about for a while now. We monitored a phone call Gatsby made to a bank in Switzerland. There could have been more. We don't know. Two days after we bugged his phone, he replaced it. That same day he also bought a pay-as-you-go phone. Since then, he's replaced the pay-as-you-go phone three times. Someone tipped him off, or he suddenly wised up. I don't know which. What I do know is he's up to something and is seriously trying not to get caught. Just think about it, will you?"

She slouches backward. "God, Hawke." She crosses her arms and continues, giving a quick glance around the hangar. "My dad had his yard landscaped, all new, all different, very beautiful with a 10-foot waterfall. That was four months ago.

Now he's redecorating, new appliances, new furniture, the works. I admit it did need updating. Still, ever since I can remember, he's always had money. Don't get me wrong. He inherited a hell of a lot of money. And the bank in Switzerland, he's dealt with that bank as long as I can remember. But God, he goes through money like an alcoholic goes through booze. He's got to be spending above his pay grade. You were right to suspect him."

"Since he all of a sudden caught on to us, we think someone's helping him. Pax, whoever that is, could be arrested for perverting the course of justice. And the Feds play hardball."

"One year after moving to the ABQ, I got an apartment. He pays for it, and all my other bills. On top of that, there's an automatic deposit into my bank account for five thousand dollars every month. My lifetime allowance, he calls it. I never use it all, so I've been increasing my savings with it. Two months ago, he deposited fifty thousand into my savings account. When I got used to being able to see again, he told me I should take a trip and see the world. Even I thought the timing of that was pretty stinky.

He loves me, no question. And he loved Mom too. Which side do you take your stand on? Is it family, or is it the truth? I've been struggling with that one all morning. You think to yourself nothing is more important than family. Everybody says it, but is it really true? So, what is the answer? I think I figured it out. Selling the sensory chip technology would cause the most deaths. That's the truth of the matter. In this instance, the truth is more important than family. I'm going to tell you something, something I should have already told you. I don't know if you've considered it or not. It's the Russians."

"The Russians?" Hawke exclaimed. "What are you talking about?"

"Gatsby wanted me to let them extract the chip and analyze it. I wasn't about to let that happen. I'm not stupid. They'd steal it and leave me blind as a bat and bleeding."

"The Russians. You're sure?"

"Gatsby told me. I think he's sold them technology before."

"Could he be lying?"

"*Lying!* He didn't have to tell me in the first place."

"That's exactly my point. Why did he?"

"I might have given him the impression that I would tell him my location if he would tell me who he was working for."

Hawke grabs one of the drinks, pulls the tab, and the sound of fizz can be heard all around. He takes a slow swallow. "So, the Russians?"

"Think about it. With the sensory chip, they match the U.S. in the latest technology."

Chapter 29

Now

Inside the Pentagon safe room Pax stands before a select group of men. First in charge is General Stackhouse. Edward, Gideon, and Nate are to his right and left. Hawke is absent due to an urgent trip to the psychologist's office. His evaluation will determine if he stays on the team.

Pax glances past the men to the only entrance and motions toward it with her head. She says, "That door has an electronic lock with a touchpad. I'd like to think I can go out for a sandwich or soda when the mood hits me. Do I get the code, or should I consider myself a prisoner?" When nobody commented, her brow compressed, and her lips tightened together. She shook her head. "I guess no answer is an affirmation."

General Stackhouse nods to Edward. Edward returns the nod and looks at Pax. He says, "The door is pneumatic. The guards outside operate it. If you need anything, push the button above the touchpad and talk."

She glanced at the door again, then around the room. "I suppose going out for a jog is out of the question?"

Edward smiles and rubs his forehead. "Anything you need, say the word. It doesn't matter what it is. We can have a treadmill here within the hour if you like." He points behind her to a minibar. "It's fully stocked, including your favorite sodas." Pointing farther back, he continues. Behind the bar is the rest of the suite. You have a bedroom, a full bath, and a living room complete with a TV."

"And if I want to go outside, do I just tell the guard?"

Edward rubs his forehead again. His smile fades. "I thought you understood. It's not a safehouse unless you stay inside."

Pax glanced back and forth between Edward and the general. "Can you give me an idea of how long I'll be here?"

Walking away from the group, the general turns and faces the others. He leans against a mahogany desk, almost sitting on it, and crosses his arms. He says, "Making sure you're safe, Paxton, is the first of several phases." He sighed deeply, then resumed. "Maybe now would be a good time for a drink." Unfolding his arms, he motions at Gideon. "Would you mind, Gideon? You do make the best martinis."

He grins as Gideon heads for the minibar. "Now, where was I? Oh, yes, the phases. We have an investigation to complete. Fergus, our tech man who helped make the sensory chip operational, is already in lockup. He communicated to the Chinese that the sensory chip was a finished product and undergoing testing in a subject. Hopefully, after we've made a couple more arrests, things will be safer for you."

"You think it's the Chinese that are after me?" Pax asked.

"Yes." The general responded.

"Why would they do that if they already have the technology?"

"It's a good question, one I don't have an answer for. Maybe they want to check it with what they have. Our sources tell us they will be testing their version of the chip by the end of this week. The good thing is, they only have the version we want them to have. Neither Fergus nor Dr. Tennison was ever aware of the chip's other capabilities. And that gets us to the next phase. I'm going to turn this one over for Edward to explain. It's his domain, not mine. I'll help Gideon pass the drinks out."

After receiving her drink, Pax takes a long sip and turns her attention to Edward. She had no clue that she was about to find out how little she still knew about the technology built into her brain.

Edward had yet to take a sip. He just holds his drink, staring down into it. He says, "The pneumatic door we discussed a moment ago is for security, not convenience. However, having you here is for both purposes." Looking up, he makes eye contact with Pax. "I could try to explain it to you but showing you would be more effective." Turning up his drink, he gulps a swallow, punches his phone, and holds it up to his ear. He only says one word. "*Now.*"

Immediately the lights went out. The safe room is an interior room with no windows. The results are cave-like darkness.

Edward continues. "I don't mean to alarm you, Paxton, but in a few seconds, you will notice something about yourself that is strikingly different. Here, now," again he punches his phone. "Can you describe to us what you see?"

"I can see everything. The lights are still off, though, aren't they?"

"Yes."

"All of your pupils are dilated. That's how I knew. And the room isn't as bright as before. How did you do this? Was it built into the sensory chip to begin with?"

"It was." Holding the phone back to his face, he repeats the same word. *"Now."* Instantly the lights come back on. "I have an app on my phone that controls the chip's functions."

"Are you telling me you can even control my eyesight?"

"Everything the sensory chip does we can control. If something goes wrong, we need to be able to shut it down. There was no way to know how you would adapt."

"Don't you think you should have told me all of this before installing it into my brain?"

"Under ideal conditions, yes."

"What does that mean?"

"It means we would've had to know, for sure, that you would have accepted the chip even after understanding everything involved. If we had been transparent with everything, and you turned us down, you would've known highly classified information. The information would have put you in danger. Instead of taking that risk, we decided to install the chip and seek forgiveness later."

The general interjects. "There are times, Paxton, when we make life more difficult, not by what we do, but by what we fail to do. At some point, whether we had someone's permission or not, we couldn't not do this. But, if you decide you don't want the technology implanted in you, we can deactivate it. Later we can retrieve the chip."

"I want to know everything, what all my capabilities are. I don't want any more surprises."

General Stackhouse dips his head and makes his drink swirl in the glass. "It's time, Edward," he said, nodding and looking back into Edward's face.

After acknowledging the general, Edward, looking a little weary and showing signs of sweating on his cheeks, spoke cautiously. "Adding to the things you already know, you can run faster, jump higher, hold your breath longer, and even sense fear or anxiousness in a person. Of course, we would need to test you, but I think it's reasonable to expect you to run 40, maybe 50, miles per hour. Elite athletes can run in the low twenties, and the fastest human ever recorded ran 27.5 miles per hour. We believe you could double that without any adverse effects on your tendons or muscles. And we think you can jump to a height of about ten feet. A man in Texas holds the record for a vertical jump of five-feet, five inches. You could probably double that, meaning you could easily jump onto the roof of a one-story building. As far as holding your breath, carbon dioxide buildup in the blood is the problem because it causes a person to pass out. Still, the world record was set by a diver in 2016. She held her breath for an astonishing twenty-four minutes and three seconds. With your capabilities, you could double that. And one other thing. You have what we call projection. Oh, it may take a while, but when your brain fully integrates with your senses, you'll be able to project actions."

"Actions."

"You know, a person's actions, what his next move will be, even days in advance."

"How on earth do you know this? And tell me how it works?"

"It'll take some time to explain. Tell you what, I'll come back tomorrow morning, and we'll talk, just the two of us. Pax, I want to make something else clear. There could be other abilities or changes that happen. The sensory chip is so new that it's impossible to foresee everything. And the short-term effects could be followed by other long-term effects. We can't tell you everything, Paxton, because we don't know it all ourselves."

Pax rubbed her weary eyes and closed them for a moment. She had just flown a long distance from Albuquerque to D.C. without any time to rest. From the day the sensory chip was implanted in her, she had been running around searching for answers. She raked her mind, frantically comparing notes. Everything seemed so bizarre- the Iranians, Chinese, Russians. What kind of spy games had she fallen into? She could not be sure she was anywhere close to the truth yet.

"Oh my God," she whispered and opened her eyes. She felt like lightning had just struck, and she jumped on it and rode it across the sky to the ground. "You guys need to start connecting the dots. You're locked onto the Chinese so much you're missing things."

"What dots are you talking about?" The general asked.

She drew a deep breath. "What about the Russians?"

"What about them?"

"Have you ever considered that they might be involved?"

"Of course, but all of our intelligence points to the Chinese. The Russians aren't a player in this."

"Yes, they are."

"Did Gatsby tell you that?" The general asked.

She hesitated, just staring at him.

"Could you give us his location?"

Visibly agitated she says, "I don't know his location. And anyway, you've suspected him from the beginning, haven't you? I know Hawke has."

"We've been troubled about him, yes."

"Your cheeks are suddenly flushed. How troubled, General?"

The general looks at her sympathetically. "Did you know Gatsby was the one that gave us the recommendation to use you to test the sensory chip?"

"Yes. He told me. He wanted me to have my eyesight back."

"Of course, you were already on our radar. Your math capabilities sealed the deal. Anyway, we trusted Gatsby, thought for sure he was a company man. We've had eyes on him for a while, trying to connect those dots you mentioned. A few days ago, he gave us the slip. That's when things became dangerous for you. You and I both know it wasn't a coincidence. If you know his whereabouts, you need to tell us."

"I already told you. I don't know."

"Whoever he's working with will keep after you. The only way you get out of this safehouse is if we can find out his location. Once we know that, we can send a team and retrieve him."

Pax's agitation is growing. "You can't be serious. My dad's just after money like he's always been. It's the Russians you should be after."

General Stackhouse went silent. He set his drink on the desk, glanced down at his shoes, then up around the room. "If this drags on, it becomes a bigger problem. We're not talking about Fergus or Dr. Tennison here. *Your dad* knows everything about the sensory chip. He knows the implications, and he's got an army behind him trying to steal it."

"An army?"

"Yes."

"You mean the Russians?"

The general was becoming annoyed with her. "No."

"Then, who? Is it the Chinese? Why won't you tell me?"

The general knew that she'd held back information. He moved his shoulders uncomfortably. "You've been protecting Gatsby. You had information that implicated him. How can you justify your actions?"

Here it was, the confrontation Pax knew was coming. The general was right. She was holding back. She wanted to protect her father and give him up at the same time. She was trying to think of a way to do both. There was a difference between justifying and trying to understand. She felt her throat tightening up. At what point does she stop trying to understand her own father. He raised her. She owed him ninety mules and ten hundred acres. She knows he's always been sort of an ass, but now, the stuff that is going on is an entirely different territory. Before they sweep in and take him, she wants a second chance to talk with him.

Her father was a brilliant lawyer, and still is. But there was always that other side, that thing that was a little dysfunctional. He would make stupid decisions. He left Sloan because she was CIA and wanted to be an operative. That was crazy because when they first met, she had already applied to the CIA, hoping for an undercover career. Pax walks around the general to the other side of the desk. She plops down in the seat holding up her hands and analyzing her French manicured nails for a moment. Her father was always chasing the other side, she knew that. He recommended her for the sensory chip and look what's happened. "My actions? Yes, you got me on that one. Still, I think you should consider that the Russians might have played him or taken advantage of him."

The general stands up from the desk, twists around, and sits again, this time facing Pax. The others gather around the desk. "If Gatsby seriously thinks the Russians are behind this, then, yes, he's being played," the general said. "We've checked all the addresses where he could be hiding. Does he have a place we don't know about, a desert house, or maybe a cabin somewhere in the mountains?"

"He sometimes stays at the Crown Plaza, and you might check the Hotel Chaco. That's in Old Town, Albuquerque."

"We knew about those already."

"He doesn't have a second home that I know of, but have you checked my apartment? He has a key. And since he's trying to find me, it would be the perfect spot."

The general turns and says to Nate, "Go. Now. Check with our eyes in the area. If he's there, take him. I want him here in D. C. by tomorrow."

Ten seconds later, Nate is gone, and the general has again focused on Pax. "We're moving to phase three. You have a visitor that's been waiting to get in. Special Agent Hannagan."

Pax jumps up from her seat. "Darcie's here?"

The general raises his phone and punches a button. "Send her in."

She didn't stop when she walked in, not until she stood in front of Pax. The two women exchange hugs. "Since you ran out on me, I've been worried sick," Darcie said, giving Pax one more quick hug. "Rosie said he gave you the keys to his Hummer and told you to... how did he put it, to *skedaddle.*"

"That's Rosie. How's he doing?"

Darcie is holding Pax by both her arms. She slides her fingers down and takes Pax by the hands. "After you left, the next morning, all hell broke loose. A weaponized drone and an attack force of about twelve or fourteen showed up. After the shooting, the drone was a burning pile of rubble, and Hawke had fled. When I left, Rosie was preparing to move the RVs. I have no idea where his next location will be, so don't ask."

Pax clears her throat and squeezes Darcie's hands. She says smoothly and in a low tone, "But you see, it's not like Hawke to run."

"I was as surprised as you," Darcie replied. "It's clear now that he gave up our location. If Rosie hadn't sent you away, you wouldn't be standing here right now. In a way, he saved your life."

"Saved my life. You could be right about that."

Darcie watches as a smile blast across Pax's face. Instead of smiling back, she frowns, tilts her head sideways, and rubs her brow with her hand. "Anyway, I'm glad you got out. It looks like Hawke went to the other side, went rogue. Or maybe he just went crazy. You've probably noticed he's been hallucinating."

"Yes, he's been seeing his dead daughter."

Darcie raises her head. "Right, so he's lost it."

"You told us he fled. How did he do that? Did he leave on foot?"

"He managed to get to his Nissan. It took a few bullets, but he got away."

"So, I took Rosie's Hummer, and Hawke took the Nissan. How did you get back to town?"

Darcie lets go of Pax, moves her hands out open-palm, and starts motioning like a frantic mother. She says, "The attack force, the soldiers, they ran off after that drone blasted away at them. I took one of their jeeps."

For the second time, a smile blasts across Pax's face. "*You're LY-ING.* In case you didn't know, I can sense it. Plus, your body temperature suddenly went up. It's obvious by the color of your cheeks."

"No, really. I took one of their jeeps."

"And the keys just happened to be in the ignition?"

"That's right."

"Tell me then, did you leave by yourself or with the attack force?"

Knowing that she's caught, Darcie steps backward and goes into complete denial. "That's absurd. I'm an FBI Special Agent, loyal to my country. My record speaks for itself."

"Your record, that might be true. But everything else is *a lie.*" Turning to her right, Pax makes eye contact with General Stackhouse. "What are you waiting for, another drink? Take her, question her. Maybe you can get the truth out of her. If nothing else, a name, a number, or an address."

His only response was to raise his phone again and punch. "I want two guards in here now." When they walk in, he points at Darcie and continues. "Take her to interrogation room 106A and post guards."

After they take her, Pax continues. "General, sir, if you've got the manpower, could you have someone check on Rosie. He's got nothing to do with this, and I think he might need some help."

"Do you have the coordinates?"

"Yes. I'll write it down. It's about twenty miles outside of Bear Canyon."

Chapter 30

Now

Not too far away, in a different wing of the Pentagon, Hawke sits waiting as Mona skims through some paperwork. "I guess they flew you here just for me?" He asked, then laughed disparagingly.

Once she finishes glancing at the papers, she shuffles them together, squares them up, and shoves them to the side. "It's good to see you, Hawke. You've gotten yourself in the doghouse with the higher-ups."

"You think so?"

She grins and shakes her head at him. "They bring me to the Pentagon about twice a year, sometimes three. When they do, it's usually pretty important. I don't pretend to know why they wanted this done here instead of Albuquerque. The secrets of this place go way above my pay grade. I'll try to ignore the basement office they stuck me with and just focus on you. Your friends are concerned, you know that, right?"

"I know."

"It's the same thing as last time. They see you talking with people who aren't there. If you keep it up, you'll be retired. Is that what you want?"

"Not particularly."

"Other than drowning yourself in vodka, do you have a plan? Because it looks like that's where this thing is heading."

"When I was in college, I used to write some. I could publish a book about my FBI experiences."

"Seriously? That's your plan?"

Hawke shuffles his shoulders and readjusts himself in the chair. "I was good at it at one time."

Mona glances at the paperwork again, crosses her hands on the desk, and leans slightly forward. "You make a pretty decent living as a special agent. Did you know that most writers, no matter how talented, are poor?"

He doesn't answer.

"It's sad too because they entertain us, inspire us, even teach us. And all the world is willing to give back to them is a small apartment or two-bedroom house. I don't mean to make it seem so bleak, but for 90 percent of writers, that's how it is. Maybe you could think about that. Your salary is increased twelve and a half percent each year. That's way better than most people.

Okay, look, you are your own villain here. Do you agree?"

He looks beyond her to a blank, mauve-colored wall. "Yes."

"You can keep your job, Hawke. But not if you willingly keep giving your cheek for someone else to strike. I understand your hallucinations. I know where they're coming from. It's not like you're insane, but if you don't start ignoring them, then your days in the FBI are over. Is Ginger in the room right now?"

"Yes."

"Has she talked to you?"

"No, she's just staring at you."

"Will you work with me on this?"

He cups his hands together in his lap, squeezing them tight. "What is it you want me to do?"

"I thought I made that clear. When you are in public, you have to ignore the hallucinations."

Ginger jerks her head around, looking at Hawke. "Tell her, Daddy."

Hawke tries to ignore her, glancing at her, then back to Mona.

"She's trying to make me go away. *Tell her, Daddy.*"

For a moment, he peers down into his lap. When he looks back up, he is eye to eye with Ginger. He asks, "What do you want me to tell her?"

"Tell her you're not going to ignore me."

"But it's only in public."

"It's just the start. She's trying to make me go away."

"If it means I get better, don't you want to go away?"

"No, I want to stay. I can stay, can't I?"

"As long as you want, yes."

"Then tell her, Daddy. Tell her to stop it. Tell her you want me to stay."

"Are you talking to Ginger?" Mona asked.

"Yes."

"She's not happy with me, is she?"

"I don't know. I mean, no."

"I never told you to do away with her."

"I know."

"The last few months, is Ginger the only one you talk with?"

"Mostly, and Callie some too."

"Callie?" Mona gives a quick glance at the papers. "That was your wife?"

"Yes."

"Do you have any thoughts on why she's showing up?"

"Not really. I mean, maybe she wants me to know how unhappy she was."

"I doubt it. She made that clear a long time ago."

"Then I guess she just wants to torment me."

"I promise you that's not it. The kind of hallucinations you're having are like a masquerade. They can be mysterious and difficult to understand, but they're there for a reason. Something was left undone. That something needs to be worked through. You are the one that will have to take the mask off. Your hallucinations of Ginger are easier to see through. She was so young when she died. You're still trying to bring the relationship to closure. With Callie, the relationship was over, which turns us back to you. What is it, Hawke, that you left undone with Callie? Is there something you need to say to her, something important? Can you think of anything?"

Hawke jumps to his feet. His hands are shaking nervously. "But it's so silly."

"What's silly?"

"She didn't like movies, no, that's not what I mean. She was intimidating. No, sorry, that's not it either." Hawke sits back down, interlocks his fingers, and sucks in a deep breath. "I think what I mean is, she could dismiss you with a look. Her mother was like that too. If she didn't want to do something, like go to the movies, which she hated to do, she would give me that look. If she didn't agree with me about, well, anything, she would give me that look. If I made the wrong choice, did something to upset her, came home late from work, she would give me that look. After a while, I just stopped trying, not because it was intimidating, but because I didn't want to feel like a failure."

"And you never discussed it with her?"

"I didn't think I needed to. *Callie knew what she was doing!*"

"Most of the time, the notion of something seems better than doing it. To Callie, she was just giving her opinion. She probably thought she was making things easy for you. When she gave you that look, it meant less confrontation, less disagreeing, less arguing."

"I didn't realize that."

"Over time, I think you stopped communicating. She saw it as if you were disengaging from the marriage. She probably thought you didn't love her anymore and started looking elsewhere."

"But I was crazy about her, couldn't have been more in love. She was the prettiest woman I'd ever met. When she laughed, her cheeks were like a fireworks display. And when she smiled, her eyes would nearly close. I loved that about her."

"It's easy to know what's in your own heart, but if you never told her or showed her. I don't think she ever meant to hurt you. To her, it looked like the marriage had run its course. It's why they have marriage counseling, to work these things out."

"I guess the breakup *was* my fault."

"Not entirely, but yes, taking ownership of that is essential. Sometimes we get a rare opportunity to find out something about ourselves. And sometimes what we see we don't like. When that happens, we need to change. It's called character building, and it's not easy.

I'm going to encourage you to do three things, Hawke. One, the next time you see Callie, tell her how you feel. *I mean it, take your heart out, shove it into your mouth, and tell her how you feel.* Don't leave anything out. Tell her the good, the bad, the wonderful, and the horrible, everything. Two, you need to meet with the support group. And don't tell me how busy the FBI life is. If you don't turn this thing around quickly, you won't be in the FBI much longer. I'm arranging a flight for both of us tomorrow morning. Tomorrow evening you meet with the support group."

"I don't need a support group. My situation's different."

"Doesn't matter what you think. This is no longer a suggestion. If I'm to sign off on you, I must know you'll see this through. If you refuse, the next report goes against you, and we both know what that means.

And three, right now, your hallucinations are understandable. That said, you need to be working through them. Say what you need to say to Callie and Ginger. The more you hold back and fight it, the longer you'll be talking to people who aren't there.

This is important, Hawke. I told you earlier, and I'm telling you again. Only talk to them at home. When you're in a public place, ignore them. Don't give your superiors a reason to retire you. They need you on the team. They made that clear. If they don't see improvement soon though, they'll do what they have to do."

Chapter 31

Now

At precisely nine-thirty, Pax heard Edward calling for her. She walked out of the living area where she had been watching CNN. No sooner than she turned the corner around the dividing wall, her hand went up, acknowledging him. "This place has no windows," she said with exasperation. "All I wanted to do this morning was to see outside. I pushed the intercom button and asked the guards to let me out for fifteen minutes. I told them they could escort me and that I just needed some sun. They politely told me *HELL NO*." She squeezed her hand into a fist. "Is it too much to ask that I be let outside for a few minutes? I've done nothing to deserve house arrest."

Edward acknowledges her with a nod. He says, "What you're doing is called righteous indignation. To a degree, it makes sense, and I understand how you feel, but it's not house arrest. It's protective custody. We went over this yesterday. If you're not in the safehouse, you're not safe. We don't want to take any chances. You're too valuable. Is there anything I can do to make you more comfortable?"

She tilts her head toward the minibar. "Whatever that stuff was that came out of the coffee machine was pathetic. Is there a Starbucks in the Pentagon?"

Edward laughs and shakes his head. "There's one at the Pentagon City Hotel, and they deliver. I'll have the guards call in your order. What would you like?"

She wanted fiercely to go herself and smell the aroma of a coffee house, but she knew it was out of the question. "A large dark roast with creamer and a croissant."

Edward held up his phone and punched a button. "I need a delivery from Starbucks, guys. Two large dark roasts and a tray of croissants and bear claws. And have them send plenty of creamer." Holding his hand over the receiver, he looks at Pax.

"Anything else?" She shakes her head, and he removes his hand. "Get that in right away."

"I was beginning to think you wouldn't show up this morning." Pax spoke as Edward punched off his phone. "I'm glad you're here. I would've gone crazy wondering what's happening."

Before he can answer her, his phone rings, and it goes right back to his ear. "Nate, did you make contact?" After a brief silence, he continues. "I see. Yes, yes. No, there's no time. Get him on a plane. I want him here, asap. Are we clear? Good. And Nate, I want to be the first to know of any surprises." This time Edward shoves his phone into his suit pocket. His attention goes back to Pax. "A strike force confronted Gatsby twenty minutes ago. It was early in Albuquerque, so he was caught off guard. Nate said your father was worried about you. He thought you might be hurt or worse. After what happened, I tend to believe him. Your father is pretty shaken up. We'll have him here sometime this afternoon. I'll allow him to speak with you in private when that happens. Our chances of getting what we need out of him are better that way."

"And what would that be?"

"Who he's working for."

"I told you, it's the Russians."

"That's what they want him to think. They're probably just privateers looking to sell the technology to the highest bidder. Doesn't matter. We just need to know. When we get confirmation, we'll strike hard and fast. I'm talking a Chinese fireworks show. Once they know they've been outed, they'll back off. You'll be safe then. They won't take a chance of being targeted again."

"That's how it works?"

"Yes. It's sort of like a board game. Once we find out who they are and strike, the game's over. Espionage is a dirty, tough profession, but it can be predictable."

"*Then* I can go back to Albuquerque?"

"You can go back home, yes. I'll keep a team close by, led by Nate or possibly Hawke if he's cleared. I'll know that by tonight. Now, for the business at hand. You want to know about your ability to project."

"That's right. And how is it you know that I have that ability? I mean, how can anyone know that?"

"It has to do with how the brain functions. I'll try to explain it by illustrating how the brain works with the sense of touch. For example, pickpockets don't stand around discussing how the brain works, but their profession requires at least some understanding of the subject. A common pickpocket technique requires two partners. One of the thieves will bump into the victim on one side. He does this to distract him from the other thief's hand, taking the wallet from the other side. Why does this work? It works because it distracts the brain from the events on the side where the critical action takes place. Signals coming from receptors in the body send reports to the brain about any touch activity. It's how we know we've touched something hot or cold or were pricked by a sticker bush.

In some cases, these signals don't get passed along at all. This is often apparent in pickpocketing, where you're bumped into so hard on one side that the receptors ignore the other side. It's called expectation of response. The expectation is that the brain needs to give its full attention to the side that receives the hard bump. This response of not sending out a signal can also happen with something like pain or even ticklishness. If there is expectation, the signal is often not sent out. It's the reason a person can't tickle himself. Their brain is focused on other, more essential stimuli. It knows the body is tickling itself, so the receptors don't send the signal because the expectation of being tickled is already present. This allows the brain to focus on other stimuli. Most of the time, we are unaware of the feel of a hat, the texture of our socks, or the tightness around our ears due to eyeglasses. It's the same premise. The signals don't go out because it would distract the brain from more important stimuli."

"What does this have to do with my projecting someone's actions?"

"Everything. You already know when someone is lying to you, which itself is a projection of their actions. Your senses are doing this because they can focus entirely on the individual, blocking out all other stimuli. As your senses continue integrating, they will go beyond deciphering a lie. They will start to anticipate the next move. All of this is due to your focus on the person. Because of the sensory chip, your brain acts like the zoom function on a camera. The only downfall is that you may not recognize something else happening around you because those stimuli are blocked.

In the brain, all the senses are organized into maps. These maps overlap so the senses can work together. Gradually, due to the sensory chip, all of your senses become one singular map. Because of our understanding of how the brain functions, we came to realize you would be able to project actions. There are some exceedingly rare cases where people have displayed the ability to foretell something hours or days ahead of time. Some say they are prophets. Others say the spirit realm is involved. In actuality, it's a rare genetic disturbance where the senses merge, becoming one. It can be brought on by a head injury or a severe sickness. It generally goes away when the body heals. It's another reason we knew what would happen to you. I hope that makes sense."

Suddenly, Pax and Edward are interrupted as two guards walk into the room. Edward smiles and points to the guards. "Looks like your Starbucks order has arrived. I'll head out now."

"Before you leave, could you check on something?" Pax asked.

"What is it?"

"I need you to check who occupies office 4S7 at Quantico."

"Quantico?"

"Yes."

"Why?"

"I have reason to believe the person in that room is a mole, probably working for the Russians."

"A spy in the middle of our FBI training facilities?"

"I'm not certain, but if you could just follow up on it."

Edward rubs his forehead and smiles. "Enjoy your Starbucks, Pax." He turns to leave.

"You will look into it, won't you?"

He throws up his hand and continues walking. "I'm pretty sure we don't have a spy at Quantico, but yes, I'll check on it."

Chapter 32

Now

Mona asked, "Who would like to start us off today?" She was sitting at the top end of a circle of eight people. For the past year, the Albuquerque Public Library has provided the room. Before that, the support group met in the back of a closed-down fire station on the north side of town. The new location afforded a better atmosphere and was more central for the group to meet. Mona hurriedly accessed the group. She didn't want to be confrontational, but someone had to talk. "Amy, could you tell us how things are going?" We haven't heard from you in a couple of weeks."

"Um, I guess so. Sure." Amy was a thirty-eight-year-old white Hispanic, whose husband died while stationed in Afghanistan. He was part of an army mission to rebuild Afghan firebases. He did not survive a series of cruise missile strikes. A few months after his death, the hallucinations started. At first, she would see him in a crowd or on a street corner. Before long, he was making passing comments about trivial things. Eventually, this worked its way into a daily relationship. "Okay. So, yesterday he wanted to touch me. I mean, we've been kissing some, but this was different. I was in the shower. I told him, *you are my husband. You can touch me whenever you want.* After that, he hugged me, and we just stood there with the water sprinkling down over us."

"Why do you think that happened?" Mona asked.

"I don't know."

Colton, a fifty-something white man, shifted uneasily in his seat and then spoke to Amy. "You need a boyfriend," he shook his head. "Your cheeks are flushed, just talking about it."

"Thank you, Colton, for your comment," Mona said. "Do you have anything else to add?"

"No. I mean, a boyfriend might be good for her, don't you think?"

"Not necessarily. Amy misses the intimacy she used to have with her husband. She needs to work that out and tell her husband how she feels. A boyfriend might complicate the situation. It could even make matters worse by affecting her conscience, causing feelings of guilt. What do you think of Colton's suggestion, Amy?"

"I don't need no boyfriend."

"Okay. Colton was just trying to help. The next time your husband wants to touch you, tell him how you feel, how you miss being intimate with him. Talking it through is the most important thing. Now, who's next? We're just getting started."

"I got an email today," another white-Hispanic girl said with a soft voice. Her name was Lucy. She stood out because of her blue-dyed hair and butterfly tattoos that partially covered her neck and arms. A year earlier, both her parents had died in a freak boating accident. At the time, Lucy was only nineteen. The last year had been a tough one, filled with attempts to find a job and a place to live before the money inherited from her parents ran out. After the hallucinations started, she showed up one day at Mona's office. "It was from a girl I knew in high school," she said, twisting and slumping down in her seat. "We were close in school, but she moved away after graduation. Her name's Reese. She lives over in Las Cruces. It wasn't a message as much as a list of job openings. I told her last month I wasn't ready to make a change, but she doesn't have many friends there and wants me to move in with her." Lucy glances slowly around the group and asks, "What do you think I should do?"

"How long before your money runs out?" Colton blurts out.

Lucy crosses her arms and then her legs. "If I'm careful, I could go another year. If not, I got maybe eight or nine months."

Colton continues. "Does she know you hallucinate?"

"No, do you think that should stop me?"

He shrugs his shoulders. "If you haven't found suitable work here in three months, I think you should go. If you wait too long, you'll end up homeless."

"So, you don't think she'll mind my mental problem?"

"If you can't find work here, I don't think you have a choice."

"*You always have a choice,*" Hawke interjected. "Heaven's sake!"

"Everyone," Mona announced. "This is Hawke Gentry. He lives over in Rio Rancho. He's going to be a part of our group now. Hawke, do you have anything else to add?"

"Is everyone here so…" He stopped and glanced around the group. "So crazy free to share things."

"It's how the process works, Hawke," Mona responded. "You'll get used to it. You were saying something about having a choice? Were you speaking from experience? Go on. We want to hear."

"I can say anything I want, doesn't matter?"

"Yes, anything. What is it you want to say?"

"I don't want to be here." He throws his hands up and lets them fall back into his lap. "Just so everybody knows." He made a face that showed his contempt. "If I don't come to these meetings," he points with both hands to Mona, "she gives me a bad report, and I lose my job. It's ridiculous how they turn to the *psychoanalyst* like she's a genius. The point is, I wouldn't be here unless I was forced. *I don't need this.* Someone says I'm talking to myself, and they think it means something. It doesn't mean *anything* because there's always someone there. I don't talk to myself."

"It's the same thing," Lucy replies.

"What's the same thing?"

"You're making them up in your mind, so you're talking to yourself. It's the same thing. We all do it. It's why we're here."

"We're here because Mona wants us to be here. Isn't that right, Mona?"

"Partly, yes."

"And what do you think of me now that I've crapped on your party?"

"The same thing I've always thought. You're a good person who's been through a lot."

"Is that all?"

"No. Everything shows in your eyes, the sadness, the pain, the anger, everything. It helps me to know what I need to do."

"And what might that be?"

"To stop you from giving up." Mona places her thumb under her chin, rubs, and attempts a half-hearted smile. "When your life turns out to be something entirely different than expected, it's easy to give up. My job is to not let that happen."

"Well, I want everyone to know that I don't believe in this process or whatever you call it. And...," he points around the group, "I'm not like the rest of you."

"You can say that again," Colton replied. "Nobody else here is an ass."

"You do hallucinate, Hawke," Amy interjected. "You just told us."

"Yes, but," he points again around the group. "What's happening to me is different. They help me."

"Who helps you?" Lucy asked.

"Mostly, my daughter, Ginger. She tells me where I need to improve or when I'm taking too much crap from people."

"Right!" Colton snaps. "She's just bossing you around, is all. I agree with you. You're not like us. You're way more pathetic."

"And who else?" Amy asked.

"What do you mean?" Hawke asked.

"You said mostly your daughter, Ginger. So, who else?"

"My wife, Callie."

Amy continues. "How did they die?"

"Why? What does it matter to you?"

"It doesn't affect me in the least. But it's why we're here, and I want to know. How did they die?"

Hawke shakes his head. "It caused a big outrage in the community. A tour bus broadsided their car."

"I'm sorry, Hawke." Amy said, trying to console him.

"Me too," Lucy interjected.

"Was there a lawsuit?" Colton asked.

"No, the bus driver died, too, and the company lawyered up and denied responsibility."

"Would you tell the group how it made you feel when they died?" Mona asked.

"It's freaking obvious, isn't it? I mean, God! When they left, all the air was sucked out of my lungs. One month later, it was the same. And now, today, it's still the same." Hawke's hands go up as he begins gesturing. "They were so damned annoying, and I miss that. I miss having my sentences completed or having to get dressed late at night and go out because Ginger couldn't go one day without chocolate. It's so irritating how much I miss them, my wife, my baby girl."

His voice softens, and his hands fall into his lap. "When I first met Callie, everything was beautiful. She was trying to make my life better, and I was trying to make hers better. We shared everything, especially the good stuff. You know, the late-night dates, the fizzy drinks, and those long kisses that make you think you're merging into one." Hawke points around the group again. "What we had, none of you mixed up people ever spent one minute experiencing." His voice raises, and his hand points even harder. "None of you! So don't tell me we're all the same freaking thing here because we're not...we're not...we're not! Callie and I had that thing that holds everything else together. It was our own perfect world!"

Hawke points around the circle to everyone. "Your lives were full of crap and stress and emptiness. That's why you're here, but not me. This is just a waste of time!" He stands up, ready to walk out, and suddenly sees Ginger run past the group. She stops, turns, and looks at him.

"Why don't you tell them, Daddy?" She starts giggling and runs around the group behind him. Whirling around, he sees her standing there. She's barefoot, and in the yellow dress he likes so much. Cupping her hands around her mouth, she whispers. "Tell them, Daddy."

"Tell them what?" He answers and then sits back down, facing her instead of the group.

"Tell them about your mommy and daddy."

Callie comes walking up next to her daughter. "Go on, Hawke, tell them. They need to know, and you need to talk about it."

"I don't think I can."

"Sure, you can, baby. What happened to you doesn't make you. It can't. You're a good person, loyal and true, always have been."

"They don't want to hear. I've been rude, a real ass."

"Tell them your story," Callie re-emphasized.

"Yes, tell them, Daddy."

"Hawke?" Mona asked. "Are you talking with Ginger and Callie?"

"Yes."

"And they want you to tell us something?"

"Yes."

"Then go on." Mona glances around the group. "We all want to hear. Don't we guys?" Everyone nods.

"I'm dying to hear," says Colton. "You've made my day, livened up the whole group. We've all been where you're at. Listen to your family and talk."

Hawke smiles, nods, and painfully turns to the group, who are staring at him. "You are growing into a fine young boy," Hawke said and then hesitated, wiping tears from his eyes.

"Who said that to you, Hawke?" Mona asked.

He rubs his hand on his pants and frowns. "I didn't say?"

"No."

"That's what my father told me on that night. You are growing into a fine young boy."

"Was it your birthday or something?" Amy asked.

"My birthday? No. It was just a regular day. It was good. We had spaghetti, which was my favorite. Mother didn't eat much. She'd been watching her weight. She had a glass of wine. She didn't do that unless she was feeling good. Dad had two helpings. It was," Hawke smiles. "It was really nice. After supper, Dad turned on the TV to that station that plays all those old shows. He loved that stuff, and so did Mom. After a while, I got bored and crawled behind the sofa, where I kept my baseball cards. I opened the shoebox and piled them in stacks according to their teams. I started flipping them over and checking statistics. Batting average and home runs determined who were the best players. It was one of my things, statistics.

About that time, I heard other voices. I didn't recognize them but was too involved with my cards to think anything of it. And then I heard my mother's voice change. I had heard it like that once before when her grandmother died. We were at the funeral home, and she was talking to her grandfather. I remembered her voice because it was my first time in a funeral home, and everything seemed creepy. *You don't have to do this, mister,* she said in that voice. I could tell by the sounds that my father was holding my mother. It was the sound of tears, and it kept getting louder, and I could tell they were squeezing each other harder. I almost stood up, but something made me stay put. One voice I didn't recognize said something about my mother's jewelry and my dad's wallet. And then another voice shouted, *Just do it!* It was strange because I only heard one more word. My mother said, *PLEASE.* After that, the explosions started. Later they told me what I heard was twelve gunshots. For the longest time, I couldn't move. I just sat there behind the sofa, holding cards in my hand. It took some time, and I don't know what it was, but whatever was keeping me from moving started to go away.

My eyelids blinked, and some cards fell out of my hand. When I leaned onto the sofa, the sofa didn't seem real. I could hear my shoulder scrape against it, but I couldn't feel anything. I put my hand on the sofa's edge, pulled myself over, and peeked out. There were splotches of red everywhere, and then something dripped on my face from the top of the sofa. It ran down my cheek, and when I touched it, it smeared. I could see it was also red. I stood up and walked out in front of the sofa. Twisted together, my parents lay on the floor in front of the sofa. They were all red like someone had poured ketchup on them. I placed my hands on them, and they were warm, and I knew that they were not sleeping.

When I walked outside, I wiped my hands on my shirt and headed down the street to the closest neighbor. For some reason, I was calm. I rang the doorbell, and it felt like I was just paying a visit. When the door opened, a tall man was standing there. *Christ's sake, son,* he said. *What's happened to you?* I told him that someone poured ketchup over my mommy and daddy and that now they can't breathe. He brought me inside, closed the door, and looked out a window. Then he had me sit down, and I could tell that the chair was new because of the smell. He went over to a phone, and I could hear him say his address and to hurry."

"How old were you, Hawke?" Amy asked.

When he looked at her, his eyes had turned glassy, and then one single tear slipped down his left cheek. "I don't remember. I think I was in the second grade."

Chapter 33

Now

Pax sits in the bedroom of the Pentagon saferoom wishing things could be different. She hopes Gatsby won't make another mistake by refusing to cooperate. He had done some things to be sorry about and reflecting on the situation made her uncomfortable. A degree of damage had been done and couldn't be repaired. If convicted of espionage he would end up in prison for a long time. It was a dreary outlook, his future being in the hands of people who neither loved him nor understood him.

A few minutes earlier, the guards had informed her of his arrival. He was waiting on the other side of the wall, looking around, wondering where she was. When he realized there was another wing, he gathered his thoughts and began walking toward the bedroom.

Pax lay across the bed, trying to think of what her first words should be. She was angry at Gatsby for what he had done and, at the same time, excited to get to see him. She checked a clock on the wall. It had been five minutes since the guards had escorted him inside. She took several deep breaths to fill her lungs and ready herself to face him. But before she could move, she heard his voice.

"What do we have here?"

At first, she froze. Then slowly, her face turned toward the voice.

Gatsby was smiling at her. "Odd time of day to be taking a nap, don't you think?" he asks, quickly glancing around the room.

Pax swung her legs around, and her feet hit the floor light and soft. Even with his balding head, Gatsby was still a handsome man. His blue eyes were still bright, and his smile was as beautiful as ever. "You're crazy, Dad." She pushed herself to her feet. "You know that, right? The things you've done. What the hell?"

His stomach muscles clenched, and his lips twisted as he looked down and then back up. "I never meant to put you in danger."

"Then right the wrong. Is it really the Russians you're working for or someone else?"

"It doesn't matter."

"Yes, it does. The Pentagon orders a military strike, and it's all over."

"Doesn't that bother you?"

"Why should it bother me?"

"When our country steals technology from another country, they call it a game and go out for drinks to celebrate. But when another country even attempts to steal technology from them, they start killing people."

"I just want this to end!" she exclaimed.

"It will never end until the Pentagon's enemies have what they want. And they want everything."

"You mean the sensory chip?"

"That's only part of it."

"Then what?"

"They want the Timeship technology. They know you've completed the math, and they know you've tested it. They also know that the Pentagon plans to use it to gain a significant advantage."

"What kind of advantage?"

"The boot on the neck kind. They're willing to go to war over this."

"Who, Dad? You have to tell me."

He could keep his secret from anyone but Pax. She was too much a part of him to block her out. His face was expressionless as he quickly scanned the room. He was looking for a chair to sit down in, but he couldn't find one. "The Russian Federation," he looks back at her.

"So, you've been telling me the truth. Are you a double agent, a Russian spy?"

He shook his head. "No, but you're on the right track. I must be careful about what I say. The Russians got an ex-CIA

Black Ops working for them. If they suspect I'm turning on them, we're both dead."

"How long have you been in bed with the Russians? Was it before I went blind?"

"No. Look, Pax, darling, if we just give them what they want."

"Right, and then we'll be safe. I don't think so." She suddenly lifts her hands grabbing both sides of her head. "Wait a minute."

Her brain takes off racing with probabilities, calculations, and end results. The sensory chip was doing its thing, aligning her senses, and producing a best-case scenario. In only seconds she had designed a master plan.

She lowers her hands. "I want you to go back to your boss or whoever communicates with you. Tell them I've changed the math calculations on the Timeship. If I die, the calculations show up in the emails of three generals stationed at the Pentagon. If I live, the calculations stay with me."

"And the sensory chip?"

"Make it clear to them that they're not doing brain surgery on me. That's Pentagon technology, so they'll have to negotiate with them. The Pentagon will probably give them a diluted version to appease them, but at least it's something. The first attempt they make to extract it from my brain, the math calculations for the Timeship get emailed, and they got bigger problems to face."

"You think this will work?"

"The one sure thing is that both sides are arrogant. The Russians will think their scientist can take the diluted sensory chip and figure the rest out on their own. Who knows, maybe they can. The Pentagon will hedge that they can't. Me, I could care less. I just want this over with."

"So, that's it, that's the plan?"

"It's the best chance we got. The Pentagon won't be happy when they realize I'm preventing them from using the Timeship, but it's the only way out of this mess. Anything else, and you and I are dodging bullets with a third world war on our hands. How soon can you relay my message?"

"They know I'm in custody. They won't risk contact with me until I'm released."

"I think I can arrange that with General Stackhouse."

"Then, after that, it's just a matter of time. They have people here in D.C., so probably within one or two hours of my release, they'll contact me."

Relieved, Pax inhales and nods. People are unpredictable. She hoped that she and her dad wouldn't end up on the losing side. There was no way to tell for sure. But the plan was solid. She pushes her hair back, squints, and shakes her head. There was something else she needed to get off her chest.

Gatsby, who by now had sat on the edge of the bed, stands back up. He could see her eyes watering. He says, "Don't start crying on me now."

"I'm not."

"You say that, but…"

"I'm not!"

"Okay, then. What is it?"

She dries her eyes with her hands. "For a while there, I thought you had just changed. I mean, it happens to a lot of people, especially when money gets flashed in front of them. The thing is, you've always been greedy. I can see that now."

"That's not why I did this."

"Of course, it is. And shame on me for not seeing it from the start."

"I don't blame you for thinking it, but you're wrong."

"Then, why? If you didn't sell out for money, tell me."

"I can't."

"You can, but you won't because you know I'm right."

Gatsby didn't respond. He just looked at her with a blank face. Worlds had converged and forced his hand. He wasn't in control of his life, hadn't been for a long time.

"Say something!" Pax demanded.

"All actions have consequences. That's the best I can do."

"Seriously? Not exactly touching or sentimental, is it?"

"No. And once again, I've disappointed you."

"How did you manage to do such a good job raising me?"

"I got through it. That's all I know."

"You didn't just get through it. You were wonderful, the best father I could've hoped for."

He smiles. "You didn't need anything that sensory chip gave you for strength; not eyesight, not super reflexes, not super-duper senses, none of it. I know because it was in your eyes from the time you started school, and it still is. You're a strong woman, Pax, and I'm proud of you." He twists his head and nods toward the flatscreen TV. We've got some time. Why don't we watch a movie?"

"I don't want to watch a movie."

"Your mom and I used to love watching movies."

"If it was so great, why did you divorce her?"

"Things were good for a long time. When you came along, we were riding a pretty good high. Even when we started disagreeing, things weren't crappy. They were *never* crappy, Pax."

"It was all about her becoming an operative, which I still don't understand, Dad. She had already applied to the CIA when you met her. And she was upfront with you about her goal of being an operative."

"All of what you say is true."

"Then why did you allow it to break up the marriage?"

"I didn't."

"Yes, you did. You gave her an ultimatum. When she accepted the position as an operative, you divorced her."

"That's not how it went down."

"You're just in denial."

"You need to go back and rethink the timeline. My issues with Sloan started a month or two before the CIA offered her an operative opportunity. She had waited for years, but they had never offered. Even though she was qualified and had the training, she began to think it wasn't going to happen. When they finally offered, yes, I fought it. But her being an operative is not the reason we divorced. She became involved with something.

When I tried to help her, it was too late. She couldn't back out of it."

"Something so bad that you divorced her?"

"Yes."

"You're just making things up."

"Now, who's in denial? Your mother was an amazing person but far from perfect."

"Then tell me what she did that was so bad it made you divorce her?"

"It's water under the bridge, now. Besides, it'll just ruin your day."

"Look around, Dad. I'm a prisoner. My day is already ruined. Tell me!"

"First, you have to promise me you won't hate her."

"Hate her? What are you talking about? I could never hate my mother."

"Promise me."

"Okay, I promise."

"I divorced your mother because of a loyalty problem."

Pax throws up her hands in disbelief. "You want me to believe that she was running around on you?"

"That's not the kind of loyalty I'm talking about."

"This isn't a board game, Dad. Just tell me what the hell you mean?"

"To begin with, I want to make something clear. When you work for certain branches of the government, it's not uncommon to be approached by another country."

Trying to understand, Pax scratches her forehead. She asks, "And the CIA is one of those branches?"

"Yes."

"I don't believe it. You're saying she was a spy for a foreign government."

"She waited for years to be an operative. She was losing. No, she had lost faith that it was going to happen. When the opportunity arose to do the same thing for another government, she jumped before thinking it through. It was a terrible mistake. I tried to reason with her that she could back out. I even assured her the CIA would help; nothing I said or did would make a difference. It killed me to divorce her. Regardless of my feelings, I had to distance myself from her. If she got caught, I would be implicated by association. With both of us in jail, who would care for you?"

"It was the Russians. She was a Russian spy?" Pax asked.

"It was the Iranians that contacted her first. Within days of that, it was the Russians. The Iranian offer got her thinking. But when the Russians contacted her, she was beside herself with excitement. She had always dreamed of being an operative on that level. She knew the language and had the training.

I didn't want her to become an operative. But our real problems started when the Russians entered the picture. It was a question of loyalty. You can't work for the CIA and the Russians. The penalty for that is life in prison."

Pax felt a surge of joy because she knew that Gatsby was telling the truth. He had been protecting her from the ugly truth about her mother. Her suspicions had been wrong about him. He was the same caring father he had always been. She took a step toward him, and he gracefully did the same toward her. The two embraced with her high cheekbones shining above his shoulder. He began stroking his hand through her hair. She squeezed tighter, realizing that he had always let her into his life more than he did anyone else. All the years she had spent with him. The bond that nothing, including espionage, had been able to break. "Since I moved into the apartment," she spoke softly. "I've missed you, Dad."

"I've missed you too. I was so proud of how you adapted to living by yourself."

Suddenly Pax felt something hot deep inside her. It was as if she had caught on fire from the inside out. Loosening her grip, she moves back and looks Gatsby in the face. And then it hit her, a powerful surge that nearly knocked her down. It was her first projection causing her vision to blur. For the next twenty seconds, she saw only strange outlines, half of them in blue and half in red. This visualization transitioned into the spinning view of a tunnel where she had feelings of falling rapidly. Still, even the tunnel appeared in blue and red outlines. At the same time, her mind was racing through the events of the next several days. Gatsby's life was in danger, but it would only make matters worse if she told him. This city, where she was born and raised, was no longer home. It was crawling with spies and creeping with money-seeking, double-crossing politicians, and assassins.

The Russians had enough plants in D.C. to force Gatsby's hand and ultimately cause his death. On his release, after they made contact, she would need to get him back to Albuquerque before they had a chance to eliminate him. And there was something else that kept flashing through her mind. The Argonauts were on to Gatsby. They had been following him for months, but who were they, and from what country? All she could picture was a tattoo of an eight-legged octopus.

She let go of him. She says, "You mentioned an ex-CIA agent working for the Russians. Could there be more? Do you know anything about the Argonauts?"

"In the espionage world, D.C. has a nickname. *The Land Of 10,000 Spies.* I know the Russians are embedded here. I just don't know who or how many. As far as the Argonauts, I've never heard the term."

"I think they're a group of eight Russian spies, planted here for years. Their mark is the octopus. Have you ever noticed an octopus logo on any paperwork?"

"Not that I can recall, no."

"I think they might be silent, invisible plants in the Pentagon."

"It makes sense. It's been thought for years that the Chinese have been stealing technology. There have been suspicions that it's Russia making it look like the Chinese. That theory holds a lot of weight because Russia usually deploys the stolen technology first. So, eight Russian spies are hiding in plain sight under our noses? How did you find out about the Argonauts?"

"A hacker friend of mine. He hacked into the Pentagon website. When he discovered the octopus logo and the term Argonauts, he tried searching for more. There was very little information. It appears the Argonauts started up during World War II. There was a lot of spying taking shape in America, especially in D.C. If he's right, the Russians have managed to implant spies and keep them invisible for the better part of a century. The Pentagon building opened in 1943. My hacker friend traced the Argonauts back to that time."

"Do you think my Russian contact is one of these Argonauts?"

"I don't know. Right now, I'm having the guards contact General Stackhouse. He needs an update, and we need to get moving with the plan."

Twenty minutes later, the general is standing next to Edward Cotton in the safehouse. He's eyeing Pax and Gatsby. "Do you have something for me?" He asked. "Tell me you do, and we can end this situation before it goes any further."

Pax and Gatsby exchanged looks. The general could tell something was smoldering. Pax was having an awful time speaking, but finally raised a question. "You're not seriously going to approve a military strike on Russia?"

"It's the Russian Federation?"

"Yes."

"We'll take down one of their jets or sink a ship. In a hostile world, this is how it works. We'll deny involvement, but they'll know what it was about. They'll back off, and in a few months, we'll provide them with the technology. It won't be exactly what they want, but it will be enough to appease them."

"I figured as much." Pax continued, "The Russians want the Timeship, sir."

"Then we'll give them a Timeship."

Pax glances at Gatsby and shakes her head. "They know it's operational, sir."

If what she said was true, the groundwork had been laid for war. Nothing short of giving the Russians the Timeship technology could prevent it, and that was out of the question. The Argonauts' involvement would be useless. The general wanted the information authenticated. "How did they find out?"

He asked. Even Gatsby didn't know that. "Gatsby, you got anything to say?"

Gatsby sighs, shakes his head, and says, "I left D.C. years ago to get away from this Chinese fire drill. Still, here I am today, with poop twirling like a tornado. I don't know how they know, but they know. And if they don't get what they want real soon, they'll invade Alaska. In less than a month, Alaska would be under the Russian flag. They already made that clear. They don't plan on waiting around for that thing to be used against them."

"I came up with a plan," Pax interjected. "It's not an end-all, but it buys us some time."

"Let's hear it," the general demanded.

"We release Gatsby. They'll contact him within an hour or so. He informs them of a truce I came up with. For the time being, I'll withhold the Timeship calculations from the Pentagon. In return, the Russians stop chasing me. If I'm harmed, the calculations will be emailed to three generals stationed at the Pentagon."

"And the sensory chip?"

"They won't start a war over the sensory chip. Gatsby will inform them that the Pentagon will negotiate the release of the technology in good faith. He can give them a timeline of six months. Meantime, before they get wise to the plan, I go back in time and see what can be done to fix this mess. Are we agreed?"

"Yes. I want this show on the road now. As soon as the Russians contact Gatsby, I want you and one of our team to make use of that Timeship."

"I'm good to go. Two days ago, we agreed that if Hawke was cleared, he would be the representative. Is he cleared?"

"He's cleared, but he's in Albuquerque."

"Perfect. I don't like being in D.C., so get me on a plane. Oh, and my dad's in danger here." She glances at Gatsby for a moment. "He doesn't know it yet, but he's going to threaten the wrong person. It has something to do with my mother, probably her death."

"How do you know?" The general asked.

"A few minutes ago, I had my first projection. I want him followed and protected. When he's done informing the Russians, I want him on that plane with me."

Chapter 34

Now

Flying back to Albuquerque, their talk turned to the future. Gatsby wanted to spend more time with Pax and had just asked her to move back in with him. But Pax was not eager to pursue the subject because her projection capabilities were kicking into high gear. One scene after another would come into view, heighten, and produce an infusion of visible clips of the future. Each scene would linger for a moment while she absorbed it like some new energy source. Dates and decisions came into view like ripples working their way across a pond. Slowly the water would calm, the final date and decision clearly seen, forming a single overall picture, a projection of the future.

"Well, what do you think?" Gatsby asked.

She was looking straight ahead down the aisle of the plane. "I'm sorry, Dad." She waves at a flight attendant. "Wait a second." The flight attendant approaches. "Could I get a bottle of water? You know what, a Coke would be better." The flight attendant nods.

"What do you mean you're sorry?" Gatsby asked.

"It's just that moving back home would be a step back. Besides, I like having my own place and meeting new friends. You understand, don't you?"

He placed his hand over the top of hers, and says, "I'm suddenly reminded of when I first moved out on my own. It was scary and exciting at the same time. It was an amazing experience."

Later that night, Pax was guzzling wine in her apartment while waiting for Hawke to come over. They had talked earlier and made plans to meet. When she heard a knock at the door, she didn't get up, just shouted out. "Come in."

Seeing Hawke headed in her direction, she took a drink of wine and gazed at him. His eyes were bright, his beard glittering handsomeness just the way she liked. Reaching to the coffee table, she poured a second glass of wine and handed it to him. While in D.C. it had been difficult, and she wanted to put it all behind her. And there was something else on her mind, something she had been wanting to mention. She gushed, her face turning pink. "Last week when we were together, I had a negligee on. And we…, well, you remember."

"I remember." He sits down in a cushioned chair across from her, holding but not sipping his wine. He's trying not to fixate. Her dress is cut low. He thinks it's on purpose.

Pax swallowed another drink and poured herself a refill. There was a longing for him that had been there for a while. But since their one encounter he had been deflective, and she was concerned. Her perception of their relationship was strong. He liked her, yes, but going to the next level didn't look good. She says, "Look, just tell me, is this thing between us gonna end before it starts?"

At first her question freezes him. He didn't expect they would get to this point in their relationship so quickly. He nods, not the kind of nod that means yes, the kind that says you deserve an answer. He says, "I have issues, haven't you heard? In two weeks, you'd walk out, hoping I hadn't already driven you to lunacy."

"I don't think so. Besides, I like it when you talk to people, I can't see."

"Really?"

"Uh-huh. I spent most of my life listening to people talk to people I couldn't see." She takes another drink, feels the first wave of alcohol connect to her brain, and begins motioning with her hand. "The way I see it, we'd marry in a couple of months. We would never fight unless it were really bad, like, you know, attacking each other's character. Any other fight would be too boring, too meaningless. Within three years, we'd have two kids, one girl, and one boy. We'd give them old-fashioned names like Evelyne and Godfrey."

"Then what?"

"Not much. We'd be happy but grow old, really fast. I'd die first, then within a month, you'd die, and Evelyne and Godfrey would say you died of a broken heart. All the neighbors would agree."

"Other than the growing old fast thing, I love it."

Their romance was starting to smolder like a fire. It was either going to burn bright or go out, neither one of them knew which. Hawke stared back at her, deep into her eyes, thinking, hoping his condition wouldn't prevent a relationship with her. He is surprised to see Ginger run behind the sofa. She waves her hand at him and giggles. She says, "Listen to her, Daddy. She's like a little girl. She doesn't know what the world can do."

"I think she does know, Ginger. I think she's all grown up now." He grins and takes his first sip of wine.

Ginger runs around the sofa up to Hawke, placing her hands on his knees. "She likes you, doesn't she, Daddy?"

He reaches out and rubs her cheeks, then begins stroking her hair. "Yes, baby girl, and I like her too. What do you think about that?"

"It's good, Daddy. It's what mommy and I have been waiting for." Suddenly as quickly as she appeared, she was gone, evaporating into the air.

Hawke turns his attention back to Pax. "As you can see, I'm certifiable. I'm not exactly husband material."

Taking another gulp of wine, she smiles at him. "I wish I could have known your daughter."

He shakes his head, wishing the same thing. He says, "I'm supposed to ignore her when I'm around other people. The situation is pathetic. I can't seem to stop."

"Is she still here?"

"Not anymore, no." With Ginger gone it would be easy to give in to his fixation and just stare at her. Instead, he takes his second sip of wine and leans back in his chair. Not to be deterred, Pax pours yet another glassful and turns it up, gulping down several more swallows. A wooziness rushes in like a surfer's wave overtaking her, a second wave, and she starts laughing.

"Are you trying to get drunk?" Hawke asked.

"Yes!" She immediately burped and laughed again. "Now you see, see, um. Now you got it." Reaching out for the wine bottle, she almost knocks it to the floor. "Oops-zee-day-zees."

Hawke catches the bottle and holds it. "You've been through a lot the last week or two. So, you just want to get blasted? Is that it?"

She reaches for the bottle, but he pulls it back. "Well, is that it?"

"No! Okay, yes."

"Mission accomplished. Maybe I should go and let you get some rest. We've got a big day ahead of us tomorrow. General Stackhouse informed me we'd be testing the Timeship. To be honest, I'm a little nervous about it—actually, a lot nervous."

"No," Pax responded, her head dipping woozily to the right before jerking back.

"What do you mean?" Hawke asked. "*You do* have the Timeship with you, don't you?"

"Yes."

"Then what?"

"First, Rosie."

"Oh, you want to know how he's doing. My boss at the Albuquerque FBI checked on him. The RVs are still there, but he's nowhere around. My guess is he's lying low. We can drive out there tomorrow morning if you like?"

She nods, yes, and takes a deep, exhausted breath.

"So, then," Hawke sets the bottle back on the coffee table and stands up. "You get some rest, and I'll be back tomorrow morning."

"No!" Pax points for him to sit back down. Her head bobbles backward as she tries to focus.

He sits down and says, "Look, I see two issues right now. One, you're not thinking straight for obvious reasons. And two, if you would just go out and meet other guys, you'd see that you can do better than me."

She interrupts, pointing her index finger at him. "We alone, and dinking... drinking wine, and-I-don't," she presses her finger into his chest, "care."

"Deep down, you know that I'm right, Pax."

She waves him off. "You seem forget why I'm 'tracted you, to… you. Not cause I'm dunk… but cause you 'tractive and cause you fun-nun-nee. Um, and kind. And honest. And cause maybe we not fit right way 'round. God, I'm so drunk. Maybe we don't fit together the right way. But I don't care. You-should-be-angry-for-all-happens, has-happened-to-you. Oh crap! Juss kiss me." Pax slips off the sofa onto her knees, a third wave hitting her. "Juss kiss me." She lunges forward, pushing the coffee table up on two legs. The bottle of wine flips over, slides into Hawke's lap, spilling what's left of the semi-sweet red juice. Slapping at the table several times, she finally shoves it out of the way, falls forward, grasping at Hawke and locking her lips onto his.

Even in a drunken state, her kiss electrifies him.

After a long wet one, she moves back with her nose still touching his. "Sorry 'bout the-wine-on-your-pants."

"It's okay." He didn't want her to move. "Best accident I ever had."

She lays another one on him, deep and long. He liked it. She knows because she can feel his heart beating out of his chest.

He wanted so badly to just light his hair on fire and go for it, but lurking back in the crevices of his mind was Callie and Ginger. It was the thing that was holding the relationship back. He knew he needed to move forward. The thought of them was working on him, partly because kissing Pax felt good and partly because he knew he would be spending the night.

The following day it was gloomy out due to heavy overnight rain. Pax had a hard time getting Hawke out of bed. When she finally did, they sat at the kitchen table, attempting to drink lousy coffee but mainly reflecting on the night before. "So, what did you think?" Pax asked.

"You mean about last night?"

"Yes."

"That's easy. I thought you were sexy, soulful, and sinful. The sinful part was probably due to the wine, but it's all good.

The next time you get drunk, though, I might get excited, so don't hold it against me."

"I won't."

"And what about me?"

"You?"

"Yes. It's only fair. I told you what I thought about you, so."

Pax lifts her coffee cup, then, remembering how awful it tastes she sets it back down. "You won't let it go to your head, will you?"

"Of course, I will." He waves her on. "Let's have it."

She cups her hands together and rests her chin on them. "Last night, you got into the tips of my toes."

"Is that like a metaphor for I'm sexy, soulful, and sinful?"

"No. It just means I like you."

"Oh."

"I'm not finished."

"Sorry."

"And it means my being with you feels good."

"I feel the same way."

"I'm still not finished."

"Crud, sorry." He waves her on.

"I've been waiting for someone I feel comfortable around." Pax looks away from him around the room for a few seconds. "And it's you."

"Are you done now?"

"Yes."

Hawke sinks back into his chair. "This could get complicated. I'm FBI and," he points to his head, "a little off up here."

"I don't care."

"You probably should."

"Maybe, but I don't think so." She sips her coffee and cringes at the taste of it. "Do you have regrets about last night?"

"No. I mean, it's just that I'm in some hot water already with my mental state. Keeping this quiet would be in my best interest. I love my job. If I lost it," he looks at her and smiles. "I'd probably get drunker than you did last night."

"Hahaha. It felt so good letting go for a change," she laughs again. "But seriously, I can't imagine what you must have gone through."

My psychologist instructed me to talk through any issues I had with them. She says once I do that, the hallucinations will go away. But I don't seem to be making much progress."

"It's not easy discussing problems."

"I couldn't agree more."

"One thing I learned when I lost my eyesight was you have to get past the unfairness. I dwelled on that for months, not having my mom, not having my vision." She lifts her cup and takes a sip. "God, this coffee is terrible!"

"But you made it."

"I know." She sets the cup down and pushes it away. "Maybe that's it, accepting your role in the breakup, acknowledging your part."

"I'm not sure that's fair. I never wanted to break up."

"And I never wanted to make bad coffee. You played a role, and subconsciously it's wearing you out. Find out what your part was and take ownership."

"My psychologist told me the same thing. What do you think will happen?"

"It seems to me that if you want to make things right, you have to start with where things went wrong. Once you've figured that out, you'll know what to do." Pax glances down at her coffee cup. "And since I obviously destroyed the coffee this morning, how about I treat us to Café Bella?"

"I'm glad you're taking ownership."

"My subconscious feels better already."

Chapter 35

Now

Driving through the desert in Hawke's repaired Nissan Rogue, sprinkles of rain spat down like tiny missiles on the windshield. Pax gazed to her right, noticing scattered cactuses and lots of rocks and desert weeds. Farther up ahead at the intersection of two dirt roads was a stone gate leading to a large courtyard. Beyond the courtyard was a deserted two-story stone building. At one time, the building operated as a makeshift fort, housing a garrison of soldiers. The troops defended against marauder bands that ran during the late nineteenth and early twentieth centuries. At this intersection, Hawke slows the car and takes a sharp right. In another five minutes, he veers left, slows the Nissan, and maneuvers beyond two rose-colored dunes. They are now eyeballing Rosie's RVs and hoping he's somewhere around. The Nissan slows, rolls past the first RV, and comes to rest in front of the second.

"Do you notice anything strange?" Hawke asked as he opened the driver's side door.

Pax shoves her door open and canvasses the area. She says, "Other than it looks like it's been raining like a pissing cow, no. Why?"

Holding umbrellas, they both stand up outside the car. "Unless I dreamed it all up, there's been a cleanup crew here." He glances at Pax while tilting his head down with a serious look. "And I wasn't dreaming. When I blasted my way out of here in my Nissan, at least two Hummers were blazing away in a screaming fireball. And this should be the crash site of a nice-sized drone with missile capabilities. It's gone, all of it. They've made it look like nothing ever happened."

"Do you think they took Rosie?" Pax asked.

"Don't you think Rosie could have been working with them?"

"Absolutely not."

Hawke lifts a hand and wipes his forehead. He says, "Then, I don't know. But if he wasn't working with them, he was in some serious danger."

Pax cups her hand around her mouth and shouts. "Rosie, are you here!" Walking over to the second RV, she pounds it with her umbrella and opens the door. She and Hawke scramble inside. She half expected to see him brutally murdered or at least tied up and gagged, but she found neither. Pointing to a desk, she glances at Hawke, and says, "Rosie's not the type to leave his computer behind."

Hawke stares at the same computer. "I'm going to have to agree with you on that one. That computer was his life, which means he either ran off or has come to a bad end. I have no idea which."

"Where would he run to?" Pax asked. "You could do that in the old days, maybe. Back then, they didn't have military-grade Hummers and drones to track you down. He wouldn't have gotten far. He's one of the best hackers in the country. So long as they needed him, they would have put up with him."

Hawke nods and his face tightens. He says, "And if they didn't need him, they would have discarded him with no regrets."

"I know." She sounded dejected.

"I realize he made a good impression on you, Pax, but since we don't know what happened, best not to think about it."

She nods and continues looking around the RV. "No sense in us hanging around here any longer." Before she could finish her words, there was a noise outside the RV. Hawke twists to his left, swings the door open, and the two walk back outside into the pouring rain.

A girl in pigtails not more than twelve is standing in front of the Nissan with rain pouring off her face. With both hands, she nervously points a Glock at them. "You killed my Gramps!" She shouted. "You killed him and left him to rot!" She had big round eyes, long blond hair, and her cheeks were heavily flushed from fear.

"No!" Pax responded, throwing a hand up in the stop position. "We're his friends."

The girl was blinking her eyes in a nervous fit and looking around, hardly able to focus. "Yes, you killed him." Like a fish out of water, the girl's mouth fell wide open, and tears burst out, rushing down her face and mixing with the rain. "He was my Gramps!"

"How do you know he's dead?" Hawke asked, trying to keep the rain out of his eyes.

Letting one hand go of the gun, she points past the RV, out in the distance. "This morning, when I arrived, I saw some big ass rats over there. When I walked over, they were feeding. I don't have to tell you on what."

Pax motions downward with her hands, trying to calm the girl. The rain was now drenching them all. "I'm so sorry. What's your name?"

The girl drops the gun to her side and wipes her eyes. "Samantha. Gramps called me Sam."

"Sam," Pax continued. "In the RV, there's a storage compartment with a shovel. We could bury him. Then the rats couldn't get to him."

"I killed them. There were like eight of them. I killed them all with this gun."

"And how is it you know how to use that thing?"

"Gramps taught me. He said everybody should know how to use a gun. It was in his desk drawer. I couldn't find his AK47. Somebody must have taken it." Her eyes opened wide, and her forehead scrunched up in an absurd way. "I thought for sure it was you." She bursts out crying again.

"No, Sam," Hawke replied while cautiously reaching into his pant pocket and pulling out a leather holder. In the pouring rain, he flips it open and holds it out for her to see. "I'm FBI, and Rosie was trying to help us with something when things got out of control. I'm afraid he was caught in the middle of some bad people. It wasn't his fault. It's just that it was a bad situation."

"I'll get the shovel." Pax turns around and yanks at the latch on the RV storage compartment. It was stuck, so lifting a foot, she gave it a swift kick. The mechanism releases, and the door falls open, hitting hard against the ground. Reaching in, she grabs the shovel, slams the compartment door shut, and turns back around. Sam was still wide-eyed. She wore a pink T-shirt and blue jean shorts that only half covered her thighs. The three walked toward a rise in the landscape.

When they top the hill, they are met with an unpleasant odor. The body lay on its back, the face and arms badly eaten by the pack of rats.

"Why don't you let me dig the grave?" Hawke asked, reaching for the shovel.

"No," Pax responded. She places the sole of her shoe on the beveled edge and presses it into the sandy soil. "With the sensory chip, I can do this in like half the time." She continues digging.

Hawke turns his attention to Sam. "How did you get here?" He looks around. "Surely you didn't walk."

"My Honda dirt bike," she answered, pointing back behind them. "I hid it behind the first RV in case the un-friendlies showed back up."

"And where do you live?"

"Not far." Again, she points. "Five, maybe six miles west. It used to be farther until Gramps moved his RVs."

"Do your parents know where you are?"

"I never knew my dad. They tell me he was killed in a cave-in at work, but I know better. I overheard Momma and Gramps talking one day. He was a drug dealer that died in a prison fight. Just last year, my momma died of breast cancer."

Pax hesitates with the shovel. She remains silent for a moment, her striking green eyes glistening in the rain. Her face softens as she looks up from what is already a shallow grave. She asks, "Do you live with relatives?"

"No. When Momma died, Gramps brought me from Philadelphia. They were gonna put me in a foster home, so he adopted me. He paid a family to let me stay with them because he said the RV wasn't a proper place."

"And what now? Will they adopt you?"

"They're illegals." She paused awkwardly. "So, I don't think so."

Pax studied Sam's face. "We'll figure something out, Sam. I promise, okay?"

She nodded, and Pax started digging again with more determination than before. Within ten minutes, she finished burying the body, and they were walking back to the RV. The rain had picked up and was getting heavy. It felt refreshing because the temperature was quite warm. Once they reached the RVs, a government car came driving up. Two men that Hawke recognized pile out and flip open umbrellas. They are FBI, and Nate is one of them.

"Are you alright?" Nate asked as he walked up to them.

"We're fine," Hawke answered. "How did you know we were here? Please don't tell me you planted a GPS tracker."

"No, we tracked your phone. I got some news. General Stackhouse asked me to tell you in person." For a few seconds, Nate looks up, angles the umbrella backward, and scans the cloud-covered sky as if he is looking for something or expects something to happen. The rain poured over his face, wetting him and his nice blue suit. When he looks back at Hawke, he continues. "First off, the general says it's time." Nate glances at Pax, and Hawke nervously follows suit.

"Crazy timing," Hawke answered, wondering how Pax would take it. "I hope you trust me." He was still looking at Pax.

With rain dripping from her she shrugs her shoulders.

Hawke glances back at Nate, rubs his face impatiently, and nods, yes.

Immediately Nate looks over his shoulder at the car and waves for someone to come. Two more people pile out of the car, open umbrellas, and walk up to the group.

Pax couldn't believe her eyes. She appears startled, staring into the faces of Josie and Chili Pepper.

Josie reaches out her hand, her palm touching Pax's cheek. "What's wrong, Honey?" She seemed calm and gentle.

The sound of Josie's voice and the way she touched her reminded Pax of how her mother used to wake her up for school. For a moment, it takes her back in time, and she can see herself crying and her mother consoling her. She can feel her arms wrapped around her, can hear her whispering *my sweet baby girl*, a very peaceful feeling. She snaps out of it, glaring into Josie's eyes. Even though it was raining, her voice suddenly went dry. She tried to swallow but couldn't. "Yo," she sounded hoarse and spoke with considerable effort. She coughed into her hand, trying to moisten her mouth. "Josie, you never talk like that. What's going on?" She looks at Chili Pepper. "And what are you guys doing here?"

After glancing at each other, Josie and Chili Pepper slowly reach out their left arms showing Pax their wrists. Both have identical octopus tattoos. Almost in sync, Nate, Hawke, and the other FBI agent follow up by doing the same. Tension rips through Pax as she stares at five octopus tattoos. She could feel herself, the veil lifting like a spaceship, lifting into the misty, dark afternoon. In three seconds, her brain made the connection. Her head lifts, looking at Hawke. She did not realize that she had reached out and taken his hand. She says, "So, *you guys* are the Argonauts?" Her voice was so hoarse it was nearly unrecognizable.

Hawke nods. "The more you learned, I thought you might figure it out. You sound like you could use a cup of hot coffee. I think all of us could."

Pax twists her head back to Josie and Chili Pepper. "That street talk was just a front, right? I mean, both of you were like, amazing."

Chili Pepper throws up his arms. "Hey, yo, it's all sick, huh? Imma tell you right now, New Eyes like a flash of lightning, a fire shooting from a belt buckle. Café Bella her portal to the underworld." He laughs. "I practiced for weeks getting ready to meet you. And that first encounter where I shoved you against the car. We were trying to test your capabilities."

"Our assignment was to watch you and make sure you were safe." Josie spoke while reaching out and giving Pax a hug. We were on the lookout for enemy spies. "Also, to test you, see how you adapted to the sensory chip." Backing up, she lets Pax go and smiles. "Yo, it all like the dark side of YouTube. True that, true that, but we with you, we fight for you. This ya war, but we fight for you."

"Yo," Pax responded, laughing. "I'm glad you guys are on my side. Now what? Where do we go from here?"

"I'm afraid it's bad news," Nate interjects. "But here goes. "Darcie produced a video that makes Hawke look guilty of treason." He stares at Hawke. "It shows you aiming a gun at Darcie." Motioning outward with his arm, he continues. "Then running and shooting your way out of here. She said if it weren't for her and her hacker friend, Rosie, Pax would be a captive right now. After showing the video to the team, she called for a no-confidence vote and asked that you be suspended. After discussing the matter in private, General Stackhouse and Edward agreed and released her.

Before you get upset, you need to know they put a tail on her and are tracking her phone. They suspect she's working with the Russian Mafia. They've been stealing and reselling technology for a few years now. They're adding to their loansharking, racketeering, and gambling operations.

We did some digging around, and Darcie was in Russia five years ago. It was a shared information program between the FBI and Russia's Federal Security Service. We think the Russian Mafia made contact there. If she's in bed with them, we'll know in a day or two.

There's more, Hawke. The Russian Federation made a power move this morning, invading Alaska. They've taken control of the Diomedes Islands and engaged in an air battle at Tin City. The air force base there fought courageously. After losing a dozen aircraft, they had to surrender. The Navy didn't fare much better. It was a complete surprise. By the time radar detected the invasion, it was too late to stop it. The President will address the nation tomorrow. He's going to downplay it as much as possible. For their part, the Pentagon has demanded the immediate withdrawal of all Russian troops. They've been given two days before war is declared."

"I thought they accepted Gatsby's terms." Hawke quipped back.

"That was just to throw us off, and it worked. They've had this in the planning stages for some time now."

"I see," Hawke said. "Makes sense. What are they asking for?"

"They want transparency with the sensory chip technology and the same with the Timeship. They understand the ramifications."

Hawke continued. "And if the U.S. doesn't comply?"

"Nuclear missiles are aimed at seven major cities, including D.C. Looks like a repeat of the Cuban missile crisis. It's doubtful that they would engage in a nuclear war over this, but it's a good move on their part. In the end, it looks like the Pentagon will have to comply. If not, at the very least, Russia will occupy Alaska for the foreseeable future. And at the worst, well, nobody wants to think about that."

"What does all this mean for me?" Pax asked, pulling Sam close and holding on to her shoulders.

"That's the main reason I'm here," Nate responded. "In five days, two meetings will take place. One's at the Whitehouse. The President and the Secretary of State, along with the Joint Chiefs of Staff will meet with several Russian officials. The other is in Albuquerque at the same hospital where you had the sensory chip implanted.

I'm sorry to have to tell you this, but the Russians want the chip taken out. Until the technology is made available to other countries, they insist on it being non-operational. They've made this clear to the Chinese also. Hopefully, this all gets sorted out within a few weeks, and you don't have to suffer very long. General Stackhouse and Edward wanted me to tell you how bad they feel about this situation. The President has made the call in what he hopes is a show of good faith to the Russian Federation. There's nothing else for us to do but comply. I hope you understand."

Pax moves her arms, wrapping them around Sam and pulling her tight. Next, she reaches out, grabbing Josie by the hand. "I never asked for the sensory chip superpowers to begin with. As far as my eyesight is concerned, I've been blind before. I'll manage it. If it's alright with you, Nate, I've got two requests?"

"Let's hear them. I'll see what I can do."

"First, this girl here, her name is Sam. Sam's grandfather was the hacker friend Darcie mentioned to General Stackhouse. She and her Russian friends killed him. Sam's mother and father are deceased, and there are no other relatives to care for her. I want the Pentagon to intervene and make sure she doesn't end up in foster care. For the time being, she can stay at my apartment. Can you make that happen?"

"Absolutely. What's the second request?"

"The Timeship has been tested once, but Hawke and I were supposed to test it together. General Stackhouse requested it. We planned on that later today. I know things have changed since, but I want to see it through."

"As long as you turn over the Timeship by tomorrow evening's meeting, I got no problem with that."

Suddenly, the rain takes a turn for the worse. They are standing in a torrential downpour. "I think it's time we head back to Albuquerque," Hawke shouts over the stampede of moisture.

"Roger that," Nate replies, tipping his head. "Call me tonight when you've finished testing the Timeship." As quickly as they arrived, Nate and the other FBI agent, along with Josie and Chili Pepper, piled back into their car and drove away.

Chapter 36

Now

The government car carrying the argonauts disappears into torrential rains. "How about that coffee now?" Hawke asked. "And I'll bet Sam could use something to eat." He notices that Pax has closed her eyes and is aiming her head at the ground. "You, okay?" He asked. "Something the matter?"

At first, she does not answer. Instead, she just holds her head, rocking it back and forth. After a few more seconds, she shakes her head and looks up. She says, "We need to go, now!"

"Why? What's going on?"

"While I was touching Josie, I received a projection. I didn't understand it at first, but now I do. She's in danger. They're all in danger. It could be any minute. We have to go before they're attacked."

In another twenty seconds, the three of them were in the Nissan driving away. Pax could see that the wet weather had picked up even more in intensity. She stifled a sigh that was part fear, part impatience. She knew that somewhere, somehow, the rain was going to be trouble.

Hawke maneuvered the Nissan around the dunes, pulled the steering wheel hard right, and belted the car onto the highway. He could not help thinking how millions of dollars a day are made from the sale of technology. And he cringed to think that the Russian Mafia was a player in the game. He slammed the accelerator to the floor and blasted the Nissan into the angry rainstorm. He was certain of one thing. He had to catch up with Nate and the others.

Up ahead, he noticed red and yellow lights. It was obvious there were too many lights for one car. As they drew closer to the lights, three cars came into view, two of them Hummers. Sparks flashed from the Hummers, indicating a barrage of bullets aimed at Nate's car. Suddenly all three vehicles topped a hill, veered left, and went out of sight. To keep the Nissan under control, Hawke locked down on the brakes. The car slowed, and all appeared fine. But when they entered the curve, it spun out, doing a 360 and coming to a screeching stop. Up ahead, the two Hummers crashed into Nate's car. Hawke and Pax watched in horror as the car flipped off the road into a ravine filled with a raging river of water.

Not even on her worst day had Pax seen something so disturbing as Nate's car sinking under the water. She had to act and pressed the button on her seatbelt. As soon as she opened the door, she felt Hawke's hand grab her shoulder. "It's what they want, Pax. If you go out there, they'll shoot you full of holes and take the sensory chip."

Sam is looking over the seat at Hawke and Pax. Sam unknowingly bites at the cuticle on her index finger. She asks, "You're not going to die, too, are you?"

Pax reaches back, gently rubbing Sam's cheek. "No, baby, but I've got to do something. Now sit back and try not to worry. Gazing back at Hawke, she slaps his hand away, reaches over, and grabs his Glock. "If I wait any longer, all our friends are dead!" Twisting to her right, she jumps from the car and runs to the spot where Nate's car had entered the water. She aims and pumps out several shots hoping to keep the bad guys at bay. When a hail of bullets came blasting back, she tucked, rolled, and, lying on her stomach, fired several more rounds. She attempted to get to her feet but was pinned down by a barrage of gunfire.

Inside Nate's car, everyone is unconscious except Josie. Frantically, she attempts to open her door as water fills the car. She tugs at the handle, then twists around and kicks with all the force she can leverage. It's no use. The door is jammed from the impact of the Hummers.

A strange sort of loneliness suddenly hits Josie. She pictures herself drowning and trapped in this car for the next hundred years. And she feels a mysterious connection to the others in the car, as if they are all together in the same suffocating coffin.

The rising water has reached her shoulders, and she is fighting panic. The car is lodged sideways against a large rock. The passenger side doors are blocked, leaving her only one other door to try to open. As the water reaches her neck, she lunges half her body over the seat, reaches past Nate, and attempts to open the door. It, too, is jammed. The water is now at her mouth, and as she thrusts her whole body over the seat, panic sets in. Maneuvering her feet around, she begins kicking at the windshield. Suddenly she is underwater and holding her breath. Her mind is racing.

She had wondered many times when it would happen, and now she knew. Would it be like sleep? Would she be invisible, spiritless? Suddenly, things she had never got to do started blasting away at her. And then, a picture of her father settles in her mind as if he is trying to calm her. Josie can hear his soothing, peaceful voice. She comes back to her senses and realizes that she is still kicking away at the windshield.

Pax has made two more attempts to get to her feet, but with so many guns aimed at her, it's no use. She knows if something doesn't give soon, her friends will drown. She hears the unusual sound of blades slapping air, hitting their own wake vortex. Spotlights from a helicopter come flashing into view. Nate had made a phone call earlier when the two Hummers showed up. This was not an ordinary helicopter. It was a four-blade UH-60 Black Hawk with a top speed of 222 mph. It lowered and hovered like a fire-breathing dragon about fifty yards away. Without warning, two missiles were launched, and after an explosion, the Hummers were turned into a three-hundred-foot-tall mushroom cloud. Darcie and her Russian friends were gone forever.

Seeing her opportunity, Pax springs to her feet, sprints down the road like a Triathlon contestant, veers right, and jumps headfirst into the angry river. Her senses blend together, her arms pulling, her legs kicking, her body streamlined at ten times the thrust of top athletes. She cuts through the dangerous water, swimming as easily as a dolphin. The propulsive forces created by her enhanced senses shoot her like a projectile missile toward the submerged car.

It had been this way forever, sudden cloudburst causing flash floods to fill ravines almost instantly. It was the desert's way of wreaking havoc, of making you long for the wet stuff, and then as soon as it comes, making you fear it. It had taken unsuspecting lives before, animals and humans alike. And at this moment, it is on the verge of taking four more.

When Pax made it to the car, she could see Josie's eyes bulging with fear as she attempted to free herself. Due to the water, she could not get the kind of leverage needed to kick out the windshield. Pax motions for her to stop, then swimming to the other side of the car, she plants her feet against the rock and starts pushing with a herculean effort. The rushing waters push against her, but she manages to free one door. Flinging it open, she waves her arm at Josie, motioning for her to swim out. When she does, so that she is not swept away, Pax takes her with one arm and pulls her through the raging waters. Once they surface, Josie sucks in a huge amount of air and collapses on her side.

Plunging back into the river, Pax wasted no time swimming back to the car. Due to the sensory chip, she effortlessly holds her breath while unbuckling Nate and freeing him. After getting him to the surface, she directs Josie to start CPR, and for the third time, she dives back into the river. Next up was the other FBI agent. Again, she directs Josie to give CPR. When she reaches Chili Pepper on her final descent, a piece of metal caved in by the rock has his arm trapped. She tries but cannot bend the metal back without cutting up her hands. His lungs had filled with water at least three minutes ago, so she knew there was no time to spare. Swimming to the front seat, she pops the trunk release, turns, and swims out of the car around to the backside. She searches for something to bend the metal back, but there is nothing. To the side of the trunk, she notices a twist lever. When she twists it, a panel releases, and she removes it. Inside, there is a bar used to change flats. She must unscrew a nut to free the bar, which takes her a few more seconds. Finally, she has the bar and swims back inside the car.

Wedging it under the metal, she forces it back away from Chili Pepper's arm. She pulls him from the car and rushes him to the surface. Once at the bank, she frantically begins CPR.

Ten minutes later, they were all safe, sitting on the bank of the ravine. The rain had lightened with the sun half peeking out at them behind a few remaining clouds. After a moment of silence, they hear clacking and look up to see dozens of sandhill cranes floating southward toward the horizon. The cranes continue clacking away as if they are resuscitating the exhausted group back to life.

Chapter 37

Now

Standing outside her apartment, Pax yawns, stretches her arms, and catches sight of a stray dog. She had noticed it coming around the last few days. It would stay at a distance but always keep her in its sight. She didn't know if the dog was watching over her or looking for somebody to watch over it. A few days ago, she had started leaving food out. She shoved a bowl with her foot, then backed up several steps. Cautiously, the dog came over. A curious thrill shoots through her as she observes the dog in a feeding frenzy. It was the first time the dog came and fed while she stood there. Usually, it would wait until she went back inside, and the food would always disappear while no one was looking. As it lapped up the food, she wondered how long the little brown mongrel had been searching for a place to call home. She scooted down on her butt, cupped her hands around her knees and watched. When the dog gulped its last bite, it sat on its hind legs and then plopped down on its stomach, never taking its eyes off Pax. It was the first time the two of them could relax around each other.

"What's his name?" A voice asked from the doorway. It was Sam. She was leaning against the casement staring at the dog. The annoyingly cute mutt jumps to his feet.

"Careful. You'll scare him away. He showed up a while back and keeps snooping around. I haven't thought of naming him yet. I wasn't even sure he would stay."

"You should call him Snoop since he keeps snooping around."

"Snoop? I think I like that, Sam."

"He looks like a Jack Russel mixed with Cocker Spaniel. Pax, can I pet him?"

"I don't know. You can try but go slow."

Sam takes three steps and leans down. The dog moves back nervously. "Come on, Snoop," Sam says softly. "I don't think I can take rejection right now."

Snoop glances at Pax as if asking permission. "You can do it, boy," Pax whispered. "Just give her a chance."

He stepped forward and plopped back down on his belly. When Sam started petting him, he rolled over onto his back.

"That's it," Pax said. "He's yours for life if you want him."

Turning her head toward Pax, Sam smiles. "We could get him a leash. They feel safe on a leash like somebody cares about them."

"If that's what you want, sure." Pax stands back up. "Listen, Sam, after a while, Hawke and I have some important work to do. We can't be interrupted for any reason. It'll probably take two or three hours. I can get Josie to come over and keep you company. She lives in the neighborhood, and I think you'll like her."

Sam doesn't look up but just keeps petting the dog. "I'm twelve years old. I don't need a babysitter."

"You're sure?"

"Do you have Netflix?"

"Yes."

"I'm sure."

"Suit yourself. I'll leave her number on the fridge just in case you need something."

After breakfast Hawke and Pax retreated to the bedroom. It would be used as their launching pad to the past. They had an hour before leaving, plenty of time to review the plan. Pax hadn't decided what to say to her mother, and there would be only a small window of time to convince her. She had gone over it a few times in her head, but everything she came up with was over complicated and would take too long to explain. She needed this to be straight forward with as few words as possible.

It would be cold and snowy in D.C. A day earlier they had dug out winter coats, scarves, gloves, and warm boots in preparation. Jack had even purchased hand warmers at Wal-Mart in the sporting goods department. They were usually used by deer hunters for extended time outdoors. They didn't know how long they would be in freezing temperatures, so they were trying to be as prepared as possible.

Pax takes the Timeship and carefully calibrates the coordinates. When finished, she looks up and sees Hawke standing by the door staring at her. He looks like a car salesman waiting for a customer to decide on the red or black one.

"Have you decided what you're going to say?" Hawke asked, leaning back against the casing, and crossing his arms. He seemed concerned or maybe nervous. He had been on edge about time traveling. She had tried explaining to him what to expect, but it hadn't done much good.

She takes him by the hand and pulls him away from the door. Wrapping her arms around him, she softly kisses him. "I can't seem to come up with anything that makes sense. I need to be convincing. To do that I would have to explain some things. There won't be time for all that."

"Have you considered telling her point blank that if she goes back into the house she'll die?"

Pax loosens her arms and steps back. "Just like that?"

He nods and smiles. "Simple is good, don't you think?"

She wraps her arms back around him. Finally, she had some clarity. It would only take a few seconds, and history would be changed. Her mother would be alive. The two fall together onto the bed, rolling and kissing.

"Does this mean you like my idea?" Hawke asked.

"Yes." She sits up on the side of the bed and stands up. "I almost forgot. We need to get our winter clothes on. It's time to go."

Chapter 38

No Second Chance
Twenty Years Ago

Gatsby hesitated, squeezing ten-year-old Paxton's hand, sensing that this had the potential to be a career decision. Churches were supposed to provide sanctuary, but that was not what was happening tonight. A chill from the cold D.C. air had crept under his coat, so he pulled it tight, then reached out and attempted to open the door. The handle was locked to protect against intruders. For the second time, he pulls his coat tight, reaches out, and knocks loudly. Soon an elderly priest opens the door. He looks at Gatsby with compassion and a sense of sorrow as if he were looking at a wounded animal. Next, he glances down and forces a slight smile at little Paxton. Turning to his side, he lifts an arm pointing the way. Looking straight ahead past two dozen or more church pews, Gatsby catches sight of one solitary man. He wears a three-piece suit, and there's a trench coat folded over one of the pews next to him. "Could you watch my daughter?" Gatsby asked the priest. After the priest nodded, he continued. "She's blind, so you'll need to keep hold of her hand." Again, the priest nods.

While Gatsby walked, he peered up at the cathedral ceiling. Paintings of angels marked its exquisite beauty. Other paintings of the apostles along with one of Jesus walking on water gave the illusion of tranquility and peace. The towering stained-glass windows only added to this perception. When he reached the man, he stopped and placed his hands in his pockets. "I'm here as you directed. What is it you want with me?"

The man's chin rises. He says, "You are aware of Sloan's agreement with us?" He spoke with a Russian accent.

"I am," Gatsby responded.

"Good, that will save us some time." The Russian tilts his head, pointing his forehead.

When Gatsby looks behind him, he sees two more men standing with Paxton and the priest. "Say here, what's going on?"

"Did you know your ex-wife tried to back out of our agreement?"

"No, but to begin with, I tried to tell her she was making a mistake."

"In Russia, our agents remain agents for life. If they want out, they are considered a threat and are executed. However, in this case, there's more involved. You already know of her agreement with us. The only way we can be sure you keep this confidential is to take your daughter."

"But I haven't said anything, and I won't. I promise."

"*There is* one other alternative."

"I can't lose Paxton. What is it?"

"*You* replace Sloan."

"What does that mean?"

"It means you will provide us with military technologies."

"But I'm just a lawyer."

"Our intelligence tells us that any new tech comes across your desk before it goes to development."

"Yes, but just the generalities, not the actual drawings."

"You're in charge of protecting the intellectual property in its early stages."

"That's right," Gatsby replied.

"You'll provide us with any new technology that crosses your desk. We'll take it from there. In return, your daughter stays with you."

"What about Sloan?"

"Sloan has already written her future. Russia doesn't give second chances."

"That's not what I'm asking."

"Then what?"

"Don't execute her. Let her live her life out there in Russia. With her education and training, she can be a valuable asset. If you agree, I'll do what you want."

"Sloan's been classified as a threat by my superiors. I'll pass along your wishes, but don't expect anything to change. Now, do we take your daughter or not?"

"No. Leave her be. I'll do what you want."

No Second Chance, Number Two
Three Years Ago

There was silence in the bedroom. A narrow beam of light shot past a tiny crack in the drapes and ran like a child across the carpet. Hawke Gentry hadn't slept a bit that night, which was new to him. Usually, it was waking up that he struggled with, but not since Callie had left him. She had taken Ginger, officially destroying anything good left inside of him.

He watched as Callie stood beside the bed packing the last few things she had in the house. Hawke closed his eyes. He was scared, thinking how stupid he was for letting it get this far. When he opened his eyes, Callie had a small suitcase in one hand and an even smaller box under one arm.

"This is the last of it," she said tiredly as if worn out with the whole subject of separation.

He watched her eyes seeking more words as though they were fleeing before she could articulate them. She gives up, looks at the open bedroom door, and gives an empty stare. "Well, I guess that's it."

Hawke moved forward a step, his head held low, trying to think of a way to release the pain he was carrying. He was hoping to make one last push, anything that might keep Callie and Ginger with him.

To Callie, it seemed that Hawke was thinking deeply or maybe listening to something far away. And then he looked up at her, quiet and serene as if his eyes were talking, telling her things about herself, things that she wouldn't like if he said them out loud. "Did you hear what I said?" She asked.

He realized he was making direct eye contact and hesitated to reply. Then he dropped his head a little and gave a soft smile. He was beginning to cry. "Callie don't do this. I'll try harder. We can work this out."

"It's not you. It's me." She spoke in a low tone just loud enough for him to hear.

His head jerked back up. "Seriously! Now you patronize me."

"Well, it is. You're like the perfect husband, always supporting me when I've had a bad day. You play with Ginger like you were her best friend, and I love that. And your unexpected spaghetti dinners just when I needed a night off were the thing of dreams. I'm tired of making a fool out of you. I don't love you, and I don't even know why."

"You're just confused. We could see a marriage counselor."

"What do you think a counselor will tell me that I don't already know?"

"Then we can take a trip to the mountains. You love Aspen. We could plan a skiing trip. Ginger could stay with your mother. It would work. I know it would."

"Stop it, Hawke. Stop it right there. A skiing trip won't make me love you."

"Just give me a second chance?"

"It's over. I've got to go now. Ginger is with my mother, and I'm running late."

"Then I'm sorry."

"What! I told you it's not you. It's me. God, what's wrong with you?" She turns to leave.

"I'm sorry my being supportive wasn't what you needed. I'm sorry the spaghetti dinners made you feel guilty. And I'm sorry you don't love me anymore, but I'm glad you finally had the courage to tell me."

She stops in the doorway, twisting her head back. For a few seconds, she scrutinized his face, realizing he was finally giving up. Pained by the moment, a sinking feeling hits her in the stomach. Glancing one last time around the room, she remembers when they moved in and when she first realized she was pregnant with Ginger. He didn't deserve what she was doing to him, which pained her even more. Without saying another word, she turned and walked through the doorway.

Hawke closed his eyes, feeling faint, and leaned on the bedpost. Remembering his first date with Callie, he wipes tears from his eyes. After watching an early movie, they had gone to the park that day. They couldn't seem to keep their hands off each other. Their first kiss was deep and long and blew in the summer scented air. Hawke opened his eyes, and for a second, he could still taste her sweetness on his lips. He sits down on the bed and falls back, laying horizontally. He thought about that day until he heard himself crying. Deeply pained, something was breaking inside of him.

No Second Chance, Number Three
Now

Thanks to her calculations, the Timeship had landed Hawke and Pax twenty years in the past. One glance at her childhood house told Pax that there wasn't much time left. She smiled when she noticed her ten-year-old self playing in the snow. It was different than she remembered, the snow not as heavy, the temperature not as cold. The snow animals little Pax is molding seemed different too, not as big, or pretty as she remembered.

"It must feel strange," Hawke notices her staring.

She glances at him, then back to little Pax. "I guess, yes."

He continues, "I love all the colonial-style homes. Is the neighborhood like you remember?"

Pax looks down the street. "The houses are smaller. In my memory, they're much bigger. Everything is smaller, even the mailboxes and trees and cars. I was so certain how this was going to go, how it was going to feel. Now, my memory seems to be unraveling."

Hawke looked surprised and then shook his head. He says, "Perceptions change." He points at little Pax. "That was then." He points back to Pax. "This is now. You can sort it all out later." He looks over the yard. "Are we closer to the house than you expected?"

She nods. "Looks like only fifty or sixty feet from the street."

"That's about right." Hawke looks up into the sky, sticking his tongue out and tasting the snow. After a few seconds he surveys the neighborhood. "God, what a beautiful day. The snow's perfect. The trees are loaded down, the roofs are covered, and there must be about six or seven inches on the ground." He holds his hand out, letting some fall between his fingers.

Pax shakes her head in agreement. "D.C. can be beautiful in the winter." She shifted uncomfortably, noticing a man coming from down the street. "That's him." She points in his direction. "He's the one that goes into the house with my mom."

That means she's going to come running out in a few minutes. Have you thought about what you're going to say, about what we talked about?"

"Yes, but somehow it seems inadequate now."

"Don't overthink it. Simple is good."

"I hope so."

"Besides, you visited her once already."

"I know, but she can be stubborn."

"Don't worry. She'll listen to you. Just tell her straightforward."

"Straightforward. Right. Got it."

And then it happens. Sloan comes blasting out of the house, shouting, *mister, mister.*

Pax has been so obsessed with this moment that she freezes. When Hawke notices, he winces and gives her a shove. "Don't stop breathing. Go, now!"

She darts out into the yard, jumping in front of Sloan and throwing up a hand. She stops her in her tracts. "Mom, it's me. I'm back."

Sloan's eyes are wild looking. She has confusion and surprise written on her face. She says, "Right! And you choose now to show up? What the hell's wrong with you?"

"I came to warn you. If you go back in the house, you will die."

"You might be twenty years older, but you still don't know what you're talking about."

"I do, Mom. I know the history. You die, and I get blinded. But it doesn't have to be that way."

"So, you think you'll just get involved and save me."

"Of course. Like I said, you don't have to die."

"If I don't get that man and go back into the house, *you will die*, and probably Gatsby."

"What?"

"You don't know the first thing about the Russian Federation. I'm doing exactly what they instructed me to do. If I don't, you die. Get it! Now get out of my way before you ruin everything." Sloan shoves Pax to the side and runs up to the man. Ten seconds later, Pax and Hawke watch as the two of them rush back into the house.

With no time to waste, Hawke grabs Pax by the hand and pulls her toward the road. "If you don't want to die here in the snow, you'll run. Come on, run!" The two sprint to the road and duck behind an oak tree. Twenty seconds later, all hell breaks loose, the exploding house rocking the neighborhood. A giant crater opens up along the street, gases ignite, and fire shoots a hundred yards into the sky. In a domino effect, houses, one after another, explode like they're being hit with nuclear missiles. Fiery projectiles from the homes shoot hundreds of yards, sprinkling the landscape. Flashes of light make it appear the snowflakes are on fire.

Shaken but not injured, Hawke and Pax stand cautiously next to the oak tree. "Look, Hawke," Pax shouts. She's pointing at little Pax, who is lying on her back. By the time they reach her, she has stood up. Pax grabs little Pax by the shoulders, and as she pulls her close, she can hear Hawke talking about how damaged the neighborhood is. At this point, little Pax looks up into her face, the two making eye contact. In her memory, Pax realizes that there had been this strange physical connection all along. She remembers it now from when she was ten years old. The man and woman that so kindly helped her through this situation had been herself and Hawke. Warmed by the profound moment, she wondered how it could be. Later she would have to work out the math involved to try and make sense of things.

Suddenly, something even stranger happens. Little Pax, still looking her in the eyes, started talking. "Do you want to help me? Is that why you've come?" Little Pax smiles and continues. "I'm glad you came. You're going to call my daddy now, aren't you? He's going to come and take me home with him. And I'm going to live with him. And one day, when I grow up, I'm going to be you."

Pax was trying to understand how little Pax knew all of this, then it hit her. She had been holding onto her shoulders. Since the two were the same person at different times in their lives, the sensory chip had created a significant projection. It had somehow gotten into little Pax. Little Pax had just witnessed a projection of the future. "I'm going to play it straight with you. Everything you just said is true. Does that scare you?"

"No. Are you going to call our daddy now?"

Chapter 39

Twenty-One Years Ago

Dear Momma

It's been one year and eight months since you died and two months since I made a tape for you. It was a very hot summer, but the heat faded with the passing of August and September. There are cool nights now and damp, chilly mornings here at Daddy's house. I probably should admit something to you right now. At first, I hated living in the city, but now, I am increasingly glad to be here. I don't hurt anymore from the explosion, not even my eyes. Daddy says I have a renewed body. And I don't worry much now. For the last three weeks we've had a cat. It likes to lay in my lap and purr, and I think that's why I feel better. Day by day things are calmer because of the cat, and I don't think so much about the explosion.

Before everything happened and I came here, I was not thankful to you. I know that now, but back then, I did not. I would not pick up my toys, and I was always picking petals off the cherry trees. You would give me glances and tell me where I needed to improve, but I never listened. I liked picking petals very much. But I would listen now, Momma, cause I'm more grown up. I told Daddy that if you were here right now that I would apologize. He said that you would appreciate that and that I should keep on the way because I am headed in a good direction.

Last month at the doctor's office, I met a girl who was not blind but had poor eyesight. She was sitting next to me and spoke in a raspy whisper. She talked about being lazy and thoughtless and said that girls our age should always be having fun. She was nothing like me, but I was at ease with her in a way that I had never been before until that moment. I didn't have to say much because she talked a lot, and I liked that. She told me that she lives in the country and that coming to the city is more eventful. Then she took my hand and said, life likes to play lovely, beautiful tricks on little girls. After that, she started laughing, and I laughed with her. The girl's name is Mary. Daddy told me she could visit me sometime if she likes. Mary's momma agreed, but I think she was just being nice. When Mary was leaving, I told her to keep on the way, but she looked confused like she did not know what I was talking about. Anyway, I really liked her and hope to see her again someday.

While I am recording this tape, I am pretending to look out my window. Pretending makes me feel normal, so I will tell you what I see. It is the twilight of the day on an October evening. A pink color is floating on the border of the horizon, and there is some purple mixed in with it. Some early stars are popping out, and I think it will be dark soon. The moon is sitting on top of a big oak tree in the front yard, and the neighbor across the street is looking out her window at it just like me. Yesterday, Daddy told me I have a good imagination, and I thought you would like to hear an example of it. I do miss the outdoors. Since I have been blind, I don't get out of my room much, so I like to picture it in my mind.

Momma, I like spending time with you when I make these recordings. It makes me think you are sitting right here beside me. I want you to know that other than missing you, everything is alright. Daddy has been good to me, even playing French music that I like very much. He said the singer's name is Edith Piaf. Have you heard of her before?

In case you haven't kept up, this is my twelfth recording. I hope that you have enjoyed them as much as me.

Your daughter, Pax

P.S. I apologize for pulling the petals off the cherry trees.

Chapter 40

Now

Due to an unusually crowded restaurant, Hawke, Pax, and Sam sit at the far end of Café Bella's tables. It's like they're burrowed into a tunnel on the side of a mountain because their view is blocked, and it's dark inside.

Pax has been without the use of her eyes for one month now. Her adjustment has been more difficult than she anticipated. The sensory chip had been taken out to appease the Russian Federation. It was part of a list of agreements with the Pentagon. She's been in darkness ever since. Sam living with her has been helpful but not easy.

Sam sits with one leg crossed over the other, leaning against the wall and playing video games on her phone.

Pax twists a lock of hair around a finger as she sometimes did when nobody was around. Only this time, somebody was here sitting with her and watching her.

"What are you thinking about?" Hawke asked, breaking a lull in their conversation.

His voice sounded distant to her like he was across the room instead of sitting at the same table. She had started to concentrate, separating dreams from memories and just wishful thinking. It had almost lulled her to sleep. Although she didn't mean to, she gave out a restless sigh. "Why are you whispering?" She asked.

"I don't know. I guess because you seemed in deep thought. Did you hear my question?"

"Yes."

"And?"

"I was thinking it would've been nice to have had a best friend growing up. I mean, I had a few friends at school and stuff, but, you know, it's not the same."

"I had a best friend growing up." Hawke said. "It lasted for a couple of years. Then he went away."

"It's always tough when parents move their kids to another town." Pax said.

"That's not where he went away to."

"Then where? Oh, God, I'm sorry."

"It's okay. A drunk driver ran a stop sign. It's been a long time."

"I didn't mean to remind you."

Hawke just waves her off.

As soon as he did, Pax started crying like some slow rain that you know won't end for days.

Sam lowers her phone and glances at her. "What's the matter?"

"It's okay, baby. I'm just, you know, just." She attempts a smile. "Play your games, sweety. The food will be here soon."

"It happened when I was a kid, Pax. Seriously, it doesn't bother me anymore."

"That's not what I'm crying about. A few days ago, I stopped...." She sighs again. "I stopped dreaming. I guess I forgot that would happen. After what I've been through, I thought all the pain had a purpose, that I could get over anything. Then, the dreams stopped. It's the one thing I just don't know about. I don't think I can deal with it."

"They'll come back, Pax."

"When?"

Maria interrupts them. "Okay, guys, One Redeye with a breakfast burrito." She slides them off the tray in front of Hawke. "One cinnamon latte and order of scrambled eggs, and one dark roast with butter croissant." After setting the food in front of Pax and Sam, she points her thumb behind her. "Sorry about the seating arrangement this morning. We're not usually this crowded." She notices the tears dripping from Pax and glances at Hawke. "Is she crying again?"

Pax shakes her head. "Hey, you know I can hear you, right? I'm blind, not deaf."

"Sorry, it's just that you've been doing that a lot lately. Oh, before I leave, in case you didn't know, the President addressed the country a little while ago. Google YouTube, there should be a video on it by now. It's about the Russians and some spy stuff. I'll see you guys later."

"What do you think?" Hawke asked after Maria had gone. He pulls open the coat of his blue suit and takes out his phone. "We should watch it. Hold on. I just received a text. Looks like we got company on the way."

"Who?" Pax asked in between her bites of the croissant.

"Nate, Josie, and they're not saying, but it looks like a surprise guest. They won't be long." He takes a small bite of his burrito. "I'm going to YouTube now." After pulling up YouTube, he turns his attention back to his burrito. Three minutes later, he shifts his chair next to Pax, so she can hear clearly. He punches his phone, and watches as the President speaks.

"*Good morning to all viewers in the North and Southwestern United States, including Alaska. Every American should know that our nation, our freedom, is under constant attack. The two flags you see blowing behind me remind us that we have endured before and will endure again.*

Four weeks ago, several individuals within our country's defense framework were arrested and charged with espionage. Homeland Security uncovered a plot to sell U.S. Military Technology. These traitors were aligned with others around the world who would do our country harm. It is my promise to you that all parties involved will be prosecuted.

This past month has been a difficult one, especially for those Americans living in the great state of Alaska. We want to inform you that, as of right now, the Russian Federation is withdrawing all troops from Alaska. Within the next seven days, our country's borders will be secure again. The unprovoked invasion has allowed for a closer look at all Pentagon policies. To avoid future military confrontations, American and Russian officials have agreed in writing to a much more open sharing of all advanced military technologies. This understanding has put our two nations on stable ground with each other. We anticipate our relations only getting better with continued future dialogue.

In conclusion, I would like to express my thanks to all of you who have shown courage and patience during this time of peril. Thank you for tuning into today's broadcast. More information regarding the traitors will be given in due time."

Hawke slides his chair back to the other side of the table. "You know what this means, don't you?" He asked with a hint of excitement in his voice.

Finishing off her croissant, Pax shakes her head. "No, what?"

"It means the negotiations are over. You get your vision back."

Pax fell back in her chair, almost spilling her coffee. "Are you serious? How soon?"

"I don't get to make that call, but sooner than you think. Wait, I just got another text. Nate says to come outside. He's here with Josie. He says, look for the large white van." Hawke glances at Sam. She'd been listening and was smiling back at him. "Sam, take Pax by the hand."

Sixty seconds later, the three are standing next to a cargo van in the parking lot. Nate's positioned at the back end of the van. Without a word, he grabs hold of a handle, presses down with his thumb, and opens the door. Inside the van was Josie, sitting at a metal table with a small box. Farther back in the van is the surprise guest. It's Gatsby. Nate motions with his arm, and they help Pax inside, seating her at the table.

"Yo, it's me, Pax," Josie said. "I need you to relax and hold your head back, okay?"

"I'm a little nervous. Could you tell me what's happening?"

"I'm going to put some drops in your eyes. After that, I install the contacts."

"Do you mean the ones with cameras?"

"Yes."

"But what about the sensory chip? They took it out a month ago. The cameras won't work without it."

"That's true. The Russians insisted on it. However, another one was installed in its place. What they don't know won't hurt them. You won't suddenly turn into a ninja, but your eyesight will return. Now, lean your head back. That's good." Josie applies two drops to each eye. "How does that feel?"

"It's fine."

"Close your eyes for me. That's good. Okay, open. Now for the contacts. First, the left. This won't take a second. Perfect. Blink a few times. Now the right. Just a few more seconds. That's it. Now, blink for me again. Good. Everything feel, okay?"

"Yes. I hardly notice them."

"Give me a minute. I need to switch them on." Josie turns to her left and punches away at a computer. "Fergus, the technician, would normally be doing this, but he and Dr. Tennison are sitting in jail for espionage. But don't worry, I've been trained, overtrained, actually. And I have a medical background. Okay, just a little longer. There's a little bit of a delay while they connect with the sensory chip. You might want to close your eyes and open them slowly. There, all done. You can open your eyes now."

When she opened her eyes, the scene was crystal clear. "Dad? I didn't know you were here. I'm so excited. My heart's beating out of my chest. Finally, a face and feelings that go together." The two quickly embrace.

"The President pardoned me," says Gatsby. "Have you heard?"

"No, Dad."

"When Homeland Security investigated, there were some extenuating circumstances." Gatsby let her go and stepped back. "There are some things you need to know."

"I don't understand. What things?"

"It wasn't about the money."

"What are you talking about?"

"The money. You thought I sold secret technology for money. The Russians never paid me a dime."

"Then why would you do something like that. You made yourself a Benedict Arnold."

"No."

"Yes. You betrayed your country."

"It's not what you think."

"Then what? Tell me. Help me understand."

"The story is complicated. First, there's someone I want you to meet. After that, you can decide if I'm a traitor for yourself. Why don't we get out of this van."

When Pax stepped outside, she grabbed Hawke by the arm. "Do you know what this is about?" She asked.

He shook his head. "I don't know any more than you do."

Gatsby directed her to a gold SUV next to the van. The windows were tinted too dark to see inside. He points. "Go to the passenger side and get in."

She could not picture what was in the SUV, so she walked over, opened the door, and sat down. In the driver's seat was a middle-aged woman looking straight ahead. She appeared nervous or agitated and, at first, just sat there quietly. After about a minute and without turning her head, the woman started talking. "Paxton, you need to pay close attention to what I'm about to say because it's important. I want you to know that I made a terrible mistake. I was eaten up with ambition, and it cost me everything. It's my fault that you were blinded all those years. All the pain you have experienced is my fault. When I realized the explosion blinded you, it was like my heart shattered into a thousand pieces."

Shaken by the raw, aching words, Pax reaches over and turns the woman's face. "Momma." Tears are running down the woman's face.

"It's me, Paxton. I'm your mother."

"But you died. I saw the house explode. There was nothing left of it." Now Pax is crying.

"It was all staged." Sloan continues, "The Russians needed the CIA to believe I was dead. I walked straight through the house, right into Russian hands. Of course, they didn't expect it to blow the whole freaking neighborhood up. It was only supposed to blow the kitchen out."

"I don't understand."

"No, you wouldn't. You're completely innocent. When I finished my training at Langley, they didn't use me as an operative. I had waited so long and done everything they asked of me. The Iranians wanted me to work for them, but it was the chance to work for Russia that got me. To me, it was my *James Bond* moment. It sounds silly now, but at the time, it meant seeing my dream come true. After I had done the deal, my superior at Langley informed me I was approved as an operative. I thought, God, seriously, now you approve me. He said that they wanted me to go through three more months of specialized computer training, and then I would receive my first assignment. I was in a group of six that would receive the training. They would then plant us deep undercover in Europe and the Middle East. It's what I had always wanted. I also got an offer from another secret government organization. When I backed out of my deal with the Russians, I had no idea they planned to kill me. If it weren't for Gatsby, they would have. In the end, they agreed to keep me alive as long as Gatsby funneled them information on any new Pentagon technologies. He's done that for the past twenty years. After this month's agreement with the Pentagon, the Russians no longer need me. For the last two weeks, Gatsby's been working on my release. Your father is not a traitor. It's because of him that you and I are alive today. I'm so sorry that I ruined your life. I ruined my life, Gatsby's life, our whole family. When the weight of what I had done hit me, I didn't want it to be real, but it was too late."

"But why, momma? Why did it mean so much to you?"

For a moment, Sloan twists her head, looking out the window. She sees Gatsby talking with some others that she does not recognize. She wonders if they are CIA and figures they probably are. She moves her head back and gives out a little sigh. She says, "Being an operative means living life at its highest level. It's as demanding as any form of human activity, as satisfying as a fine work of art, and as thrilling as a duel to the death. I was addicted to the idea; I was obsessed." Again, Sloan glances out the window at Gatsby. She notices a little girl standing close to him, a skinny girl with a pretty face. For a few seconds, she tilts her head back, rubbing at her brow, realizing that there's so much she's missed out on. "There is always a price for obsession." She spoke with pain knotting in her jawbone, pulsing through her voice. "It will dangle its opportunity and then assimilate you.

When it's all over it has destroyed your life. My obsession cost me everything. All it gave back was isolation and estrangement. I parachuted into the middle of it, and I was trapped. Maybe that's the point. Maybe you must go to that other side where there's no way out to entirely understand what you've become. Now that I've been rescued from the trap, I can say with sincerity that falling into obsession is falling into madness. Once you've done it, you'll spend a lifetime trying to escape."

"Well, if it means anything, you didn't ruin my life. I still love math and had a great education." Pax slowly scoots over and places her head on Sloan's shoulder. "I used my math skills to prove time travel. I'm closer to Dad than ever, which is really saying something. I even met a man and fell in love. So, you didn't ruin anything."

"You *would* say that. You're so much like your father."

"No, we're nothing alike. He can be a real ass."

"He changed; I admit. But that was my fault. Before I walked out on him, he was the kindest, most giving person I had ever met. And he could be funny too, especially when he was trying to impress me. I did love him, God, I still do."

"When I fell in love with Hawke, that's his name, it happened when I didn't expect it."

"Love comes into your life in its own time, not when you're ready. How does he make you feel?"

"When I'm with him, everything is clearer, deeper, more beautiful. I'm comfortable being me. He's like home."

"He sounds like the one."

"He is."

"I had that with Gatsby. Did you know that he was dating another girl when he met me?"

"He never mentioned it."

"I guess he wouldn't. She was prettier and more appealing. He chose me anyway. I don't know how, but I had his heart. I had it until I went and blew it all to smithereens. That poor man, he tried to tell me, to help me. He warned me over and over. My biggest regret is that I loved my job more than him. That's a terrible thing to realize about yourself. I walked away from the best thing that ever happened to me. I lost him, and I lost you. It's strange too because I didn't realize it when it was happening. I generalized it. I would talk about the issue at work and sometimes with the neighbors. I made it seem unavoidable, a once good marriage where two people are just moving in different directions. When talking about it didn't work, I would just grab the scotch and get drunk.

There was nobody to talk to in Russia. I had to deal with things on my own. For years I would lie awake at night. I used to wonder what Gatsby saw in me. And I used to wonder why we decided to have a kid. We were both happy and busy with work. Why did we want a family when we were still getting to know each other? It wasn't like we had this giant need to get pregnant. I guess a lot of men and women wonder about that, but in Russia, I had a lot of time on my hands. For years I couldn't figure it out, and then one night, it came to me. It was just there, so beautiful, crystallized in my mind."

Pax lifts her head off Sloan's shoulder and looks her in the face. "What was it?"

Shifting her feet, Sloan crossed her legs and angled herself straight at Pax. She softly kisses Pax on the cheek and rubs both hands on her face. "I think everyone, subconsciously, knows it. Procreating, giving life is the greatest act of love. Together, Gatsby and I wanted to be a part of that. Once you've done that, there's no going back. You've participated in something bigger than all of us. It's the reason for everything. The one thing we got right was having you."

Chapter 41

Now

Hawke has left for work already, backing out of the parking spot in his Nissan Rogue. It had become a habit of his, staying with Pax and Sam. From the time they had met Sam, they had been like a ready-made family.

Suddenly a voice comes from the Rogue's back seat. "Are you going to marry her?"

Taking a deep breath, Hawke squeezes the steering wheel, trying to steady himself. Moving only his eyes, he peers into the rearview mirror. "I haven't seen you in a while."

Ginger lunges forward, placing one hand on his shoulder and one on the passenger seat. "Are you going to answer my question?"

"We haven't discussed marriage."

"That's not what I asked."

"Okay, then probably."

She falls back into the seat. "Good. I like her."

"Why do you like her?"

"Because she's like me. She's just a little girl. She doesn't know what the world can do."

"You keep saying that? But she's a grown woman."

"She's been blind since she was a kid."

"But she's got her eyesight back now."

"Then she can grow now, like me. She can find out what the world can do. We can find out together."

"I guess you're right. I guess she's just now learning."

"Can I have some breakfast?"

"Of course. What would you like?"

"A cheeseburger."

"You can't get a cheeseburger for breakfast. We've talked about this before. Nobody sells them."

"That place that has the firetruck sitting out front does."

"That's on the other side of town. How about some eggs and toast?"

For the second time, she lunges up in the seat. "Can I have French toast?"

"I think we can work that out."

She throws both arms straight up. "Yee-hah! Yee-hah! I love you, Daddy. Yee-hah!"

Hawke had always been captivated by her energy, so honest, so relentless. He waves a hand at a fly buzzing around the cab of the car and suddenly notices how bright the sky is today. A redbird lifts from a tree branch, and he watches as it shoots down and zips across the road in front of his car. When he looks back into the rearview mirror, Ginger is gone.

Later that day, Hawke sat staring around Mona's office. On a desk was a photo of Mona and her husband. More family photos seemed to be showing off as they stretched the entire length of a wall. Another wall had two rows of framed citations, proof of the psychologist's excellent education. "How long do I have to do this?" Hawke asked, slumping back in a chair.

Mona taps a yellow pencil on her desk. "Nobody's holding a gun to your head."

"So, that's it then? I don't have to come back?"

"If I release you, no, you don't. I think it would be a mistake. However, if it's what you want?"

"I'm all better. It's what I want."

"Are Ginger and Callie still a part of your life? Do you still communicate with them?"

"Yes, but it's all good."

"We've been over and over this. They're not real."

"They don't have to be real. They just have to feel real, and they do."

Mona taps her pencil a few more times and forces a smile. "What do you think of your progress? Do you think I'm helping you?"

Hawke sits up in his chair, right to the edge, almost standing up. "Absolutely! You helped me to see that my being happy is not a betrayal. And I don't blame myself anymore. Oh, and your patience with me, it's..." He glances around the room a second before settling back on her. "I don't know how you managed it."

"You still hallucinate. In the world of psychology, that means I've failed you."

Hawke places his hands on his knees and then on the edge of Mona's desk. "I suppose in some cases, that would be true. But I don't want Callie and Ginger to go away."

Mona smiles again, this time it spread across her face. "Then they won't."

Leaning his weight on the desk, Hawke stands up. "You've helped me to see that there are things that happen that I can't control. We all deal with life, right?"

"Yes."

"All the little cuts that life gives you year after year, right?"

"I couldn't agree more."

"Well, I'm dealing with life now. And I think that's the most any person could ask."

In Mona's heart, there was a struggle taking place. It was clear to her that Hawke was in a good place, the best he had been in years. However, her training told her that he was in a battle, one he didn't even know he was fighting. In the end, she decided to let things play out. He was doing better now, so the hallucinations would eventually stop. It was a judgment call, one she thought was the right one under the circumstances. If she pushed him now, it would only reverse the progress made. "I'm going to sign off and release you. Don't be surprised, though, if I ask you how you're doing once in a while."

"If you didn't, I'd be disappointed."

Back at the apartment, Pax stood completely nude in front of her dresser. She had just finished showering and was picking out panties and a bra. To her surprise, she hears Sam's voice. "I hope I look like that one day."

When Pax looks up, Sam is standing in the doorway. "You're barely twelve, Sam. You have the frame and a pretty face. There's plenty of time. What really matters is being happy."

"I'm already happy."

Pax pulls out a pink mini-mouse t-shirt and holds it up for Sam to see. Sam nods in agreement with her choice. "So, you like living here?" She asked and slipped the shirt on.

Sam walks farther into the room. "Yeah. Do I get to stay?"

"I'm going to adopt you if that's what you want." Pax sits on the side of the bed, leans back, and slides both legs into a pair of jeans. After she stands up, she buttons and zips up. "Could you hand me those black and white Converse shoes? They're next to the closet door."

Sam quickly retrieves them, takes a few steps, and hands them over. "Does that mean you'll be my mother?"

Pax hesitates a moment before putting on the shoes. Both she and Sam are staring at each other. "It means I'll be your guardian, the person responsible for you."

"Is that the same thing as a mother?"

"Yes. I would be your mother by adoption, and you would be my adopted daughter. But look, Sam, you don't have to call me mother."

"I want to."

"You do? You're comfortable with that?"

"Yes. Are you?"

Hit with an unexpected rush of emotions, Pax glances down. Suddenly, she drops the shoes, springs to her feet, lunges over, and embraces Sam. "I want to, Sam, darling. I want to, I want to, I want to."

"Mommy you're squeezing me too tight."

"Oh, god." She releases her. "Sorry, I'm just, would you like some eggs? I can scramble some up for us. And we have waffles."

"Okay, but first, can I feed Snoop?"

"Yes, feed Snoop. Then get dressed and walk him through the apartment complex. When you get back, I'll have breakfast ready."

Twenty minutes later, Pax is in the kitchen finishing up breakfast when she hears the door open. "Sam!" She shouts. "Do you want orange juice?" She walked the eggs and waffles to the dining room table, which was mostly open to the living room.

When the door shuts back, her eyes glance over. Across the room stood a surprise guest, Darcie Hannagan.

"You sleep late these days, Pax." Darcie reaches around to her back, pulling a Glock handgun out. "It's already a quarter of ten. I think Hawke's been a bad influence."

Pax nervously sets the food on the table and rubs her forehead. "What is it you want?"

Darcie smiles and shakes her head. "I didn't think you would need to ask. I want the same thing I've always wanted."

"Then you must've been in a commune somewhere because they uninstalled my sensory chip. All you'll get is the vision technology."

Again, Darcie shakes her head. "If I take it, I get ten million dollars. I'm not sure the sensory chip is worth all the fuss. Nevertheless, I'm here to retrieve it because that's a hell of a lot of money. I'll sit on a beach sipping umbrella drinks and saluting the Pentagon with my middle finger."

"I told you they uninstalled it."

"What they did was a pretense. Oh, I don't blame the Pentagon, and neither should you. Espionage is a dirty game, and nothing will ever change that. Besides, it was nothing compared to the Russians invading Alaska. Now that was a dirty rotten move. My sources tell me you have the same chip in your brain. They just used a computer geek to deactivate it."

Grabbing hold of the back of a chair, Pax squeezes tight and audibly sighs. "How did you survive?" She asked.

"I was wondering when you would get around to that. It was a close call." She lifts one arm and shows Pax a severe burn on the backside of it. "I have a larger one on my back. That freaking Black Hawk chopper nearly got me. As soon as I saw it, I knew the drill. Get the hell out of Dodge or die. I jumped, rolled, and ran. The others weren't so lucky."

"What now?"

"Now the sensory chip. After all the crap I've been through, I'm gonna take great pleasure watching them dig that thing out of your skull. And if you're thinking about trying something." Darcie makes a fist and pounds the door three times.

Two men walk in. One carries a medical-style briefcase. The other one has Sam clutched in his hands and a gun pressing against her head. "If you try anything, the girl's dead."

"You can take the chip. Just don't hurt her."

Darcie waves the gun at the kitchen table. "You're gonna lie down there, on your stomach. Clear the table and do it now."

Before Pax can pick up the plates, there is a hard knock at the door.

Surprised, Darcie backs herself against the door wall. She motions for the others to do the same, then lip-syncs for Pax to get rid of the visitor. Waving Pax to the door, she repeats her lip-sync. "*Get rid of them, and don't try anything.*"

As soon as she swings open the door, words come blasting back at her. "Yo, New Eyes, where you been, girl? I been asking round. And why you dodgin' me? What's up with that? You like turtle in a shell. You ditch Café Bella."

Chili Pepper was back to his street talk, which told Pax the Argonauts knew what was happening. They probably had her apartment bugged. "Yo, Chili Pepper, sorry about the hiatus. I've been busy lately. And besides, sometimes you do the same thing. I don't see you for days."

"True that, true that. I been wondering is all. If New Eyes need backup, Chili Pepper way onto that."

"No, no, I'm good here. I'm just really busy. In fact, I need to go check on Sam right now. Tell you what, I'll see you tomorrow at Café Bella. Sound like a plan?"

"Yo, see ya on the flip. You come chill, have fun." Chili Pepper lunges forward, giving Pax a tight hug. Almost immediately, she feels a surge inside her. It's a projection, which means the sensory chip is fully activated. She sees Josie and Nate close by, armed and ready. Things are about to get seriously hairy. Chili Pepper releases her and turns to walk away. "Later, New Eyes."

Once the door is shut, Pax is again staring into the barrel of a Glock. "What the hell kind of talk was that?" Darcie shouted.

Pax shrugged her shoulders. "It's just street talk. I kind of like it."

"He sounds like somebody hit him in the head with a shovel. Now get back to the table."

Pax isn't budging this time. Her eyes squint, and her head tilts downward. She's pushing down with the ball of one foot, twisting it on the floor like an auger bit. She's slightly bent at the knees, and her arms are in the karate position.

"Get to the table, now! You know what happens if you don't."

Darcie could have never anticipated how lightning-quick Pax would move. Springing from the ball of her foot, she does a back twist followed by a lunge. The move was made with the speed of a striking snake. By the time Darcie pulled the trigger, Pax had slipped behind her. She slams a fist into Darcie's arm, and the gun flips through the air. In continuous motion, she raises a leg and kicks behind her, catching the man holding Sam directly in the head. Both Darcie's gun and the man hit the floor at the same time. The man is out cold. The other man holding the medical briefcase wraps his arms around the case and backs against the wall.

"Sam!" Pax screams. "Get the guns!"

Quickly, Sam takes one gun from the knocked-out man and the other from the floor. Everything happened so fast. Pax had appeared to make one move, but in reality, it was a series of moves.

Standing there with one gun in each hand, Sam seems startled by Pax's abilities. She moves back, putting as much distance between them as she can. While doing this, she watches Pax shove Darcie to the floor.

Darcie's next words take Pax completely by surprise. "Now, Sam, shoot her. Do it now!"

Sam aims both Glocks at Pax. She says, "If you move, I'm gonna have to shoot you. So, don't."

"Sam! What are you doing?"

"How do you think we knew the time was right to come here today," Darcie shouts. "I really appreciate you giving her a phone. It made things a lot easier. She works for us, dumbass. She's been feeding us information the whole time."

"What? No. It makes no sense." Pax looks hard at Sam, her face pleading with her. She says, "Everything we've been doing. I mean *everything!* It was all for you. Darcie killed your grandfather. You can't let her get away with that."

"I'm sorry, Pax. Rosie's not my gramps. I made it all up."

"I don't believe you. I would've known."

"And yet, you didn't," Darcie interjects. "That freaking chip in your brain's not that perfect after all."

Pax looks down beside her at Darcie. "The chip's just fine. I don't know what you did to her, what you're holding over her, but she's lying. With the sensory chip, *I see everything.*" Pax isn't close enough to make a move on Sam. And she doesn't want to risk the nervous girl pulling the trigger.

And then, unexpectantly, the man squeezing the briefcase grabs a gun away from Sam. At the same time, the front door swings open. The man wastes no time firing several rounds at Pax. Two miss, instead, zipping through the room and blasting the kitchen table. Another hits Pax in the shoulder, and still, another is a direct hit in her chest. Several more shots ring out as Josie and Nate rush into the room. Blood is spattered on the wall as the man with the briefcase falls over dead. Sam is struck in the abdomen. The blast knocks her to the floor. During all the shooting and confusion, Darcie bolts out the door, escaping.

Both Sam and Pax lie on the floor, bleeding badly. Josie punches frantically at her phone.

"911, what's your emergency?"

"I got two victims with serious gunshot wounds. I need an ambulance at 238 Bogdon Street, apartment 112."

"Are they conscious and breathing?"

"One of them, yes, but I think the other might be dead."

"Can you check for a pulse?"

"Have you sent the ambulance?"

"Yes, ma'am, that's already done. Now, could you check for a pulse?"

With her tongue partially hanging out, Pax lies with her head to one side. Josie winces, kneels, and is overcome with emotion, nearly passing out. There are no signs of breathing as her hand falls upon Pax's neck, searching for a pulse.

"Ma'am," the operator said. "If she has a pulse, move her on her side. She can breathe better that way."

"I think she's dead," Josie responded. Suddenly, on the other side of the room, Sam jumps up, holding her abdomen. Attempting to escape, she takes two steps and collapses halfway into Nate's arms.

Meantime, Pax is unconscious and near death. Her brain is being deprived of oxygen. This causes her to sink into a hallucinatory dream state. Although she is cold and lying in a pool of blood, she feels a hazy warm air casting down on her. To her, it is a sunny day at the beach. She lies on a blanket listening to the ocean water splashing on the beach. Her golden tanned body is lying between a cooler of drinks and several beach towels. While she stares up into the sky, she can feel beach foam on her feet. Running passed her and giggling are several girls wearing strawberry-colored bathing suits. She hears the voice of Hawke and can see his eyes looking straight down at her.

In reality, it really is Hawke. He had been informed about the situation and had rushed back to the apartment as quickly as his Nissan would carry him. He is kneeling over her talking to her. "Pax, Pax, can you hear me?"

She has no idea that she is lying there about to bleed out. "Hawke," she responds weakly. And one more time, "Hawke?"

He kneels even closer, their faces almost touching. "What is it you're trying to tell me?"

"I love it when I get caught in your stare." Her conscious moment was brief. Barely clinging to life, her eyes close, and her body goes limp.

Hawke hears sirens roaring inside the apartment complex.

Chapter 42

Six Months Later

Hawke waited on the front porch of a small white house. A soft clicking sound could be heard from behind as Nate walked up the steps. "Did you see all the apple trees?" Nate asked as he reached the top step. "There must be two dozen or more."

Turning to look, a sudden burst of wind blows Hawke's tie over his shoulder. He pulls it down and holds it in place, then glances across the side of the yard and notices the fruit trees are so thick that they are touching each other. The day is bright, the wind stirring wildly, rustling a group of hedges adjacent to the porch. Shadows are darting around the ground beneath the trees due to the stiff wind.

He acknowledges Nate as he walks up next to him, then as he turns, he sees his reflection on the glass transom running up beside the door. It hits him that he has the classic look of FBI and for a fleeting second, he is filled with pride. He reaches out and gives several firm knocks.

When Darcie's mother opens the door, she looks the suited men over. She says, "Let me guess, more private detectives. You guys are younger and more handsome than the last ones."

Reaching into his coat pocket, Hawke pulls out a leather holder, flips it open, and displays his FBI badge. "Are you Dorothy Hannagan?"

"Yes, but they call me Dora. Been that way for sixty-eight years."

Hawke smiles, nods, places his badge in his coat, and continues. "Dora, are you the mother of Darcie Hannagan?"

"Yes."

"Could you tell us what detectives were doing here?"

"Someone hired them to look for Mousey."

Both Hawke and Nate give a glance at each other. "Who's Mousey?" Nate asked.

"Why don't you two step inside before the wind blows you off the porch." While they walk in, she continues talking. "It's Darcie. Her father, Pete, we both called her Mousey because she was sneaky and quiet, showing up when you least expected. I can't tell you how many times she came into our bedroom without us knowing."

"Is Mr. Hannagan here?" Hawke asked, turning, and looking around the room. Instead of drapes on the windows, there were California Shutters. All of them are open, allowing in the bright sunshine. There was a leather sofa, walnut in color, with four blue pillows. Directly in front of the sofa was a glass-top coffee table with painted figurines in the shape of people. Beyond the table were two Stonehurst accent chairs with vegetable motif patterns. The room is nicely decorated. However, nothing is hanging on the walls other than a couple of paintings with French city scenes.

Dora had a narrow face framed by gray hair and wrinkles. Even so, there was a cuteness and openness about her. "Pete's in a nursing home suffering from Alzheimer's. He's in the final stage, on death watch. It could come at any minute."

"Sorry to hear that, ma'am," says Nate.

Hawke lifted a hand and scratched at the side of his neck. He asks, "Have you seen Darcie lately or spoken with her?"

"She showed up three weeks ago to visit her father. She spent the night, which surprised me. She doesn't care too much for Pennsylvania, especially the Philadelphia area. She loves D.C. You probably already know that's where she lives. So, after that, she said she had some business to take care of out west. Albuquerque, I think."

"Did you know she was in some trouble," Nate asked. "Did she talk about that?"

"I hadn't heard from her in several months. Then she shows up out of the blue. I figured something was up. No, she didn't mention anything. A week later, those detectives showed up. They wouldn't give details, but it was clear that she was into something serious. You should probably know that Mousey was a suspect in a missing person's case when she was just sixteen. It was a girl she knew in high school. The girl's family thought Mousey was involved, they still do. Due to lack of evidence, Mousey was cleared. I always wondered about that because that girl was in our house a lot. She had been with Mousey every day when she suddenly went missing. Mousey swore she didn't know anything."

"What do *you* think?" Hawke asked.

"I always thought she had to know something."

"Did you know she was FBI and had connections to the CIA?"

"FBI, yes. CIA, no. It fits her, though. That quiet, sneaky thing is what the CIA is all about. What's she done? Is someone else missing?"

"She's suspected of involvement with an organized crime ring," Hawke replied. "We can't tell you specifics while the case is under investigation. Dora, Mousey could be out there right now hurting someone. Is there anything else you can tell us that might help us track her down?"

Even at sixty-eight, Dora's eyes were still filled with a deep blue color. She attempted a grin, but it didn't last. Cowering her head, she gave out a sigh. "There are two things. One of them I'm certain of, the other, well, I'm not as sharp as I once was. When her father dies, she will come back to kiss his coffin." Dora's head pops back up. "You can bank on that. She was way closer to him than she ever was to me. When they thought she had something to do with that girl's disappearance, Pete hired the most expensive lawyer. We had to hock our house to pay that man. But it worked. He knew every button to push. Mousey was a minor, so the police had to go through that lawyer. They quit looking into her real fast. The second thing is I can't find my cellphone. I've been looking all over, but it's nowhere to be found. Now, I could have misplaced it. I am getting up in years. Truth is, though, I suspect Mousey took it. She didn't have one when she was here. Those two things are all I got."

When Dora first answered the door, she was cheerful and lively. That was before discussing Mousey. The complexion in her face has whitened, her words coming out slower. "Did you know Mousey had a twin?" She asked.

For the second time, Hawke and Nate glance at each other. "No," Nate responded. "Girl or boy?"

"Girl."

"Does she live around here? Can we get her contact information?"

"That would be impossible. Jessie, that was her name. We always called her Jess. She died when she was nine years old. Accidental drowning, that's what the coroner said. He found doxylamine in her system. That's an antihistamine used in some cough syrups. It makes you drowsy. The coroner noted from the levels he discovered that she must have drunk a whole bottle before getting in the bathtub. She fell asleep. You can guess the rest. When I found her, it was way too late. She was as purple as a plum.

I'm going to tell you something I never told anyone before. I don't think it was an accident, never did."

"What makes you say that?" Nate asked.

"For one thing, Jess wasn't sick. Physically there was nothing wrong with her. Why would she drink cough medicine? And then there was that other thing that always bothered me. Most twins are drawn to each other, some even inseparable. With Mousey and Jess, it was the opposite. They bickered and fought all the time. Mousey weighed more and was more assertive. She was the dominant, smart one. I can't prove it, but I think she forced Jess to drink the cough syrup and, when she fell asleep, held her under the water. There was water all over the bathroom floor. To me, it looked like Jess woke up and fought like hell. Mousey had her pinned down. She never had a chance.

About a year later, I couldn't take it anymore. I point blank asked Mousey if she killed her sister. She wouldn't answer me, so I squeezed her arm and forced her. She jerked her arm right out of my hand and looked at me, all red-faced and pissed off. That's when it got really weird. She suddenly calmed down and got this large smile on her face. Then she started laughing, I mean like out of control laughing. She never said a word. I just turned and walked away. I've never mentioned my suspicions before because who would believe a nine-year-old could do something like that. I don't know what she's into right now, but you guys had better stop her. I got a bad feeling that if you don't, someone's going to die."

"Dora, would you be willing to help us?" Hawke asked.

"What is it you think I can do? I've told you everything I know."

"Ordinarily, I would never ask something like this. It's just that I don't see another way. We need you to fake your husband's death."

"But that's illegal."

"I promise you won't get into any trouble."

Dora's eyes start wandering around the room. "Oh, dear, I didn't even invite you to sit down. Go on now. The sofa's comfortable, and I'll get you a glass of Iced tea."

"That won't be necessary," Hawke said. "Thank you just the same. Will you help us, Dora? Will you help us stop Mousey?"

She reaches up, placing one hand on her forehead. "I always used to think I was a horrible person because I wished it had been Jess that survived. Can you imagine a parent thinking like that? I still feel that way. Jess was kinder, softer, and she wasn't a sneak. The only reason she fought with her sister was that she knew how cruel she was." Dora drops her hand and looks Hawke straight on. "Just tell me what you need me to do."

Chapter 43

Timing is Everything

Darcie Hannagan was a chameleon. She had a knack for looking like one thing when she was the opposite. Case in point: how she confused and manipulated Sam.

When she made it as an FBI agent, she quickly became their number one investigator. Interviewing suspects was her specialty. She was super tough and relentless, but she transformed herself when she walked into the interrogation room. She started with an affectionate tilt of the head, nurturing smile, and a courteous approach. Suddenly, she was so damn friendly and nice that she could get into anyone's mind and slide unsuspectingly into their heart. She became the fragile face and the gentle voice of a best friend. Anyone would tell her anything, which earned her the admiration of her superiors. They had no idea that she had been doing this her whole life.

At the moment, she sits in a Rio Rancho parking lot, eyeing an apartment building. Her car is a gray Grand Cherokee with dark tinted windows. It's a color that quietly blends in, going unnoticed like a mouse.

Her face is pale and a little drawn in due to a lack of sleep. The Russian Mafia haunts her now and keeps her looking over her shoulder. It has been that way since she failed to deliver the sensory chip. The mafia had a deal to sell it to the Iranians for half a billion dollars. Losing that amount of money is a solid reason to be pissed. So, she's been moving around a lot, from D.C. to Philadelphia and out west to L.A. and Albuquerque. If they ever catch up with her, it will be her demise. She knows the business all too well, though. If she can stay ahead of them long enough, they'll lose interest and move on.

Here comes the reason she has been waiting in the parking lot; it's walking out of the building. It's a woman, a girl, and a dog. She swallows hard, trying to remain calm, but anger is building in her. Next to her in the passenger seat is a shoulder holster with a Glock 19/9mm. In one smooth move, she picks it up, leans forward, and slips it on. After throwing on a fleece jacket, she flips the hood over her head, zips it halfway up, and steps out of the Cherokee. She waits next to the car until she sees the threesome headed back to their apartment. That is when she makes her move walking directly up to them. Tossing the hood of her jacket off, she grabs the Glock and points it at their backs. She says, "You must be near thirteen by now, Sam. After what happened, you're lucky I let you live that long."

Caught by surprise, Pax and Sam quickly turn around. "Darcie!" Pax spoke as if she were out of breath. "What are you doing here?"

Darcie has the gun aimed at Sam. That way, she knows Pax won't try anything. She will not risk Sam getting shot. She says, "Oh, I thought I would visit you and talk about art or music, or wait, no, *technology.* For a minute, it skipped my mind. You remember the technology I'm talking about, don't you, Paxton?" She glances at Sam. "And don't you, Sam, the little girl who wouldn't pull the freaking trigger. You cost me a lot of money. I should've killed you when I killed that pathetic grandfather of yours."

Pax throws one arm across Sam's chest and steps toward Darcie. "What is it you want?" She asked.

"I've been thinking about that a lot lately. Money is still the number one answer, but that train has left the station. So, what is it that's so important that I would risk coming back here again? I could say revenge, but that doesn't do it for me. Satisfaction is a better term. There's something inside of me that needs, you know, fulfillment. It's like an itch. Anytime I don't get my way, it just takes over. Unless I scratch it, I can't get comfortable. That's why I'm here, to scratch an itch and get satisfaction."

For a fleeting second, Pax thinks about disarming Darcie. The last time they were in this situation, Darcie got one shot off. With the gun aimed at Sam, attacking wasn't an option. "You're not making any sense. Just tell me what you want." She is hoping for the best.

"You sound like my mother. I never made any sense to her either. Okay, I'll rephrase it. I'm here to do you both harm." In the middle of her sentence, Darcie's phone (the one she took from her mother) starts vibrating. Careful to keep the gun pointing at Sam, she reaches into her pant pocket and pulls it out. So that she can keep one eye on Pax, she holds it up and starts reading a text message. *Your father has passed. There will be a viewing tomorrow from 5-8 at the funeral home on Jackson Street. The day after is the burial. I'm sorry for the short notice. I've been upset and only in the last half-hour did I get a new phone. If the one reading this message isn't Darcie, please disregard it.*

A rush of emotions sweeps over Darcie. The woman filled with confidence only a few seconds ago takes a step back, lowering the phone. She had been waiting for her chance, and now that everything was perfect, all she could think about was her father. She was thinking, wondering about the man who had always protected her. Pete was the one person she loved without having to think about it. And now he was dead.

"You're sick," Pax shouted, clutching Sam with both arms. "You know that don't you?"

Without even noticing, Darcie takes another step back. "Sick, no, no. That's what momma thinks. She's wrong, though. My energy just always seemed to go in a different direction. That's all it is. It's not the same thing. Sometimes I get these flashes, and I can't stop myself. It's something mystical, magical, beautiful. I think it's the power of the universe leading me. When I follow through, it's the best feeling in the world. I'm not sick. I just know what makes me happy. And being happy is the reason for everything." Suddenly, Darcie begins waving the gun toward the apartment building. "Go, now, before I shoot you where you stand."

Pax could read her face and voice inflection and knew she was telling the truth.

Darcie continues, "I just found out I have more important things to do. Today is your lucky day. Now go before I change my mind."

A half-hour later, Pax and Sam sit in the kitchen eating pancakes. Looking at her phone, Pax reads a text that is a reply to one she had sent out twenty minutes earlier. After setting the phone on the table, she picks up a cup of coffee, leans back in her chair, and stares in wonder at how Sam is growing into her body. Her face is rounder, her body still thin but plumping up in all the right places.

Sam notices her staring and makes an absurd face, pulling her eyes down at the corners and sticking her tongue out. She follows this up by pressing her nose into the shape of a pig.

Pax grins and then laughs out loud. When she settles down, she is still smiling. She says, "We've been talking about you. Do you know what next week is?"

Stirring a piece of pancake around the syrup-saturated plate, Sam crams it into her mouth, chews, and talks. "Our last visit to the hospital."

"It's a rehab center. No, you have full use of your arm now. Considering what happened, we both recovered quickly. It's crazy because when I first met Darcie, she was amazing, protecting me like a mother. I thought she cared about me. It turns out she was just keeping someone else from stealing my sensory chip. She had 10 million reasons to protect me till she could take it herself."

Having finished her food, Sam pushes her plate away, crosses her arms, and rests them on the table. She asks, "Is Darcie like Jack-the-Ripper bad?"

"I'm not sure what category to put her in," Pax replied. "I just know what she did to you and me. And I know she repels me; repels every ounce of human decency I have. Poor Rosie. She used him and killed him. The more I think about it, the more I think you're right. Darcie Hannagan is Jack-the-Ripper bad. But enough about her. Next week we finalize the paperwork on your adoption."

"Can we celebrate?"

"We sure can. What would you like to do?"

"Can we have a party at Café Bella?"

"That's a great idea. I'll talk with Maria and have her set it up." Suddenly, there is a knock at the door. "That's for me," says Pax. "I sent a text to Hawke informing him about Darcie's surprise visit. He said someone's coming over from the Albuquerque FBI. Don't worry about the dishes. I'll clear them later. But it's dog wash day, so take Snoop to the bathroom, and remember warm, not hot water."

Chapter 44

One Hour Later

A knock comes from the door. Pax jets over, quickly opening it. She stands there looking into the eyes of her second surprise guest of the day. "Why Edward Cotton. How long has it been now, five or six months?"

Sharply dressed, as usual, he's wearing a dark blue suit with a matching tie. "You were still in the hospital in pretty bad shape."

She's looking him up and down. "I could use your shoes as a mirror to put my makeup on."

"Really?"

"Yes, they're super shiny."

"Do you mind if I come inside?"

"Oh, of course." She motions him over to the sofa, follows, and sits in a chair across from him.

"You have a nice apartment," he slides a pillow to his side and gets comfortable.

"Gatsby pays for it. He won't let me spend my money. I guess I'll be a millionaire in a couple years."

"I take it you two are close these days."

"It's taken some time, but, yes, we're good."

"What about your mother, Sloan?"

"Last I talked with her, she planned to stay with Gatsby. She likes Albuquerque, and they've hit it off again."

"I couldn't be happier to hear that."

"Thanks. I keep pinching myself. It's like a fairytale where everything is a disaster, and then at the end, it all works out."

"I'm happy for you, all of you. So, Paxton, Hawke told me about Darcie showing up here today."

"It was quite a surprise. There would've been trouble, but she got a text message and left faster than a man who learned he got a girl pregnant."

A smile quickly comes across Edward's face. "I'm glad you haven't lost your sense of humor. Darcie's been a tough one to track. She keeps moving around. Every time we get close, we end up back at square one." Edward shifts his body forward to get closer to Pax. His knees bump into the coffee table as he maneuvers to the sofa's edge. "We think we have a plan that will work. Hawke devised it. The one person in the world that Darcie is close to is her father. Right now, she thinks he's dead and is rushing back to his funeral. We've got a team of agents waiting to pick her up. By tomorrow night, your troubles with her should be over."

"If it's okay, I would like to be there for that," Pax replies.

"You would need to leave by tonight."

"All I need to do is pack a bag and drop Sam off at my mom and dad's."

"If you're that serious, I have a military flight scheduled for seven o'clock. You can go with me."

"Thanks. I want to see her captured with my own eyes. I think I need that, Edward."

"I understand. There is one other thing I was hoping to discuss with you, actually two things."

"You want to know how my senses are integrating, don't you?"

"Yes, Pax. You'll keep going through changes for about another year. That's just an estimate."

"I already am."

"What else? Tell me?"

She stands up. "How about I just show you?"

"Go ahead."

Pax scratches just above her eye and smiles. "It's good you're sitting down. You'll know what I mean in a minute. Okay, I gained this ability a couple of weeks ago, so I'm not very good at it." Lifting her arms out next to her, she squares them up horizontally like the wings of a plane. After taking a deep breath, she lowers her arms, and her body lifts off the floor.

Edward is astonished. For so long, he had wondered if his invention would bring about abilities never before seen. And now, floating in front of him, here it was.

Pax giggles. "Pretty cool, huh?"

"That's one way to put it."

"When this first happened to me, I did the math because I didn't think it was possible. Sure enough, there is a mathematical function that reverses gravity."

"Can you move through the air?"

"When it first happened to me, no." Pax makes a swimming motion with her arms and darts across the room. "I'm doing better now. Why didn't you tell me this was going to happen?"

"I didn't know what would happen when your senses came into perfect alignment. Reversing the effects of gravity? Never would I have expected that."

Pax makes a backward swimming motion and glides to the floor, landing next to the sofa.

"You've been practicing that, haven't you?" Edward asked.

"A little every day, yes."

Standing up, Edward turns, facing her. "There is one other thing I was hoping to discuss with you."

"Of course. Ask away."

"First, I should explain something. The Russians don't have the same version of the sensory chip we installed in you. No one does, including the Iranians. They think they bought the same one from one of their underground connections. We made sure they got the version we wanted them to have. We were able to do this because we found Russia's contact. It was Gideon."

"Let me guess, room 4S7?"

"Yes. You put us onto him. Thank you for that. They had a mole right under our noses. We offered him a plea deal, and he gave up all the other moles."

"Other moles. Why am I not surprised to hear that?"

Edward just gives her a grin. "We're all happy they've stopped chasing you. That said, I've been authorized to make you an offer. Let me just cut to the chase. We would like you to be a member of the Argonauts. Before you turn us down, please take some time to think about it. And there's more. We're starting up a youth division of the Argonauts. We surgically install the sensory chip at 13, and at age twenty-one, they become active agents. This allows plenty of time for the assimilation of all the senses. When it's all said and done, there will be eight additional Argonauts. We would like to offer Sam one of the youth positions. Other than taking the time to explore her new abilities, we wouldn't expect her to do anything until she turns twenty-one."

"And if I say no, the Pentagon uninstalls the sensory chip?"

"Not if I have anything to do with it. You've earned the right to keep it for life."

"My gut tells me I might regret it, but my senses are aching to use my abilities. I guess I have a little of my mother in me. Would my home base be Albuquerque?"

"If you like, yes. We need you in one of the southwest states."

"How much international travel?"

"Our main objective is the defense against the infiltration of spies. Specifically, spies that are here to steal technology. You'd mainly be working in this part of the country and in conjunction with other Argonauts. Basically, that means Hawke, Nate, who we've already reassigned to Albuquerque, and me. Out of the country assignments will happen from time to time. Because of the extremely private nature of the Argonauts, we'll arrange for your training here in Rio Rancho."

"When do I start?"

"As soon as we can rent a space for your training. That shouldn't take long. There's also Sam to consider here."

"I'm inclined to let her make her own decision. What happens if she turns twenty-one and changes her mind?"

"Only Argonauts will have this particular sensory chip technology. It's only for those in defense of enemy spies. We would have to replace it with one of lesser capabilities."

"She told me she wants to be just like me. I have a feeling she'll jump at the opportunity. But…"

"What is it?"

"My god, she's so young. She's still learning to dream."

"Try to think about it this way. *Timing is everything.* If she were older, she wouldn't be in consideration. Going through these years with the sensory chip will make her youth much more amazing."

Chapter 45

Now

Hawke stands next to a stained-glass window, partially hidden by dozens of floral arrangements. Going unnoticed, he swivels his head, staring intensely, searching back and forth. It was a simple plan. They would back off when Darcie was spotted while she said her goodbyes to a closed casket. As soon as she exited the building, several agents would converge, de-arm, and handcuff her. He and Nate would place her in a police car, bind her with leg irons, and detain her in a Philadelphia precinct. It was a simple plan, but nothing about Darcie Hannagan had ever gone in a simple way.

Five o'clock turned into six, six into seven, and seven into eight. Darcie did not show. At nine o'clock, Hawke, Nate, and Pax stood in an empty parking lot, wondering what had gone wrong.

Pax asked the obvious question. "Do you think she was on to you?"

Both Hawke and Nate shook their heads. "I don't see how," Hawke spoke, turning his eyes toward the funeral home, gazing, thinking. "Unless..."

"Unless what?" Nate asked.

"Unless she just hasn't arrived yet." He'd been so immersed in thinking she would come during visiting hours that he never considered the alternative.

Pax stepped next to Hawke, looking with him at the building. She says, "What you mean is she's coming in the middle of the night when no living person is around."

"That's exactly what she's going to do. Nate, could you get on the phone. We need those agents back asap. Pax, you come with me. I want to make sure nothing changes with the room. Let's get a move on. Management's about to lock up." They ran out of the lighted parking lot onto a dark walkway and back into the light of the building's entrance. They were resetting the trap.

Ten o'clock turned into eleven, eleven into twelve, and twelve into one. Hawke's phone vibrates with a text from one of the agents. *"She's just drove into the parking lot."* He whispers to Nate and Pax, who sit against a wall behind the floral arrangements. "She's here. Get up. Things are about to get interesting."

Sitting in her car, Darcie carefully eyeballs the place. After a minute, she opens the door, steps out, and eyeballs some more. Walking to the front of the building, she continues her methodical inspection. When she reaches the entrance, she takes a narrow piece of metal and jimmies the lock. In five seconds, she is inside.

Hawke receives another text. *"The mouse is in the trap."*

"It's showtime," Hawke whispers. "When she reaches the casket, we give her a few minutes to get comfortable before we make our move."

After Darcie creeps into the room, she hesitates suspiciously, swiveling her head back and forth before walking up to the casket. Pictures of her father are taped to a poster board and sitting on an easel stand. Taking her time, she uses the tips of her fingers, touching each photograph as if she were remembering, attempting to reconnect with him. Next, she leans slowly over the casket, kissing it like a newborn baby. And then she does something Hawke wasn't expecting, lifting the casket lid, and peering inside. At first, she just stares into it like she sees him and is reminiscing. Then she notices that it's empty and is confused.

Hawke realizes that she could flee at any moment and does something that surprises even himself. "Mousey!" He spoke in an altered, low, pitched tone.

Darcie turns in the direction of the voice. "Daddy?" All she sees are dozens of floral arrangements. The whole thing strikes her as very ghost-like but very real. "Daddy?" She repeats. "Is it you?"

"It's me, Mousey." Hawke steps out from behind the flowers into a darkened part of the room.

Darcie steps toward him. "Daddy? Oh, God, I've missed you. Momma told me you passed, but you've come back, haven't you? You've come back to see me one last time."

"No, Mousey." Hawke steps into the light and draws the Glock from his holster. "I've come to arrest you for murder and treason. Hands up where I can see them."

Darcie is still locked in a confused state when several FBI agents suddenly rush the room. When she sees them her eyes bulge with comprehension, and she darts down low, rolling underneath the casket. When she stands back up, she is protected by the casket and is aiming her Glock at the agents. With two successive shots, she drops them in their tracks. "Hawke!" She screams, pointing her gun in his direction. "I got you in my sights. Put the gun down. Do it now, or I swear I'll shoot."

Lifting his hands in a defenseless position, he slowly lowers and lays the gun on the floor. "You won't make it out alive," he says, standing back up. "We've got the exits covered."

Nate walks out on the opposite side of the flowers. He has a Glock aimed straight at Darcie. "Drop it, Darcie. It's over."

Looking anxiously around the room, she starts talking wildly. "When I first looked into the casket, I saw my father's face. I thought how strange. He didn't look real. And then he just vanished, and I realized the casket was empty. I came to see my father buried, but he's not dead." Her voice rises. "*He's not dead, is he Hawke*?"

"No." He shrugs his shoulders. "You probably should have checked with the nursing home before coming here. Not a good move for you."

"In truth, he was more than my father," Darcie shouted.

"Put the gun down, Darcie." Nate continued, "You're not making any sense."

In a fast motion that catches everyone by surprise, Darcie reaches behind her, pulls a second Glock from her jeans, and aims it at Nate. The scene is crazy. Her arms are now stretched in opposite directions, each holding a gun. Everybody is deadlocked, unable to make a move. "Daddy always knew what

I was," Darcie shouted, continuing her wild talk. "He even knew I killed my sister. I think we were the same, he and I. I could always talk to him, really open up about all the things I did, the people I hurt, tortured, killed. He killed too. He said it was before he married my mother. He said that after the wedding, he didn't feel the need. I've killed over twenty people. Twenty-four, I think, but I'm not sure anymore."

"Darcie!" Nate shouted. "Please, let's end this. No one has to die here."

"You guys haven't figured it out yet." She replied. "There is a thin line between fighting for something and dying for nothing. You think you're better than me because you're loyal agents, don't you? But when your career is over, you won't have pretty girls serving you wine and rubbing your feet. The best you can expect is a plaque hanging on a wall with your name on it. You are all unenlightened if you think that means a damn thing. Stop fighting the power of the universe. Give in to it and let it guide your energy. Give in, and you'll see what real happiness is all about. If you don't, you'll have so many uncertainties and regrets when the act of dying finally comes. Time loses all sense when there's none of it left. The parties where you could have danced and the songs you could have sung. All people, great and small, are equal when that time comes. And that time, special agents, has come."

Just as Darcie was about to pull the triggers, something slammed down on her shoulders, sending her arms upward. The bullets fly harmlessly into the ceiling. She crashed to the floor, knocked out cold.

Pax had used her ability to defy gravity. She silently elevated to the top of the twenty-foot ceiling, used a swimming motion to maneuver above Darcie, and reversed the swimming strokes, sending her 135 pounds smashing down on her. She stood hovering over the evilest person she had ever known. Hawke and Nate quickly rush over and secure both of Darcie's guns.

Soon Darcie awakens and looks up into Hawke's eyes. "Is it over? Are you taking me in?"

He lifts her hands and slaps the cuffs on. "Yes, Darcie." Helping her to her feet, Hawke walks her to a chair, and motions her to sit.

Nate wasted no time rushing over to one of the agents shot by Darcie. He snatches his phone from a belt clip and punches 911.

"911, what's your emergency?"

"This is Agent Nate McMillan of the D.C. FBI. I need an ambulance sent to Jackson Funeral Home at the corner of Jackson and Denton. There's been a shooting. I got one dead and one shot in the chest."

"Is the person conscious?"

"No, but he's breathing."

"Keep pressure on the wound, and if possible, raise his legs about a foot or so. I've dispatched an ambulance. They're close by. It shouldn't be long."

Pax and Hawke stand next to Darcie, looking over the situation. "Is he going to make it?" Hawke asked.

"I'm not sure," Nate responded. "The bullet missed his heart, but it might have punctured his lungs."

By now, the other two agents have entered the room. When Pax and Hawke turn to acknowledge them, Darcie jumps up and snatches Hawke's Glock. She puts the gun to his head and screams at the agents. "You two, move over there next to the flowers. Do it now, or you'll end up like your buddies."

In the corner of his eye, Hawke noticed a little girl had run out from behind the flowers. She runs across the room, not stopping until she is a few feet behind Darcie. "Ginger?" Hawke thinks, but he keeps silent.

"Daddy, I'm scared."

"You shouldn't be here," he answered, again only in his mind.

"But I want to help."

"You should leave. I don't want you to see her pull the trigger."

"She doesn't want to hurt you."

"How do you know that?"

"I know because you know. She just wants to see her daddy one last time. You know that don't you?"

"I guess I do."

"Then let her, Daddy. There's something wrong with her, but she doesn't know it. She's living inside the madness. She thinks it's normal. *She thinks the madness is the real world.*"

"Go back to your mother, now. I'll take care of this."

Ginger darts back across the room, disappearing before she reaches the flowers.

"Don't shoot, Darcie," Hawke shouts. "I know what you want."

Pushing the gun hard against his head, she scrapes his skull and draws blood. "You don't know anything! Down on your knees."

Dropping to his knees, he stares up at Pax, smiling, hoping she won't try to save him. "You want to see your father, don't you?"

Darcie drops to one knee and places her head next to his. "Can you make that happen?"

"You already know the answer. I can have you there in less than fifteen minutes."

Darcie looks wildly around the room, laughing. "It's the power of the universe. It's giving me what I want, guiding my energy like it's always done!" As quickly as she started, she stopped laughing. "Get up now. We're leaving, just you and me." After he stands up, Darcie shouts at Pax. "Back up, super-girl or your cute boyfriend is dead."

Once Pax has moved back, Darcie turns toward the exit and unexpectedly stares into a semi-automatic rifle. A sniper in the Russian mafia's employment presses the trigger twice, hitting Darcie in the head. She collapses to the floor. Without ever having visited her father, she dies. Her reign of madness is over.

Chapter 47

Three Weeks Later

An early rainstorm meant an empty restaurant as Pax waited for Hawke at Café Bella. Sam was spending a few days with Gatsby and Sloan, hoping to get to know her new grandparents better. Hawke had been away, too, giving details to the Joint Chiefs of Staff at the Pentagon about Darcie Hannagan and the Russian Mafia. He had arrived by military plane an hour ago and was enroute to meet Pax.

When she noticed him walking in, she was excited to see him. As he reached her, she stood up, gracefully leaning into him and kissing his cheek. She asks, "Is it wrapped up?"

He smiles and nods. "It took a little longer than expected because they wanted to cover details of the new Argonaut program. That took an entire day. We finalized the selection of the youth participants." Flipping over his wrist, Hawke displays his tattoo. It's an octopus. "I'm to inform you that you start your training in one week. On the first day, you'll get one of these."

"Does Sam get one too?"

"Not until she receives the sensory chip. Next month is the surgery date."

"She's going to be so excited. Actually, she already is. When I discussed it with her, she jumped out of her seat and spilled a Coke all over me."

"I wish I could've been there for that."

"You're here now. I'm glad too because I miss the sound you make when you're sleeping and that nasal thing you do when you first wake up."

"You should have heard me when I was a kid. When I was twelve, I had those cracked tones in my voice."

"Lots of boys get that."

"You don't understand. I sounded like I sucked in a helium balloon, and the sound stayed. They called me crack boy and not for the drug. If you'd known me back then, your opinion of me might be different. I was pathetic."

Under the table, Pax is rubbing her foot on Hawke's leg. "Haven't you noticed that's what I go for?"

Hawke's face crinkles up. "So, you think I'm pathetic?"

Her foot rubs harder, moving and pressing against his ankle. "Absolutely. Otherwise, I wouldn't give you the time of day."

"Really?"

"Yes, but don't worry. You're pathetic in all the right ways."

"Well, I'll keep working on that. Is there something you *don't* like about me?"

She jerks her foot back and bursts out laughing. "Are you kidding? You seriously don't know?"

"Know what?"

"When you wake up in the morning, you're slower than a constipated turtle!"

"Okay, I get it. I'll work on that too."

"Good then. And don't even think about bailing on me. I love everything else about you, including how your eyes roll back in your head after you kiss me. It's like I killed you, but in a good way."

Hawke rubs his cheek and throws up his hand. "Don't stop talking. I think I can get used to this."

After laughing themselves out, Pax places her hand over the top of Hawkes. "Life is larger when I'm with you. I like that feeling."

"I know what you mean."

"It's weird too because I used to care a lot about what kind of person I would be. It's not that I don't care anymore. I do. But now that my brain functions on a higher level, it doesn't seem to matter."

"Did I tell you that all of the Argonauts are getting the sensory chip?" He continues, "I get mine the same day as Sam."

"Hawke Gentry and the sensory chip, now that's a combination I'd like to see."

"I'm feeling really good about it. In fact, I'm going to give you a deep tissue massage. Go ahead, turn around. Let's do this."

Pax stands up, turns her seat around, and sits back down.

Hawke rubs his fingers deep into her shoulders. He says, "Right here around your shoulders and the back of your neck?"

"Oh god, that feels so good."

"Now, who's your man?"

"Who's my man? Who's my superhero?"

"Now you're talking."

"When you finish with her, can you do me?" It was Maria. "I'll buy your breakfast." She pulls up a chair next to Pax, and the three friends burst out laughing.

A half-hour later, they're finishing breakfast and have settled into a nice conversation. The sun is out now, so customers will be coming in soon. Unexpectedly Hawke sees the shadow of a little girl run by the table and stop. He hears a giggle, and the girl turns around, facing him. It's Ginger, and she's wearing his favorite yellow dress. She points at Pax and smiles. "You did good, Daddy. Just look at her." She points again. "No, no, I mean it, look at her." Hawke glances at Pax, watching for a few seconds as she talks with Maria. When he turns back to Ginger, she blows him a two-handed kiss. "You did good, Daddy. You helped her. *Now she knows what the world can do.*" After another two-handed kiss, Ginger turns around, opens a glass door, runs out into the sun, and evaporates into a group of sandhill cranes landing in the parking lot.

Hawke leans back in his chair. A warm feeling jutted through him. "*The cranes are back again.*" He rests his arms comfortably on the table.

Pax and Maria glance outside at the beautiful birds, and suddenly Pax's phone starts vibrating on the table. She picks it up and punches it. It's Sloan. "Momma, I was just thinking about you."

"Me too, dear. I was just sitting here having breakfast with Gatsby and Sam and wanted to hear your voice."

"Momma, I've been meaning to tell you something."

"What is it?" Sloan asked.

"After I was blinded and thought you were dead, I started making recordings for you just in case, you know, you came back. I know that sounds funny, but I was just ten years old. I hope you don't mind, but I saved all of them. It would mean a lot to me if you would listen to them."

"I'll come over today and pick them up."

"Don't bother. I'll come to you. I've been wanting to show Sam my old room."

"Speaking of Sam, she wants to talk with you. Here, I'm giving her the phone."

"Mom, I love you," Sam blurted out.

"I love you too, darling."

"It stopped raining."

"I just noticed that. It's going to be a wonderful day."

THE END
OF
BOOK 1
GIRLS, GUYS, & SPIES SERIES
SEVEN SENSES

Acknowledgements:

For all writers there is always that time during the process of writing when you look around in need of something to spur you on. The verbs inspire, motivate, and fire-up come to mind. More than anything else it is my manuscript readers that do this for me. They are my shot-in-the-arm, a refreshing breeze which stimulates, invigorates, and revitalizes me.

First, I want to thank Becca, my wife. Your hard work and dedication to my work is vitally important to me as you push through the mundane but challenging steps: proofreading, formatting, book cover construction, and all the other steps to get it ready for print. You always make me look better than I am. Your initial excitement for this book was for me like hooking a big, elusive fish just when you thought it was not possible. (I'm never sure how well my books will be received.) Thank you for your spirit that lit a fire of confidence in me!

I also want to thank John and Janette Innes. You have been readers for me since my first novel. Your feedback is invaluable, your enthusiasm for my work is inspiring. You are my pep rally that incites me to be my best. Thank you, a thousand times.

And I want to add a special shout out to one of our dear friends, Alisha Cromie, who volunteered to assist with editing. Another set of eyes is ever so helpful. Thank you, thank you, thank you, for catching everything we missed. Without your effort, my finished work would not reach its full potential.

Coming soon:

Girl Traveling Solo by H. G. Shuler is a gripping and atmospheric novel that takes readers on an emotional journey through the Pacific Northwest. The story centers around Frankie Lyn Jones, aka 'Ladybug,' an 18-year-old girl who mysteriously vanishes after hiring an Uber to the airport for her return to Anchorage, Alaska. What begins as an exciting trip to visit her cousin in Seattle quickly transforms into a suspenseful and heart-wrenching tale of disappearance and the relentless search for answers.

Shuler masterfully captures the essence of two distinct yet equally captivating cities, Seattle and Anchorage. Seattle's bustling urban environment and rich cultural backdrop provide a stark contrast to Anchorage's rugged natural beauty and the mystical allure of the Northern Lights. These settings are more than just backdrops; they become integral to the narrative, each city contributing to the unfolding mystery in its own unique way.

The characters in *Girl Traveling Solo* are deeply engaging and well-developed. Frankie, or Ladybug, is portrayed with a blend of youthful curiosity and maturity that makes her disappearance all the more poignant. Her family, known as Aurora Hunters due to their passion for chasing the Northern Lights, add layers of depth and intrigue to the story. Shuler's exploration of their dynamic and the impact of Frankie's disappearance on them is both touching and thought-provoking. He uses POV brilliantly to reveal the tale from unique perspectives. The plot is intricately woven, with suspense building steadily as each clue and revelation brings readers closer to the truth. *Girl Traveling Solo* is a compelling read that keeps you on the edge of your seat, filled with twists and turns that will leave you pondering long after you've turned the last page.

www.ingramcontent.com/pod-product-compliance
Lightning Source LLC
Chambersburg PA
CBHW071302140726
47996CB00005B/1600